THE
DARK
ROOM

JONATHAN MOORE

First published in Great Britain in 2017 by Orion Books,
an imprint of The Orion Publishing Group Ltd
Carmelite House, 50 Victoria Embankment
London EC4Y 0DZ

An Hachette UK Company

1 3 5 7 9 10 8 6 4 2

A CIP catalogue record for this book is
available from the British Library.

ISBN (Hardback) 978 1 4091 6502 6
ISBN (Export Trade Paperback) 978 1 4091 6503 3

Printed in Great Britain by CPI Group (UK) Ltd, Croydon, CR0 4YY

www.orionbooks.co.uk

For my son, Bruce Nathaniel Moore Wang.

我愛你王小龍

THE DARK ROOM

1

IT WAS AFTER midnight, and Cain and his new partner, Grassley, watched as the excavator's blade went into the hole, emerging seconds later with another load of earth to add to the pile growing next to the grave. On the phone that afternoon, the caretaker of El Carmelo Cemetery had asked if they could do this at night. There were burials scheduled all day, and he didn't want to upset anyone. The time of day hadn't made any difference to Cain. Staying up all hours was his business. He just wanted this done.

After three more scoops with the backhoe, the caretaker rotated the arm out of the way and his assistant jumped down into the hole with a long-handled spade. As he did that, the van from the medical examiner's office arrived. Its headlights scanned across Cain and Grassley, and then paused over the exhumation. The caretaker's assistant climbed out of the hole, blinking against the bright light. Then he took the lifting straps from his boss and jumped back into the open grave.

Cain watched the technicians climb from the van and start up the hill. A man and a woman, young, no more than a few years out of college. Grassley's phone rang, and he checked the screen before he answered. He looked at Cain and took a few steps back.

"Yes, ma'am," he said, and then he paused a while to listen. "No, we're out at El Carmelo, in Pacific Grove — you know, the Hanley thing?"

Now Grassley was listening again, pressing his finger into his free ear to dull the excavator's diesel rumble.

"He's right here. Hold on."

Grassley handed him the phone.

"It's the lieutenant," he said. "She wants to talk to you."

He took the phone, stepping through the long shadows of the

1

headstones toward the cypress trees at the top of the hill, where he would be farther from the excavator's idling engine.

"This is Cain," he said. "What can I do for you, Lieutenant?"

"Something came up. I need to reassign you."

"We're right in the middle of something."

"I wouldn't pull you off if I had a choice," she said. "But I don't. Grassley can take Hanley from here."

"We're two hours south."

"That's not a problem," the lieutenant said. "You're — Where exactly are you?"

"El Carmelo," he said. "The cemetery."

"Hold on, Cain."

He knew she was checking her computer, pulling up a map. There was too much noise on the hilltop to hear her keystrokes. In less than twenty seconds she was back to him.

"There's a golf course," she said. "Right next to you. They can set down, pick you up."

"They?"

"The CHP unit."

"You're sending a helicopter?"

"It'll be there in ten minutes," she said.

"What's going on?"

His mind went first to Lucy, but the lieutenant wouldn't have called about her. She didn't even know about Lucy.

"We'll talk when you get here, face to face. Not over the phone. Now give me Grassley. I need another word with him."

He started toward Grassley, then stopped when he saw the hole. He had to try one more time. He cupped his hand over the phone's mouthpiece, so she'd hear him clearly.

"I spent three weeks setting this up."

"It's a wild-goose chase, Cain. One that's been sitting thirty years. I've got a problem that's less than an hour old. Now it's your problem. Put Grassley on."

He came back to Grassley and handed him the phone. It wasn't any use wondering why the lieutenant was pulling him away. Instead, he walked to the edge of the excavated grave and looked down, shining the flashlight he'd been carrying. The caretaker's assistant was kneeling on top of the casket. He'd dug trenches along its sides and was reaching down to fasten the lifting straps.

Three decades underground, the kid wouldn't weigh much, at least. And from what Cain understood, by the time he'd finally died, there hadn't been all that much to put in the casket anyway. The assistant climbed out of the hole again and handed the ends of the four straps to his boss.

Cain checked up the hill and saw Grassley standing under the tree, one finger in his left ear to block the noise as he talked to their lieutenant.

"Inspector Cain?"

He turned around, putting his hand up to block the light shining in his face.

"That's me."

The woman from the ME's office lowered her light and came around to stand next to him. She leaned over to look down into the hole.

"You're riding back with us in the van?" she asked. "We heard something like that."

"Not me," Cain said. "I just got reassigned."

He gestured up the hill toward Grassley.

"He'll have to go. You or your partner can follow in his car."

"Reassigned? It's two a.m. and we're —"

She stopped, following Cain's eyes to look at the light coming toward them from the north. When the helicopter broke out of the clouds and into clear air, they could hear the *whump* of its rotors. Cain pointed up the hill toward his partner.

"That's Inspector Grassley," Cain said. "Make sure he gets in the van, that he rides with one of you. He might want to drive back on his own, but don't let him. We need the chain of custody. You understand. I don't want any problems later, some defense lawyer picking us apart."

"I get it," the woman said.

"I've got to go," Cain said. He looked back into the hole, shining his light on the casket's black lid. "Let's get this one right."

He paused on the way down the hill and looked back up at Grassley. They met each other's eyes and nodded, and that was all. Then he hurried across the access road, toward the long fairway that stretched between the graveyard and Del Monte Boulevard.

. . .

3

When he reached the golf course and felt the short grass under his feet, he checked the sky to the north and saw that the helicopter was less than a minute away. He took out his cell phone and dialed Lucy's number.

"Gavin?"

"Sorry—I didn't mean to—I thought I'd get your voicemail."

"I was up."

He looked at his watch. It was a quarter past two. The grass on the fairway was slick with dew, and he could smell the ocean.

"You're okay?"

"I'm fine."

"You're feeling sick again," he said. He could hear it in her voice.

"It's not such a big deal," she said. "Really."

"Okay."

"Where are you?" she asked.

"Down south, near Monterey. For Hanley."

"Hanley?"

"The video we got, the guy who—"

"That's enough," she said. "I remember. I can't stomach it right now."

"No more," he said. "I promise."

"Are you coming soon?"

"Something came up," he said. "They're sending a helicopter, but I don't know what's going on."

"You have to hurry?"

He glanced up at the helicopter, saw it swing around as it lined up for the fairway.

"I ought to go."

"Then call when you can," she said. "Or better yet, just come."

"As soon as I can," he said.

"Be careful," she said. "Gavin, I mean it."

"Try and get some sleep."

They hung up and he put the phone away. Then the helicopter came in just above the line of trees, and when it was hovering over the fairway, its spotlight lit up. He walked toward the white circle, one hand in the air to call the CHP pilot in.

2

IT WAS HIS first time in a helicopter. The SFPD had scrapped its aero division before he'd even joined the force. Now whenever his department needed helicopter support, it called the California Highway Patrol. The agencies were friendly, but arranging anything was a bureaucratic and logistical mess. Which meant that this flight, on short notice at two in the morning, could only have happened if someone far above his lieutenant had stepped in.

He put on his headset and bent the microphone toward his lips.

"Where we headed?"

"Civic Center Plaza," the pilot said, and Cain had to press his earphones tight to hear her voice over the engine. "I'm supposed to set you down on the lawn at the corner of Polk and Grove."

"They tell you what it's about?"

She shook her head.

"I'm just a taxi service tonight. That's all I know."

They were racing above Monterey Bay. Five, six hundred feet up, with wisps of fog between them and the black water. Ahead, he could see Santa Cruz, its lights spread between the bay's curved shore and the low, silhouetted mountains.

"What were you doing in the cemetery?" the pilot asked.

"Exhumation."

"Cold case?"

"That's right," Cain said.

It was no ordinary cold case, but he wasn't going to explain that now. He hated to be reassigned right at the cusp, a moment before they pried open the lid and found out if they had a case or nothing at all. It wouldn't wait for him, either. The lieutenant had been clear — Grassley would handle it without him. He was supposed to be good, but he'd been Cain's partner for only three weeks. Cain hadn't seen enough to have an opinion either way, and that made him nervous.

When they reached the northern edge of Monterey Bay, the pilot came up high enough to pass above the Santa Cruz Mountains, and though they were flying toward the city's gathering orange glow, beneath them, the woods were dark and untouched.

Twenty-five minutes later, the pilot circled Civic Center Plaza once, and then put the helicopter down on the lawn, slipping easily between two rows of flagpoles. Cain took off his headset and stepped out, closing the door behind him.

Lieutenant Nagata was waiting for him across the lawn, standing clear of the wind. Behind her, on Polk Street, a yellow cab and a pair of private cars had slowed to a crawl to watch the helicopter.

Cain straightened his suit and went to his boss.

"Lieutenant," he said. "Where are we going?"

She nodded toward City Hall, which rose into the dark across the street. The gold leaf on the dome glowed against the night. Lieutenant Nagata waited for a car to pass, and then led him across Polk Street. A policeman opened the main door for them, and Nagata led Cain into the building. She stopped beneath the rotunda, at the foot of the grand staircase.

"He wants to see you alone. Go on up, and when you're done we'll talk down here. I'll introduce you to Karen Fischer."

"Who wants to talk to me?"

"Castelli."

He thought about that, what it might mean. He'd never been inside City Hall in the middle of the night. The lamps next to the staircase were lit, and there were a few spotlights farther off, illuminating the bust of Mayor Moscone and the spot of floor where he'd died. He could hear someone pacing in one of the marble-floored galleries above, and he looked around until he spotted the patrolman up there.

"Karen Fischer—who's she?"

"Your contact with the FBI," Nagata said. "Starting tonight, and until this is over. But go up. He's waiting, and he's had a long night already. It'll just get harder for him from here."

It wasn't like Nagata to show sympathetic concern for anyone holding an elected office. The one exception was the mayor. It almost never came up, but when it did, she could be fierce about it. She owed him her job and paid that debt however she could. With her hand at the small of Cain's back, she pushed him toward the grand staircase. He climbed up, passed under the ceremonial rotunda, and then nodded to the patrolman who stood between the flags flanking the mayoral suite.

Cain stepped inside the reception lounge, the red carpet thick underfoot. There was a glass-shaded lamp on the receptionist's desk, and it was the only source of light after the patrolman closed the door behind him.

There was no one else in the lobby. Cain wasn't sure if he was supposed to sit. Maybe in the mayor's mind it made sense to pull him out of El Carmelo, fly him back into the city, and then make him wait. He crossed through the lobby and found the door to the mayor's office. He knocked once with the back of his hand, then opened the door.

Harry Castelli was bent over his phone when Cain stepped in. He glanced up, then cupped his hand over the mouthpiece.

"He's here, and I'll —"

But Cain couldn't make out the rest of it.

The mayor hung up, then pointed at one of the two chairs that faced his desk. Cain pulled one out and sat looking at the man who'd brought him. He was wearing a white dress shirt and a pale blue silk tie. His suit jacket lay atop his desk. His hair was black but must have been dyed because the stubble on his face was all white. His face was fall-down tired. Nothing like the man Cain had seen on TV, leaning with his elbows on a podium in the rotunda, facing a crowd of reporters that pressed all the way down the stairs.

"You're Cain — Inspector Cain?"

"That's right."

"I called your lieutenant and asked for a name."

"Okay."

"I wanted the best, and that's why you're here," the mayor said. "I see you wondering."

"I appreciate that."

If this had happened at the beginning of December, Nagata would have picked a different inspector. But December had been a hard month, and she didn't have much choice. A pair of inspectors and the Office of the Medical Examiner had lost control of an investigation, and three of Cain's closest friends had been killed. By New

Year's Day, he was the most senior man left standing in the Homicide Detail. He was thirty-seven years old.

The mayor reached halfway across the desk and lifted his suit jacket. There was a manila folder under it. He looked inside, then put it on the desk and weighed it down with his palm. He was wearing a thick gold wedding band. No scratches on it. He must have been in the habit of taking it off whenever he did anything with his hands — or else, there'd always been someone else to do those sorts of things for him. Any kind of real labor.

The mayor leaned forward. He may have looked exhausted, but when he spoke, his voice was deep, each word a jab.

"Let's make one thing absolutely clear."

"All right."

Castelli took the folder again, holding it up without opening it.

"I don't know what this is," Castelli said. "And I don't have anything to hide."

"Okay."

"We're clear?"

"I heard you," Cain said.

Usually, the first thing a witness said was a lie. This wasn't starting well for the mayor.

"This — this *thing* — it's bullshit."

Cain didn't answer. He looked at the mayor until the man put down the folder and opened it. There were only a few pages inside. Five, at the most. Cain could see a letter on top, upside down. Its author had conveyed his message in just a few lines. No letterhead, no signature. A nice, clean typeface. Cain didn't need the mayor to tell him what kind of letter it was.

"This came today, in the regular mail."

"It came today, or it got opened today?"

"Both — we open all the mail, every day."

"Who opened it?" Cain asked. He looked at the mayor's hands again. "Not you, I'm guessing."

"My chief of staff. And then she brought it straight to me."

"And she's —"

"Melissa Montgomery. She's giving her statement to the woman from the FBI."

"All right," Cain said. "Is that a copy?"

8

"The FBI's got the original. This is your copy."

Castelli took the top page from the stack and passed it across, closing the folder before Cain could get a good look at the photograph underneath it. Cain took the letter and turned it around.

Mayor Castelli:

1 – 2 – 3 – 4!

All this time, and you're really surprised? Or are you just feigning it, like everything else? Nothing stays in the dark forever.

I'll give you until Friday. Or else: 5 – 6 – 7 – 8. Those go to everybody. Even if they've never seen you that way, they'll recognize you. You didn't forget 9 – 10 – 11 – 12, did you?

When it's dark, you think about her. You imagine what it must have been like. Should your wife start thinking about it too? What about your daughter? Could she be the next Sleeping Girl?

There's an easier way out: *bang!*

—A FRIEND

Cain read the note twice, then put it on the desk in front of him. He studied Castelli for a moment. He looked at the note and read through it once more.

"The numbers — one, two, three, four — those are photographs?"

"Yes."

"Show me."

Castelli passed him the folder. Cain put it on the desk's edge, then flipped the cover back and looked at the first photograph. It was a copy, but a good one. A glossy, full-page print on good photo paper.

"You sent this out, had it done somewhere?"

Castelli shook his head.

"One of my staff — he's got a photo printer. Here, in the office. Melissa used that."

"It was black-and-white to start with, or just after she copied it?"

"Black-and-white."

"It would be," Cain said, speaking mostly to himself. "Wouldn't it?"

"I don't understand."

Cain lifted the photograph from the folder and laid it on the desk, sideways, so that they could each lean in and look at it.

"These distortions," he said, touching the photo with his fingertip. "Here, and here."

"Yeah?"

"This isn't digital, unless it's seriously touched up."

"It was shot on film, is what you're saying."

"You get an amateur in a homemade dark room, you see things like that — ripples, bright spots. And it's easier to develop black and white than color."

"You're a photographer?"

Cain shook his head.

"My line of work, I see a lot of photos," he said. "You know what it tells me, that he didn't shoot color? He didn't want to take these out, let someone else see them. He used black-and-white, and developed them at home. Your friend has his own dark room."

"He's not my friend."

"That's not what he thinks," Cain said. "He's pretty familiar."

"Not to me."

"And what about her?" Cain asked, touching the young woman in the photograph. "You know who she is?"

"All this, it's bullshit. I told you already. I don't know anything about this."

The mayor stood up and went to the cabinet behind his desk. He opened it, his back to Cain. When he turned around he was holding a bottle of bourbon and a pair of tumblers.

"Drink?"

"I'm on duty."

"And I'm your boss. Have a drink with me."

10

"I'm on duty, sir."

Castelli put one of the tumblers away, then poured three fingers of bourbon into the other. He sat again, putting the open bottle and the glass in front of him. Cain looked back to the picture, let himself go into it. The young woman wore a one-sleeved black dress held together at the front with a jeweled clasp. She held her hands out in front her, her fingers splayed in a gesture of self-defense. He couldn't read the look on her face. She hadn't expected the photograph to be taken, and she was afraid. But it wasn't the camera that frightened her. It was the man holding the camera. She was begging him not to come any closer. That was it — that was the look: she hadn't given in to full terror yet; she thought she might have a chance.

She still thought she could beg.

Behind her was a brick wall. In the middle of it, a padlocked steel door. It might have been a warehouse, the storeroom of a bar. The basement in a forgotten apartment block. It probably hadn't mattered to her where she was. She just wanted a way out, but there wasn't one.

In the left corner of the photograph, someone had used a black marker to write the number *1*. There was a loose circle drawn around it.

"You've never seen her?" Cain asked.

"No."

"She look like anyone you know?"

"No."

"Could she be someone's daughter — a niece, something like that?"

"I said I've never seen her before."

"Listen to the question," Cain said. "I didn't ask if you'd seen her. I asked if she looks like anyone you know. If she could be related to someone you know. Look at the picture — look at her face, and answer the question."

Instead, Castelli took his glass of bourbon and drank half of it. He set it down, topped it off, and then started coughing into the crook of his arm.

"Mr. Mayor."

But he was still coughing, and his face was going crimson. When he finally stopped, he took a tissue from the box at the edge of his desk. He used it to wipe his face and nose.

"Mr. Mayor," Cain said. "I need you to look at the picture.

"It's all bullshit—a hoax, whatever you want to call it," Castelli said. "I told you."

"You called me. Not the other way around."

"I'm being blackmailed."

"Because of something you know?"

"I don't know her, and she doesn't look like anyone I know."

"She's a pretty girl," Cain said. "I'd remember her if I saw her— wouldn't you?"

Castelli looked at him. Then he nodded.

"Sure," he said.

"You'd remember, if you saw her?"

"I'd probably remember."

"Because she's a knockout, right?"

The mayor glanced at the photograph. Cain wasn't sure if he nodded or not.

"She looks like one of those old film stars," Cain said. "Lana Turner, maybe."

"You got it mixed up," Castelli said. "It's Lauren Bacall you're thinking of. She looks like Bacall."

The Big Sleep—that was her?"

"Bacall and Bogart," Castelli said. "Yeah."

"One of your favorites?"

"It was okay."

"I meant Bacall."

"Bacall?" the mayor asked. He took another drink. "She was before my time."

"Way before mine," Cain said. "But you see her on the screen, and it doesn't really matter."

"Maybe for some guys."

Cain took out the next picture and set it on top of the first. This one showed a cluttered bedside table against a water-stained plaster wall. He could just make out the edge of the iron bedframe beside it. At the table's edge sat an empty tumbler, a lipstick mark kissing its rim. There was a man's wallet, and a set of house keys. An empty ashtray. There were a dozen white pills in a loose pile, and next to them there was a silver flask, its cap unscrewed. Behind the flask were two pairs of handcuffs. Not the toys they sold in sex shops, but the real things, like the pair strapped to Cain's belt.

"Recognize any of this?"

"No."

"Not your keys, not your wallet?"

"Not mine."

"The flask?"

"I've never seen it."

"How about the handcuffs?"

"Come on."

"Come on?" Cain asked. "Did we read the same note? The guy who sent it, he's pretty sure this stuff means something to you. The next ones — the photos he's holding back — those might mean even more."

Castelli took a swallow of his bourbon.

"Go on," he said. "Make your point if you've got one."

"Right now, it's just you and me. But on Friday, when he sends it out? You'll be talking to the cameras."

"Or you could find him."

"That's what I'm trying to do," Cain said.

"Arrest him. Lock him away."

"I can't if you don't cooperate," Cain said. "So far, everything you've told me is bullshit."

The mayor stared at him. He glanced at his phone, and Cain thought he might call someone in. Have Cain muscled out of the office, out of City Hall. But then he shook his head. He held his glass close to the green-shaded desk lamp and looked at the glowing bourbon.

"I'm trying," Castelli said. "Nothing like this has ever happened to me. I'm not lying to you."

"The handcuffs — you own any like that?"

"Never," Castelli said. "Not like that, and not any other kind."

He set his glass down, then picked it up again. He was nervous about his hands, wanted to keep them busy. When he spoke on TV, he was always gripping the podium. If he didn't have a podium, then he was holding on to something. A cup of coffee, a rolled-up newspaper. Cain wondered if he'd been a smoker at some point.

"It's you and me right now," Cain said.

"We're not into anything like that, is all."

Cain nodded. He waited for the mayor to start talking again.

Sometimes a man wouldn't answer a question but would talk to end a silence. This silence stretched for ten seconds, and then Castelli took another sip of bourbon and spoke into his glass.

"My wife and I, is what I mean. When I say *we,* I'm talking about me and her. The two of us, we're not into anything like that."

"Okay."

Cain could think of half a dozen follow-ups, but this wasn't the time. The mayor had opened the door a crack, but was ready to close it if Cain started to press. Instead, Cain opened the folder and took out the third picture, putting it on top of the others. Castelli glanced at it, then looked away, picking up his drink. Cain could smell the bourbon fumes in the air between them. Sweet and sharp, like sugar burning in a pan.

The photograph showed the woman, this time from the knees up. She was still wearing the black cocktail dress. Her back was against the wall, the nightstand at her left hip. She was drinking from the silver flask, her features caught in a painful wince. Her eyes were focused to her right. Someone must have been standing over there, out of the shot. Cain took the photograph and held it up, tilting it toward the light. He took off his glasses and leaned close to look.

"Did you look at these?" he asked. "All these pictures?"

"I saw everything in the envelope."

"You understood what's happening here?"

"I don't know."

Cain slipped his glasses back on, then set the photograph with the other two.

"The pills — they were on the nightstand before. Ten, twelve of them," he said. He pointed to the empty space where the pills had been in the second picture. "They'd be right here."

"Okay."

"They made her swallow them," Cain said. "Don't you think?"

"I don't know."

"Any idea what they were, those pills?"

"Of course not."

"You see her eyes, how she's looking to the right?"

"Yeah."

"What do you think about that?"

"She was looking at something. Or something caught her eye."

"Does she look scared to you?"

"I guess," the mayor said.

"Come on," Cain said. "We're cooperating. Right?"

"She looks pretty scared."

"Could someone have had a gun on her?" Cain asked. "Outside the shot?"

"Inspector — I don't know what you want me to say. I can't tell you what's happening outside these pictures. Not what she saw, or what she thought about it. I don't know who she is. I don't know what they paid her to pose for them, what they told her she was doing. Maybe she thought it was nothing — spread for some magazine, get a little cash."

"You think it's staged? That's what you think?"

"I don't know anything," the mayor said. "Except that it's got nothing to do with me."

"It does now," Cain said. "Sir."

The final photograph in the folder was turned face-down. Cain picked it up.

"I'm telling you —"

"You don't know anything," Cain said. "Right?"

"I just want us to be clear."

"I heard you the first time."

Cain turned the photograph over.

Now the woman was on the bed. Either she'd taken off the dress herself, or someone had taken it off for her. She lay on her back, her head on a pillow. She wore nothing but a pair of black panties. One knee was bent, so that her left foot was hooked across her right ankle. She'd painted her toenails. The polish looked black, but it was a black-and-white photograph. Cain supposed it could have been any dark color. Her right arm came up past her head, her hand shackled to the bedframe above her. There was no cuff on her left arm, which rested across her chest. If she'd been conscious, it might have been a gesture of modesty, of defense. An attempt to shield herself from the men in the room with her. But she wasn't conscious. Her eyes were closed, and her lips were slightly parted.

Cain studied her, and then looked at the nightstand next to her. It had been cleaned off. There was just the empty tumbler, the dark lipstick stain on its rim. He looked back at the woman. He'd seen enough death in the last eight years to guess he wasn't looking at it right now. It was just a photograph, and a poorly developed one at

15

that. But he could almost see the rise and fall of her chest, could feel the warmth coming off her. She wasn't dead; he was sure of that. But she wasn't asleep, either.

There was no way to gauge how much time had passed between the third photograph and the fourth. Enough to put her in the bed, to clean the room up a bit. They'd stripped off the dress and maybe put a comb through her hair. She'd taken at least twelve of the pills, and she'd had whatever they'd put into the flask. By the time they took the picture, the drugs were working on her.

3

CAIN LOOKED UP from the photograph. Castelli was no longer across from him but had gone over to the window. He'd parted the curtains to look down at the street. He stood sideways at the window, his body hidden from the exposed slit of glass. As if someone out there might take a shot at him. Or snap a photograph to run in tomorrow's paper: *Beset by a blackmailer, Mayor Castelli peers from City Hall.* The problem was only a few hours old, and it was the middle of the night. But the mayor had to be worrying about leaks. The moment he'd picked up the phone, letting someone other than Melissa Montgomery know about the letter, he'd become vulnerable.

"When you read the letter, did you have an idea who wrote it?" Cain asked.

"No."

The mayor let the curtains fall back into place. He came back to his desk and stood behind the chair.

"What about enemies?" Cain asked. "You've probably got a few."

"Which kind?"

"There's more than one kind?"

"Start with the enemies I see every day. The ones I deal with in public — in the papers and on TV," Castelli said. "There's the guys I don't know for sure, but suspect. And then you've got the crackpots I've never met at all."

"The first two, that could include your friends, your family?"

"There'd be some."

"Can you make a list?"

"My staff's working on it."

"The FBI asked already?"

The mayor nodded.

"What about business interests? Not enemies, but people waiting on your decision—building permits, contracts. People who think they'd have a better shot if someone else were behind your desk."

"They're working on that, too."

"The FBI is, with your staff."

"That's right."

"If they're doing all that, why am I here?"

"You'd have to talk to them. To Lieutenant Nagoya."

"Nagata."

"Nagata, then," Castelli said. "But I already told them what I think you should be doing: tracking down the girl."

"You give me three pictures of a woman and I'm supposed to find her."

"You're supposed to be the best," Castelli said. "The best guys, they get an assignment and they do it. That's how it used to be, anyway."

Cain let that slide past. He gathered the photographs and put them back into the folder. He read the letter once more before he added it to the stack and closed the cover on it.

"Everyone's going to recognize you in the next set of pictures. That's what your friend says."

"I read that."

"Have you ever been in that room?" Cain asked. "Do you recognize it?"

"It could be anywhere—I've never seen it."

"What's in the next set of pictures?"

"How should I know, Cain? It could be anything. Think how easy it is to doctor a picture, to pay someone to do it for you."

Cain stood up.

"Is there anything you want to tell me before I find it out on my own?"

"What's that supposed to mean?"

"Nothing," Cain said. "Just, now's your chance."

The mayor squeezed the back of his office chair. He turned his head and coughed into his right bicep. Then he sat down and picked up his glass. It was nearly empty.

"I've got nothing else. You should go meet with Nagoya and that girl from the FBI. Take your folder."

"Fine," Cain said.

He crossed the wide office to the door. When he had his hand on the knob, he turned and looked back at the mayor.

"I'll need to know a good time to drop by your house."

"What?"

"Your wife, your daughter — I'll be interviewing them."

"You're not doing that. You're not going anywhere near them."

"I get an assignment," Cain said, "and I do it. I don't ask permission."

"Inspector —"

"And so we're clear? I run my investigations. I see anyone, I ask anything. And there's no interference from the top down. I'll set something up with your staff."

He opened the door and stepped into the reception lounge. A woman in a charcoal skirt and matching jacket was waiting at the threshold, balancing a tablet computer on the stack of documents in her arms. She stepped back too quickly when Cain came out and nearly tripped. When she'd caught her balance again, he recognized her. He'd seen her standing with the mayor on television. Until tonight, he'd never put a name to her face.

"You're Melissa Montgomery," Cain said. "The mayor's chief of staff."

"I'm not sure I got your name."

He took a business card from his badge holder, but her hands were too full to take it. He set it on top of her tablet's screen.

"Gavin Cain. Call in about an hour," he said. "We'll set it up."

"Set what up?"

"Let's not pretend you weren't listening," Cain said. "Just get a time and call me."

He stepped around her and went out.

Lieutenant Nagata was leaning against the brass and iron railing at the top of the grand staircase. She pushed off it as he came toward her, and then they stood in the shadows of the marble columns. She looked at the manila folder in his hand.

"How'd it go?"

"It was an honor, Lieutenant," he said. "A pleasure and a privilege. It reinforced everything I already thought about him."

"Cain."

"He's an alcoholic, and a liar."

19

"Are you finished?"

"He's an empty suit, and he's soft. You see his hands?"

"Can you do it?"

"You want me to find the girl."

"The FBI's got the rest," Nagata said. "We just have to find her, see where that leads. Can you do it?"

"Anything's possible."

"You don't have to vote for him next year."

"He might not be in a position to run."

She took his elbow.

"Come on — she's waiting."

When they reached the staircase, instead of leading him down the steps to the rotunda, she guided him to the left. Another patrolman was guarding the entrance to the Board of Supervisors' chambers. He pulled back the door as they approached.

"This is our headquarters," Nagata said. They stepped into the antechamber. "But just for tonight. Tomorrow we're getting a conference room."

"In City Hall?"

"In the Burton Building. The thirteenth floor."

"We need a headquarters in the FBI office?"

They stopped before opening the second set of doors to the main room. Nagata gestured at the folder in Cain's hand.

"We work it until it's done," Nagata said. "We have one priority and it's this."

"I've got other cases, things that won't wait."

"That's why we brought in Grassley."

"We don't even know what this is," Cain said. "My others — I've got bodies in the morgue. Grassley's good, but he's never worked a homicide on his own."

"We're talking about the mayor. That's the whole discussion, right there."

She opened the second oak door and they stepped into the main chamber. A wooden rail cut the room in half, separating the supervisors' tables from the rows of benches in the public gallery. A woman was sitting in one of the supervisors' seats, and otherwise, the chamber was empty. He and Nagata came down the aisle under the dim chandeliers, opened the gate, and came through it. Agent Fischer was typing something on her phone and didn't look up until she was done. Then she stood and shook Cain's hand.

"Karen Fischer," she said. "I've heard good things about you."

"Okay."

She pointed at the table opposite her, and they all sat. He guessed Fischer was a year or two older than him. She had a bit of gray in her short hair, and, unlike Castelli, she wasn't trying to hide it with dye. The checkered grip of her service weapon was visible under her suit jacket.

She looked at Nagata and then at Cain.

"You know why we're here? You talked to Castelli?"

"Yes," Nagata said.

Cain just nodded.

"We're tracing the letter—"

"I never saw the envelope," Cain said. "Castelli gave it to you?"

"Not him, but his staff—and we're putting everything we have into tracking it. It was postmarked from North Beach, no return address."

"You can follow it past that?"

"If the lab doesn't find prints or DNA, we have—let's just say, other resources. And by lunch tomorrow we'll have backgrounds on the names we get from Castelli's staff. The enemy lists."

"Lieutenant Nagata says I'm supposed to look for the woman."

"Finding her—we see that as more of a local law enforcement issue."

"You don't know she's local."

"You don't know she's not," Fischer said. "And it's moot, anyway."

"How's that?"

"The mayor," Lieutenant Nagata said. "He wanted you. He insisted."

"He wanted his police to have a part," Fischer said.

"It took him five minutes before he told me how to do my job," Cain said. "If you think he brought me in to look over your shoulder—"

"I don't, Inspector Cain," Fischer said. "We'll work just fine together. You and I will, anyway."

"All right."

"We don't know if the woman's local or not," Fischer said. "We don't know if she's a coconspirator, an actress hired to play a role, or something else."

"A victim."

"It's a possibility," Fischer said. "One you'll have to check."

"I'm doing this on my own?"

"On your own. We'll meet twice a day," Fischer said. "At noon and at seven p.m. If I find anything that could help you, I'll give it to you. Nothing held back. I expect the same from you."

"You can count on it," Nagata said.

"You have the letter and the photographs," Fischer said to Cain. "You'll need to show them to people. I know that. But try to be discreet. You're looking for the woman — that's all."

Cain nodded.

"We'll want to keep this as quiet as we can. We don't want to telegraph every move we make, or he might move up his timetable. Whoever did this, he'll be watching for anything out of the ordinary."

"Like a police helicopter landing on Civic Center Plaza at two in the morning?"

"Things like that," Fischer said. She looked at Nagata. "Starting now, we'll want to avoid things like that."

"That was the mayor's call."

"But he's not running this investigation, is he?" Fischer said to Nagata. Then she turned to Cain. "Our next meeting's in nine hours. Hopefully you'll have something by then."

4

THE PATROLMAN LEFT him in front of the Hall of Justice at four in the morning. It took him five minutes to pass through security, get a cup of coffee, and reach the sixth-floor office he shared with Grassley. He shut the door behind him, then sat in his chair and looked at his name, written backward, on the frosted-glass window. He took a sip of his coffee and then put the cup on the desk. It was still too hot to drink. They hadn't painted Grassley's name on the window yet, but his old partner's name had been scraped off.

He logged in to his computer, then pulled up the SFPD's public webpage and clicked through to the gallery of missing persons. There were twelve on the main page, and another thirty in the archives. Half of them could be ruled out right away. He wasn't looking for a man. And none of the women were anything close to the pictures he'd seen in Castelli's office. From the missing persons gallery, he went to the collection of unsolved homicides—known victims killed by unknown assailants. There were forty-seven, going back to 1991. He clicked through each picture and dismissed them all.

The last stop was the medical examiner's website, where he scrolled through the thumbnails of unidentified corpses. Bodies pulled from the alleys behind the Tenderloin's SRO hotels; bodies drifting back and forth between the pylons along the Embarcadero. Most of them were men, and every one of them looked homeless. Some of the pictures were pencil drawings, and Cain knew they were just approximations. The sketch artist, sitting seven floors below him in the basement, could only guess what their faces might have looked like. A week in the water, a month in a trash pile, and there wasn't much left.

He hadn't expected this to be easy. But he'd learned early on that you had to exhaust the simplest options before you committed to

23

anything else. He looked at his watch. His contact in Menlo Park wouldn't be awake for another four hours. He sent him a text, asking if he could come down. He wouldn't get any closer to finding the woman until Matt Redding answered. Lucy was surely asleep. But Grassley might be back by now.

He dialed his partner's number, and Grassley answered after three rings.

"Cain — where are you?"

"Sitting in our office."

"I got here thirty, forty-five minutes ago."

"You're in the morgue?" Cain asked. "Have they started?"

"Shit, Gavin," Grassley answered. "I'm all by myself. The ME's not coming in till ten thirty."

"What about the techs, the ones you rode back with?"

"Those guys? They went home."

"You're just sitting with the casket?"

"That's what you wanted."

"You're all right, Grassley," Cain said. "You know that?"

"They brought it in. They wouldn't open it without the ME, and I didn't ask them to. But they put it on the x-ray table. I figured no harm doing that."

"You figured right."

"They took the shot, put it up on the screen. Then they took off. Left me looking at it."

"They locked up and left you?"

"You should come down here," Grassley said. "See what I'm seeing."

"Okay."

"I mean," Grassley said, "I think I know what it is, but I'm not sure. We never saw this shit where I came from."

"Grassley — are you okay?"

"This is fucked up."

Cain left the office and started walking to the elevator. In the three weeks they'd been partners, Grassley had been game for anything. Not that they'd seen much so far, but he'd put up a calm front. A couple shootings, a partial dismemberment.

He'd never heard Grassley sound like this.

"I'm on my way," Cain said.

"I don't know about this shit, is all I'm saying."

"Give me a minute."

He reached the elevator and hit the button. The car was already there. At this hour, the Hall of Justice was dead. The elevator hadn't been called away since he'd ridden it up from the lobby.

"I'm about to lose you," Cain said. "I'll be right down."

He hung up and got in the car, then hit the button for the basement.

Cain tapped on the locked door to the medical examiner's suite of underground offices. The door pushed open and Grassley stepped out of the shadows.

"The lights," Grassley said. "I can't turn them back on. Maybe they got a key card, something like that."

"Don't worry about it."

Cain still had his flashlight. He took it out, switched it on, and stepped inside. Grassley let the door close behind him and then turned on his own light.

"It's over here."

Cain had never been here in the dark. The office used to be open twenty-four hours a day, but it was running short-staffed now.

They went into the main autopsy room.

The stainless-steel tables stood out in their lights and cast stilted shadows up the wall. There was the long sink. Above it, another familiar sight: the hanging-basket produce scales, used to weigh internal organs. Cain let his light slide along the particleboard back wall, where the black-bladed cutting tools hung from hooks like the display in a pawnshop. The cutting shears were from gardening stores; the cleavers from Chinatown shops. There was a hacksaw no different from the one in a plumber's truck, except for what it had done.

Then they came to the x-ray room. It was off in a corner, separated from the rest of the room by a heavy, lead-plated partition. Even here there were drains on the floor, and Cain watched a half-dozen cockroaches scurry across the tiles to reach them as he and Grassley approached with their lights. The casket sat on a table beneath the ceiling-mounted x-ray. Cain could smell it. The scents of fresh earth, of rotting wood, rode above the morgue's background stench.

"Here," Grassley said.

He'd stopped in front of the x-ray's control desk. Cain's light moved across a dark computer screen. Grassley tapped the keyboard, and the screen came to life.

"Look at this," Grassley said.

Cain rolled the chair back and sat down. He took off his glasses, then leaned close to the screen. It showed an x-ray image of the casket, taken from above. He could see the casket's elongated outline, could see the sharp white spikes of the screws and nails holding it together. The interior was a jumble of ghostly white bones. The image made no sense. Either the focus was off or there was some kind of doubling effect in the x-ray.

"You see it?" Grassley said. "You get it?"

"There are too many bones."

"The guy — he was really onto something, wasn't he?"

"I guess so."

"What now?"

"We seal it, sign it, and go home."

"That's it?"

"For now," Cain said. "You'll be here at ten thirty, when the ME gets in. You'll have to watch."

"What about you?"

"I'll make it if I can," Cain said. "But I don't know."

"What's she got you working on?"

"She didn't tell you?" Cain asked.

"She didn't give me anything."

"Then I better not say."

Cain looked at the x-ray again, then stood and went back toward the morgue's work areas. It didn't take him long to find a roll of tamper-evident seal tape. He plucked a permanent marker from a pencil jar on someone's desk, then went back to the x-ray room. The casket overhung the table on each end. There'd be enough room to run the tape all the way around it, so that after he and Grassley signed it, it would be impossible to open without breaking the seal.

"Here," Cain said. "Let's find a roll of paper towels. We need to wipe some of this dirt off. The tape's got to stick."

His coffee was still warm when he got back to his office. By then, he wasn't sure he wanted it. But he took a sip anyway and then went to

26

the filing cabinet. Three weeks ago he'd put a TV on top of the cabinet and hooked it up to a JVC camcorder he'd found in a thrift shop.

Cain unlocked the filing cabinet and took out the tape. He'd watched it first by himself, and then he'd played it for Grassley. They'd brought in Lieutenant Nagata, and she gave her blessing to show it to an assistant district attorney. Cain and the ADA had copied the file onto a CD, had submitted it to the Superior Court of Monterey County with their application for an order of disinterment. Before that, they'd gone up to Napa to see Chris Hanley's mother. They didn't show her the tape. They hinted at what was on it, but that was all. She let them come back later in the afternoon, with a notary, so that she could sign the affidavit supporting their application.

Now he put the original tape into the camcorder, turned on the TV, and played it. He leaned back against his desk's front edge and watched. He'd seen it two dozen times, but it still transfixed him.

In the beginning, the first twenty seconds, there was white snow. And then, with the suddenness of a finger snap, the image appeared.

The old man sat in a leather-bound recliner chair. There was an IV stand beside him, some kind of apparatus on the floor next to it. The light was all fluorescent. The wall behind the chair was painted pistachio green. The man was stone bald, and an oxygen tube dipped past his ear on its way to his nostrils. Cain had taken a still image of this opening shot, had shown it around the sixth floor. Half a dozen people told him he was looking at a chemotherapy administration room.

"My name — my real name — is John Fonteroy," the man said. He was looking into the camera. Tubes disappeared into the turquoise hospital gown he wore. "I owned the Fonteroy Mortuary, on Geary Boulevard, in San Francisco."

He gave his old address and his social security number.

He reached to the table next to him, picked up a cup of water. There was a flexible straw in it. He drew it into his mouth and took a tiny sip. Then he put the cup back and looked to the camera again.

"I'm about to die," he said. "And this is my confession."

Now, an offscreen voice cut in. A woman's voice. She spoke with a light midwestern twang, but they'd never figured out who she was. They hadn't located the hospital where Fonteroy was sitting, hadn't tracked down where he'd gone after running away from his mortuary. They didn't know what name he'd been using since he'd fled the city, what name he'd used to check into the hospital.

"Tell them who you're talking to."

"I'm talking to you," the old man said. "My lawyer."

"You're telling me this because you want to?"

"Yes."

The tape had arrived in a plain envelope, postmarked from Chicago O'Hare. When Cain opened it, there was a handwritten note on white cardstock.

My instructions were to deliver this to you upon my client's death, which condition has recently occurred. My duty to him is discharged, and I have none to you.

It had been addressed to the SFPD Homicide Detail, and Cain had been the one to open it.

On the screen, John Fonteroy was staring at the camera. His breath whistled around the oxygen tubes in his nostrils.

"Did anyone coerce you?"

"No — I don't have to do this. I have the right to remain silent. I can die, silently. But I don't want to. I want to speak."

"Are you taking medications — pain medications — anything clouding your thoughts?"

"I won't have them until we're done here. They won't help, though. They won't stop what's happening."

"Did I tell you what to say?"

"You asked me not to say your name, and I won't. But you didn't tell me what I should say — you told me not to do this at all."

"By making this statement, you could be prosecuted. I told you that. You understand that."

"Yes."

"How long do you have to live?"

"Too long," he said. "Days. Maybe even a week."

The assistant district attorney had paused the tape here the third time they'd watched it together. He'd asked Cain if he understood

28

what she was doing, this twang-voiced midwestern lawyer. Cain had shaken his head, and the ADA explained it. She was trying to do them a favor. Her client was going to die, and she wanted to stay invisible. But she knew there would come a day when a judge or a jury had to see it, that this would have to be admitted into evidence. So she was laying the best foundation she could set down to overcome a hearsay objection. It might not work. All the rules of evidence cut against her. But her client hadn't left her much to work with.

"Why are you making this statement, Mr. Fonteroy?"

"I'm afraid of Hell."

Fonteroy looked into the camera, and Cain felt the old man's fear. Hell wasn't waiting for him; he was already in it. It was creeping up on him, hiding in every shadow. It was pumping through the tubes and into the port on his chest, yawning at him through the lens of the camera he was facing. He'd been feeling it consume him since 1985.

"Tell them what they need to know."

"I had a wife," Fonteroy said. "And a little girl. I didn't think much, when I started taking the money. It was for them, is what I told myself. I was doing it for them."

"You have to explain. Who was giving you money, and why?"

"They'd been looking for someone like me. They knocked on my door in 'eighty-one. Christmastime. I had something they wanted, and they were ready to pay. And —"

He glanced up at the IV above him and then, longingly, at the cup of water. He began to reach for it but stopped. It occurred to Cain, now, that the cup must have seemed very far away. That it must have been so heavy for him. The act of reaching — of holding on to it and bringing the straw to his dry lips — so burdensome. The combination of its proximity and its impossibility must have been maddening.

"And what?"

It took ten seconds for Fonteroy to turn back to the camera. Another five before he was focused again.

"And I was a coward," Fonteroy said. "So I said yes. Maybe anybody would've done it. I don't know. I just know I did."

"What did you have to do for the money?"

"Look the other way."

"When?"

"When they wanted me to. It'd be before a funeral but after the wake. When the coffin's getting sealed and no one sees inside it again."

"That's all?"

"I took the money, and I didn't look."

"But one time, John, you saw."

The man swallowed, and it made a dry sound, like rocks grinding against each other. His eyes shifted again to the cup of water.

"It was the Hanley kid, Christopher Hanley. The last visitation had just ended. They were waiting when I brought him into the back. They told me to step outside."

"Did you do it?"

"I took the money — I took it, and I did what they told me."

"But you saw something."

"I saw through the back window — only a little."

"But you saw. It's not something you heard about. Not a hunch you had. You saw."

Fonteroy nodded, or tried to.

"I didn't know what they'd been doing. What they were doing with the coffins. No clue, until that day, when I decided to look. I swear to God, ma'am — until then, I didn't know."

"What did you do?"

"Nothing. I should have tried to stop it, but I didn't."

"Why?"

"I was scared of them. You see a thing like that, and you find out what kind of man you really are. That's what I've been living with since."

"And after the burial?"

"I didn't go. I was supposed to drive the hearse that day. But I got my brother-in-law to do it. And then I took Marianne and Beatrice, and put them in the other car, and we left."

"Why did you run?"

"I couldn't do it again. Not after what I saw, what I overheard. But if I stopped taking the money — the next time, it'd be me. Or it'd be my wife. My little girl. I knew too much."

"What do you want the police to do?"

Fonteroy looked up, focused his eyes into the camera. The next words he spoke, he pronounced very carefully.

"You need to dig up Christopher Hanley. They buried him

July 17, 1985, in El Carmelo. That's down the coast from the city. A good spot, by the ocean. I could only wish for a place like that. And once you open the lid, you'll understand."

"Who were the men, the ones paying you?"

Fonteroy shook his head.

"I don't know."

"Mr. Fonteroy — you can't hold anything back. It's too late for that."

"I never knew their names. But if the police go to El Carmelo, they'll understand. They've got tools now. Tests that weren't around back then. Maybe they can put it together."

"What are you talking about?"

"Turn off the camera. I'm done. Either they'll figure it out or they won't. But we're done. Okay?"

The screen went to snow.

Cain turned the TV off. He rewound the tape, then took it from the camcorder and locked it in the file cabinet. He finished his coffee and put the paper cup in the trash. He looked at his watch. If he hurried, he might make it to Lucy before she woke.

5

SHE OWNED A row house on Twenty-Second Avenue, a block north of Golden Gate Park. He climbed the steps from the sidewalk and stood on the tiny porch to look through the predawn rain to the crowns of the eucalyptus trees on the other side of Fulton Street. When the wind came from that direction, Lucy's entire home had the clean, medicinal smell of the trees. But when it blew from the north, the house seemed like it was alone on a mountaintop. Wrapped in clouds and cut off from everything. They could stay in her upstairs bed all day and listen to the foghorn beneath the Golden Gate Bridge. There was nothing empty about that low note as long as he was with her.

He let himself in, took off his shoes, and went upstairs. The bedroom door was open, and he tiptoed past it. There were two boxes of his things in the hall. To reach the bathroom, he had to step around them. Lucy hadn't said anything yet, but he kept expecting her to bring it up, to ask when he was going to move the rest. He showered, then went to Lucy's bed wearing one of her towels around his waist.

"Hey," she said.

"Sorry."

She moved toward him when he dropped the towel and got under the covers.

"You're all wet," she said. "Shit, Gavin."

He started to pull away, but she followed him.

"I don't care," she said. "Hold me."

He put his arm around her and tucked his knees into the bend of her legs, so that the length of his body followed hers. She pressed her back into his chest. Her T-shirt had been through the wash so many times, it was as thin as tissue paper. Warmth radiated through the cotton.

"My first lesson's at eight," she said. "That's just three hours."

Once her lessons started, he wouldn't be able to sleep. But that didn't matter.

"This is just a little nap. I've got to go to Menlo Park early enough to be back by noon."

"Then let's go to sleep," she said. "Quick."

"Okay."

He woke, briefly, when Lucy left the bed. She crossed the room wearing nothing but her old high school T-shirt. As she disappeared into the hall, he wanted to lift himself and follow her. But he was asleep again before she started her shower.

The doorbell woke him the second time. Her first student had arrived. He heard their voices back and forth, the mother greeting Lucy and then saying goodbye to her daughter. The student was a little girl. Her voice, coming up from the lower floor as they crossed through the length of the house, sounded like the warbling of a small bird. He listened to them go into the music room that overlooked the garden.

When Lucy was teaching a new piece, she'd usually play it first so that her student could listen and watch. Cain sat up when she started, looking across the bed to the window. There were raindrops on the glass, backlit by a gray sky. Beneath him, Lucy hit the first eight or nine notes. He tried to think of the name of the piece. She'd been teaching it to several of her students lately, but before that, she'd played it for him. Just the two of them in the music room. Her wineglass was perched on the piano's lid, the water in it trembling with each note. They'd left the bay windows open a crack, and the wind had pushed in, carrying a fine mist of fog and the scent of lavender from the garden.

He got out of her bed, wrapping her towel around himself again and listening as she played. It was a calm thing, this song. The first time he'd heard it, he'd imagined Lucy on a tiny island, playing the song as the moon came in and out from behind the cover of slow-drifting clouds. The water around her was dappled with shadow, and then, suddenly, lit silver-white. The image fit her well. She needed an island like that, a place of refuge where she was cut off from everything but the weather and the heavens. Maybe she'd already built it in her mind, and when she looked out her living room windows, she didn't see the street or the cars parked on it. She saw the dark water. The moon lighting a path across its rippling surface, inviting her to walk to the opposite shore.

When he turned off the shower and went to the empty guest room to dress, he could hear the piano again. Now the student was playing. The notes were correct, but the timing was off. She wasn't used to the piece yet, this little girl. The song stopped and he heard Lucy's voice. They talked back and forth, and there was a bit of laughter. The student began to play again, and Cain stood in front of the closet and picked a tie. There were only two to choose from, so it was easy. He strapped on his shoulder holster and then knelt at the little safe. He punched in the code and took out his gun, then closed the door. Lucy hadn't asked him to buy the safe, but when he'd brought it one day, she looked at it and understood. If he wasn't wearing his gun, he'd have to lock it up. There were children in and out of this house, something they needed to get used to.

He holstered the gun, then stood and put on his suit jacket. He headed down the stairs, and when she heard him, she broke away from the lesson. They met in the entry hall. She reached up to his shoulder, then kissed the corner of his mouth.

"The thing last night, with the helicopter?" she whispered.

"It's still going on," he said. "It's why I'm going to Menlo Park — Matt Redding can help me find somebody, maybe."

"Is everything okay?"

"For me it is," he said. From the music room, Lucy's student stopped after the first five or six bars and then started from the beginning. "It's not going so well for the mayor."

"Is this even a murder case?"

"I don't know. Someone's trying to blackmail him, and we want to know who."

"Will it be in the paper?"

"They're trying to keep it out," Cain said. "We'll see how that goes. Either way I'll tell you."

"I'd like that."

He looked again toward the music room. The little girl was getting it this time. It wasn't the calm moonlight that Lucy could find in the piece, but Cain could tell that the girl sensed it there, that she was trying to catch it. And now he remembered the song's name.

"It's that Debussy piece, the one you played for me," Cain said. "*Clair de lune,* right?"

She took both his lapels and pulled him to her.

"You're good."

"You should get back to her. Tell her she's getting it."

"I should," she whispered. "I'll play something else for you, tonight."

"I might be late coming back."

"You're always late," Lucy said. "But I'm always here."

He put his hands on her waist and held her close before he went out. She followed him to the door but no further. She hadn't left this house in more than four years.

Matt Redding's office was a garage off Johnston Lane in Menlo Park. He had three desks and a dozen computers. Having perfected what he'd sought to build, he spent most of his time waiting to be bought out. The last time he'd spoken with Cain, five companies were courting him. He was giving demonstrations, taking limo rides down to Mountain View. He spent his free time on websites specializing in Caribbean real estate. Once, while they were sitting outside a courtroom before Redding testified, he'd asked Cain what he'd do if he owned an island. What if there was a settlement on it? Would he relocate the villagers, or let them stay?

That was the thing about Redding: In a year, he might be worth a hundred million dollars. Or nothing. The last time they'd met, he needed Cain to pay for lunch.

Cain pushed open the door and stepped inside. Redding was at his desk, but came around from behind it to shake his hand.

"I got your text," he said. "Did I answer it? I forget."

"I figured I'd just come anyway."

"Sit down," Redding said. "Show me what you have."

They sat at a beige couch that Redding had probably found on a curb somewhere. Cain slid the coffee table closer and set the folder on it. He took out the pictures and handed them to Redding.

"I'm trying to find this woman," Cain said.

Redding went through the photographs. He spent a minute or more with each one.

"What do you know about her?"

"Nothing," Cain said. "She's in these pictures. That's it."

"Is she dead?"

"I don't know."

"Okay," Redding said. He had to have known there was more to it than that. "We've got three shots of her, three different angles. That's good. What about the rest of it?"

"What do you mean?"

"The rooms, the stuff on the night table. You want me to run it?"

"You can do that?"

Cain had used Redding twice, and both times it had been to run down faces. He hadn't realized the program went past that.

"We'll see."

"How long will it take?"

"I've got to scan the photos, upload them. I might touch a couple of these up, get rid of the distortions. So, figure thirty minutes."

"You want a cup of coffee? Some breakfast?"

"If you're buying."

Cain walked through Menlo Park's small downtown strip until he found a coffee bar. He ordered an espresso and sat at a table in the corner. He'd mentioned Matt Redding's name to Lucy this morning. It had come out naturally, no warning of any sort to precede it. He'd been so tired he'd forgotten his usual caution. But if it affected her, he hadn't seen it.

And he'd been noticing things lately. Small indications. This morning, for instance, there'd been a bar of handmade soap in her shower. It was the kind they sold at the farmer's market in the Inner Sunset. Maybe someone had brought it to her as a gift — one of her students, or one of their mothers. But that was an intimate gift for a piano teacher, and he didn't think Lucy's grocery delivery service covered the farmer's market. She couldn't have ordered it online, because she had no computer and no cell phone. An Internet connection would be a window, one that commanded landscapes she had chosen not to see.

That left open another possibility: she might be going out. Putting on shoes, getting a coat if it was raining. He couldn't imagine what that would cost her. The strength she must be calling upon to take her fear and carry it with her out the front door. It stung a little that she hadn't told him. But maybe she was saving it. Maybe she didn't want to get him excited until she was sure she could sustain the outings.

He set the bag with Redding's sandwich on the desk and handed him a paper cup of coffee.

"Anything?"

Redding took the lid off the coffee and brought it close to his face to smell it.

"No luck on the woman," he said. "But I think I know why. All you've got is the pictures, right? You don't know when they were taken?"

"No idea."

"They're thirty years old, and she's dead."

"Explain that."

"If she died in 1985, she wouldn't have a footprint on the Internet. I can't find what's not there."

Cain reached to the desk and turned the first photograph around so that he could study it. There was nothing that explicitly dated the photo, other than the fact that it was probably shot on black-and-white film. The woman could be walking on the street today. She wasn't wearing jewelry or makeup, and her hair was pulled into a messy ponytail. There was nothing about her that announced itself as any particular decade.

"Ask me: *Why 1985, Matt?*"

"Why 1985?"

"First, the dress. It's a Jean Patou design. You heard of him?"

"Is that even a real question?" Cain asked. "Come on."

"Patou, he died in 1936. But in the mideighties, a couture house in Paris started licensing his designs. You know that word — *couture*?"

Cain looked up at him, then turned back to the photo.

"Thin ice, Redding," he said. "Go on."

"Look at her. At the dress."

Redding took the third photograph and set it alongside the first. Now Cain had one shot of the woman backed against a brick wall, her hands held up in a gesture of panic. Next to it, in the third image, she stood against the nightstand, pain and fear on her face as she drank from the flask. Her dress was striking, though not as much as she was. It had a full-length sleeve on the right arm but didn't even cover her left shoulder. To balance that asymmetry, there was a half-train coming down the left, hanging past the back of her knee. The hem on the right side didn't reach the halfway point of her thigh. The dress was wrapped around her, the fabric gathered and held in place with a jeweled pin above her hip.

"It looks black in the photograph," Redding said, "but it might've been green. See?"

He swiveled his computer screen so that Cain could see the website he'd been studying. It was a couture resale store, and the dress Redding had found was exactly what the woman was wearing. Cain could order it right now if he had sixteen thousand dollars.

"If they're still selling them," Cain said, "we can't be sure of the year."

"That's not all, or I wouldn't be sure."

Redding lifted the second picture from the folder, the one showing the nightstand and its contents. He tapped the pile of pills.

"This is your crack in the door—enough to get your foot in, maybe," Redding said. "You ever heard of benzyldiomide?"

Cain shook his head.

"Me neither, until fifteen minutes ago. How about Thrallinex?"

"Never heard of it," Cain said. "What was it?"

"The trade name, here in the U.S. It came in five- and ten-milligram tablets. These are the tens."

Redding passed the photograph up to Cain so that he could take a closer look at the pills. They were elongated ovals, pale white even in the underexposed image. Each one had a break-line indentation across the middle so they could be split into half-doses by hand. And along the edge, each pill bore the same imprint, but it was impossible for him to make out. He didn't understand how Redding's algorithm actually worked, how it could take such small details from a blurry image and produce accurate search results.

"Thrallinex went off the market almost as soon as it came on," Redding said. "It got approval in Europe, then here. But five months later—I'm talking October 1985—they withdrew it worldwide."

"They?"

"The manufacturer," Redding said. He looked at a sticky note on the edge of his desk. "Raab and Weisskopf AG. A German company."

"I've never heard of that, either."

"It didn't outlive the lawsuit."

"What was it for?"

"It caused acute liver failure. Also, some kind of skin thing."

"Not the lawsuit, the pill—what was it supposed to do?"

"It was a hypnotic. And a muscle relaxant."

"Like Valium?"

"More like Rohypnol," Redding said. "But you should talk to a doctor. That's not my expertise."

Cain looked at his watch. He'd be able to talk to a doctor in about forty-five minutes, if he didn't hit any traffic on the way back.

"Is there anything else?"

"The keys, here on the nightstand?"

"Don't tell me you know what they fit."

"Not all of them," Redding said. "But the one on top—the long one—that's the ignition to a 1984 Cadillac Eldorado."

"You're sure about that?"

Redding nodded toward the bank of linked computers on the back wall.

"They're sure," he said. "So I'd swear to it. Hand on a Bible."

"You've got three reference points tying it down," Cain said. "So either the photos were taken in the eighties, or someone hired a Hollywood prop coordinator to make sure everything fits."

"Pretty much."

"All right," Cain said. "I've got to get back."

Redding stood and reached across the desk to shake his hand.

"Maybe I'll get to testify again?"

"We'll see," Cain said. "I don't know where this one's going."

"The first one, that was a good time."

"Not for everyone."

Cain slid the photographs back into the folder, then put it under his left arm.

"I didn't mean it like that," Redding said.

"It's okay."

He walked Cain to the door.

"Seriously, Gavin. I didn't—"

39

"I said it's all right," Cain said. "And she's doing a lot better now."

"Both of you—you're okay?"

"More than," Cain said.

Redding opened the door.

"Give me a call if you get anything else I can run," he said to Cain. "We'll find her."

6

CAIN STOPPED AT a light on Santa Cruz Avenue, put his phone on his knee, and began to dictate a note to himself. This didn't require any real precision. He just spoke in a free flow of thoughts.

Thrallinex. Benzyldiomide.

Redding thought the drug was the key, and he might be right. In an hour, the ME could tell Cain how it compared to a hypnotic like Rohypnol, what a dozen pills would have done to the girl. Then there was the dress. When it came to high-end fashion, he had no idea where to begin. He'd been wearing the same suit three days running, and knew switching ties and shirts wasn't fooling anyone. But every problem had an entrance. Maybe a clerk in one of the shops around Union Square could point him in the right direction.

The '84 Cadillac Eldorado was something he might be able to work with, though. No one had to register a dress. Pills got passed hand to hand. But cops knew how to find cars.

As he was driving past the airport, his phone rang. He picked it up on speaker, without looking at the screen to see the caller.

"This is Inspector Cain," he said.

"And this is your partner," Grassley answered. "Where are you?"

"Twenty minutes south. They open the casket yet?"

"We're waiting on the ME."

"You in the morgue, or the office?"

"Morgue — you're gonna be here for it?"

"That's the plan."

"We start in fifteen minutes. That's why I called. If you're not here, I'll make them wait."

"Good," Cain said. "Hey, Grassley?"

"Yeah?"

"Think you could borrow a computer?" Cain asked. "I need you to look something up."

"Hang on," Grassley said, and then he must have put the phone on mute. Cain drove in silence, watched a mile tick past on the odometer. Grassley came back. "I got a Web browser. What do you want?"

"Harry Castelli," Cain said. "Where he was thirty years ago. What he was doing from 'eighty-five to 'eighty-six."

"This have to do with that thing you can't talk about?"

"Yeah."

"You gonna keep me hanging?"

"For now," Cain said. "Until I convince Nagata to bring you in."

"All right," Grassley said. "I got his Wikipedia page."

"Anything about the eighties?"

"Hold on. It's loading."

Now Grassley was mumbling as he scanned through the page. Cain pulled into the left lane and accelerated to pass a corporate shuttle bus. Then Grassley was back.

"I got it, right here," he said. "'Eighty-one to 'eighty-four, he was living with his parents in London. His dad—"

"Was the ambassador, right? I remember that now."

"—a Reagan appointee, yeah," Grassley said. "But in 'eighty-four, Harry came back for college. At Cal."

"So we can put him in Berkeley, more or less, for the next four years?"

"He graduated in 'eighty-eight."

"With honors?"

"It doesn't say."

"That means no," Cain said. "What'd he major in?"

"Political science."

"And after he left?"

"He went back to London. It says he was a freelance consultant."

"For what?"

Grassley was reading to himself, maybe following links. Then his voice came back, clear enough for Cain to hear.

"There's nothing solid. U.K. businesses, is what it sounds like."

"He was selling his connections," Cain said. "Access to his dad. That's not a minor position."

"Makes sense."

"Dad was still the ambassador in 'eighty-eight?"

42

There was more silence while Grassley chased that down.

"He stayed on through Reagan, and Bush reappointed him. Clinton replaced him in 'ninety-three. February 1993."

"And then Harry had to go look for his first honest job."

"You're not a fan."

"You can hear that, even over the phone?"

"I didn't hear anything, sir."

"That's right," Cain said. "What'd he do after 'ninety-three?"

"Came home. He got an MBA at Stanford, worked for a couple startups. He got in at the beginning of the bubble. Cashed out in 2001."

"That's when he ran for the Board of Supervisors," Cain said. "There were signs all over town."

"It says he split with his dad, rebranded himself as a Democrat."

"Didn't he have a stint in Congress?"

"Two, or one and a half — he left in the middle of his second, and ran for mayor."

"Ambitious," Cain said. "Working his way up."

"All of them are. You know the type."

"Sure."

"What's he gotten into?" Grassley asked. "I mean — is he some kind of suspect?"

"Nice try," Cain said. "I'm not biting. See you in ten."

Cain buzzed into the medical examiner's suite and met Grassley in the bare-bones waiting room. An intern was spraying Lysol onto the painted concrete walls, then scrubbing the mildew off with a grime-caked rag. Nothing could mask the smell down here, though.

"She's waiting back there," Grassley said. "But they want us to suit up first. Respirators, hoods. The whole thing."

"You'll be glad for it."

Grassley followed Cain to the double doors leading from reception into the main examination room. So far, he'd seen three autopsies, each time with Cain at his side. Those bodies had come to the morgue still warm. They'd been at the scenes, had knelt next to the dead and searched their pockets with gloved hands. By the time they got to the morgue, there weren't any surprises left.

But anything could be waiting inside this casket. Cain paused at the door and looked at his partner. The x-ray was only a hint of what was beneath the lid. Judging by the look on his face, Grassley knew it.

"Let's do this," Cain said. "I've got to meet Nagata at noon."

They suited up in a spare office. A pair of Tyvek body suits had been laid out on the desk. Full-face respirators lay nearby. Plastic booties to go over their shoes, thick rubber gloves.

"Nice they got this out for us," Cain said.

"It was that kid, the one disinfecting the lobby."

"Suit up," Cain said. "Bag your feet first, then pull the cuffs tight. Same around your wrists. You want to seal out the air, or you'll be going to the dry cleaner."

"You've done one like this?"

"I did one twice as old," Cain said. "They'd buried her in 'fifty-two. It was bad, and she was nearly a skeleton. You get a casket with a good seal, and it locks everything in — unless the gasses blow it open from the inside."

"That happens — they blow open?"

"Sometimes," Cain said. "But it didn't happen to Chris Hanley. His casket's intact. And it hasn't had so long to dry out . . . You didn't eat a big breakfast, did you?"

Grassley glanced at his feet.

"Shit."

"Come on — you saw the x-ray."

"I thought it'd just be bones. Just — a whole lot of bones."

"Coming back up from El Carmelo in the van, what'd you smell?"

"Dirt," Grassley said. "Wood."

"It's got a good seal on it."

"You think?"

"We'll see."

Rachel Levy, the acting medical examiner, was waiting for them in the autopsy suite. The casket was on one of the six tables. Cain's tamper-evident seal tape circled each end of the wooden box. Dr. Levy nodded to each of them. No one shook hands in here. Two tables over, another autopsy was in progress, an assistant medical examiner elbows-deep. A lab tech stood behind him with a glass specimen jar. As for the cadaver, it was so thoroughly disassembled, Cain could guess neither the sex nor the age.

"I watched John Fonteroy's video," Dr. Levy said. Cain turned back to her. She was gathering her curly hair into a tight bun. Her face shield lay on an empty table nearby. "You ever see anything like it?"

"Not even close," Cain said. He handed her the face shield when she was finished with her hair.

"Maybe you should talk to some of the old guys," Dr. Levy said. "The ones who worked homicide in the eighties. Fonteroy's place was on Geary. Find some guys who worked that neighborhood, and maybe one of them will know something."

"Are there any left?" Cain asked.

"I wouldn't know," Dr. Levy said. She'd been brought in from Seattle after the last medical examiner had been dismissed for compromising a case. A month in, she was still learning her way around the office and didn't even know the current crop of inspectors, let alone the retirees. "It's just a thought."

"Not a bad one," Cain said. "You saw the x-ray?"

"Ten minutes ago."

"How hard will it be, opening this?"

Dr. Levy turned to the assistant medical examiner and the technician helping him.

"Jim — you guys got a casket key collection?"

Jim didn't look up from the chest cavity. He was using a metal probe, maybe tracing a bullet's trajectory.

"By the wash station," he said. "Third drawer down, green plastic pencil box."

"Thanks."

"I'll get it," Cain said. He looked at Grassley. "Double-check that camera. Make sure it's rolling, the battery has enough juice."

"Bring her the pliers," Jim said, still concentrating on the problem in front of him. "Same drawer. Thing looks rusted all to hell."

The drawer had come off its slide tracks, and he had to kneel down and jiggle it to coax it open. The pencil box was beneath a pair of short-handled bolt cutters — useful, Cain supposed, if a body came wrapped in padlocked chains. There was a ring of assorted handcuff keys, a scatter of pliers and vise grips. Cain grabbed a couple sets of pliers and the green box.

When he came back, Dr. Levy was using a wet rag to wipe the dirt from a small metal protrusion at the foot of the casket. He put the box and the pliers on the edge of the table.

"You rolling?" he asked Grassley.

"We're on."

"Dr. Levy," Cain said. "It's your show."

She took a pair of pliers and gripped the rusted knob. Cain watched as she flexed her arms and strained against the pliers' rubber grips. She let go, clamped on at a different angle, and tried again. The knob, which was no bigger than a half-inch hex nut, didn't budge.

"All right," Dr. Levy said. She brought her face shield up and looked at Cain. "I hate this — it's like asking my husband when I can't open a jar. Do you mind?"

"It's nothing."

He stepped up and took the pliers from Dr. Levy.

"What is it?" he asked. "What do I do?"

"It covers the casket lock — protects it from corrosion, we hope. Either it'll unscrew counterclockwise, or it's got a rubber gasket and just pushes on. So grab on hard and twist it, and give it a yank at the same time."

"Okay."

Cain fit the pliers over the rusted metal. He found a good hold and then put both his hands on the pliers' handles. He clamped down and began to twist, but the cap disintegrated beneath the force of his grip. It fell away in dust and flakes of oxidized metal.

"Or you could just break everything," Dr. Levy said. "That's another way to do it."

"Sorry."

Cain used the pliers to tap at the last pieces of the cap, and they fell off. He'd uncovered a screw-threaded throat that came out of the casket wall. In the middle of this, there was a hexagonal hole, and he could see the green patina of bronze. He set the pliers down and stepped back so that Dr. Levy could look at it.

"Maybe we're in luck," she said.

She opened the pencil box. Inside it were half a dozen bronze and steel casket keys. They reminded Cain of miniature engine cranks, the kind of things you might have used to start a Model-T. Dr. Levy sorted through them until she found one she liked. She fit it into the lock and put her weight on it, and it began to turn. Grease-starved gears groaned inside the casket walls, and then the lid rose a few millimeters. There was a long hiss, as if Dr. Levy had given a slow twist to a soda bottle's cap.

"The smell of success," Jim said.

"Jesus," Grassley coughed.

"Inspector?" Dr. Levy asked. "Would you like to remove your seals?"

"Yes, ma'am," Cain said. "You getting this, Grassley?"

"I'm getting it. You don't have to ask."

Cain found the edges of his seals and inspected them. He turned to the camera.

"For the record, neither seal's been touched," he said. "Zoom in, get that."

"If anyone had messed with that thing," Jim said, "it wouldn't have hissed. That's a solid casket."

"Thank you, Jim," Dr. Levy said. "We'd like a clean tape from here on."

"I'm just saying."

"From here on."

"All right."

Cain popped the seals off and put them into a zip bag while Grassley filmed him.

"Okay," Dr. Levy said, when he was finished. "Let's lift this lid. You're at the head, and I'm at the foot. The hinges might be a little stiff."

The lid swung up ninety degrees, and the smell that wafted up with it had reaching hands and an implacable grip. Cain stepped around and took a place next to Grassley. Dr. Levy was on the other side of him, and Jim and the lab tech left their autopsy and came to look inside.

"Oh, Christ, do you see that?" Grassley whispered. "Do you *see* it?"

7

"WE SEE IT," Dr. Levy said. She pointed at the inside of the lid. "Here — and here."

At some point in its three decades underground, the casket's lid liner had fallen apart. The yellowed silk had dropped away from its padded underlayment, detaching completely from the lid. Now it lay atop the corpses like a shroud. There were rips and holes near its top, and through one of the larger ones, Cain could see a jawbone, all its teeth still set. The silk covered everything else.

No one reached to remove the shroud, because they were still looking at the inside of the casket's lid. Where the wood was visible through the shredded padding, the scratch marks were clear.

"Is that — Are you getting that?" Cain asked.

"I'm getting it," Grassley said.

"Wait," Dr. Levy said. "Wait a minute."

She went to one of the drawers and returned with a pair of tweezers. Carver stepped aside to give her space. She leaned over the casket and delicately plucked something from between the wood-planked lid and the polyester batting. When she turned, with the object in the tweezers' grasp, Jim wordlessly held out a plastic sample tube. Cain couldn't see what she was gripping, but after she dropped it into the sample container, she took it and held it for the camera.

"This is a fingernail," she said. Looking into the lens, putting it on the record. "Dark green polish that chipped off and stuck to the wood. It was embedded in the coffin lid."

"It was a woman, and she was alive when she went in," Cain said. "They put her in there, on top of Christopher Hanley, and buried her alive."

"It looks that way, but —" She turned toward Grassley, who had backed up to the wall and was leaning against it. "Are you okay, Inspector?"

"Yes, ma'am," Grassley said. "I just need a minute."

"Don't hold your breath," Dr. Levy said. "You need air."

"Here," the lab tech said. "I'll shoot it."

"Don't turn it off," Cain said. "It has to be one shot."

"I've got it."

The technician took the camera from Grassley and went up to the casket. Cain stood next to him, and then Grassley came reluctantly to his right. They all looked down together as Dr. Levy and Jim pulled off the silken shroud.

Cain hadn't been able to find any records about Christopher Hanley, and didn't know anything about the kid until he and the assistant DA were sitting in Marjorie Hanley's breakfast nook in Napa. She poured them each a cup of coffee and told them her son had died of AIDS. He was seventeen years old. He'd spent most of the last year of his life on a hospital bed set up in the living room. They'd lived in the Haight then. From his bed, he'd been able to look across Buena Vista Avenue at the park. In the beginning, when he wasn't strong enough to get in and out on his own, she'd needed her husband's help to lift him into the bed. At the end, she lifted him out of the bed and carried him from the house herself. He weighed just eighty pounds.

Now, standing over Christopher's casket and looking down, one hand pressed to his respirator to keep it tight, Cain thought how tight a fit it must have been. Even with the kid shrunken down to nothing, when they pushed the woman in on top of him and shut the lid on her, there would have hardly been room for her to move.

She must have run out of air quickly. Ten minutes. Less, even: in her frenzy to escape, she'd have burned through the oxygen in a hurry. She'd clawed through the liner and the padding, had dug her nails deep into the wooden lid. Her hands were frozen beside her face. Her skin was black and purple, her features completely indistinguishable. Her teeth were intact, visible because her jaw hung open. That was something they could go on, if she had dental records in a database somewhere.

She had blond hair, and had gone into the coffin naked. Underneath her, Christopher Hanley wore what was left of a white suit.

49

"How come he's in better shape than her?" Cain asked. "You can make out his face."

"He was embalmed," Dr. Levy said. "She wasn't, if she went in alive. He might look even better if he hadn't spent thirty years underneath her."

"I'm getting a crime scene team in here," Cain said. "I don't want you to do anything else until they're here."

Dr. Levy looked up at him.

"Fingerprints?"

"That's right."

"Anything on the outside, that's all gone. Thirty years in the dirt, no way."

"But the inside?"

"Maybe."

Cain leaned over the casket again. Driving up here, he'd almost talked himself into believing that if he found a second corpse in this casket, she'd be wearing the rotten remains of a Jean Patou cocktail dress. That there'd be a jeweled pin in there somewhere, and a set of handcuffs. What were the odds that on the same day he was asked to track down a woman from a 1985 photograph, he'd find a woman in a 1985 coffin? She had the right color hair, and polish on her toenails. But none of that proved a thing.

There was only one way to check that he could think of, but it was a long shot. She wasn't handcuffed, and she'd gone into the coffin lively enough to rip up the lining and claw into the lid. If it was her, a long time must have passed between the last photograph and the moment they put her in the box. Long enough, anyway, for the drugs to wear off.

"Can you have a lab run toxicology on her?"

"I can run it," Dr. Levy said. "I don't know what I'll find. And you know our backlog. It'll take months. If I gave you samples, you could get a private lab. It'd be faster."

"Just run it and see."

"It'd help if I knew what you were looking for—this long, the drugs won't be there, but maybe their decomposition products will be."

"Tell the lab to look for everything. But especially Thrallinex."

"You know something you're not telling me?"

"I don't know anything yet," Cain said. He turned to Grassley. "Get that team in here. I've got to go."

Cain found a meter on Turk Street, directly behind the federal building. His phone rang as he was unbuckling his seat belt. It wasn't a number he recognized, but he took the call.

"This is Inspector Cain."

"It took me longer than you wanted, but I did it."

The caller was a woman. Late twenties or early thirties, her voice either very professional or extremely distrustful. Or maybe both, he thought, once it clicked and he realized who she was.

"Melissa Montgomery," Cain said.

"Yes, and I don't have long. They'll be at the house at two o'clock. They'll be waiting for you."

"It's got to be me and them," Cain said. "The wife and the daughter. Castelli doesn't get to sit in."

"He won't get in your way. I've got him booked through eight o'clock."

"Did you tell him where I'm going?"

"It might have slipped my mind," she said, and hung up. All business, this woman. If she felt anything at all about what she was telling him, Cain hadn't heard it.

His phone rang again before he made it out of the car. Grassley this time. He sat back down and answered.

"What's going on?"

"The techs are going over the casket. The good one, the guy you like, he's in charge."

"Where are you? You should be there."

"Christ, Cain — I'm watching from the other side of the room," Grassley said. He was keeping his voice low so that no one would hear their conversation.

"You want to know why I asked about the Thrallinex."

"If I'm working this, I need to know what you know. You can't keep all the cards."

"You're right," Cain said. He stepped out of the car and shut the door. "What Nagata's got me on, and what we've got in the morgue — they might be two sides of the same thing. It's just a hunch, but it feels right."

"You'll bring me in?"

"Not officially," Cain said. "But let's do this — I'm already late for my meeting. And I've got an interview at two. So stay with the body, and get as much as you can from Dr. Levy. I'll buy you dinner at the Western, at five. Bring Inspector Chun, if you can find her."

"You think I'll want to eat after this?"

"Up to you," Cain said. "If you don't, I save money."

He hung up, went through the federal building's glass doors, and handed his badge to the guard at the security checkpoint.

Lieutenant Nagata and Special Agent Fischer were waiting for him in a windowless conference room on the thirteenth floor. The walls were battleship gray, and the wooden table was so pitted, it might have been used as a chopping block. The contractors who had re-done the rest of the place must have missed this room. But some-one had brought in an urn of coffee, and it smelled like it had been brewed that day. Cain poured himself a cup and then sat next to his boss, across from Fischer.

"I'll start," Fischer said. He liked the way she got right into it. "We rode herd on the guys at the lab, got them to expedite. But it's like we thought — no prints anywhere, no DNA on the flap. Whoever mailed the letter wore gloves, used a sponge instead of licking the envelope."

"You said you had other resources?"

"I'm getting there," Fischer said. "Since the anthrax attacks — 2001, we're talking — the Post Office has a program called Mail Isola-tion Control and Tracking. You're familiar?"

"No," Cain said. Nagata shook her head.

"The system, it photographs every piece of mail that comes in, in the order it's received. So if you get a letter and you don't know where it came from, you can go to the MICT database and look at every letter that got processed just before and after."

"You know where he mailed it?"

"We pulled the MICT photographs, found the letter, then looked at the twenty pieces on either side. Most of those had return addresses, all in North Beach. So at seven this morning, we went knocking on doors. We woke up a lady on Chestnut Street, showed her a photo of the envelope she'd mailed — birthday money for her grandson, she said. And she dropped it in the blue box at Bay and Stockton."

"Did you —"

"We had a fingerprint team at the box in fifteen minutes. Right now, we've got agents running down prints from everyone we know about who mailed a letter from that site. But that's a long shot, the prints."

"If he wore gloves and used a sponge when he did the letter, he would've used them when he mailed it," Nagata said.

"That's what we think," Fischer answered. "But we've got to check — and we're also fanning through the neighborhood, looking for cameras."

"Bay and Stockton," Cain said. "That's residential. Pretty quiet."

"Right. There aren't any storefronts, but we're looking for web-cams, private security systems. At least two hundred apartment windows look down on that intersection."

"Another long shot," Cain said.

"But it's like I said — we've got to check. Turn every stone."

"Where are you on the enemy list?" Cain asked.

"It's progressing," she said. "A man like Castelli — let's just say he's got as many enemies as friends."

"Anybody stand out?"

"Like I said, it's progressing." Her eyes cut to Nagata, and Cain wasn't sure if his lieutenant noticed or not. She was busy taking notes. "I'll let you know when we find something."

"All right."

He wondered what had happened that Fischer already distrusted Nagata. Maybe Fischer distrusted everyone, as a way to save time.

"What about you?" Nagata said to Cain. She underlined something on her spiral pad. "What have you found?"

"The woman in the photos, she died in 1985," Cain said. "She came in wearing a sixteen-thousand-dollar Jean Patou dress, was force-fed an incapacitating dose of Thrallinex, and disappeared. The guy who brought her was probably driving a 1984 Cadillac Eldorado."

Agent Fischer was staring at him, waiting for him to go on. But he didn't say what he thought had happened next. That they'd put her back in the Cadillac and driven her to the mortuary. Someone had gone inside and handed John Fonteroy an envelope, then told him to step out back and have a smoke. They'd have had to bring her in quickly, because Christopher Hanley's family would've been milling around out front. She hadn't been gagged and she hadn't been bound, so they must have been confident they could control her.

That she wouldn't scream or fight back until after they forced her on top of Christopher Hanley and closed the casket. The last light a narrowing crack, and then nothing but blackness for thirty years.

He couldn't prove any of that yet, but that wasn't the only reason he kept it back. He might have trusted Agent Fischer with it, but he didn't think Nagata would go five minutes before she reported it to Castelli. Agent Fischer must have been thinking the same thing when she dodged his question about the enemy lists.

"You went to see Matthew Redding, didn't you?" Nagata said.

"This morning."

"Explain how you know all that," Fischer said. "And who's this guy Redding?"

8

THERE WAS A flagpole in the Castellis' front yard, the gold-trimmed San Francisco ensign showing a phoenix rising from a ring of flames. Cain looked at it, and then beyond at the Spanish-style house that clung to the sea cliffs above China Beach. He'd checked in with the patrolmen stationed on the lower portion of the street before coming the rest of the way up. A squad car parked next to a fire hydrant, keeping out of sight of the house, so they wouldn't alarm anyone.

Cain looked the place over as he walked up the driveway. It was a good thing Castelli had made some money in Silicon Valley before the crash. The only thing Cain knew for sure about real estate was that he didn't have any, but he did know Castelli couldn't have picked up a house like this on a politician's pay. There must have been twenty rooms in the place.

He stepped off the brick driveway and followed a path lined with waist-high rosemary bushes to the front door. Everything was wet and cold, and smelled of the ocean and the pine bark mulch that was spread through the flower beds. He rang the bell and listened to the heavy chimes echo inside the house.

Castelli's daughter, a dark-eyed nineteen-year-old, opened the door. Alexa Castelli. The patrolmen down the street had plenty to say about her, and now he understood why. She was using one hand to keep a bath towel wrapped across her chest, and the other to hold her wet hair in a pile atop her head. Steam rose from the back of her bare neck.

"You're the cop."

"Your mother's here?"

"She's in the back, waiting," Alexa said. She opened the door the rest of the way. "We've never had a detective come and see us."

She let go of her hair and shook it out, so that the dark pile fanned across her shoulders. Rivulets of bath water ran past the rise of her clavicles and then down her chest to the towel.

"Why don't you go get dressed?" Cain said. "And I'll start with your mom."

"Why don't I?"

She didn't sound the least bit interested in putting on clothes. But she turned and went back across the Saltillo tile floor, leaving small wet prints behind her. Cain waited until she was out of sight, and then he stepped inside and closed the door after himself. The only sound was a bathtub draining.

"Mrs. Castelli?" he called. "Mona Castelli?"

"*Back here.*"

He crossed the entry hall and entered a room that didn't seem to have any purpose except to be large. The carpet underfoot was thick and white. He was probably supposed to take off his shoes, but he didn't. Mona Castelli was nowhere to be seen.

"Ma'am?"

"*I'm in the sunroom.*"

He wandered through more of the house — a vast stone and stainless-steel kitchen, a den, a humidor larger than Lucy's bathroom — and then he found a tiled staircase that led down to a glass-walled room at the cliff's edge.

Mona Castelli was perched on a pair of floral print cushions on a wrought-iron chair. There was a round table in front of her with a silver pitcher atop. She was balancing a martini glass between two fingers, her nails painted like the insides of polished shells.

"You're Cain?"

"That's right."

"Sit down," she said.

He sat opposite her. He could smell the gin and vermouth when she spoke. She had frosted highlights in her auburn hair, and a carefully made-up face. It was cold in here, the wind and mist beating against the glass behind her. She wore a fur-trimmed cashmere shawl, but it did nothing to hide her figure. She looked ten years younger than she probably was, but as far as Cain was concerned, nothing would hide the fact that she was drinking a pitcher of martinis alone at two on a weekday afternoon.

"You met my daughter already, I assume."

"Yes. I'll talk to her after."

"When she answered the door, was she dressed?"

"She had a towel."

"Thank god."

"I already did."

She smiled at that, and he couldn't help but like her a little for it. At least she understood how this looked, and had enough sense to be embarrassed.

"She likes to find the boundaries, and then cross them," Mona Castelli said. "With her, it's always been *push push push*."

"Okay."

"Now she's at the Academy of Art—which hasn't suppressed her penchant for streaking. Apparently, they encourage it. She volunteers as a studio model."

He let that sit on the table between them, not sure what she wanted him to do with it. She sipped her martini, then put the glass down. Behind her, there was a wall of fog moving off the ocean toward the Presidio. It would hit the cliffs and stall, piling along the shore toward the north until it could spill under the bridge and into the bay.

"Do you have children, Mr. Cain?"

"Not yet."

"God help you if you have a daughter," Mona said. She looked across the rim of her glass and met his eyes for the first time. "The Montgomery girl—*Melissa*—said this was important. And I know there's a police car down the street. Men posted there, to watch us. Are we in some sort of danger?"

"Ms. Montgomery didn't say what's going on?"

He wondered at the way she'd just referred to Melissa Montgomery but knew better than to ask about it. Either that would come out, or it wouldn't. Asking wouldn't make any difference.

"You needed to talk to us. That's all she said."

"What about your husband?"

"What about him?" she asked. "Did he say anything to me? Is that what you're asking?"

"Did he?"

"Since when?"

"Since last night. Or this morning."

"He slept in his office last night," she said. Her laugh sounded like ice swirling in a glass. "He does that sometimes, when he's busy. It's such a long way, from City Hall to here."

Cain had just driven it, and had watched the odometer so he could claim the mileage. It had taken him eighteen minutes, in traffic.

"He didn't call, or email?"

"Call? Email? This is Harry we're talking about?"

"Did anyone call for him?"

"Besides Melissa, to set this up?" she asked. "Nobody."

"He didn't get any message to you? I'm talking about the letter."

"What letter?"

No wonder Castelli hadn't wanted him to come anywhere near his family. The man had political aspirations that ran to a national scale. He probably already had a guest list for his next inauguration party. But his home life belonged on cable TV.

"Let me ask you something else," Cain said. "How'd you meet Harry?"

She looked at the martini pitcher for a long moment but didn't touch it. He thought of John Fonteroy, dying of cancer and longing for a plastic cup of water that lay cruelly out of reach.

"He was at a San Jose startup. NavSoft is what it was called," she said. That icy laugh again. "This was after he got his MBA, and they hired him as a vice president."

"You're talking, what, 1996?"

"Closer to 'ninety-seven."

"So he was an executive," Cain said. "What were you doing?"

"I was in college — I was his intern."

"College where?"

"Stanford."

"Undergrad?"

"A freshman," she said.

"You finished in 2001?"

"I didn't finish."

She gave the pitcher a stir and then refilled her glass. There was no way to tell how much was left in the pitcher. For that matter, there was no way to guess how full it had been when he'd arrived, or how many she'd gone through earlier in the day.

"Why not?" he said.

"Why do you think? I was an eighteen-year-old intern. He was — Whatever. It doesn't matter what I thought back then."

"What do you think now?"

"You know the story," she said. She used her glass to gesture at the Pacific where it crashed against the cliff beneath her house. "And now here we are. Here I am. I won the lottery, right?"

"It looks like it."

"Then why are you here, Mr. Cain?" she asked. "Why do the police have the street blocked off?"

"Someone's threatening him," Cain said. "Trying to get at him with a letter. We don't understand it—maybe it's something from his past?"

"Is that a question?"

"Is there anything we need to know?"

"Know about what?" she asked. "He's an open book. The most boring man you'll ever meet. If you want to know something about him, you can Google it."

She drained another glass. Christ, Cain thought. These Castellis. He hadn't come here looking for much more than a sense of who they were. How they behaved on their own ground, how they worked as a family. He was getting about as much as he could stand.

"What about Melissa Montgomery?" he asked. "What's her story?"

"She's his chief of staff," Mona said. "She started as his intern. She was in college, and he was in Congress. And then she worked her way up."

"Okay."

"Okay, what?" she asked. "I thought you were asking questions."

"Do you trust her?"

"She's my husband's chief of staff."

"She called you and set this up," Cain said. "She didn't tell him. So that makes me wonder about her loyalties."

"I don't know what she tells him. I don't know her thoughts on loyalty. I don't know anything. I'm here, and she's over there, with him, and that's all I've got."

"So then, you don't trust her."

"I didn't say that," she said. "She's doing what anyone would do. What I did."

He watched while she refilled her glass. When she was done she straightened up and put her hair back behind her shoulders again. She must have practiced in a mirror, the way she moved her hands through her hair and looked up. There was probably enough gin in

59

her blood that she'd go up in flames if she lit a match. But when she moved, she was as steady as a surgeon. There was no natural talent for that. She'd been training.

"Are we done?" she asked.

"For now."

"You really have to talk to Alexa?"

"Yes."

"If Harry's done something—"

"I won't tell her anything I didn't tell you," he said. "I'm not here to upset her."

"Thank you."

He watched her gin-wet eyes. Shouldn't she have tried, just a little, to find out what he was holding back? What he might say that would upset Alexa?

"I'll talk to her in the kitchen," Cain said. "You'll sit in the den, so you're out of sight, but you'll still be able to hear. Sound good?"

She nodded, then stood up.

"I'll make sure she's got clothes on—I know that's what you're worried about."

It wasn't the only thing on his mind, but he was happy to let Mona Castelli think it. Assuming it was what she actually thought.

Alexa came to the kitchen wearing a checked gingham dress. She pulled out a stool and sat with her elbows on the marble center island. The window behind her looked across a garden in the side yard. A bronze birdbath, wrapped in ivy, caught the rain. He watched the water and thought about where to begin with Alexa. It always made sense to start with something he knew. The more he seemed to know, the less likely she'd be to tell him a lie.

"You're an artist. Your mom and I were just talking."

"Yeah."

"Painting? Sculpture?"

"Both," she said. "Mostly painting."

"You must not live here all the time, if you're going to the Academy."

"I've got an apartment South of Market. A studio. It's close to school."

"How come you're here?" Cain asked.

"Melissa asked me."

"You know her pretty well?"

"She's family, almost."

"Explain that."

"She was at the house all the time when I was younger," Alexa said. She was looking at him, winding a lock of her wet hair around her index finger so that the water dripped onto her chest. "She'd pick me up from school, stay over for dinner. Stuff like that."

"Did she tell you why I want to talk to you?"

"No."

"Did you ask?"

"I guess I figured —"

She trailed off, glancing at the doorway to the den.

"You figured what?"

"He's the mayor," Alexa said. "So there's always something going on. Is he in trouble?"

"We don't know," he answered. "It might be nothing. That's what I'm trying to figure out."

"What does that mean?"

"There was a letter, someone trying to blackmail him."

"Blackmail him with what?"

"He says it's a hoax," Cain said. "But it has to do with a girl. Something that happened to a girl, in 1985."

He made sure his voice would carry to the den.

"That was before I was born."

"I don't expect you to know anything about it," Cain said. "And even if it's a hoax, like he thinks, we have to follow up. The girl was a blonde. Your age, maybe, or a couple years older. A good-looking girl, like Lauren Bacall."

Without getting off her stool, Alexa leaned to a drawer on the far end of the bar and quietly slid it open. She brought out a pad of stationery and a pencil, her eyes on the doorway to the den.

"How often do you see your father?" he asked. They'd have to keep the rhythm of the conversation going.

"Besides on TV?"

"Face to face."

"A couple times a month. He's busy, and so am I."

She wrote something on the pad and slid it over to him. He glanced at the words — *China Beach in 2 hrs* — then tore the top sheet from the pad and put it in his pocket. Maybe there was more to this visit

61

than just lifting the lid on their home and seeing the Castellis in their natural habitat.

He started to ask the questions he had to ask. Throwaways that didn't matter, except to let Mona Castelli hear them.

"In the last couple of weeks, have you seen anyone following you?"

"No."

"Have you had any conversations with anyone — especially anyone your father knows — that seemed unusual?"

"No."

"Have you bumped into anyone on the street you hadn't seen in a long time, maybe just someone who looked familiar?"

"No."

"Strange phone calls or emails?"

"Nothing like that," she said. Then she mouthed the words *two hours* and pointed toward the ocean.

"All right," he said. "Thank you for your time, Miss Castelli. This is my card. You can call me day or night if you think of something."

9

HE DROVE FOR five minutes, long enough to put some distance between himself and the Castellis, and then he pulled to the curb and called Grassley.

"Buddy," he said, when his partner picked up. "You have no idea how much I've missed you."

"You never call me buddy."

"I should start. How's it coming?"

"Four hours since we opened the lid," Grassley whispered, "and they've just got them out of the casket. The crime scene guy came, got whatever prints he could inside the lid — it was that guy you like."

"Sumida?"

"That's him — Sumida," Grassley said. "This is taking forever."

"That's good."

It meant they weren't rushing, that they were documenting everything. The casket wasn't just a burial. If they'd read it correctly, it was both the murder weapon and the crime scene. Moving her out would destroy it, and then the only record would be the photographs.

"Christopher Hanley, too?" he asked. "They took him out?"

"The longest part was getting them separated. Sorting them out — this bit goes with that body. But now all of her is on one table, all of him on another. More or less."

"What's Dr. Levy doing now?"

"She was just getting to the surface examination," Grassley said. "And then Mrs. Hanley showed up. I don't know who leaked it, but someone did. She knew about the girl."

"Shit."

"What I thought," Grassley said. "I did my best to get her to calm down, but how's she going to do that?"

"She isn't."

"She wants us to ID him, and that's it — no autopsy. And wash him. She's pretty clear on that, she wants him washed. A fresh suit, too."

"Anything else?"

"A new casket. And so, I said: Lady, sure. Anything. You bring us the new suit and a new casket, and we'll wash him up and take care of him."

"Grassley —"

"Now I know. Okay? Dr. Levy took me aside — and I'm not shitting you, she took me by my ear, and she pulled me around a corner — and then she lost her shit."

"She's not a funeral director."

"She said that," Grassley said. "And some other stuff."

"Did you go back to Mrs. Hanley and walk it back?"

"I'd already said it. How could we walk it back?" Grassley said. "Even Dr. Levy said we couldn't do that."

"So now she's on the hook to wash him and dress him up."

"And ID him first, which she would've done anyway," Grassley said. "We gave Mrs. Hanley an oral swab. The lab can ID him with a DNA match to her."

"Did she say how she found out?"

"Found out what?"

"How she heard about the girl," Cain said. "We need to know who told her."

"It was a reporter. Lady called from the paper, wanted a comment."

"Shit."

"What I thought."

"Dr. Levy's going to finish today?"

"No way — they'll keep going a bit, but she's putting them in the icebox at five o'clock."

"Fine," Cain said.

He guessed Rachel Levy would've pushed through, however long it took, if Grassley hadn't pissed her off by volunteering her as an undertaker.

"Did you track down Inspector Chun?" Cain asked.

"She can come. She says she's got time."

"Five thirty," Cain said. "At the Western."

"We'll be there."

64

Cain hung up, then looked at the clock on the dashboard. There was time before he had to meet Alexa Castelli. He drove to the Deli Eliseevski, on Geary, and picked out a half-dozen things he knew Lucy would eat. He bought a bottle of sparkling mineral water for her, a can of Baltika for himself. She liked lemon in her water, but there were lemon trees in her backyard. As long as it was dark, she'd even go out herself to pick them.

The house was quiet when he stepped inside, balancing the deli packages and putting his keys away.

"Lucy?"

No answer. He went through the living room and the dining room. The kitchen, to the left, was empty. A pair of French doors led to the music room, and he could see through the glass panes that she wasn't there. The piano's lid was closed. The windows overlooking the garden were open a crack, the wind coming in and putting rain-drops on the sill. He slid them shut.

He went to the kitchen and put his packages away, and then he went upstairs.

He found her in the walk-in closet, leaning against the back wall, half hidden by the sleeves of the coats hanging above her. The light was off when he opened the door, and he didn't see her at all until he turned the switch.

After a moment, she looked up at him.

"You're early."

"It's just for a minute," he said. "I have to go out again."

"Okay."

He took off his shoes and came into the closet. It smelled of leather and wool and Lucy's shampoo. He moved a shoebox out of the way and sat beside her. She took his hand in hers and laid it above her navel.

"I come in here sometimes," she said. "It's just — I like to think in here."

"Okay."

"I'm getting better, Gavin."

"I know."

"You don't have to worry about us."

"I don't."

"You do," she said. "I know you do. But you don't have to, is what I'm saying."

"Okay."

"How long do you have, before you need to go?"

"Not long," he said. "I have to meet the mayor's daughter. To interview her. Then meet Grassley and Inspector Chun."

"When will you be back?"

"After dark. But not too late. Maybe nine?"

"I'll be here."

"Right in here?"

"I don't know."

"I brought you blinties. And that salmon you like."

She made a sound and he looked over, not sure if she was laughing until he saw her face.

"*Blinis,*" she said. "Not blinties."

"Okay."

"That was cute."

"Are you really going to sit in here?"

"If I want to," she said. "It's up to me, isn't it?"

He had no answer to that. For months, he'd been thinking that he ought to leave. Not because he didn't love her, but because he didn't know how to help her. And he was sure that every time she woke up next to him, he made it a little harder for her. She wouldn't forget how they'd met, what he represented. It wasn't fair to her that he'd wanted her, that he'd pursued her.

But any thought of leaving had disappeared in December.

Maybe she never left the house. Maybe the first time he'd seen her, Lieutenant Nagata and the district attorney had been with him, and Lucy took too long in coming to the door because she'd been hiding in the closet. They hadn't meant to get where they were, but they hadn't done much to stop it, either. Everything about their love had been reckless, so that eight weeks ago, when he came in and she met him at the door, he'd known. She hadn't said a word to him, but he'd known.

She'd led him to the music room. As soon as she sat down, she began to play, swaying in the current of cold air rushing through the windows. It was nothing he'd heard before, played in a way he'd never seen. Maybe this was something she saved for herself. In the quietest stanzas, the Golden Gate's foghorn rattled low through the windows. He thought of the path it took, that sound, traveling over the Presidio and down the long avenues, a mile and a half or more to reach them.

She'd gone on and on, one piece after another. Debussy. Chopin, and Brahms. Clementi. He didn't think of getting up, of disturbing her. The music held him in place.

"Are you pregnant?" he said, at last.

He thought she'd stopped, but she hadn't. He knew the answer to his question, but he needed to hear it from her. But she didn't say a word that night. She just nodded, and didn't miss a note.

He came to sit on the bench next to her, as her students did when she was showing them something new, her hands folded on top of theirs. Two bodies, and four hands, coming together to find one song.

He'd never wanted her more than he had right then.

In the closet, he stood to go. He kissed the top of her head and she looked up at him.

"Hey," she said. "Did you want me to save you a blintie?"

"Now you're just making fun of me."

"But do you?"

"You have them," he said. "I told Grassley I'd buy him dinner."

"Then you have to do better than that," she said. "Before you go, I mean. The top of my head, that's nothing."

He knelt down next to her, slipping his fingers into her hair. She lifted her face to his, and he kissed her the right way. It didn't matter if they were in the bed, or pressed against the kitchen counter, or on the floor in the back of her closet. The instant they came together, there was nothing else. Maybe that's what he'd been fleeing.

Jesus, he thought. This woman.

This fiercely brave, and totally fucked-up, perfectly wonderful Lucy.

Half an hour later, he was at the China Beach parking lot. It was late January. Four thirty in the afternoon, and dusk was already closing out the sky. He got out of the car and put on his jacket, then walked down the concrete ramp that switched back and forth to the beach. The surf was running out of the north, and it curled and boomed into the sloped dark sand. He stepped off the pavement and onto the beach and followed the shoreline toward Castelli's house. To his left, across the water, the Golden Gate Bridge came in and out of the weather.

He slowed a moment when he first picked out her silhouette, and then went up to meet her. She was standing on a promontory of rock, the surf breaking on either side of her.

"Good," she said. "I wasn't sure you'd come."

She was barefoot but still in the gingham dress she'd worn that afternoon. It couldn't have been very warm, and was already sticking to her thighs and stomach where it had gotten wet in the windblown spray. From down here, in the last of the light, he could see the path she must have followed to reach this spot. A winding boardwalk clung to the cliff's face beneath her parents' house. It descended from her mother's sunroom, then zigzagged to the tide pools a hundred feet beneath. A few lights glowed through the windows, but it was one of the darker houses on the cliff.

"Your mom and dad up there?"

"Just my mom, and she's getting ready to go out," Alexa said.

"That's normal?"

"Normally, she'd be passed out. But tonight she's hosting a thing in Monterey."

"You wanted to tell me something?"

"You said a girl disappeared, in 1985."

"Maybe."

"Maybe?" Alexa asked. "Which part don't you know?"

"What do you know about her?"

"Nothing."

He started toward the walkway, his back to her.

"Mr. Cain, wait."

He turned around, and she was lifting up a black plastic bag that had been near her feet. She'd weighted it with a rock so the wind wouldn't take it.

"I found this," she said. "When I was little. He probably thought the maids threw it out — but it was me, and I had it hidden."

"Show me."

She put it behind her back.

"The girl from 1985 — she was a blonde?"

Cain nodded.

"And she would've been a good model," Alexa said. "Fine features, beautiful lines."

"What's in the bag?"

She ran her free hand up the bodice of her dress, cupping herself.

"Full figured, up here," Alexa said. Then she touched her face. "And all the right angles, here. A face you want to see. A face you can't stop seeing."

Now she kissed her fingertip.

"Perfect lips," she said. "Full and soft."

"What's in the bag, Alexa?"

"Am I right about her?"

"Yes."

She handed him the bag, and he pulled out an eight-by-ten photograph. He took out his flashlight, and there she was: the woman from the photographs he'd first seen in Castelli's office. She was handcuffed to the bed, wearing nothing but a pair of dark-colored panties. This wasn't a picture he'd seen before, but it must have come from the same roll of film as the first four. The differences were obvious. There was no number in the corner. The woman was in the same position, but the angle was slightly different. The photographer had moved around to the end of the bed. Cain slipped his glasses off and held the glossy print close enough to study it carefully. It had the same subtle distortions as the others, everything warped just a little bit.

"You found this where?"

"In his study."

"How old were you?"

"Ten."

"It wasn't just sitting out," Cain said. He switched off his light and put it away. "He wouldn't leave this in plain sight."

"It was under his desk. Upside down, on the floor."

"Why did you take it?"

"Why wouldn't I take it?" she asked. "Look at it. It's wrong. It scared me — and attracted me, too. I wanted to know more."

"After you took it, did he ever say anything to you about it?"

"Of course not."

"But he must've asked if you'd been in his study."

"Never."

"He was normal, that day and the next few?"

69

"That day, he'd gone to Washington — to his apartment in D.C. I didn't see him for two months. By then I was back in school, and I'd mostly forgotten about it. I'd found other things to do."

"He'd left that day?"

"That morning."

"What'd you think, when you found it? The first thing you thought."

Alexa looked up at the sky, used one fingertip to trace her throat.

"That he'd dropped it when he was packing his briefcase," she said. "It slid under the desk and he didn't see it."

"That's what you thought then? When you were ten years old?"

"Then, and now, Mr. Cain," Alexa said.

"The desk, how many drawers does it have?"

"Four," she said, right away. "The big one's on the bottom right."

"Are they locked?"

"Just the one — the big one."

"You'd never seen inside it?"

"Not then, and not now, either."

"He still has the desk?"

"In his study," Alexa said. "Upstairs."

"Does he lock the room?"

"Not so much anymore."

"But back then?"

"More often — but I knew where he kept the key."

"Where?"

"His medicine cabinet," she said. Again, there was no pause at all. "Behind the Clive Christian cologne."

Cain wondered if it was possible to keep a secret from your own child.

"Why had you gone into his study?"

Her finger had traced down from her throat to the neckline of her dress.

"He had a *Playboy* collection in there, on the bookshelves. The old issues, from the fifties — you know the ones. I didn't read them for the articles."

"You didn't — what?"

"Marilyn Monroe. Jayne Mansfield. Yvette Vickers — I wanted to see what a woman looked like."

She reached behind her neck and undid something on her dress, then opened it from the back and slipped out of it. It only took her a second, and then it was hanging around her waist. She splayed her fingers into her hair and arched her back, presenting her bare breasts to him.

"Miss Castelli."

She closed her eyes, turned her face toward the nearly dark sky.

"Yes?"

"Cover up."

She dropped her hands to her hips, thumbs under the waistline of her hanging dress, and opened her eyes as if she'd just been struck with the greatest idea she'd ever had.

"Let's go swimming!"

"No."

"You don't need a suit on this beach. Especially not at night."

She pushed the dress off her hips, then flicked it at him with a kick of her toes. He stepped aside and it brushed past his face. He heard it hit the wet sand behind him.

"The water's so cold, it makes you feel every part of yourself. You know—I mean, you know for certain—that you're alive. You could dive under, when the water's this cold, and breathe it in. You wouldn't even know you'd drowned."

"I'm keeping this," Cain said. He put the photograph back into the plastic bag. "We'll finish this conversation. Probably in an interrogation room."

"Swim with me, Gavin Cain."

"Good evening, Miss Castelli."

He walked along the sand and then caught the concrete path up the hill to his car. He didn't look back to see if she'd gone in the water.

10

"THAT WAS IT," Cain said. "The last straw."

He slid the fifth photograph onto the table, next to the other four. He'd told it to them chronologically, starting with Lieutenant Nagata's call while he was at the exhumation in El Carmelo.

"I mean, keep in mind she answered the door in a towel. She'd known I was coming and she was waiting for me like that. Don't forget that. And then for some reason, I still went and met her on the beach."

"What are you saying?"

"I'm saying I shouldn't have gone down there to begin with. But when Carmen Sternwood tossed her dress and asked me to go skinny-dipping, I finally got it. I took this, and I left."

"Wait," Grassley said. "Who's Carmen Sternwood?"

"An actress," Chun said. She looked from Grassley to Cain. "Right?"

"Never mind."

"*Rebel Without a Cause,*" Grassley said. "The one with Cary Grant. Way before my time."

Cain shook his head. They'd be here all night, if he tried getting into that.

They were in a booth at the Western, on Fillmore Street. Their table was on the diner side of the business, but they could hear a loud game of darts from the dubiously legal bar in the building's back half. Both the bar and the restaurant were cop hangouts, and that was the only reason the building wasn't posted and padlocked.

"What else did Levy get from the autopsy?" Cain asked.

"So far, not much," Grassley said. He picked up his iced tea and made a face when he sipped it. He sniffed the rim of his glass, then checked the cuff of his sport coat.

"It stays with you," Cain said. "It's probably your imagination. But if you can smell it tomorrow . . . You got a good dry cleaner?"

Grassley shrugged out of his jacket, folded it roughly, and then put it on the bench behind him.

"She won't start cutting until tomorrow," Grassley said.

"She finished the surface examination?"

"What she could. It's just — when they lifted the woman out, a lot of her skin was stuck to the kid's suit. I don't remember exactly what the doc said."

"It's hard to examine the surface when the surface isn't there," Chun said.

"That's it."

"There weren't any entry wounds? No ligature marks?" Cain asked. "Tell me what she saw."

"Nothing that changed her mind."

"The woman went in alive," Cain said. "Dr. Levy still thinks that."

"She found wooden splinters in the woman's fingertips," Chun said. "I saw her pull them out."

"How long were you there?"

"Just for the last part," she said. She tilted her head toward Grassley. "He called, and I came as soon as I could."

"There's one thing I have to clear up," Cain said, "before we go any further."

"I've got time," Chun said.

"But it's off the books. A lot of overtime that's not getting paid, because you can't even request it."

Chun glanced sideways at Grassley, who looked away.

"Yeah," she said to Cain. "Okay. It's fine."

"Same," Grassley said. "But I'm on this anyway — the girl in the coffin is my case. And if I'm on my own because Nagata put you on a blackmail note, she can't say no if I bring Angela in. So everyone gets paid."

"That might work," Cain said. "Just watch how you talk about it, especially at the division meetings. We'll be able to move fast and quiet if Nagata doesn't connect the cases."

"Moving fast is good," Chun said. "But where are we going?"

"We'll split it up. The goal's to tie Castelli to the photos . . . You live in the East Bay, right?"

73

"Oakland."

"Then Berkeley's your new pastime. Castelli was there in 'eighty-five. Maybe some of his friends are still in the area, or you can track them. Find out what kinds of things they were into."

"And the car—I won't forget the Eldorado."

Cain hadn't worked with Angela Chun before today. But her reputation in the Homicide Detail was solid.

"Castelli didn't meet his wife until 'ninety-seven," Cain said. "So find out who he was seeing back then. We'll want to talk to her. Or them."

"Understood."

"But use a soft touch," Cain said. "Some of these people might still be his friends. You don't want them picking up the phone."

"What about me?" Grassley asked.

"The pills and the dress," Cain said. "You know what I want?"

"For the pills—you remember Frank Lee talked to that guy at UC-SF's pharmacy program? He'd drawn an OD in the Ritz and wanted some background on all the shit they found in the guy's bags?"

"I remember," Cain said. "That came up in the roundtable."

"Frank liked the guy, said he was pretty good. He might know how Thrallinex was being prescribed, what the doctors were doing with it. I'll start there and see where it goes."

"Okay," Cain said. It was what he would have done. "And the dress?"

"Back to school again," Grassley said. "There's got to be a fashion program at the Academy of Art. That's all I can think of—find someone who's plugged in to that kind of thing and ask where you would've gone to get that dress."

Cain glanced at Chun.

"Don't look at me," she said. "There's nothing like that in my closet."

"I just wondered if you had anything to add to Grassley's plan."

She looked at her phone's screen, then switched it off.

"Sixteen thousand for a used dress seems pretty steep," she said. "You wouldn't buy something like that off the rack."

"But they're selling one online."

"Used," Chun said. "When they're new, dresses like that, you get them made for you. So it's not like you're looking for a department store clerk who remembers taking the girl to a fitting room with a couple different sizes to try on."

"Who am I looking for?" Grassley asked.

"I don't know—there'd have been people who measured her for it. They might've sat down with her a couple times to look at fabrics, to go through style books. If she was a regular customer, they might've come out to her. Otherwise, she probably did it in Paris."

"How do you know all this?"

"*Vogue.*"

Grassley looked at Cain.

"Maybe she should take the dress and I should canvas Berkeley."

"I like it the way we have it," Cain said.

He'd already decided that Angela Chun would do a better job in Berkeley, which was the more sensitive task. But he didn't want to explain that to either of them.

"What'll you be doing?" Grassley asked.

"What Dr. Levy said I should do—find some of the old guys and talk to them."

"That's why you wanted to meet here."

Cain nodded. Even if there weren't retired cops drinking in the bar, there'd be a few guys close enough to pulling the pin that they'd remember the ones Cain really wanted to see. All he needed was a name, and he could take it from there. He turned when he heard a swirl of noise from the kitchen. The waitress backed through the swinging door, pushing it open with her shoulders. She crossed to their booth and set down three plates.

"You're Inspector Cain?" she asked.

"Yeah."

"And you're parked outside, on Fillmore?"

"Is there a problem?"

"Somebody called the kitchen just now. They left a note on your windshield. They said you had to go get it right now, before someone comes along and takes it."

"They?" Cain asked.

"He—it's loud back there, and it was loud wherever he was. But it was a man."

Cain looked at Grassley.

"Follow her to the kitchen and see if you can get the number." He slid out of his seat and looked down at Chun. "Inspector, you come with me."

At a run, they reached his car in less than a minute. The manila envelope was tucked under the windshield wiper on the driver's side. The glass was beaded from an earlier rain, but the envelope was still dry.

"Hold up," Cain said. "Let's do this the right way."

He used his key fob to pop the trunk, then unzipped his crime scene bag and put on a pair of latex gloves. He handed a plastic evidence bag to Chun. Then they went back to the front of the car and Cain slipped the envelope from beneath the arm of the windshield wiper.

"More photos?" Chun asked.

"It's too light."

The flap was held closed with a piece of red thread wrapped in a figure-eight around a pair of thin plastic buttons. He unwound it, then eased the envelope open and looked inside. There was just a single sheet of thin typewriter paper, folded in half. Cain took it out and opened it, holding it so Inspector Chun could read alongside him. In his pocket, his phone began to vibrate, but he ignored it.

Cain:

If he hasn't called you already, then he's hiding them. And if he's hiding them, he must not like what he sees. Ask him what he did to her.

Maybe you should ask yourself some questions too. Like, why even look for me? He's the one that did it; I'm just reminding him.

—A FRIEND

Cain turned the page over, but the back was blank. He tilted the open envelope up to the streetlight and looked inside again.

"Empty?" Chun asked.

He nodded, then put the note and envelope into Chun's evidence bag. Now he pulled out his phone, checked the missed call, and tapped Grassley's name to call him back.

"Buddy," he said. "What'd you find?"

"The phone didn't have caller ID, so I star-sixty-nined it and got the number."

"Okay."

"It's a pay phone, in the Elite Café."

Cain turned around, then stepped into the street. One block down, on the other side of the intersection with California, the Elite's neon-traced sign flickered through the canopies of the Chinese banyans that lined this section of Fillmore.

"The waitress," Cain said. He was scanning the sidewalks on both sides of the street. There were a lot of shadows here, the streetlights no match for the trees. "She's sure it was a man?"

"She's sure."

"She took the call, not someone else?"

"It was her. Then she got our plates and came out," Grassley said. "This is three minutes ago — max."

"Thanks, Grassley." He hung up and turned to Chun, then pointed at the café's sign. "The guy called from up there."

"The Elite?"

Cain nodded.

"Let's go — watch this side of the street and I'll take the other."

"What am I looking for?"

"Anything."

"That narrows it."

They jogged to the corner and crossed the street without waiting for the light. The guy must have planned this for a while, if he already had a note typed out. Otherwise, he would've handwritten it on a scrap of paper. So the note was planned, but maybe the call was a sudden decision. He couldn't have known where Cain was going, couldn't have planned for a pay phone within a block of the car. And if he'd started acting on impulse instead of on carefully thought-out plans, maybe he'd make a mistake.

On the other side of the street, a man came out of the Elite Café and tucked himself into the recess of a dark storefront two doors down. There was a point of light when he drew on a cigarette.

"Cain?"

77

Angela Chun was tugging at his elbow, whispering.

"What?" He didn't take his eyes off the smoking man.

"That man —" She turned him so that he was looking back toward the intersection.

A man had slipped past them on the sidewalk, but Cain hadn't paid him any attention because he was focused on the other side of the street. Now he just saw the tall man's back. Charcoal gray running jacket, matching pants. His hands were in his pockets, his head down as he strode away from them.

"That's our guy," Inspector Chun whispered. "I think."

The man couldn't have heard her, but at her words he set off at a sprint. The traffic signal was against him, but that didn't seem to matter. He dove through two directions of traffic, dancing sideways along the center line as a panel truck brushed past close enough that he had to duck its side mirror.

Then they were racing after him, coming off the curb and into the street without even looking. An eastbound BMW skidded sideways and laid on its horn. Chun reached into her jacket and came out with her badge, and the driver let up on the horn as they skirted past his front bumper. As they threaded through the westbound traffic, they spotted the man a hundred feet ahead of them. With each step, he increased his lead. Tall and thin, this guy. Built to run.

"SFPD!" Cain yelled. "Stop!"

Instead, the man found even more speed. They were following him up a hill, the man moving in a straight line, an easy target. It would have been a simple thing to end this with a bullet, but there was no justification for it. It'd be a bad shooting, and Cain knew it.

Near the hill's top, the man grabbed on to the corner of a shingle-sided row-house and hooked out of sight into the alley that ran alongside it. That changed everything. They couldn't confirm he was an unarmed suspect anymore, fleeing in plain sight; he could be waiting around any corner now, with anything in his hands.

Now was the time to draw his gun. Next to him, Chun did the same. He stopped running before they reached the alley, holding out his left arm to block Chun from running past its mouth. He nodded at the cedar-shake wall of the row-house, and she stood against it, close to the corner. She held the evidence bag in one hand, her gun in the other, its muzzle pointed at the sidewalk a few feet in front of her. Its illuminated sights glowed softly in the dark, three points of dull green. She looked at him.

"Ready?" she asked.

She didn't sound like she'd just raced through traffic and sprinted up a hill. He took a breath before he answered.

"Wait," he said.

"For what?"

He tried to remember her age. Ten years younger, maybe. That would put her at twenty-seven, twenty-eight. Young, sure. But she ought to know why he'd paused at this corner.

"Guys who run into something without looking first, those are the ones who get killed," he said. "That's not us."

"He's . . . the guy's —"

"I know it," Cain said.

He stepped to the right and dropped to one knee, looking down the alley's length over the barrel of his gun. There were dumpsters at the fence blocking the far end. To the right, a medical building. Its ground level was a parking lot. Twenty spots, max, and maybe half of them taken. A gateway opened to a set of stairs that led up to the cross street.

"Shit."

"What?"

"It's no good."

The guy might have run all the way down the alley, then climbed onto a dumpster to vault the fence. Or he might have dodged right, under the medical building, and taken the gate out. Then again, he might be behind any one of the parked cars, waiting for Cain and Chun to step a little closer.

"What do we do?" Chun said.

Cain stood up and holstered his gun, waited for Chun to do the same. He wasn't even sure why they'd been chasing the man in the first place, except that he'd run. That wasn't a good enough reason to keep going.

"We'll go find Grassley," he said.

"That's *it*?"

"You're not getting shot for Harry Castelli," Cain said. "That's the first thing."

"And the second?"

"I told Grassley I'd buy him dinner. If we don't get back, he'll get stuck with the bill."

Angela Chun went past him and stood at the entrance to the alley. She looked down it, toward the chainlink fence and the dumpsters. Then she turned to study the parking lot beneath the medical building, her eyes flicking to each car, to all of the shadow-heavy corners.

"All right," she said. "If there's nothing else we can do."

11

ON THE WALK back down the hill to Fillmore Street, he asked Angela Chun how she'd known. He'd seen the man briefly from the back, and then they were running and the only thing that had mattered was the chase. Now he couldn't even say for sure the color of the man's hair. He'd been tall and fast, and that was all Cain knew.

"It wasn't anything, really," she was saying. "It was just the way he looked at me and then looked away."

"That's it?"

"That's it."

"If there'd been shots fired, if he'd been hit by that truck while we were chasing him, we'd have to face a board of inquiry. What would you have said then?"

"He ran."

"But you knew it was him before he ran."

"I knew," she said.

They reached the bottom of the hill and turned onto Fillmore. She didn't say anything else until they'd gone half a block. Then she stopped, next to Cain's car, and touched his elbow to turn him.

"He didn't look at me the way a man looks at me. Even if it's just for a second — a half second — most men do it. They don't even know it, maybe, but they do. It's like an appraisal, their eyes flicking up and down. It looks like a blink, but it's not."

They started walking again, the Western's yellow-lit sign blinking in front of them like the marquee at an old playhouse.

"And what did he do, if it wasn't that?" Cain asked.

"The opposite of it — maybe what we do, on the receiving end. He curled up inside himself. He turned sideways and tried to slide by. You think I could explain that to a board of inquiry?"

"They're usually a bunch of old men, those boards."

81

"Then I guess it's good we didn't shoot him," she said. "But you believe me?"

"Sure," Cain said. "He ran. Did you get a look at him at all?"

"Not really."

"Young?" Cain asked. "He ran like he was young."

"Nineteen, twenty. White. Shortish hair."

"What else?"

"He was tall—but you saw that. What do you think, six foot three?"

"At least."

"I could sit next to him on BART for an hour and not know it was him."

"He must be working for somebody," Cain said. "Don't you think?"

"Why?"

"Not many kids that age give a shit about the mayor. And anyway, this is about something that happened in 1985. If he was alive back then, he was in diapers. So he's working for somebody."

They reached the Western. He opened the door for her and they went back inside.

At six thirty, he gave the waitress his credit card and watched Grassley walk out with Chun. When the waitress came back, she slid into the booth opposite him.

"I asked around," she said.

"Anything?"

He'd asked her to get him the names of any retired cops who'd worked out of the Richmond station.

"John MacDowell's the guy you want, but he's not here."

"You got a number?"

"He doesn't have a phone," she said. She handed him a slip of paper. "Next best thing—I found out where he lives."

"You should be cop."

"Maybe it rubs off."

The address was north of the city, in Stinson Beach. That wasn't the first place he'd go looking for a retired homicide inspector. The SRO hotels in the Tenderloin would be a good start for the ones who'd washed out badly. Not-quite-beachfront Florida condos if they'd hung on to their marriages and guarded their pensions.

Stinson Beach, though. That was another financial planet.

"How's he a regular?" Cain asked. "He's all the way up there."

"It's been a couple years. He used to be a regular. He moved in with family, is what I heard."

"How old is he?"

"Last I saw, plenty."

"All right," he said. He put the paper in his pocket. "This is a huge help."

"It's nothing," she answered. "When you work at the Western, that's just how it goes."

This time, he got to the Burton Building a few minutes early. Instead of going in, he leaned against the side of his car and called Karen Fischer.

"Inspector Cain?"

"Are you sitting with my lieutenant?"

"She's here, but I stepped out."

"You tell her it was me?"

"No."

He'd read her the right way, this FBI agent. She had good instincts.

"I'm out front. Can you meet me?"

"What is this?"

"I want to tell you something, and I don't want it going straight to the mayor."

"Give me one minute to get down."

He hung up and went around to the front of the building. Fischer came through the glass doors soon after, paused long enough to contemplate the rain, and then walked into it to join Cain. She folded her arms together beneath the lapels of her suit jacket.

"I need to see Castelli," Cain said. "Right now. Can you set it up?"

"It depends."

"On what?"

"Why you want to see him."

"Come with me."

He started walking back to his car, not looking to see if she'd follow. When he reached it, he went to the passenger side and opened the door for her. Once she was in, he came around the front and sat in the driver's seat. He switched on the dome light, then put Alexa Castelli's photograph on Fischer's lap.

"I got this from the mayor's nineteen-year-old daughter," he said. "She stole it from his study when she was ten."

Fischer looked at it without touching it.

"It's a different shot," she said. "A different angle. We haven't seen this one."

"But she's the same person," Cain said. "The woman we saw, in Castelli's four pictures."

He told her about meeting Mona Castelli at her cliff-top house. The interview with her, and then the strange encounter with Alexa on China Beach. He put the note on top of the photograph and told her about the call at the Western, how he'd chased the man until he'd disappeared. He tread carefully as he described this. Chun and Grassley didn't need to come up. And he didn't say a word about the corpse in the 850 Bryant morgue.

When he was done, he took the photograph and the note back.

"Now you understand," he said. "I don't want him getting special warnings."

"You think she'd do that. Your lieutenant."

"You read her the same way. When we met in the supervisors' chambers, I saw it. You don't trust her."

"She's the one who insisted on these meetings," Fischer said. "I didn't think there was any point, except one."

"To keep an eye on you."

"That's right."

"Who actually called you — the mayor, or his staff?"

"His chief of staff. Melissa Montgomery. We got involved, and then he wanted SFPD in too, so he called Nagata."

"Miss Montgomery called you on her own, or with his blessing?"

"I don't know."

"Shouldn't we find that out?" Cain said.

Agent Fischer was looking out the window. Across the street, a man in a colorless overcoat pushed a shopping cart through the black puddles. A small child, wrapped in a raincoat, slept among the soaked paper grocery bags. A man going home from the store, or a man with nowhere to go? It was a toss-up, Cain decided. It could go either way. Or an altogether different story might fit the evidence even better. Cain watched the back of the FBI agent's head and waited for her to answer him.

"Wait here," she finally said. She turned back to him. "I need five minutes to set this up — while you've got Castelli, I'll pull Montgomery off into a corner."

"You know where he is?"

"Except when he's at home, we're watching him."

"Who's watching him at home?"

"Your guys."

"And you're okay if we leave Nagata sitting?"

"Someone can brief her on what we've learned knocking on doors in North Beach," she said. "Which is nothing, but it'll take an hour. After you talk to Castelli, you can tell her whatever you want."

"That should go well."

"Stay out of trouble," she said. She opened the door. "I might like working with you."

"Yeah — you, too."

She got out of the car and ran through the slanting rain to her building's entrance.

City Hall's front door was locked.

The gilded balcony above them didn't hang out far enough to block the runoff falling from above. After trying the handle, Fischer hammered on the wood with her fist. An FBI agent opened the door, looked past Fischer, and stared at Cain, waiting.

"This is Inspector Cain," Fischer said. "With SFPD. Castelli should've heard we're coming."

The agent stepped back and let them in. They crossed the empty rotunda, Cain's wet shoes squeaking on the freshly polished stone. They went up the staircase and opened the door to the mayoral suite without knocking. Melissa Montgomery was waiting for them behind the receptionist's desk. She stood when they entered, smoothing the lapels of her light gray suit.

"He's back there?" Fischer asked.

"He's waiting," she said. "He was ready to go home."

"That's great," Fischer said. She took Melissa Montgomery's wrist and put her other hand on the small of the younger woman's back. She moved her toward the exit. "We'll give Inspector Cain some space, in case they have to raise their voices."

"But —"

"But nothing," Fischer said. "You and I can talk out here."

They stepped out of the office and closed the door. Cain crossed the red carpeted reception area, knocked once on the door to the inner office, and pushed through without waiting for an answer.

Castelli turned from the window. He'd been looking down on the rows of spot-lit flags in Civic Center Plaza. Or maybe he'd just been looking at his reflection in the dark glass.

"You wanted to see me?"

"The better question is, didn't you want to see me?" Cain said. "Why the fuck didn't you call the second you got them?"

Castelli went to his desk, pulled the chair back, and sat down. He took a gold pen from its wooden stand and rolled it back and forth between his fingers. That tic again, always needing to handle something. His fingerprints must have been on everything in the room lower than the ceiling.

"I don't know what you're talking about. You think I got something?"

"Bullshit," Cain said. "You got elected to Congress. Twice. You can lie better than that."

"You bother my wife, harass my daughter. You bust into my office at night, without an appointment, and call me a liar."

Castelli swiveled his chair and opened the liquor cabinet, then came back around holding a fresh bottle of bourbon and a pair of crystal snifters.

"Call me a liar to my face — that's nerve. I actually like that. This time you'll have a drink with me. You can't say no. And honestly, Cain, I have no idea what the fuck you're talking about."

He brought a nickel-plated folding knife from his desk drawer and used the blade to slice the red wax seal around the top of the bottle. He set the knife down, pulled the cork from the bottle, and poured an inch of bourbon into each of the snifters. He slid one of them across the desk and pointed at the empty chair.

"Sit," he said. "Drink that. And tell me what's going on."

Cain picked up the glass but didn't sit. He lowered his nose to the snifter's narrow opening and smelled the good bourbon inside, and then he stepped around the desk, pulled the wastepaper bin out, and poured the drink on top of Castelli's trash. He set the empty glass on the desk blotter. The mayor started to rise, but Cain kept him in his chair with a hand on his chest.

"Who was she?" he asked.

"The girl in the pictures?"

"Who else?"

"I don't know," Castelli said. There was no one he could call, no help to come running. But he was calm and in control, even with Cain's hand pushing him down. "I told you that already."

"What's in the next four pictures?"

Castelli rolled backward in his chair until there was a foot of distance between them. He took his bourbon and drank it, then began turning the empty glass in his fingers, his wedding band clicking against its thin crystal side.

"That's what you think I'm hiding?" Castelli asked. "The pictures?"

"I'm out there, digging up your secrets. One of the things I hear is you've got the pictures. You try and bury something, it doesn't always stay down."

He was expecting more of a reaction, but the mayor didn't even look up from his glass.

"Is that all?" Castelli asked.

"When was the first time you saw those shots?"

"Last night."

"You never had another set of prints?"

"Of course not."

"You're going to sit here and tell me you never saw her until a day ago."

"I've been telling you that," Castelli said. He poured another inch of bourbon and drank it, then wiped his lips with the back of his hand. "I'm going to keep telling you until you get it."

"If you hadn't already gotten the next set of pictures, why would I get an anonymous note saying you did?"

"You got a note like that?"

Cain handed Castelli his phone. He'd taken a shot of the note and had it on the screen. The mayor held the phone close, and Cain took a bet with himself that he would pour a third drink. Instead, after the mayor handed the phone back, he corked the bottle and returned it to his liquor cabinet.

"I assume it crossed your mind he's got an agenda," Castelli said.

"Everybody in this thing has an agenda."

"Helping you catch him isn't part of his."

"I follow the leads I get."

"That's a nice idea, but it's not what you're doing. You're just doing what he wants."

"And what exactly do you think I should be doing? Since clearly you know best."

"The letter I got . . . what's he want?" Castelli leaned back in his chair. "Easy. He's fucking with me, so I won't think straight. But at the same time, he's telling me there's a way out. *Pull the trigger,* he says. *Take the quick exit — bang!* It isn't blackmail because he doesn't want money. It's just straight coercion. Isn't that right?"

Cain nodded.

"And if I call his bluff? If I won't even blink?" Castelli asked. He pointed at Cain with the glass in his hand. "Then he's got to turn up the pressure."

"Okay."

"What's the easiest way for him to do that? Look at you, shoving in here. Pushing me around, dumping out my whiskey like it's water from the tap. You're doing exactly what he wants. He's playing you — What's so funny?"

Cain was already walking to the door. He put his hand on the knob but turned to the mayor before he left.

"Assuming all I had was the note?" Cain asked. "I'd think you're right. But it's not all I've got."

"If you want to threaten me, you've got to be specific," the mayor said. "Maybe it means I'm not a smart guy. But I don't jump at shadows."

"I'm just calling bullshit," Cain said. He let go of the door and took a step back toward Castelli. "I don't care if you find that threatening or not. You've seen that girl. We both know it."

The mayor had no answer. He stared at Cain from behind the rim of his empty snifter, which he turned and turned in his cupped hands.

"If you don't want to tell it to me, then call Agent Fischer and tell her," Cain said. "Or have that kid do it, what's-his-name."

"Who?"

"That intern you had, who called them the first time. Jacobs? Jackson?"

One name was from a list of the mayor's staff that Cain had seen at the first meeting in the federal building. The other, he'd just made up.

"Jackson," Castelli said. The name from the list. If the mayor was grabbing at hints like that, it could only mean one thing. He didn't know who'd called the FBI.

Cain nodded and stepped out. This time, Melissa Montgomery wasn't there. The reception area was as empty as he'd left it.

12

SMOOTHING THINGS OVER with Nagata was easier than he'd expected, and he had Grassley to thank for it. He'd come out of the mayor's office and down the steps to the rotunda, but Karen Fischer wasn't anywhere in sight. The FBI agent who'd let them in was making rounds in the farther reaches of the building; Cain could hear his steady footfalls echoing down the marble hallways and amplifying in the vast dome above.

He stood near one of the lamps that flanked the staircase and called his lieutenant.

"What happened — and where are you?"

"With Fischer, at City Hall."

"How is it she walks out of a meeting with me and ends up with you at City Hall, and I only hear about it an hour later?"

"That was my fault," Cain said. "I ran into her before I came up, told her what I needed to do, and she wanted to come with me. It was heat of the moment, but I should've called you."

"What do you mean, 'heat of the moment'? What's going on?"

He gave her the story he'd told Fischer about finding a note on his windshield, then chasing its author through the Western Addition. He didn't mention his meetings with Mona and Alexa Castelli, or the photograph that Alexa had given him. The note was safe because Castelli already knew about it. Cain had been careful about what information he'd shared so far, but he was going to need to sit down soon and work it through. There were too many threads in the story he was telling, and if he looked away for too long, they'd tangle.

"What did he say when you showed him the note?" Nagata asked. "Did he have the next set?"

"He said I was being played."

"And you thought what?"

"That he's got it right—someone's putting pressure on him."

"You believed him."

"Maybe he's smarter than he looks."

"So there's hope for you," Nagata said. "He can make a career in the department, you know. When he takes an interest in someone."

"I'm not sure he's taken that kind of interest in me."

There was silence while Nagata considered something. Cain looked around the darkened rotunda but didn't see Fischer. The only sound was the FBI agent, pacing the perimeter. Fischer must have taken Melissa Montgomery into an empty office, or back into the Board of Supervisors' Chambers. Then Nagata was back on the line.

"I hate to do this to you—I put you on Castelli, told you to bear down like it was the only thing that mattered."

"It's not?"

"I need you to help Grassley."

"What's he got into?"

"He called a minute ago," she said. "And asked for you. He's headed to the morgue, that exhumation job. Dr. Levy wants to see him. There was a second body—you heard that yet?"

"In the casket?" Cain asked. "A second body?"

"It's a woman—she was buried alive."

"Did they ID her?"

"I wouldn't know," Nagata said. "They had the x-ray since this morning, but nobody told me anything until now. Do you see the pattern?"

"Lieutenant—"

"Forget it, Cain. I want you there. Whatever Dr. Levy's got to say, you have to hear it. We can keep the mayor out of the news, if we're lucky. But this one will get out, and when it does, we need a senior inspector standing out front."

Of course, Cain thought. How it plays on the evening news is her biggest concern.

"I'll be there," he said. "I'm on my way."

"You can handle both?"

"Easy."

"We'll talk tomorrow," she said. "I understand how it is. You have to go wherever the investigation leads. But I don't like being left out of the loop."

"Understood, Lieutenant."

He hung up and looked around again. Fischer was coming down the staircase to meet him.

They waited until they were outside, across Polk Street from City Hall. There was a burned-out streetlight there, and they stood in the column of darkness beneath it and looked back to the mayor's lighted windows above the entry portico.

"What'd she say?" Cain asked.

"That he told her to call. That she did it with his permission. I raked her back and forth, and she didn't budge."

"Then she's lying," Cain said. "Castelli, too. He didn't tell her to call, and he doesn't know who did. I threw him a line and he reached for it. He thinks it was some kid named Jackson."

A shadow passed across the windows on the other side of the street. The mayor was pacing up there. If he had Melissa Montgomery with him, what would they be talking about? Each kept secrets from the other, but they probably shared a few too.

Mona Castelli certainly believed that.

"What do you think it means?" Fischer asked. "That she'd call without telling him."

"It could be anything—she knew he wouldn't call it in himself and wanted to protect him. She saw the pictures and got scared."

"Jealous, maybe," Fischer said. "You see them in the room together, you can't help but think there's something underneath. Not just a boss and his employee."

"Or she's angry—she sees those pictures and she starts thinking, 'What kind of man gets himself into a thing like this?'"

"Then we show up and take him by surprise," Fischer said. "He's seen the letter too, so he knows why we're there. He knows that right away, but he doesn't know who called. He plays it like he was waiting for us, like he asked someone to call. He's got to, because what else is he going to say?"

"And what's that say about him?" Cain asked. "That he didn't call."

"He knows who the girl is, and what happened to her."

His phone began to vibrate, and he looked at the screen. Grassley. He put it away without answering it. He'd see Grassley face to face in five minutes, when he got to the morgue.

"You need a ride back to your office?" he asked. "I'm headed past it."

"I can walk," she said. "It's a block and a half."

There were voices coming from the main autopsy suite, three or four people in a back-and-forth murmur, words he couldn't make out over the high-pitched whine of an oscillating autopsy saw. He went into the back office and found a Tyvek suit laid out, still damp inside from the sweat of the last person who'd worn it.

When he was dressed and had wiped menthol cream under his nostrils, he tightened the respirator mask and went into the suite. Grassley and Dr. Levy were at a center table with the girl's corpse laid out in front of them. To their right, another team was cutting in to a whale of a man who looked as though he'd jumped from a high roof.

"Inspector Cain," Dr. Levy said. "I'll back up and start over."

He stepped next to Grassley and looked down at the corpse. Dr. Levy had cut her open with a Y-incision that went through her sternum and down as far as her pubic bone.

"Your Jane Doe is a Caucasian female. A blonde. She stood five eight and would have weighed a hundred and twenty pounds, give or take five. She was healthy until she died — no chronic diseases, no obvious history of malnourishment. A twenty-year-old girl, nothing wrong with her at all."

"How are you guessing the age?"

"Dental x-rays," Dr. Levy said. "Her wisdom teeth were erupting. They would've just started bothering her."

"I had mine out at twenty-five," Cain said.

"That's the back end of the range," Dr. Levy answered. "The front end is seventeen. But in this girl, the pubic symphysis — the bone connecting the two sides of her pelvis, right above her vulva — it had a nice, billowy surface. That means she was an adult, but a very young one. Done growing, but not growing old."

"Okay."

"What I mean is, twenty's an estimate. But it's a good estimate. I could be off by two or three years."

"Then she was twenty," Cain said. "Give or take."

"I did what I could, but her internal organs were fused together

— inside, she looked like black tar. That's what thirty years under-ground will do. A good casket, but no embalming. There's not enough left of her lungs and airways to say if she died of asphyxiation. Her heart's not giving anything up, either."

"Can you say how she died?"

"What we've got are the scratches inside the casket lid, the match-ing splinters under her fingernails — and nothing else. No broken bones, no obvious cuts or stab wounds, no bullets showing up on the x-rays."

Grassley was taking notes on a spiral-bound pad, writing as fast as he could to catch everything Dr. Levy said.

"What about toxicology?" Cain asked.

"It'll take a month, maybe two," Dr. Levy answered. She went to the back wall and selected a pair of forceps the size of kitchen tongs, then came back. "You know we have to send it out. Any kind of lab work, we have to send out."

"I may not have a month."

"Then you may want to look at getting a private source. What we have, in this office, is a two-month backlog. We've already called in all our favors."

She leaned over the corpse and used the forceps to pull back the skin and underlying tissue at the young woman's pelvis. The skin was leathery, the muscles underneath black and shrunken. Dr. Levy took a scalpel from the table and used the blunt side of its blade to gingerly pry open a slit she'd previously cut.

"This is her uterus," Dr. Levy said.

Cain came a little closer and tried to make it out. It all looked the same to him, an undifferentiated mass of dark tissue. He'd stood in this room often enough to know his way around the inside of a ca-daver. But not one like this.

"She was pregnant," Levy said, gesturing to a pea-size lump. "I'd say she was eight weeks along. Not much more than that."

"Would she have shown?" Cain asked.

He'd stepped back from the table. To his right, the assistant medi-cal examiner had finally put away her oscillating saw. Now the only noise came from the hooded ventilation fans above each table.

"Probably not," Dr. Levy said.

"Was there anything else?" he asked.

"The rest can go in my report," Dr. Levy said. "I just wanted to show you this. I'll preserve the fetus—freeze it, for whatever that's worth now."

"We'll get DNA?" Grassley asked, the first thing he'd said since Cain had arrived.

"It'll be fragmentary, but you'll get it."

Grassley looked at Cain.

"The father," he said. "We'll find out if he's the father."

"Who?" Dr. Levy asked.

"We're not there yet," Cain said. He took Grassley's elbow. "Thanks for walking us through it, Doctor."

"Anytime," she said. "There's a box in your office. I set it there an hour ago, before I knew you were coming. You'll want to pick it up."

They weren't alone until they got into the elevator on the way to the sixth floor.

"Cain—"

"If you'd said *Harry Castelli,* I'd have pulled out my gun and knee-capped you."

"I'm sorry."

"Everybody talks," Cain said. "You say something to Levy in the morgue, and she'll bring it up at the next homicide roundtable. Or she'll mention it to her buddy in there, Dr. Braun. Some lab tech overhears, figures it's worth fifty bucks if he knows a reporter."

"Cain—"

"And everyone down there knows a reporter—some asshole already called Christopher Hanley's mother and told her what we found in his casket. You think they'll just sit on this?"

"I won't do it again."

"I know you won't," Cain said. He forced his voice to soften. "You're a good inspector. The best partner I've had. It was just a slip-up."

Grassley nodded.

"I'll be careful."

They stepped off the elevator and started walking toward their shared office. The cubicle farm—the vast space between the elevators and the window offices—was a chaotic mess. The noon-to-eight shift was winding down; the night watch was coming on. Typewriters rattled beneath half-shouted conversations as one crew passed the baton to the next.

They went into their office and Cain shut the door.

"Unless you're sitting in court, or alone with your girlfriend, never tell anyone but me the truth. Not when half that will do just as well."

Grassley's face locked up, processing that bit of advice.

"You're telling me to lie."

"It's not your job to tell anyone what's going on," Cain said. "It's your job to find out what just happened. You go to Vegas?"

"Vegas?"

"You want to know the other guy's hand—it's not 'I'll show you mine, you show me yours.' You want to get anything, you bluff."

"All right," Grassley said. He looked at his watch.

"If you need to go home, then go. It's late."

Cain was so tired, his face was going numb. He watched Fonteroy's tape again, the old man dying of cancer and feeling hell's glow on the back of his neck. There were no answers on the tape, no details he hadn't already seen.

He stood to leave. An orange sticker by the door reminded him to kill the lights. As he was reaching for the switch, he saw a white box on the filing cabinet. His name was handwritten across the broken trefoil of a biohazard symbol.

He took it back to his desk, pulled a pair of latex gloves from the drawer, and used a pocketknife to cut the seal. There was a hand-written note at the top. He pushed his glasses to his forehead and read it.

Inspector Cain,
Enclosed are samples from Jane Doe's liver and fetus. I'll do what I can, but you can do it faster through your own channels.
— Dr. Rachel Levy

Inside the box were two glass tubes, sealed with rubber stoppers. Each held a black lump smaller than a grain of rice. If he could find someone to foot the bill, he could hire an outside expert to run the toxicology. Fischer had the deepest pockets, but he didn't want to tell her about the cadaver until he knew where it fit. He put the box in an overstuffed drawer of his filing cabinet, shut off the lights, and locked his office door.

13

SLIDING HIS KEY into the lock, he heard voices. A man speaking, Lucy laughing. He turned the bolt without making a sound, then rotated the handle and pressed the door carefully open until there was enough of a gap for him to slip inside.

" . . . we get off the jet," the man was saying, "and I don't even know where we are. Montana? Colorado? They put us in a golf cart and drive us from the landing strip up to the house. This paved pathway — and you know those little solar garden lights? Forget those. They've got actual candles, in glass globes."

"But you've got no idea?" Lucy asked. "At all?"

"Somewhere in the mountains. The air was cold. You breathe in, and it's cold and thin, and there's hint of wood smoke. There were streams nearby, and I could hear them."

"How big was it?" Lucy asked. "The house they brought you to."

"You'd think huge, right?" the man said, and by now Cain had placed Matt Redding's voice. "But it was just a little cabin. A little hunting cabin, somewhere in the mountains. With a landing strip for a twin-engine jet. And they were all waiting for —"

Cain stepped into the dining room, and Matt stopped midsentence and stood. He'd been sitting opposite Lucy at her long walnut table. His glass was empty, and the bottle of wine next to it was half gone. Lucy had a glass of water. Cain looked to her and she answered him by tilting her right palm toward the ceiling. She didn't know why Matt had come.

"Hey, Matt. What's going on?" Cain said.

"I came over to see you," he said. "And I brought you and Lucy a bottle of wine. Only you weren't here, and I find out she won't drink wine —"

"She told you why?"

"No, but I'm not stupid — and it's great, Gavin."

"Thanks."

"Really," Matt said. "You guys are going to be great."

Cain checked to his left, saw that Lucy was still okay with this. They hadn't told anyone except her psychiatrist, who still came three times a week. Then, at the shrink's urging, Cain had found another doctor who was willing to make house calls. But the doctor couldn't do everything in a house call, and they wanted to be safe. They'd talked about it, and she knew she'd have to do it, but they hadn't settled on when or where.

In front of him, Matt held out the bottle of wine.

"So, she can't," Matt said. "I get that. But you can — unless it's a solidarity thing."

"Have some," Lucy said. "He's celebrating."

"You sold the program?" Cain asked.

Matt nodded.

"For the kind of money you expected?"

"North of that," Matt said. He poured wine into his glass and put the bottle down. "Way north."

"I'll get a glass."

They talked for a while about the places Matt thought he might travel first: the Amalfi Coast, Santorini. Places Cain had never been, but he could picture them: water the color of lazurite, whitewashed houses clinging to the cliffs and catching the last of the day's sunlight. There was only so much they could say, and they went through it all quickly. Then Cain sat looking at the wine in his half-empty glass.

"You didn't just come to tell us you're leaving."

"I had another look at the photos. Highlighted some things I didn't think to check the first time, and got a couple hits." He glanced at Lucy. "It's okay to talk here?"

"I'm okay if you're okay," Lucy said. She took Cain's hand under the table.

Matt's backpack was hanging from his chair. He opened it and brought out a tablet computer, setting it on the table between them. He switched it on, then opened a file. It was the first photograph, the girl in the Jean Patou dress, backed against a brick wall with her hands up to ward off the man with the camera. Lucy leaned across to look at it.

"This has to do with the mayor?" she asked.

"I hadn't told him that," Cain said. He looked at Matt. "You'll keep a secret?"

"You know I will."

"That photo came to Castelli's office in an envelope. There were three others with it," Cain said. He took them out of his briefcase and laid them out on the table next to Matt's tablet. "And there was a note."

"What does he want?" Lucy asked, when she was finished looking at each of the pictures. "Money?"

"Nothing so simple," Cain said. "He wants Castelli to end it."

"End what?"

"His life. With a gun to his head."

Cain slid his copy of the note from its folder and put it on the table. Lucy read it, then pushed it across to Matt.

"What do you think the other eight show?" he asked, handing the note back.

Cain had some ideas about that. Castelli might be on the bed with the handcuffed, passed-out girl. The final shots might show the girl being stuffed on top of Christopher Hanley and sealed alive inside his casket. Cain couldn't rule anything out, but he didn't have enough to start speculating out loud.

"I guess we'll just have to wait and see."

"Fair enough," Matt said. He picked up his tablet and used his thumb and forefinger to zoom in until the picture showed the girl's right wrist. "I didn't run the bracelet the first time through."

She wore a silver bangle, the metal worked in a honeycomb pattern. It had no lettering, no symbols of any kind. Just the silver, hexagonal cells that circled her wrist.

"It stands out," Matt was saying. "So I figured it was worth a shot. It's an Imogene Bass piece."

"A what?"

"Imogene Bass—she's a jewelry designer, in London. She was just getting started in 1985, and her stuff wasn't all that expensive. That bracelet would've gone for thirty pounds. Today it'd be worth a lot more."

"Where would she have gotten it?"

99

"Back then, there was just the one shop — in London. But check this out," Matt said. He scrolled down the zoomed-in photograph until they could see the girl's feet. She wore a pair of heels, open at the toe with a leather strap that came across the front of her ankle. "The computer's less sure about these — a lot of shoes look alike, and there's nothing that sets these off. But the result I'm getting is seventy percent sure these are Struttons."

"That's a shoe company?" Cain asked. He looked at Lucy.

"I've never heard of it."

"You wouldn't have — they were a small name, and they never got out of the U.K.," Matt said. "They did mostly discount stuff. Cheap shoes, knockoffs."

"So she got the shoes and the bracelet in the U.K.?" Cain asked.

"Yeah. And look at this."

Matt swiped his screen to close the photograph. He opened a map and zoomed in to London, Cain quickly getting lost as the perspective fell closer to the ground. All he knew was that they were somewhere west of the river. The Thames, he remembered. He'd only been out of the country once, to El Salvador, to talk to a witness who wouldn't touch a phone.

"This is 71 Victoria Street," Matt said. "When Imogene Bass opened her showroom, in 1984, it was here."

"Okay."

"And then go one block around, into this alley," Matt said, tracing his finger above the screen. "This is Strutton Ground. Their first shoe store was here. What do you think about that?"

Cain considered it.

"She must've lived there. If she'd been an American and gone to London as a tourist, I can see her buying the bracelet. It's pretty enough. But why would a tourist go to London and buy a pair of cheap high-heels she could get at home?"

"Makes sense."

"But here's another question," Cain said. "If she's wearing a sixteen-thousand-dollar dress, why's she going to put on a pair of thirty-dollar shoes?"

Lucy reached to the middle of the table and took the first and third photographs, so that she had two views of the dress. She held one close to her eyes, then the other. Then she stood with both of them, went to the dimmer switch, and turned up the overhead light.

When she came back, she put the photographs on the table in front of Cain.

"This isn't a sixteen-thousand-dollar dress," she said. "I don't know where you're getting that."

"But it is," Matt said. "We saw it. It's going for that much *used*. It's a Jean Patou."

Lucy shook her head.

"It's not a Jean Patou — it just looks like one. And she didn't buy it. She made it. This is a homemade dress."

"How can you tell?"

"Because I used to sew," she said. She stood behind Cain, one hand on his shoulder and the other pointing to the photograph. "Look at the seams. Or here, the hem, where it turns out and you can see the inside. It's top-stitched, with a machine. You can see the stitching from a mile away."

Matt came around and stood on the other side of Cain so he could see.

"If this were really a couture dress, the hem would be pick-stitched — hand sewn so you couldn't see anything," Lucy said. "But it's fit for her. See, here, going up her torso, the way it follows her, even when she's putting her hands in the air? She didn't get this off a rack. She measured herself, and then she made it. But she did it in a hurry."

Cain put his hand on top of Lucy's fingers. What a loss that she'd spent the last four years hiding in this house. Spending days at a time at the back of her closet, her chin on her knees and her arms crossed around her shins. He wondered, not for the first time, what would change in the next seven months.

"Then the shoes make sense," Cain said.

"She wanted to look like a rich girl," Lucy said. "She pulled it off, probably for less than a hundred dollars. Even the way she cut corners, it would've taken a long time."

Cain thought about that. He let go of Lucy's hand and stood up. In the kitchen, he poured a glass of water, not sure he wanted any more of Matt Redding's wine. The girl in the photograph had wanted to look like something she wasn't. Maybe she was also pretending to be someone she wasn't. She'd come a long way to play that role. And it had gotten her killed.

14

HE WOKE AT four a.m., his phone vibrating on the bedside table, the screen lit up with Nagata's name. He got his arm out from beneath Lucy's neck, swung his legs onto the floor, and went for the door, phone in hand. Behind him, Lucy rolled over. He shut the door and answered the phone in the hallway, his voice barely a whisper.

"This is Inspector Cain," he said. "What's going on, Lieutenant?"

"How soon can you get to the mayor's house?"

He looked at his watch, struggling to read it in the dark. "Thirty minutes. I can get there in thirty minutes."

"Fifteen," Nagata said. "Ten would be better."

"Make it ten, then. What's going on?"

"I'll tell you when you get here. Face to face. And bring your scene bag."

"Shit."

"That's right," Nagata said. "A whole world of it."

"Dr. Levy's on her way?"

"With a van full of crime scene techs."

"Fischer knows?"

"Not yet. Get dressed and get up here. I've been calling you for half an hour."

Cain drove north toward the Presidio, the city motionless beneath a heavy blanket of fog. He turned on his low beams and his wipers. When he got to Sea Cliff Avenue, he parked in front of the mayor's house and looked around to see who else was there. Nagata's car was in the driveway, and there was a white van from the medical examiner's office next to it. Behind that, there was an ambulance. There were only two patrol cars on the street, and he guessed they'd been here all along, keeping watch on the house. There were no news vans yet, which meant that so far the department had managed to keep radio silence. There was a light coming from the back window of the ambulance, and that was the only light from any of the vehicles. No sirens, no rooftop flashers.

He got out of the car and went around to the trunk for the scene bag. It was so still and quiet that he could hear the surf breaking on the rocks beneath Castelli's house. When the foghorn sounded, it felt like he was standing right above it on the bridge. The note was low and bone-shaking, and then at the end, the silence was empty.

"That was fast," Nagata said. She came around the half-open gate and stood next to him on the sidewalk while he used a penlight to check the contents of his bag. "I didn't really think you'd be here in ten minutes."

"I was close."

"I thought you lived in Daly City?"

"I was at my girlfriend's place."

It was too dark on the street to know if Nagata reacted to that at all. He stood, shouldering the scene bag's nylon strap.

"I've kept everyone out," Nagata said. "I haven't even been in the room yet."

"What's in it?"

"Castelli."

"What happened?"

"Mona Castelli called 911 at three a.m.," Nagata said. They slipped through the opening in the gate, then came off the driveway and went along the wet path through the herb garden to reach the front door. "She'd just gotten home."

"Where was she until three?"

"Down in Monterey. Charity fundraiser at the aquarium. It went until midnight, then she stayed another hour talking to Meredith Miles."

"Who's that?"

"An actress. Or a singer. I forget which. I've got a list, everyone she talked to."

"She drove there?" Cain asked.

The last he'd seen her, Mona Castelli couldn't have driven down the block to the liquor store successfully. Getting to Monterey, and back again, was out of the question.

"She went in a car, but she wasn't driving. She used a limo service."

"Was she sober when you got here?"

"Not exactly."

"Are we talking a little tipsy, or light-on-fire drunk?"

"Somewhere in between, maybe," Nagata said. "She sounded like someone who'd been at a party till one in the morning, then maybe had another couple in the limo on the ride home."

They'd been standing at the front door. Now Nagata took a pair of latex gloves from her pocket. She slipped them on, then pulled plastic covers over her shoes. Cain set down his scene bag and did the same.

"When did the limo pick her up?"

"Seven o'clock."

"What'd she tell 911?" he asked.

Nagata pushed the door open and stepped into the house. There were lights in a few of the wall sconces, and farther back, the kitchen was well lit. But the entry hall was dark enough to hide anything. Cain flicked on his light and looked around. There was a wooden table next to the door. He saw a set of keys, a patent leather clutch. A half-finished martini.

"She said she went upstairs," Nagata said. "She thought he'd be in bed, but he wasn't. His study was locked, and he didn't answer when she tapped on the door. She knew where he kept the spare key, so she got it. She found him behind his desk — she said it looked like he shot himself."

"Where's she now?"

"You saw the ambulance?"

Cain nodded.

"She's in the back. They gave her a sedative."

"Not too much, I hope."

"That's what I told them. She'll be able to talk when we're ready for her."

"Did you do a GSR swab?" Cain asked. "Can we rule her out as the shooter?"

"The paramedics did it," Nagata said. "It came out negative."

"But they took samples for the SEM lab?"

"Of course."

That was good. It wasn't easy to wash off gunshot residue. If Mrs.

Castelli had shot a gun tonight and had somehow washed her hands well enough to evade the paramedics' colorimetric field test, a scanning electron microscope would catch her when the lab got around to it. But the field tests were better than they used to be. They hardly missed anything, and that boded well for Mona Castelli.

"What about the daughter?" Cain asked. "Alexa — is she around?"

"No, she's at her apartment. We haven't told her yet."

"All right," Cain said. "His study's upstairs?"

They were climbing now, the dark staircase wide enough for them to walk side by side.

"Up here. I haven't been in, but she showed me the door."

"You were the first to get here?" Cain asked. "She called 911, and then dispatch called you directly?"

"There was a directive — call me first if anything came up about him."

"Who gave the order?"

"Castelli."

"When?"

"The night he got the first note," Nagata said.

"He was worried something would happen," Cain said. "Don't you think?"

"I don't know."

They reached the top of the stairs, and Nagata led them down a hallway. The master bedroom was on one end, and Castelli's study, accessed by a pair of book-matched mahogany doors, was at the other. An antique lever lock key protruded from the brass plate beneath the doorknob.

Nagata opened both doors and he stepped inside after her. The first thing he noticed was the sharp smell of cordite gun smoke, and under that, there was blood. He closed the doors and looked at the lock. There was no thumb lever. To lock it, even from the inside, you needed a key. He scanned the room but didn't see one.

"She couldn't open this when she came home, had to find a spare key?"

"That's what she told 911."

He pointed at the lock.

"Either there's one in this room somewhere, or this is going to get complicated."

They turned to face the study. Castelli's car-size desk was parked

105

in the middle of the room, so that sitting behind it, he would face whoever came through the door. His leather chair was empty. A pair of shaded lamps stood at the desk's corners, casting interlocking circles on its surface. The rest of the study was in shadow.

Another step in, and his eyes began adjusting.

He saw the red-black splatter on the back wall and the bookcases. There was blood on the leather blotter, a wide smear of it that led to the far edge. He stepped around to follow it, and there was the mayor. After the shot, Castelli must have gone face-first into the desk. Gravity and slack muscles eased him from there to the floor.

Now he lay curled in a nearly fetal pose between the chair and the desk. There was a thick pool of blood on the rug underneath his head. Cain knelt without touching anything, and when he leaned close he could see a small exit wound far back on Castelli's scalp, the black hair around it bloody and flecked with gray-red brain tissue.

He looked around. The gun lay to the right of the chair, partially under the desk. A snub-nosed revolver, maybe a .38. He didn't touch it but leaned closer to see it. It was a Smith & Wesson, not a Model 10 but one of the earlier M&P jobs. A lot of wear around the barrel. An old gun, a family heirloom. Maybe Harry J. Castelli Sr. had worn it on his hip in West Berlin.

Nagata was at the end of the desk, watching him. He looked back at Castelli, the blood still wet and shiny under the man's head.

"Did the paramedics come up?" he asked.

"No."

"And you didn't come in here?"

"No."

He asked the next question as evenly as he could.

"No one's checked him?"

"I thought . . . the scene."

"The scene," Cain said. "Sure."

Without moving Castelli, he put two fingers on the man's jugular. His skin was cool, and there was no pulse. He was right over the body now and could smell the alcohol rising up. When he tried to move Castelli's jaw, it was locked tight. So was his neck. Blood had come out of his lips and run down his cheek to the rug. Cain didn't see an entry wound anywhere. The gun must have been in Castelli's mouth when it went off.

"Nothing? No heartbeat?"

He looked up at Nagata.

"Cold and stiff," he said. "We'll ask Dr. Levy, and she'll tell us rigor in the neck usually takes two hours. Then she'll walk that back and say it all depends on room temperature and a dozen other things. How long have you been here?"

"Not even an hour."

"Then you're good," Cain said. "He was probably dead when you got here."

"That's good?"

"You'd rather explain to Mona Castelli why you kept the paramedics out when they could've done something?"

"Shit."

"Forget it, Lieutenant," Cain said. "Gunshot or not, you were in the clear — I've seen guys who drank enough to smell like this. They didn't need a bullet to finish things off. They just dropped dead."

"I'll call up Dr. Levy."

"Not yet," Cain said. "Before the world starts walking through, I want to see the rest of the room."

Kneeling over Castelli, he patted him down. He was wearing the same striped shirt and blue tie he'd been wearing ten hours ago in City Hall, when Cain confronted him. His suit jacket was missing but could be anywhere.

The shadows were too heavy. Underneath the desk was like a cave. He looked up. Track lights ran along the ceiling and pointed to the bookshelves.

"See if you can find a switch for those," Cain said. "We need more light."

He turned back to Castelli and patted down his trouser pockets. It was hard to feel inside the right pocket. Castelli lay curled on that side. But Cain felt the distinct shape of an antique lever lock key beneath the gabardine fabric. He didn't move the body, and he didn't try to take the key out. That would all come later, after the crime scene photographers were finished.

Above him, the lights came on. One bulb went out immediately. A droplet of blood must have splattered there, cracking the thin glass when it heated. He stepped over Castelli's legs to look at the desktop.

"There's a key in his right pocket," Cain said.

"All right."

"After we move him, we'll get it out and test it. Make sure it locks that door."

On the desk, a near-empty bottle of bourbon stood next to a crystal tumbler. Farther from the bottle, there was a red wax seal, like the one Castelli had cut from a fresh bottle at City Hall. So Castelli hadn't poured a drop from this bottle until he sat down tonight, opened it, and got started.

Cain pointed it out to Nagata.

"We'll tag it and bag it," he said. "The bottle and the glass — all of this."

He knelt again, mindful of the blood on the rug, and opened each of the drawers.

"Five dollars there's a nickel-plated folding knife in here."

"What?"

"Bingo."

The knife was in the first drawer he opened. He eased out the blade and saw the red wax caught in its serrations. He put the knife down. The drawer Alexa had described was locked, but it only took Cain a moment to find the key underneath a pencil tray in the slim center drawer.

"What are you doing?" Nagata asked.

"Checking for a note."

"A suicide note."

"That'd be nice," Cain said. "But maybe he didn't put a bow on it. If he's got the next set of photos, they might have come with a note."

"He said this whole thing was a hoax."

"People say a lot of things."

Cain unlocked the drawer, then rolled it open. There were two more bottles of bourbon, their seals uncut. Castelli must have had his own delivery truck. He pictured an entire fleet of them, riding all night on the highways between San Francisco and Kentucky. Next to the bottles, there was a foot-high stack of *Playboy* magazines. Each was stored inside a separate plastic collector's sleeve. Cain lifted the magazines to look beneath them, but there was nothing. A couple of loose coins, the pennies that find their way into all drawers and never come out. One of them was from 1983, the other from 1997. And, as far as the locked drawer went, that was all.

"I'm putting this all back the way I found it," Cain said. "We'll photograph it in place, then bag it."

"Fine."

"He might've left it in City Hall," Cain said. "In his office there. Did you post a guard?"

"I didn't think —"

"Call now and get some guys. We don't want any staff going into his office. Not even the reception area."

"All right."

"We'll search that after we finish here."

Nagata left the room to make the call. It didn't surprise him how easy it was, taking this over, telling her what to do. She'd never run a homicide investigation. She'd been looking to him for direction since they came upstairs. While she was gone, Cain checked out the bookshelves behind the desk. History, organized by geography. The top shelf was California: San Francisco on the left, and everything else on the right. The middle five shelves covered the rest of the world, by continent. General reference on the bottom shelf. It was surprising, the breadth of Castelli's interests. Cain wouldn't have pegged him as a serious reader of anything beyond bourbon labels and men's club brochures. Behind him, Nagata hung up.

"What now?" she asked.

"Why don't you check the credenza over there — see if there's a note."

He was still holding the stack of *Playboys*. He knelt again and began putting them back into the drawer, one at a time. The first issue was December 1953. On the cover, Marilyn Monroe raised her bare left arm and smiled with her eyes half closed. He knew the centerfold in that one, the famous shot of Marilyn curled up on some kind of red cushion. The pages looked well thumbed. Alexa had come in here as a girl to borrow these, to sneak them off to her room, where she could study the photographs in private. They couldn't have been in this drawer back then. They must have been out on the shelves, because the drawer had been locked and she said she didn't know what was in it. He did wonder how much he should be relying on anything Alexa said. And he wondered what Castelli kept in here ten years ago. The gun, maybe.

"No note," Nagata said from the other side of the room. "His phone. His wallet, too."

He came around the desk to the credenza, where Nagata was standing in front of a shallow marble bowl. Castelli's phone and wallet lay there. Nagata reached down and picked up the phone, moving her thumb over the button to turn it on.

"Stop," Cain said.

"There could be a note — maybe something in his last emails."

"So we call the Computer Forensics Unit and leave it for them."

He pointed to the bowl, but Nagata didn't put the phone down. She wasn't like Chun or Grassley. She hadn't made lieutenant because she was a good investigator. She'd worked on Castelli's campaign, had helped him get the police union's endorsement. He'd returned the favor. Simple as that, but now all her future promotions were dead under a desk.

"Picture yourself on the witness stand," Cain said. "The lawyer's leaning over the rail, right in your face. He knows you were Castelli's friend. He knows you used the phone. He's just asked your credentials as a computer expert. What do you say?"

She put the phone back in the bowl.

"Forget it — we'll leave it for CFU."

"Good," Cain said. "They'll give us a printout and a report. They're usually pretty quick."

He picked up the wallet and flipped through it. It was thin. Two credit cards and a driver's license. No cash and no receipts.

There was a sound from downstairs, the front door clicking open. Footsteps, and voices from the entry hall.

"Who's that?" Cain asked.

"No idea."

Cain went to the window behind the desk. Both the curtains and the exposed rectangle of glass were flecked with blood. He looked down to the driveway. A black town car was parked behind the ambulance, and a patrol car was blocking the end of the driveway. A sedan, brown in the streetlight but maybe maroon by day, was parked across the street.

"Who else did you call?"

"The people who needed to know," Nagata said.

"Come on," Cain said, going for the door. "The whole house could be a crime scene, and your VIPs are about to trash it."

· · ·

They regrouped outside the front door, a loose circle of five. Agent Fischer stood next to Cain, and on her right was the chief of police, using a handkerchief to mop the rain from his bald head. Next to him was Katherine Greenberg. Until today, she'd been the president of the board of supervisors. By lunchtime, she'd be sworn in as mayor. Cain tried to read Nagata's face but couldn't.

"He's dead?" Greenberg asked Cain. "Inspector — you saw him?"

"He's dead."

"I heard it was a suicide?"

"He shot himself," Nagata said. "The gun's —"

"He's been shot," Cain said. "We don't know which gun shot him. It's too early to say he shot himself. Right now, we can't even say it was a bullet that killed him."

"You're saying this could be a murder?" Greenberg asked.

"Until we complete the investigation, it could be anything. You know about the letter and the photos?"

"Chief Larson briefed me."

"In the car, on the way over — that was the first time I told her," the chief said to Cain. The chief had never spoken a word to Cain, and now here he was, squeezing his hands together and explaining himself. "Not before this morning."

"The letter's a complication we can't ignore," Cain said. He looked at Agent Fischer and she nodded back at him: *Go on.* "And we can't investigate this in the normal course."

"What are you telling me?" Greenberg asked.

Her hair was held in a neat bun by a tortoiseshell clip, and she wore a hint of makeup. The rain beaded and glistened like amber on her beige overcoat. Of the five people crowded around the front door's entry light, she was the only one who looked halfway awake, who had dressed properly for the weather. Was she quick about getting ready, or was she already awake when the call came? It might not mean anything if she'd been up, but then again, it might be everything.

"I'm requesting a special assignment to investigate this death," Cain said. "Agent Fischer and I can run it, and we'll bring in a pair of inspectors from SFPD — Grassley and Chun. We're an independent team with no oversight from you, from the SFPD, or the FBI. We don't report anything to anybody until we're done. Or until we're about to kick down a door."

"Kick down a door?"

"Make an arrest," Fischer said. "And he's right—we need to be independent."

"This is for political cover?" Greenberg asked. "I don't go for that. That was Castelli's way."

"It's not political cover," Cain said. "It's tactical. It's necessary, in a thing like this."

"I'm not sure I follow you."

"He's being polite," Fischer said. No one here signed her paychecks. "He means until we know who wrote the letter, our suspects include any of Castelli's enemies. And anyone who stood to benefit from his death. We don't want those people looking over our shoulder."

"Now, come on," Chief Lawson said. But Greenberg stopped him with a hand on his chest.

"She's right. Inspector Cain, too. I wasn't a Castelli fan, and lately neither were you. We can't put our hands on this."

Chief Lawson shook his head but didn't respond.

"I think we're done here," Greenberg said. "I'll leave it to you and Agent Fischer. The chief and I are going to be busy today. And I'm sure Lieutenant Nagata has other business."

"Thank you," Cain said. "Your Honor."

Greenberg shook her head.

"I don't take the oath until ten o'clock," she said. "This is your investigation. But the city's resources are yours—the ME's office, the labs. If you need warm bodies to knock on doors—"

"I'll get what I need."

She reached to shake his hand, then seemed to change her mind. Instead, she went back down the stone-lined path. She and the chief had come in his car, and now his driver was opening the rear doors for them. Nagata went to her own car without saying another word to anyone.

Cain supposed she might come back to the Homicide Detail at least once, to clean out her desk. She wasn't the best lieutenant he'd ever had, but there could be worse. At least she knew her limitations. He put that out of his mind and turned to Fischer.

"Your bosses will be okay with this?"

"Yeah."

"Who called you?" Cain said. "Nagata?"

"That's right."

"I was worried she'd try to keep it in-house."

"She seemed reluctant," Fischer said. "I guess I know why."

"You got gloves and shoe covers?"

Fischer patted her purse.

"Let's go — I'd like to look the room over before the CSI stampede. If that's okay."

15

BACK IN THE study, he brought Fischer to look at the mayor where he lay beneath the desk. She got down close to him, her knees in the same imprints Cain had left five minutes ago in the rug's deep pile. She felt Castelli's jugular and tested the movement of his jaw. She pulled out a penlight and began to search under the desk.

Cain went to the far wall of the study.

There was a door he hadn't noticed on his first brief look around the room. With a light push, one of the hardwood panels slid sideways, opening to a private bathroom. Fischer leaned around the desk at the sound.

"Nice," she said.

She went back to what she'd been doing, and Cain stepped into Castelli's private bathroom. Marble tile, silk wallpaper with a fleur-de-lis print. Everything made of metal was gold plated. The faucet fixtures, the wall lamps. Even the toilet's flush handle. He knelt and opened the cabinet under the sink. Cleaning supplies in a plastic bucket, a big bottle of bleach. Rolls of tissue paper. Folded washcloths in a wicker basket. He closed the cabinet and stood. The mirror behind the basin swung out on hidden hinges. Castelli must have had another medicine cabinet in his master bedroom — he wouldn't hide the spare key to his study in a room that could only be accessed from the study. So this was his second medicine cabinet, maybe a more private one.

Cain looked through the medications. Viagra and Ambien. Wellbutrin. Tramadol. He checked that last one with his phone — a painkiller, some kind of lightweight opiate. None of the pill bottles had Castelli's name or any kind of prescription information. He might have been buying them online. One of those pharmacies from Can-ada, from Tijuana. That made sense. A man with Castelli's ambitions might not want to walk into his doctor's office and describe the symptoms that would lead to any of these prescriptions.

"Inspector Cain?" He leaned out of the bathroom. Agent Fischer was still half under the desk. "Come here a minute."

He went over, stepping around the mess on the rug until he was kneeling next to her. She hadn't moved the gun, but she was leaning close to it. Even with the track lights on, it was far enough under the desk to be in the shadows. She lit it up with her flashlight.

"What am I looking at?" Cain asked.

The gun lay on its side, and they were looking down its blue-black barrel. The rifling looked worn down, and he thought again about how old it must have been.

"Look at the cylinder, the chamber just to the right of the barrel."

He looked and saw it.

"It's empty," he said. There were flat-nosed, metal-jacketed bullets in the other three visible chambers. The view into the bottom chamber was blocked by the trigger assembly, the view into the top was blocked by the barrel.

"That's a double-action S and W," Fischer said. "So if he shot himself, there'd be an empty shell in the chamber under the firing pin. The cylinder wouldn't rotate unless he pulled the trigger again. So the empty chamber on the right, that's something else."

"The gun was fired twice, is what you're saying."

"You keep a revolver?"

"Just an automatic."

"But still—when you fire a round, what do you do? Walk around one short?" Fischer asked. "Or do you reload?"

"I reload."

"If he kept this gun sitting in a drawer, he wouldn't leave an empty chamber. What's the point of that?"

"Beats me."

Cain rose and looked around the room. There, high on the back wall and surrounded by a shotgun pattern of blood droplets, was a bullet hole in the wooden molding. After it came out the back of Castelli's head it had gone there. That was good. If it had been a little to the right, it would have gone through the window and they'd never have found it.

"What are you looking for?" Fischer asked.

"Another bullet hole—if he fired two rounds, where'd the other one go?"

Fischer pulled herself out from beneath the desk and knelt next to him. They scanned the ceiling, then the back wall.

"There," she said. "Bookshelf, bottom row. The *American Heritage Dictionary*."

Cain went to the shelf and knelt there. The dictionary was a thick, hardbound volume. The bullet had gone into its spine.

"Good eyes."

Fischer came over. Neither of them touched the book. Cain was making fast mental notes, everything he needed to say to the photographers.

"Why two shots?" she said.

"You saw the gun," Cain said. "It's prewar, don't you think? An antique. If it was an heirloom, maybe he'd never shot it. Ammunition as old as the gun—ballistics will tell us."

"So he fires one off to see if it works. Then he swivels around, downs a drink or ten. The last thing he swallows is the barrel."

"That's about it."

"It's weird."

"You've seen a suicide that wasn't?" Cain asked.

She didn't answer right away. Probably, in the FBI, they had better things to do than run out to every dead body that got called in. He thought of the calls he'd been on, just in the last month. Suicide, death by drunken misadventure. Bag the evidence, haul the body to the ME. Write the report and forget it—except this time, the corpse on the rug was Harry Castelli.

"Do you want to swab his hands now, or leave it for the ME?" Fischer asked.

"Dr. Levy can do it."

"You trust her?"

"Yes."

She looked down at Castelli's hands. There was dried blood spackled across both sets of his knuckles.

"Three feet," Fischer said. "That's how far it goes."

"What's that?"

"Fifteen years ago, when Sandia Labs did the gunshot residue experiments, they could pick up traces on anyone within three feet of a shooter. Residue on your hands, it doesn't mean you were holding the gun."

Cain knew that. If Rachel Levy pulled a positive swab off Castelli's hands, it could mean anything. To build a case, no piece of evidence was conclusive. Everything came with its own uncertainties. The only thing to do was keep going, to gather all you could and plot every point. You had to hope the line pointed in one direction, that any other explanation became an unreasonable doubt.

"There's a medicine cabinet behind the sink," Cain said. "Prescription drugs, but I don't think he got them from a doctor. Nothing over the top, but maybe worth checking out."

"Something your toxicologist can do. Make sure he gets the bottles and samples them. The pills might be different from what the labels say. Also, his browser history — you need to get computer forensics on that."

"Our toxicology lab isn't up and running," Cain said.

"Send it out, then," Fischer said. "A private lab."

"You can't help?"

"I can send things to our lab. I can't move you ahead in line."

"I keep hearing that."

"You ready to bring them in, get going for real?"

"I'll go get them," Cain said.

Dr. Levy and the vanload of techs from the crime scene unit were still sitting in the driveway. He went to get them, and Karen Fischer followed him out. He liked that she didn't stay in the room by herself, that she didn't need him to say anything. They both understood how much better it would be, testifying that no, the only person who'd ever been alone with the body had been Mona Castelli.

They didn't move the body until well past lunchtime. The techs came in with their tripods and their can lights, and they took photographs and used lasers to shoot measurements and calculate angles. A guy from ballistics got up on a ladder and burrowed into the high back wall, eventually finding the lethal bullet buried and smashed in a two-by-six heart pine stud. When the same man pulled out the dictionary and flipped it open, the nearly intact bullet fell out of the *M* section. It had punched through the spine, had gone almost all the way through the book, but had stopped just before the fore edge.

The man bagged it, then showed it to Cain and Fischer.

"Good ballistics off this one," he said. "The other — not so much. You send a piece of lead through two sides of a skull, then into a piece of wood, it gets pretty smashed up."

Cain looked around. The study was cluttered with numbered yellow signs, a hundred and seventy of them, marking the location of each piece of evidence. The photographers were moving from one to the next, taking their time to frame each shot. Dr. Levy and two assistant medical examiners rolled Castelli over and lifted him into a body bag. They'd already swabbed his hands and bagged them, and the colorimetric GSR test was developing on the edge of the desk.

"Hang on," Cain said. "I need to check something."

He stepped away from Fischer and the ballistics man, nodded a greeting to Dr. Levy, and knelt next to her at the body bag.

"I'm taking something out of his pocket — a key," Cain said. "All right?"

"Bring it back. If it's on the body, it stays on the body until we get to Bryant Street."

"I'm not even leaving the room."

Cain reached into Castelli's right pocket and found the key. He pulled it out and showed it to Dr. Levy, then to Fischer. Then he crossed to the study's door and put the key in the lock. He twisted it, and the deadbolt slid out. He turned it the same way, another half rotation, and the deadbolt disappeared.

What did that prove?

Castelli could have come into the study, could have locked the door with the key and put it back in his pocket. Then he must have crossed the room to the credenza, where he put down his wallet and phone. After that, he opened a fresh bottle of bourbon and sat down to the serious business of drinking nine-tenths of it. There was just the one glass. But if there'd been someone else in here, a shooter, that person wouldn't very well have left his glass sitting on the desk.

Cain came back to the body bag and slipped the key into Castelli's pocket. Kneeling there, he helped position the stiffened body so Rachel Levy's assistants could zip the bag closed.

"When you do the blood alcohol test, can you determine how much he had to drink?" Cain asked.

"Sure."

"I mean, you can be pretty precise about it? Whether he drank the whole bottle himself, or if he had company helping him?"

"I can't do that," Dr. Levy said. "We don't know when he started, how fast he was drinking. He'd be metabolizing it while he went."

"He was with me at seven o'clock," Cain said. "And he was dead by three. Does that help?"

"A little. I'll see what I can do," she said.

She picked up the GSR test and showed it to Cain. The circular fiberglass swab was speckled with tiny blue dots.

Cain stood up.

"Agent Fischer?"

"I see it."

"Positive gunshot residue," Dr. Levy said.

Cain nodded and looked around the room. Soon, the CSI team would start bagging everything. They'd load the bags into boxes and haul them off. It would take a moving truck to get it all—the books and the magazines, the rug that had soaked up Castelli's blood until it was black with it, the sawn-out chunk of old-growth pine that had caught his bullet. The bottles, the tumbler, the contents of the bathroom.

Next to him, Agent Fischer was putting her phone away. She took Cain's elbow.

"That was the patrolman, next door," she said. "Mona Castelli's coming out of it. She can talk to us."

"All right."

Cain checked faces in the now crowded room until he recognized the man he wanted. He went to him, a technician from the Crime Scene Investigation unit. Cain wasn't sure of Sumida's first name, wasn't sure they would recognize each other if they passed on the street. They only knew each other from crime scenes.

"Agent Fischer and I have to step next door," Cain said. "You okay if I leave you in charge?"

"Sure."

"You know what to do?"

"Bag it and tag it," Sumida said. "And don't fuck it up."

"Good deal."

He found Fischer waiting for him by the stairs. They went down together, then crossed the foyer and went out. The early afternoon

119

was dark gray, the cold air a relief. He'd been in the study too long. Blood drying on the walls and Castelli, unrefrigerated, on the floor. Mist drifted up Sea Cliff Avenue and sifted through the jasmine flowers that lined the walk next door.

Mona Castelli had gone next door when the ambulance left. The neighbors had taken her in, had walked her to a couch. They'd also let in a patrolman, whose instructions from Cain were straightforward: Watch the widow Castelli. Keep her in sight. And if she tries to take a drink, put a stop to it.

The young officer met them at the front door.

"Sir — ma'am — she's just waking up."

"And the people who live here?"

"Sitting outside, to give you space. Make yourself at home, is what the husband said."

"Did she have anything to drink?"

"Coffee, ten minutes ago."

"No brandy in it, anything like that?"

"No sir. I saw them make it."

"All right. Let's go see her."

"You want me to wait out front?"

Cain took a better look of the patrolman. A young kid. Nineteen, twenty. But he seemed sharp enough.

"Sit in. You might learn something," Cain said. "A third witness can't hurt."

"Yes, sir."

The neighbors' living room wasn't half as nice as the Castellis'. Cain supposed everything ran on a graduated scale, even the extravagant wealth on Sea Cliff Avenue. They sat down in overstuffed white leather chairs opposite the matching couch where Mona Castelli lay. Her coffee mug was on a glass table next to her. It was still full.

"Have you told Alexa yet?" she asked. "Inspector Cain — have you told my daughter?"

She hadn't opened her eyes yet.

"No, ma'am. We haven't told her. Have you?"

"I can't bear to."

"Do you want me to?" Cain asked.

Mona sat up. She put her elbows on her knees and leaned her forehead against her hands.

120

"Will you do it for me?" she asked. "Would that be okay?"

"All right."

There was no reason to tell her he preferred it that way. It was always better to see a family member's initial reaction.

"Do you know where she lives?" she asked. "I don't remember the address. I just know how to get there. It's on Montgomery — New Montgomery."

"I'll call Melissa and get it from her," Cain said. "I can go see Alexa after we finish up here."

Mona reached for her coffee. Her hands weren't steady, but she didn't spill any. She took a long sip, then put the mug down.

"I need to ask you a few questions," Cain said.

"All right."

"And just so you know, I'm recording this."

He set his phone on the coffee table between them.

"That's fine."

"Did Harry own any guns?"

"Yes, one. A pistol. A revolver."

"Where'd he get it?"

"I don't know. He'd always had it. It was his grandfather's. Or maybe it had been his grandfather's brother's."

"The gun we're talking about, his grandfather's revolver, is the one that was next to him under the desk?"

"I didn't see it under the desk. I didn't look under the desk — I saw him, and all the blood, and I got out."

"You told 911 he'd shot himself, but you didn't see the gun?"

She shook her head.

"I could smell the smoke — and the blood everywhere. The wall, the ceiling."

"You didn't touch him?"

"He was dead!"

"He was dead," Cain said. "Okay. So you didn't touch him."

"I didn't."

"This gun, where did he keep it?"

"In his study? I don't know. I hadn't seen it for years. He isn't a gun person. He just happened to have that gun."

"Did he ever shoot it, that you know of? Take it to a range, and practice?"

"I never even saw him touch it."

"How did you know about it?"

She was using her thumbs to massage her temples now. Her frosted hair hung around her face and brushed back and forth against her knees.

"I moved in with Harry when I was nineteen. Sea Cliff House, next door, is the fifth — no, the sixth house we've had since then. Six times, I've packed his stuff. Six times, I've unpacked it."

"He's not secretive about anything in his study? He let you pack it, each time?"

"You mean the *Playboys*?" Mona asked. She looked up, and her eyes were so red, she might have just stumbled clear of a forest fire. "Those belonged to his father. I already told you — there's nothing about Harry you can't find online."

She'd told him that, but she'd also hinted what she thought about her husband and Melissa Montgomery. Cain had checked online, but even the political gossip blogs had come up clean. So either Mona was wrong, or Harry Castelli wasn't such an open book after all.

"Was he depressed?"

"Not Harry. He's driven. Confident."

"But he was taking Wellbutrin."

"Not Harry."

"Trouble sleeping?"

"None."

"Any other trouble in bed?"

"What are you — Are you serious?" she asked. "He wasn't impotent, if that's what you're trying to say."

"But no problems, ever, with sleeping? Or anything else?"

She took her time thinking about it. Her thumbs were still on her temples, rubbing and circling.

"In the last five or six days, he'd been worried about something. I didn't know what, and then you came to see me, that first time. So I thought, maybe he's worried about that. But of course he didn't say anything to me."

"You knocked on the study door, and it was locked."

"That's right."

"You took the spare key and opened the door."

This time, when she looked up, her eyes were more focused.

Maybe it was because of the questions, or maybe she'd just begun to wake up.

"I told the woman cop that already. Your boss. We were downstairs, and she called you and told you to come."

"Was the study door usually locked?"

"Sometimes."

"When he was in it, or when he was gone?"

"When he was gone. He'd never locked himself in."

"If it was locked, and he was gone, would you go in?"

"But he wasn't gone, Mr. Cain—his car was in the driveway. That's why I went in. I couldn't find him, but his car was there, and his study door was locked. Harry Castelli doesn't take long walks on the beach. He's not that kind of man. If his car's home, then he's in the house."

"Okay," Cain said. He looked at Fischer. It was her turn for a while, if she wanted it.

"Mrs. Castelli," Fischer said. "I'm Special Agent Karen Fischer, with the FBI."

"The FBI?"

"We're looking into this too."

"Okay."

"After you found Harry, what was the first phone call you made?"

"To 911."

"And you made that on your cell?"

Mona Castelli nodded. She opened the purse on the floor next to her and took out a phone. She put it on the coffee table, then flipped to the call log.

"May I?" Fischer asked.

She leaned across and looked at the phone, then showed it to Cain. The call to 911 had gone out at 3:03. It was the last call she'd made or received. The next closest thing on the log was a short outgoing call at 11:05 p.m. Yesterday evening, when she was supposed to have been down in Monterey.

Fischer handed the phone back.

"What's this one at 11:05? Short call, lasted five seconds. There wasn't a name in your contacts list. Whose number was that?"

Mona Castelli looked at her phone screen. Her face scrunched up.

"I think that's Meredith Miles."

"The actress?" Fischer said.

"The actress. She was at the fundraiser. She asked for my number, but I didn't know it — I was — I'd been —"

"Drinking," Cain said.

Mona Castelli nodded.

"So she used your phone to call hers," Fischer said. "Is that it?"

"It didn't seem important. It's not important." She looked at Cain. "When will it be all right to use my house again?"

"You'll be in a hotel the next couple of days."

"I'll need to get some things."

"Tell me what you want, and where I can find it. I'd rather you not go in."

"Never mind," she said. "I'll just go to a store."

Cain resisted looking at Fischer to see how she was reacting to that. She was too good of an investigator to show anything on her face, and of course it might not mean anything at all. Mona Castelli had just lost her husband. She was in shock, humming with the tail end of the lorazepam injected by the paramedics. If none of this had happened, she would have been in bed until sunset, sleeping off the gin.

"I have one more question," Cain said. "You understand I have to ask it."

"Okay."

"Did your husband have life insurance?"

She shook her head, then nodded. She seemed to consider another sip of her coffee but never reached for the mug.

"I don't know," she said. "I'm sure he would. Probably something on top of whatever the city had for him. He doesn't believe in skimping."

"Who'd know?"

"Who do you think?" she asked. "Melissa Montgomery has all of that. If you go to his office, I'm sure she'll be able to show you where it is."

"Okay," Cain said. He looked at Fischer. "Did you have anything else?"

"No."

"The officer here will drive you to a hotel," Cain said. "He can take you to a shop, too."

"Yes, ma'am," the kid said. "Happy to."

"Just a hotel," Mona said. "The Palace — Harry and I always stayed at the Palace in between moves."

"You know where that is?" Cain asked the patrol officer.

"Yes, sir."

"All right. Go ahead and take her."

"Yes, sir — but can I have a word first, Inspector?"

The kid led Cain to the kitchen, then gestured through the window of the breakfast nook to the tiny backyard. Fischer shadowed them, standing close enough to overhear the officer without losing sight of Mona Castelli.

"You should talk to them," he told Cain. "The people who own this house. The Petrovics. Roger and Dana. They were home when it happened — they heard the shot."

Cain read the name tag on the man's shirt pocket.

"You're doing good work, Combs."

"Thank you, sir," he said. He started toward the living room to collect Mona Castelli but turned back to Cain when he thought of something else. He dropped his voice so it wouldn't leave the kitchen. "I think they know something. But they didn't tell me."

"What makes you think that?"

"They were in the study, talking to each other. Looking at the computer and whispering."

"All right, Officer. We'll check it out."

16

THEY STEPPED INTO the backyard through a sliding glass door and found the Petrovics sitting in a pair of wet redwood deck chairs beneath a canvas awning. The fabric overhead was sodden with rain, big drops beading up on the underside and running toward the edges, where it ran in streams onto the grass and onto the low rock wall at the cliff's edge. Beyond that was an empty gray void, booming with the sound of waves breaking on the rocks below them. The foghorn growled, low and long. A ship, invisible out in the Pacific, answered.

Roger Petrovic climbed out of his chair, brushing rainwater from his fleece vest with the back of his hand. He stood a head taller than Cain. White beard and close-cropped hair, the muscles in his bare forearms like coiled hemp ropes. His wife was shorter and lithe. Her tanned face was framed by brown hair, parted down the middle. Roger took the badge that Cain handed him, looking at it for a moment before passing it to his wife. He did the same with Fischer's.

"I talked to Officer Combs, inside," Cain said. "He said you were both awake and heard the shot."

Dana handed the badges back. She glanced up at her husband, and he nodded to her.

"We heard," she said.

Roger looked at the glass door. Cain had closed it after they stepped out, and from the backyard it was impossible to see into the house. The glass was glazed, mirrorlike.

"Mrs. Castelli's gone?" Roger asked. "Your officer took her away?"

Cain had no trouble reading the tone.

He wasn't worried about Mona Castelli; he only wanted to know if he could have his living room back. It wasn't surprising. Just look at them: you couldn't find two people more different from the Castellis.

126

Not on this street, anyway. But Cain knew Mrs. Petrovic had come out this morning, had talked her way past the cop in the driveway to tell the paramedics that Mona Castelli could wait in their house.

Whatever differences they had, the neighbors had some kind of relationship.

"She's out of your hair," Cain said. "Couple nights in a hotel — after that, I don't know."

Mr. Petrovic relaxed his arms from across his chest. His wife took his hand.

"We'll sit in the kitchen," she said to Cain. "You're cold. Agent Fischer, too."

"Your officer probably drank all the coffee," Roger said. "Worrying if that woman would choke on her puke."

"Roger."

"You should've seen her — passed out on our sofa and snoring like a bum in a drunk tank."

"You've never been in a drunk tank," Dana said.

"It's all right." He held her hand close to his chest as he led them across the soaked lawn to the house. "I'm just glad she's gone."

While making sure Mona Castelli didn't die like a rock star on Roger Petrovic's couch, Officer Combs hadn't drunk much of the coffee at all. There was still enough in the pot to fill four mugs. They sat at the maple-topped island bar in the kitchen, and Roger Petrovic waited for Cain and Fischer to get out their notepads and flip to fresh pages.

"We were up later than usual," he began. "We'd had friends for dinner — you need their names?"

"If I do, we'll circle back," Cain said.

"They left at eleven," Dana said.

Fischer penciled the time into her spiral pad, then spoke while scrolling through something on her phone.

"You're sure about the time?"

"Yes."

"How?"

"I flipped on the TV when they left," Dana said. She pointed at a small flat screen on the wall near the refrigerator. "The news was just coming on. The eleven o'clock news. I listened to it while we cleaned up."

"How long did that take?"

"Half an hour," Roger said. "Give or take."

"So it was about eleven thirty," Dana said. "And we were turning out the lights downstairs, about to go out to bed. And I looked out the window there, by the breakfast nook, and I saw the moon."

"A third-quarter moon," Roger said. "It rises at noon and sets at midnight."

"You knew that already, or you looked it up?" Fischer asked.

"I looked it up this morning. We'd put it together, what we heard. So I knew we'd need to know the time."

"All right," Cain said. "Go on."

Dana took her husband's hand again.

"It was so clear," she said. "It had been foggy all night, and then it got clear. So I called him down and poured us each a glass of wine —the bottle was already open, what we didn't finish at dinner. We put on our jackets and went outside to sit on the chairs—"

"Where you found us just now."

"He knows that—and we had our glass of wine and watched the moon set past the horizon. It was too beautiful to leave—"

"About midnight," Roger said.

"—and right after the last of the light was gone, we heard the gunshots."

"How many shots?" Fischer asked.

"Two," Roger said. "The first one, and then maybe a minute later, the second."

"You're sure it was a minute?"

"It wasn't like this," he said, and snapped his fingers twice, quickly. "There was a pause. Maybe a minute, maybe two."

"Could you tell where they came from?" Fischer asked.

"Castelli's house."

He pointed out the kitchen window at the broad stucco side of his neighbor's house. A low redwood fence, overgrown with ivy, separated their yards.

"That direction, at least," Dana said. "If you asked me, at the time, did I think it came from the house? Not really."

"The two shots, did they sound like the same gun?" Cain asked.

The Petrovics looked at each other.

"I wouldn't know about that—we didn't even know it was a

gun," Dana said. "There were two bangs. They could have been anything."

"A car backfiring," Roger said. "Somebody slamming a door."

"Did you get up and look around?"

"We sat another minute," she said. "And then we went to bed. We didn't think about it until we woke up —"

"— and saw the morgue van and the patrol cars," Roger finished.

Cain looked at Fischer. The Petrovics were as solid as eyewitnesses came. They'd had some wine, sure, but they could pin their story to actual times based on a measurable event. Now he and Fischer knew when the shots were fired. But Officer Combs suspected they knew something else. He might be a kid, but Cain had learned when to trust a cop's intuition. He bet Fischer had too.

She turned back to the Petrovics.

"Before you went to bed," she asked, "did you see anyone come out of the Castellis' house?"

"No," Roger said.

"A strange car in the driveway, or parked out front?"

Roger looked at his wife, and she shook her head.

"How about lights going on or off?" Fischer asked.

"Other sounds from the house, maybe," Cain added. "Something besides gunshots."

"None we noticed," Roger said.

"Upstairs, we have blinds on the windows," Dana said. "Double-paned glass. In the bedroom, we wouldn't have noticed anything — but, tell them, Roger. What we were talking about."

Roger Petrovic nodded.

"We didn't see anything. But I can tell you when the doors opened and closed — the Castellis' doors, I mean. You're probably supposed to get a subpoena. A search warrant. But I can show you now, and we can paper it later."

"What are you talking about?" Cain asked.

"Get me my laptop, hon."

Dana slid off her chair and went away, and Roger turned back to them.

"You've heard of Watchmen Alarm?"

Sure he had. Watchmen Alarm stickers were plastered on windows and doorways all over the nicer parts of town. Neat metal signs in well-kept lawns. Sleek white SUVs, the side panels painted with the Watchmen shield, rolled through the avenues.

"That's us," Roger said. "I started it thirty years ago. The old story — a garage in Palo Alto, a trip to Fry's, and a dream."

"And my teaching salary," Dana said, coming back from the study with a computer. "Don't forget that."

"The Castellis are clients?"

Roger reached out to take the laptop from Dana. She sat next to him.

"After the election," Roger said. "They'd been with another company, but Mona wanted an upgrade. Top of the line. Door and window sensors, in-room motion detectors, outside cameras, motion lights — and remote monitoring."

"You're talking about monitoring system activity," Fischer said. "Tracking the sensors from your central office."

"The Watchmen," Roger said, and now Cain recognized his voice from the radio spots. "We have an eye everything."

"You keep a log?"

"Show them, Roger," Dana said. She looked at them. "We downloaded it from the server today, while Mona was sleeping."

Roger turned his laptop so Cain and Fischer could see the screen, then moved his stool to their side of the bar.

"Here it is, top row," he said. "Mona Castelli went out yesterday evening, right?"

"To a fundraiser in Monterey," Cain said.

"So this is her, leaving."

Roger used his finger to underline the first entry in a spreadsheet labeled *Recent Activity — Last 250 Events*. The top row said, *Front Door — Opened — 7:02 p.m.* The next row down read, *System Armed (M.C.) — 7:03 p.m.*

"She stepped outside just after seven," Cain said. "That's when her car came. The next entry, she sets the alarm, right?"

"That's it."

"What's the *M.C.* stand for?"

"Mona Castelli — they've got an app on their phones, each of them. It's part of the package. They can arm or disarm the house from anywhere. But if the system interacts with a phone, it knows who it's dealing with. And keeps it in the log."

Cain pictured Mona Castelli, getting ready to go out.

Here she is, 7:02 p.m., waiting inside the house. Pacing around, a martini in her hand. Through the window, she sees the car rolling up. She puts on her jacket and grabs her purse. Sets the drink on the table by the door and goes out to the front porch, phone in hand. The door clicks shut behind her; she swipes her phone as she walks to the car. She arms the system as her driver gets out and helps her into the backseat. She either doesn't know or doesn't care that she's leaving a record.

It all fit with what he'd heard. He looked at the next two entries.

Front Door — Opened — 10:35 p.m.

System Disarmed (H.C.) — 10:36 p.m.

"Why did Castelli open the door first, and then turn off the alarm?" Fischer asked. "How would that work?"

"Maybe he didn't know it was armed," Roger said.

"Castelli's initials are on the log — if he disarmed the alarm from the control panel and not his phone, how does the system know it was him?"

"It's got a thumbprint reader. It couldn't have been anyone but him."

Cain looked at the screen. Based on the log, after Castelli had come home, the house had been quiet for nearly five hours. The system didn't log gunshots, didn't record the slack thump of a body collapsing from the desk to the rug. By midnight, Castelli was dead. But was the house actually quiet the whole time? No one had come in or out. No door swung open, no window slid up. Nothing triggered the laser trip lines protecting the backyard and the cliff stairs. Each point in the system had a status bar, and everything was quiet.

The next entry was at 2:58 a.m., when the front door opened. It had to be Mona Castelli, because her car had dropped her off somewhere close to three.

Cain let it play out in his mind: She comes into the entry hall, dropping her keys and purse on the table near the door. Stumbling to the kitchen, she pours another drink. She wanders upstairs with it, looking for her husband. The bedroom's empty. The doors to all the bathrooms are standing open, and the lights are off. She tries the study door, but it's locked. She knocks and there's no answer.

The next log entry was at 3:22 a.m. The front door opened. Cain watched that, too: Nagata steps inside, catching Mona. She'd opened the door, but now she can barely stand up. In eight minutes, Nagata will start calling Cain. First she tries to get the story. What happened? Where's Harry? She checks the house and sees the study door, the spare key jutting from the heavy antique lock. She doesn't go in.

Cain looked at Fischer.

"What do you think?"

"I think you better throw a search warrant together, unless Mr. Petrovic wants to burn a disk right now."

"Bring the paper," Roger said. "There's a privacy clause in all the contracts. No information released unless compelled by a court."

"All right," Cain said. It was only one o'clock. "You going to be here all day, or should we serve your office?"

"Here's good — I know what you want."

"I might need till four o'clock," Cain said.

"I'll be here."

17

AFTER LEAVING THE Petrovics', they'd gone briefly back into Castelli's study. Sumida's team hadn't finished photographing it yet, and the evidence was still in place. While Fischer called Melissa Montgomery to get Alexa's address, Cain gave Sumida his keys and asked him to have someone drive his car back to Bryant Street and leave it there. He looked out the blood-speckled window at the street below. There were mobile news vans everywhere, telescoping antennas rising like masts along the street. Greenberg had been sworn in at City Hall, and the CSI vans were still in Castelli's driveway. It had only been a matter of time. He could even hear a helicopter, maybe the Channel 2 NewsChopper. Whatever it was, it had been circling awhile now, invisible above the inversion layer, waiting for the fog to clear so that it could shoot something for the evening news.

But none of these people would get the footage they really wanted. Dr. Levy had backed her morgue van up to the garage and loaded Castelli's body bag directly into the back without ever taking him outside. There'd have been no way to see it from the street or from above.

When Fischer had what she needed from Melissa Montgomery, they left. They stripped off their gloves and plastic boots, then crossed the tape line at the edge of the driveway and pushed through the waiting reporters to reach Fischer's car.

"They're not following us, are they?" Cain asked.

"They'd stick out if they did," Fischer said. "Vans like that."

"Keep an eye out anyway."

Her eyes flicked to the rearview mirror, then went back to the front. She was driving down Geary, Cain sitting in the passenger seat.

"Back there, you asked me what I thought," Fischer said. She took her foot off the gas, let her sedan creep back to the speed limit. "I'll tell you — what I really think. It's got to be suicide, right?"

"It looks like it."

She swerved around a meter maid's double-parked trike, the rooftop yellow light flashing.

"His hands tested positive for powder residue," Fischer said. "The alarm log shows the rest."

"It's compelling," Cain said. "It makes a good picture."

"It's more than that — unless you want to go off the deep end and say Petrovic altered the logs."

"He seemed more reasonable than that."

"He *is* more reasonable than that," Fischer said. "So what do you think?"

"I don't know."

They passed Twenty-Second Avenue and he looked to his right. It was sunny up that way, closer to the park. Lucy would have started giving lessons at eight. This morning, before he ran out the front door, he could have taken the time to leave a note. It wouldn't have made any difference to Castelli. What was two minutes, compared to disappearing in the middle of the night without saying where he'd gone?

"You don't know," Fischer said.

It had to be obvious he was holding back on her. At some point, he would have to bring her into the basement at 850 Bryant and show her the body he had. But he wanted to develop that a little further on his own first. He still couldn't prove she was the girl in the pictures, that Castelli had anything to do with burying her alive.

"I know I don't like that second gunshot," Cain said. "There's that."

"You had an explanation — he didn't know for sure the gun would fire. He pulls the trigger, waits a minute to get his nerve back up, and then pulls it again."

"I'd like to see what Dr. Levy has to say."

"Don't get me wrong," Fischer said. "I want to hear that too. I don't want to close the book until we get to the end."

"Even if it's a suicide, we still have questions."

"Sure we do," Fischer said.

"Who sent the note? Who's the girl — and what happened to her? If Castelli shot himself, does it mean he was involved?"

Fischer caught a red light at Park Presidio. The spot of blue sky Cain had seen a minute ago was gone. They were both still wet from standing in the Petrovics' backyard, and Fischer twisted the heater knob to its limit.

"Those reporters crawling everywhere — Even if Mona hasn't called Alexa, she's got to know by now," Cain said.

"Hell of a way to find out your dad died."

"You haven't met Alexa yet."

They parked around the corner from Alexa's school, the Academy of Art, and walked the block and a half to the address they'd gotten. She lived on New Montgomery, which happened to be across the street from her mother's temporary home, the Palace Hotel. They were on the wrong side of the street and had to wait for a gap in the traffic before they could cross.

He'd lived in an apartment the last three years he'd been in college, at San Francisco State. That was a third-floor walkup with bars on the windows. Eight hundred a month, with a roommate. He learned to sleep through sirens.

Alexa's building was a different story.

There'd been a recent renovation, but outwardly it held on to its roots. It could have been mistaken for an Edwardian-era bank, but Cain knew it had actually been the headquarters of a newspaper, the *San Francisco Call*. The building's street number was displayed on a polished bronze cartouche above the oversize glass and wrought-iron door, each side flanked with an imperial crown. The lobby beyond the entrance was two floors high; behind the glass, a chandelier hung far above the floor, its lights glowing against the midafternoon gloom.

The doorman, if there was one, was drying off inside. Out on the sidewalk, next to one of the gray stone columns, a young woman watched the street. Tired-looking and too thin, she hugged her coat against her ribs. Cain recognized her first. He pulled Fischer back from the curb.

"Did Melissa Montgomery say she was meeting us here?" He pointed with a tilt of his head, then looked back into the Academy of Art so his face would be hidden.

"She just gave me the address, and that's it. I told her we needed it but didn't say when we were coming."

"She must want to talk, face to face."

"Let's go see what she's got to say."

When the light changed on Market, there was a gap in the traffic and they crossed the street. Melissa saw them when they were halfway across and she came to the curb to meet them. Her hair was soaked from the rain. The drops were so small and it had been falling so lightly that she could only have gotten that wet by standing in it for hours.

"How long have you been out here?" Cain asked her.

"Since I heard—when I came to the office this morning, it was locked and there were cops. They wouldn't let any of us in. They wouldn't tell me—or they didn't know. I finally saw something online at ten. I knew I'd find you here."

"Why didn't you call?" Cain asked. "You've got both our numbers."

She looked away.

"Can we go into that Starbucks over there?" she asked. There was one directly adjacent to Alexa's building. She'd probably been looking at it for hours, wanting to go in but afraid she'd miss Cain and Fischer when they arrived. "I'm freezing."

They took a table near the window, so Cain could watch the street. Mona Castelli was just next door, at the Palace Hotel. Officer Combs had texted him ten minutes ago to say she was checked in. Room 8064, if he wanted to see her. What he really wanted was to see if she'd come for Alexa. If she did, Cain wondered what they'd say to each other.

"I was locked out of the office," Melissa was saying. "But I could still get into the mailroom. I have an inbox there."

She held her paper cup with both hands, was leaning toward it to breathe in the coffee's warmth.

"What did you take?" Cain asked.

"I just looked inside. I wanted to make sure I knew what it was."

She reached into her coat and brought out a nine-by-twelve clasped envelope. She set it on the small table between them. Out on the street, she'd been hugging herself, and now Cain understood why. She'd been holding the envelope to her chest, under her coat. Keeping it dry. Fischer looked at the front of the envelope but didn't touch it.

"Look at the address," she said. "Same wording, same font. It's postmarked yesterday, from North Beach."

"Who opened it?" Cain asked, turning to Melissa. "You?"

"Not me. It was open when I found it."

"Then who?"

"Harry did—this was on it."

She took a yellow sticky-note out of her jacket pocket. It had been folded in half, but when she opened it and set it on the table, he could see the words. The handwriting, in black ink, was a half-drunk scrawl.

M.M.—
    Get Cain. He needs to know.
    —H.C.

"That's Harry's handwriting?"

She nodded, and Fischer asked a question.

"What time did you leave City Hall last night?"

"Right after you were done with me—seven thirty, eight. I went to see Harry, asked if he needed anything. Sometimes he just wants to sit and talk. Sometimes, there's more."

"But not last night," Cain said.

"No—he wanted to be left alone."

"What were his exact words?"

"*Leave me alone*," she said. Something crossed her face. A memory, maybe, of Castelli. "You have to understand Harry. He's not a complicated man."

"You checked your inbox before you left?"

"Yes."

"So he put this in sometime after eight last night," Cain said. "Is that right?"

"Sometime before he went home."

Cain looked at the sticky-note. *Get Cain. He needs to know.* What the hell kind of suicide note was that?

"You looked inside but didn't take anything out?" Cain asked.

"I didn't need to take anything out. I saw the pictures, and I knew what it was."

"You got gloves?" Fischer asked him. "Mine are in the car."

"One set left."

He took them from his jacket pocket and stretched them over his hands, glancing around the shop to see if any of the customers were standing close enough to see. There were a dozen people in line. By the window, a college-aged kid was leaning against the standup counter. He was only an arm's length away, but he was busy with his phone. Texting with one hand and holding coffee with the other. He had an art student's shoulder bag, paintbrushes poking from the canvas pockets. He turned and saw Cain watching him. He finished his text without looking at his phone's screen, set his coffee on the counter, and went out the door.

Cain picked up the envelope.

The address was a half-assed job — *Mr. Mayor, City Hall, San Francisco, CA 94102* — as if the sender wanted to make sure someone other than the mayor, some underling, opened the letter before him. But somehow Castelli had seen it first. It was sliced open along the end, too clean of a cut to be anything but a sharp knife. Cain nudged it open, eased out four glossy black-and-white photographs and a laser-printed note. He read the note first.

Mayor Castelli:
    5 – 6 – 7 – 8!

    I said I'd give these to everyone, but guess what? I lied. They're so embarrassing, I thought I'd give you one more chance. The rest are coming soon — if you don't get them in the mail, don't worry. Check the paper.

    Think how much easier it would be if you didn't have to see any more, if you're not around when they figure out what you did.

    BANG!
— A friend

He put the note on the table in front of Fischer, then looked through the four photographs. Each had a circled number in the lower right corner. And in each, the girl was still handcuffed to the bed. She was unconscious throughout the series. Maybe that was a good thing. Cain could see her face in each shot: eyes closed and mouth slack.

The difference this time was that now she was completely nude. Her panties hung from the bed's iron foot post. And there was some-one else in the shot — a white man, tall and well muscled. Dark hair, neatly cut. But he never gave his face to the camera. It was just his naked backside as he lay on top of her, as he knelt between her thighs and held her ankles off to either side.

"Jesus," Cain said. He looked at Fischer. She was studying the first shot he'd handed her. Melissa was staring at the surface of her coffee, not looking at the pictures at all. Her lips were pressed together, her mouth a small, tight line.

There was one identifying mark. The man had a tattoo across his right shoulder blade. It was hard to make out, except in the last shot. Cain finished looking at it and put it on the stack in front of Fischer.

The man had been inked with three Greek letters.

"Is that Harry Castelli?" Cain asked, tilting his head so he could catch Melissa's downturned eyes.

"I don't know."

"You've seen him naked?"

"Inspector Cain—"

"Have you or haven't you?" Fischer said. "We'll find out one way or another."

"Harry and I—we—it was just sometimes. Okay? And we'd stopped, more than a year ago."

"Is that him?"

"If it is, they're old pictures. This man's young. But Harry's—"

She stopped and brought her coffee up. She took a careful sip and then put it back down.

"But what?" Cain said. "You were about to say something else."

"He's got a tattoo like that."

The room seemed to go quiet, but Cain knew it was just his mind pulling into focus. He looked from Fischer to Melissa Montgomery. They were both staring at the photographs on the table. He picked them up and slid them back into the envelope, along with the second letter.

"Let me have that," Cain said. "The note he wrote to you."

Melissa gave it to him.

Last night, Castelli had wanted to see him again. Something had changed the mayor's mind—the letter, and the photos? When he'd written this, there wasn't much time left. He'd be dead at midnight. Had he known, because he planned it? This could be a half-finished confession. *He needs to know,* Castelli had said, but know what? Was he saying that he did it? Or had he wanted to meet Cain so that he could say something entirely different?

139

"Where are you going to be?" Cain asked. "Tonight, all next week."

"At home."

"Where's that?"

"Noe Valley."

She gave him an address on Cesar Chavez. A row house, broken up into apartments. She lived there with a roommate, a girlfriend from college. But she'd spent most of the last eight years in Castelli's orbit.

"Don't go anywhere," Cain said. "I'll need you in town."

"Okay."

"He means that," Fischer said. "We'll be calling on you. When we do, we'll need you right away."

"Where would I go?"

She said that, and Cain watched her shrink into herself. She must understand that it was over. Not just her job, but her entire life up to that point. Everything she'd worked for, dead.

18

CAIN AND FISCHER stood at the security desk in Alexa's lobby while the doorman, Bruno, scowled at their badges. An FBI shield, an SFPD gold star. They'd already explained they were here to see the mayor's daughter on a family matter. Bruno should have rolled over right away; any other guard in the city would have. Instead, he'd asked to see a warrant, and then, when they admitted they didn't have one, he told them to state their business or leave.

"We already told you," Fischer said.

"What family matter?" the guard said. "I'll ring up and tell her what it is. She'll tell me if she wants to talk to you."

Cain leaned over the desk and touched the man's computer screen.

"Is this hooked up to the Internet?"

"Yeah — so?"

"Do a search for *Castelli*. See what comes up."

The guard's frown said he wasn't buying it. But he took the mouse and started clicking. He typed a word and entered it. Cain watched the screen's reflection in his glasses, watched the man's eyes flick back and forth as he read three lines of text. He didn't need to finish the article.

"Shit," the guard said. "Oh, shit."

"A whole world of it," Cain answered.

"This is for real?"

"Check another site if you don't believe it."

"She's on four — I haven't seen her in or out today, so she's probably in there. I'll send you up. You need a card to work the elevator."

They heard music from behind Alexa Castelli's door. A cello concerto — Vivaldi, if Cain had to guess. It wasn't what he'd expected, didn't fit his picture of Alexa, which tilted darker and edgier. But he remembered the blood-soaked shelves in Castelli's study, which had borne the weight of a thousand years of history. Those hadn't fit in his model either. The Castellis weren't as predictable as he'd like them to be.

He knocked, and a few moments later the music switched off. The door opened as far as the chain would let it.

"Miss Castelli," Cain said.

He could only see one side of her face, the sweep of her dark hair, and her right eye. The rest of her was behind the door.

"Mr. Cain," she answered. "I don't know your friend."

"Are you dressed?"

"More or less."

She closed the door enough to unlatch the chain, then opened it to let them in. She wore a clean white bedsheet like a sleeveless gown.

"Come in," she said.

"This is Special Agent Fischer, with the FBI," Cain said.

They stepped into her apartment. To the left, there was a living room that doubled as the bedroom. A Murphy bed was folded down. A young woman sat on a stool behind a wooden easel. She was using a loose razor blade to sharpen a charcoal pencil over a wastepaper basket. She turned when they came in. Looking at her half-finished sketch, it was clear that until he'd knocked, Alexa had been on the bed, and she hadn't been wearing the sheet.

"You need to get something on," Cain said. "And ask your friend —"

"Patricia."

"— to leave for a minute."

"Maybe I want her here," Alexa said.

"I'll stay," the girl said. She set the razor on the easel's shelf and picked up a sandpaper pad to finish her pencil's tip. "I don't mind."

"Maybe I need her here," Alexa said, looking at Fischer. "After the last time I talked to Mr. Cain, I'm not comfortable being alone with him."

She came to the edge of the Murphy bed and looked at them. Then she dropped the sheet. She crawled onto the bed, finding the pose she'd been using for Patricia's sketch. Face-down, her chin just off the corner of the mattress, one arm hanging so that her fingertip touched the floor.

Patricia gave a nervous laugh, so short it came out like a cough. She looked at Fischer, her eyes wide, the pupils bigger than they ought to be. Then she picked up her charcoal and began to sketch again, refining the work she'd done earlier on Alexa's legs.

Whatever they'd taken—MDMA, ketamine—didn't seem to interfere with this girl's ability to draw.

"Why'd you come, Cain?"

Alexa was tracing a tiny circle on the wooden floor with her fingernail. She'd spoken without lifting her head or breaking her pose. He wasn't sure whether to look at her or out the window. He'd already told her once to get dressed and didn't think repeating himself was going to make a difference.

"Your father's dead," he said. "He died last night."

Alexa's fingernail stopped midway through its circle.

"How?"

"We haven't done the autopsy, but it looks like a gunshot. A thirty-eight."

Patricia tried to put her charcoal pencil on the easel's shelf. She fumbled it and it fell to the floor and rolled under the bed.

"I should—maybe I should go?"

"Maybe so," Fischer said.

The young woman threw a few things into her canvas purse. Fischer followed her to the door and opened it.

"I'll call you later?" she said, over her shoulder.

Alexa hadn't moved from her pose and didn't answer. Fischer closed the door on the other girl's back, then turned the deadbolt. When Cain looked back, Alexa was sitting up. She swung her legs to the floor, then leaned down to get the sheet. She put it over her shoulders and wrapped the sides across her chest.

"When? And what happened?"

"It happened sometime last night," Cain said. Right now there was no reason to be more specific. Telling her what he knew would only give her a liar's guide if she needed one. "I got the call at four this morning. As for who did it, we don't know."

"Somebody *killed* my dad?"

"We don't know."

"Where was he?"

"In his study, at home—your mom came home from Monterey and found him this morning. She called us."

Alexa stared at her toes. The nails were painted a shade of red so dark it could have been obsidian. Cain looked around the apartment.

There was a little kitchen, all stainless steel and blond wood. A well-stocked shelf of liquor, but most of the bottles were full. The walls, which were covered in textured black silk, displayed her work. He recognized Patricia in two of the paintings. There was a young man in two others. In one, he was sitting on the rocks on China Beach, his hand shielding his eyes from the low sun so that his face was just a shadow. You could see Castelli's house on the cliffs in the background, could see the winding stairway that worked down from the top. The kid had to be Alexa's boyfriend. She'd caught the details of his body so precisely, she couldn't possibly have been looking at him from any distance. In the other painting, he was on the Murphy bed in this apartment, his pose not much different from the one Alexa had been holding for her friend.

"He's really— This is serious?"

"Yes," Fischer said. "This is serious."

"But who?"

"We don't know," Cain said. "Did he try calling you last night?"

"No."

"What about your boyfriend? Where was he?"

"What boyfriend?"

Cain nodded to the paintings.

"Him?" she said. "He's just a guy I paint. I used to sleep with him sometimes, but not in a while. I don't know what you call that in your world. I'd forget him, but he's still on the wall. The only thing he was any good at was sitting still."

"Your phone was turned on last night?"

"It's always on."

"And you were here?"

"With Patricia—go to the drafting table and take a look."

Half a dozen charcoal sketches lay on the drafting table. Patricia was in two of them, Alexa's style fast and fluid, somehow catching movement in a single frame. The rest were of Alexa, who wore her nudity like a piece of draped silk. She lay on the bed; she sat on a stool with her legs crossed and her hair piled atop her head. She knelt in front of a stone bowl and washed her hair.

"You were here all night?" Cain asked.

"And all day today," Alexa said. "This—what happened to my dad—do you think it has to do with what we talked about? About the girl in the picture?"

144

"Whatever you haven't already told me, now would be a good time. It could help us find out what happened."

She stood, still holding the sheet around herself. A three-paneled dressing screen blocked one corner of the room. Rice paper and painted dragons. When she stepped behind it and dropped the sheet, he could see her nude silhouette against the thin paper. She knelt, and a drawer slid open. He had no idea what she might be taking out of it. To his left, Fischer's hand tucked inside her jacket and unsnapped her holster. There was nothing showy about it; she was just being careful. He could get used to working with her.

Alexa came back from behind the screen wearing a gray nightgown. It looked like it was made of wet crepe paper. Something in her right hand flashed steel when she passed under the tracked halogen spotlights.

"After that time I found the picture?" she said. "I went back and found these."

She held his wrist with her left hand and put a set of police handcuffs in his palm. She folded his fingers over them. This close, he could smell the perfume at the base of her throat. He thought of the black roses that grew on the northern edge of Golden Gate Park, the flowers rising up from thick tangles of thorns. He took a step back from her and held up the handcuffs so Fischer could see them.

"You've had these for ten years?"

"Nine, ten."

"You've used them, handled them?"

She looked around her apartment, the art on the walls, the sculptures on the coffee table and in the windowsills. Finally her eyes settled on the bed.

"What do you think?"

He thought they'd probably seen plenty of use. Which meant Castelli's fingerprints, if they'd ever been there at all, would have been wiped away years ago.

"How do you know they were his?"

"They were in his study. Hidden."

"Where?"

"In a cigar box, behind his copy of Thucydides."

"You went in there—ten years old, we're talking—because you wanted to read Greek history. You pulled the book down, found a cigar box, and opened it. That's your story."

"No."

"Then what?"

"I went in to toss the room and see what I could find. He was in D.C., not coming back for a month at least. I figured there had to be something interesting in there."

"Why didn't you give these to me yesterday?"

"Why didn't you go swimming with me?" Alexa said. "Because you didn't trust me. You thought I was trying to trap you."

"We're just asking questions," Fischer said. "But we need answers we can believe. This is important."

"I know it's important." She sat on the end of the bed. Then she fell over onto her side and tucked her knees up close to her chest. "Why would someone want to kill my dad?"

"You knew about the girl in the picture," Fischer said. "Did anybody else?"

Alexa nodded. She was crying now, tears running across face and darkening the white sheet.

"Who?"

"I don't know," Alexa said. "But he thought so. I know he thought so. There was always something wrong. He was on edge — afraid."

"What do you mean?"

"We'd be at dinner somewhere. And he'd see a woman who looked like her. He'd watch her pass, and then get really quiet and stop eating. In the car, on the way home, he'd drive in circles and keep checking behind us. But there'd never be anyone there."

"Did he ever get out his gun?" Cain asked.

"What gun?"

"You never saw him with a gun?"

She shook her head. She pushed off the footboard and swam to the top of the bed, legs kicking. She took a pillow into her arms and another between her knees, clamping onto them.

"Where's my mom?" she said. "I want my mom."

"She hasn't called?" Fischer asked.

"I want my *mom*!"

"Alexa."

He could see where this would go if she threw a fit. She'd probably start by ripping her tissue-paper nightgown apart at the seams. Then, with his luck, she'd shatter a mirror and grab for the shards.

Of course, every time he made a bet on this family, he picked the wrong number.

"Alexa."

"Mr. Cain," she answered, her voice a glassy calm.

"I want you to take a couple breaths," he said, but whatever storm he'd thought she'd entered had already dissipated.

Alexa lay still, her face half buried in a pillow.

"I've been breathing the whole time," she said.

"Still," he said. "Go ahead. Shut your eyes, if you want."

"I want you to go away, Mr. Cain."

"I will, if you tell me one thing."

He didn't want to waste his important questions here. He didn't like to ask those until he was holding enough information. Right now, he had nothing, and if he started asking the wrong questions, Alexa would see right through them. He thought of a question that wouldn't hurt to ask. It would sound like a throwaway, but it wasn't.

"Did you love your father? Even knowing about the photo and the handcuffs?"

Alexa sat up. The strap of her nightgown had fallen off her shoulder. She wiped her nose with the back of her hand, and then her cheek glistened.

"Did I love him?"

"That's all I want to know."

"When I was thirteen, he took me to London. Just the two of us. You probably already know he lived there when he was a kid. He showed me their house. The Official Residence, he called it. He took me shopping. I was thirteen, and I thought shopping in London was so glamorous. He bought me a gold bracelet."

"You still have it?"

"Of course I have it."

"Can I see it?"

"If I show it to you, will you leave?"

"We'll go."

She got up and went behind the dressing screen. She knelt again and opened another drawer. When she came out, she was wearing the bracelet. It glittered from her wrist, a golden honeycomb. Her father had taken her to the Imogene Bass shop, on Victoria Street. He'd bought her the exact bracelet the girl had worn in the photos.

Alexa sat at the foot of her bed and wrapped her right hand around her wrist, so that her fingers covered the bracelet. She held it close to her chest. She hadn't answered his question. Maybe this gesture was as close as she could come.

"If you want, I can get someone to sit with you," Cain said. "I could have a female officer come."

"I'd rather have my mom. Can you do that?"

"I can try," he said.

But he had no intention of trying. Mona Castelli knew exactly where her daughter was. They had each other's cell numbers. If they wanted to see each other, they didn't need him to arrange it.

Fischer waited until the doors closed and the elevator started moving, carrying them down to the lobby.

"The weirdest thing about that — she didn't start acting even halfway normal until you told her Castelli was dead."

"Halfway?"

"A quarter, an eighth. Whatever."

"What do you think she's on?"

"She's nineteen, and rich," Fischer said. "What else do we need to know? She's probably into things we've never even heard of."

"He bought her the same bracelet," Cain said. "What do you make of that?"

"Does she know?"

Cain shook his head.

"The picture she gave me — the girl's cuffed to the bed. They must've taken the bracelet off. It's only in the shots when she's still dressed."

"Then as far as Alexa knew," Fischer said, "her dad took her to a shop and bought her a bracelet. It didn't mean anything else to her. It was just a present."

"If she's telling the truth."

"You think she's seen the other pictures?"

"But where?"

"And the part about the handcuffs —"

"I know."

"— that didn't sit right," Fischer finished.

The elevator doors opened and they went across the lobby. The security guard rose from behind his desk to meet them.

"You told her?"

"She knows," Cain said. He gave the man his card. "If anyone else comes to see her, give me a call. Same if there's trouble — any sort of trouble."

"She's okay?"

"Just give me a call if you see anything."

"You got it."

They went under the chandelier and out the front door. The wind was blowing from Market Street, carrying steam from the subway vents. Three stretch limos went past, and then there was a break in traffic. They crossed New Montgomery, headed for Fischer's car.

"I was saying, about the handcuffs," Fischer said. "I believed her on the bracelet. I believed the tears. But when she told you about the handcuffs, my bullshit meter spiked."

"So what do you think?"

She dug her keys from her purse, then checked her watch.

"We better get to the autopsy," she said. "That's what I think."

"I called Grassley and Chun."

He'd called them from the Petrovics' bathroom. They'd already heard the news about the mayor, but they needed to know their new assignment. And Grassley, in particular, needed to know the rules. They couldn't say anything to Fischer about the girl from El Carmelo unless Cain cleared it.

"You'll like them," he added.

"If you trust them, I'm fine."

19

BEFORE HE WENT into the autopsy suite, he stepped into an empty office and closed the door. This time, there was no need for a hazmat suit or a respirator. Castelli was as fresh as they came down here. He dialed Lucy's number. It was a landline; the only phone in the house was down in the kitchen. It rang eight times and went to voicemail. He told her where he was and that he loved her, then hung up.

She didn't have a lesson now. She could be in the bath, or asleep upstairs where she couldn't hear the phone. But his instinct said otherwise. She must have gone out. She was on another one of her tentative explorations out into the world she'd fled.

There was no one Cain could talk to, no one who'd understand how good it felt to see her coming back to life.

"Decedent is a white male, six foot one and a hundred and ninety pounds," Dr. Levy said into the microphone that hung from the ceiling above the autopsy table.

Yesterday, the mayor had been tanned and muscular. Now he was like spilled candlewax. Pale and shapeless. His head was propped on a wooden block, and when Cain crouched behind him and looked up, he could see the exit wound, Castelli's scalp peeling outward like the blooming petals of a flower.

Rachel Levy cleared her throat and continued.

"Inspector Gavin L. Cain, of the San Francisco Police Department, has identified the decedent as Mayor Harold J. Castelli — Inspector Cain knew the decedent personally. Decedent was discovered by his wife, Mona A. Castelli, at approximately three o'clock this morning. He was in his home study, on the carpet, with an apparent gunshot wound to his head. I will now begin the surface examination."

In fact, she'd already done it.

She had done the entire external examination once before, committing nothing to the record until it had been rehearsed. There'd be no mistakes and no surprises. No attorney could trip her under cross-examination, no board of review or interim mayoral commission could question the way she'd handled herself.

"Decedent appears fit and well-nourished, and does not have any external physical deformities. Rigor mortis is fully progressed and the body is cool to the touch, having been in refrigeration since two o'clock this afternoon."

She pointed to the dark welting of settled blood that discolored his right side.

"Livor mortis is fixed and pronounced on the right side of the body, except over pressure points — his right hip and shoulder took most of his weight," she said.

Cain stepped between Grassley and Chun. He whispered so that his voice wouldn't carry to the official autopsy tape.

"We found the body under the desk, curled up on his right side," he said. "What do you make of the livor mortis?"

"He wasn't moved," Chun whispered back. "After he died, he stayed where he fell. The blood settled and made those bruises."

Cain nodded and looked back at Dr. Levy, who was working up Castelli's corpse, narrating as she went.

"— his genitalia are normally developed for an adult. He has a two-inch appendectomy scar on his abdomen. He's wearing a gold band on his left ring finger, and has a two-tone Rolex watch on his right wrist. I'm removing both items and giving them to Inspector Cain, who is present."

She twisted the ring off his finger, forcing it past his knuckle by wiggling it side to side. Then she unclasped the watch and squeezed the band over his stiffly splayed fingers. She put it into a property bag along with his wedding ring and set it on an empty table alongside the clothes that had been cut off of him.

"His fingernails are neatly clipped and clean. We've taken samples from each of them for DNA testing. He has three parallel scars on his right forearm. Each scar is approximately eight inches long, running from his elbow toward his wrist. Judging from the placement of his watch, decedent was likely left-handed —"

Cain made a mental note to find out.

"— so that these scars would be consistent with a prior incident of self-mutilation."

"A suicide attempt?" Fischer asked.

"Or maybe just cutting," Dr. Levy answered. She moved away from the microphone so that this would be off the record. "These scars —look at them. They're decades old. Unless you find someone who knows the story, or luck into a medical record, it'd be hard to say."

Cain looked at Chun, and she nodded. She was still tracking down leads in Berkeley. Maybe one of her contacts would know something about the scars. Dr. Levy picked up a clipboard, which held the notes she'd taken in her first run on the external examination. She flipped a page, then went to the microphone.

"Decedent has a tattoo on his right scapula. Greek—pi kappa kappa. Each letter's an inch across. Dark green ink."

"How old is it?" Cain asked.

Dr. Levy came away from the microphone again.

"No idea. It's not new—the edges aren't sharp, and the color's faded," she said. "But think about it. It's a frat tattoo. Who gets one of those except when they're eighteen and pledging?"

She lifted Castelli's head and repositioned the block under the back of his neck. She put her left palm on his chin, then covered the back of that hand with her right. She bore down, her elbows straightening as she put her weight into him. As Castelli's mouth opened, his jaw made a sound like a pencil snapping.

"Powder burns on his palate and tongue," she said. She was leaning over the mayor, a flashlight positioned against his bloody lower lip. "Entry wound at the anterior of the hard palate. It looks —"

She put out her hand, snapping her fingers. Jim slipped her a pair of inside-diameter calipers. She gave the flashlight to him and he held it for her while she inserted the calipers and dialed the knob on the right to take the entry wound's measurement.

"— four-tenths of an inch. That's consistent with a thirty-eight in soft tissue."

"All right," Cain said. Where he was standing, he couldn't see the entry wound at all. But he'd caught a little of the mayor's shattered grin as Dr. Levy had opened his mouth. "What's the story with his teeth?"

"The chipping?" Dr. Levy asked. She pulled his bottom lip out, and ran her gloved finger over the broken teeth. "You see that, this kind of suicide. End of a pistol's barrel has a raised sight. It'll crack the hell out of your teeth when the gun kicks."

"The bottom teeth?" Grassley asked. "The sight's on top."

"Most of your gun-in-the mouth guys," she said, "they put it in upside down. What else are they going to do — pull the trigger with their thumbs? So when it kicks, the sight knocks out their bottom teeth."

Cain stepped back and nodded at the microphone.

"What do you say, Rachel?" he said. "Gut instinct."

She reached up and turned the microphone off.

"Suicide," she said. "It's easy, right? We've got gunshot residue on his hands. Powder burns and stippling inside his mouth. The body wasn't moved, and the door was locked from the inside."

"Lean down and smell him," Cain said.

"What?"

"Go on."

She bent back toward Castelli's mouth, lowering her paper mask. He watched as she breathed through her nose.

"Whiskey," she said.

"Kentucky bourbon," Cain answered. "Single cask, hundred-twenty proof. And this is what — sixteen hours later?"

Dr. Levy shrugged.

"You can't just accidentally shoot one of those old thirty-eights," Cain said. "You have to put the hammer back before you pull the trigger, and there's a hard pull on that."

"I've seen drunk suicides thread smaller needles," Levy said. "They run hoses from their car exhaust into second-floor windows. They drive a hundred miles to the bridge, park, and walk to the middle of the span. So drunk they shouldn't be able to stand. But when they're ready to go, they go."

"So you'll put suicide in the report," Cain said.

"We'll see what we get back from toxicology. And we haven't even opened him up yet."

She held out her hand and Jim Braun gave her an oscillating saw.

20

AT SIX O'CLOCK, Cain was at Lori's Diner with his three new partners. They were two to a side in a red vinyl booth, plates of pasta and home-style meatloaf on the table between them. Grassley poked at his potatoes. Next to him, Chun scrolled through her phone's screen. She put it away, then pushed her plate aside.

"Pi Kappa Kappa was a banned fraternity — it got kicked off the Cal campus in 1982, and dissolved nationwide in 1983."

"What for?" Fischer asked.

"Three sophomore coeds died at a party."

"Alcohol?"

"And drugs — but it was quaaludes, not Thrallinex," Chun said. "It might've been easier to look the other way back then, but not when there's three dead girls."

"He was a freshman in 1984," Cain said. "Pi Kappa Kappa was already gone."

"Maybe it was unofficial," Fischer said. "Unsanctioned."

"Did you see that online?" Cain asked Chun. "That they went underground?"

"Nothing like that." She gathered her things and slid from the booth, leaving enough cash on the table to cover her part of the check. "But I might find out tonight — I'm meeting a guy who knew Castelli back then. Says he knew him, anyway."

"Who?"

"Dennis Herrington — a doctor up in Marin County. We're meeting for coffee, and I'll be late if I don't get going."

"You're meeting up there?" Cain asked.

"That's right."

"Take Grassley if you want backup," Cain said.

"They don't come safer than this guy — he's a pediatrician," Chun said. Cain took off his glasses to look at her, and she went on. "All right. Point taken — you never know. But he'll talk more if it's just me."

"Call me when you're done."

She nodded.

"I'll see you in the morning."

When she was gone, Cain turned to Grassley.

"How about you?"

"I met Frank Lee's pharmacy guy — the professor at UCSF," Grassley said. "But he didn't have anything new. Thrallinex wasn't common, but it wasn't a unicorn. It's not like only one doctor in the country prescribed it."

"So it's a dead end."

"That angle, maybe. But maybe something will come of it."

He knew what Grassley was thinking. At least he hadn't finished the thought aloud, with Fischer sitting at the table. Thrallinex might still be useful to tie the girl in the casket to the girl in the photo. If her liver samples showed metabolites of the drug, it would be a done deal, in Cain's mind.

"There's still the dress. You could work on that."

"I'm on it," Grassley said. "I'm swinging past the Academy of Art tonight at eight to talk to one of the fashion instructors there."

"Until then, come with us," Cain said.

"We got time to finish?"

"If we start eating and quit talking."

Grassley pulled Angela Chun's half-finished platter of linguini over and forked the pasta onto his plate.

They came in a convoy of separate cars and parked alongside a fire-plug on Polk, then hurried across the street in the rain and went up the steps to City Hall. Cain had tried Lucy again on the drive over, but there was still no answer. It had been light outside when he'd called from the morgue, but that was hours ago and now it was dark. There wasn't much he could do now except steal away whenever he could to call again.

"It's locked," Grassley said. He'd turned around, was watching Cain and Fischer as they climbed the last few steps.

"Then knock."

Grassley pounded on the door with his knuckles. He'd been a patrolman for eight years in Stockton and an SFPD inspector for just a month. He still knew how to knock on a door like a beat cop.

A contract security guard cracked the door, and Grassley glanced back at Fischer.

"Show him your star," Fischer said.

"What happened to your guys?"

"They were here for Castelli. No need for that now."

Cain and Grassley held their inspectors' stars up for the guard to see. He opened the door for them and they stepped inside. They went beneath the rotunda and up the staircase, and found a pair of black-shirted patrolmen leaning against the doors to the mayoral suite. When Cain brought out his inspector's star, they straightened up.

"How long you been here?" Cain asked.

One cop looked at his partner.

"Since noon?"

"Has anyone tried to get in here?"

"Well —"

"There was a woman. She was the only one."

"What woman?" Cain asked. "What was her name?"

The officer on the left looked at his partner, who shook his head.

"You didn't ask her name?" Cain asked. "What'd she look like?"

"Blonde?"

"A dark blonde — almost a brunette."

"And a gray suit. Expensive."

"How old?" Cain asked.

"Thirty."

Cain believed in cop instinct, but he didn't think either of these men had much of it. If they'd been half awake, they would have gotten her name. Maybe it didn't make a difference. They'd just described Melissa Montgomery.

"Did she try to talk her way past?" Fischer asked.

"Not after we told her Castelli was dead — then she went off in a hurry."

"You told her what, exactly?"

"That he ate it — bullet through the head."

"All right," Cain said. "Open it up. We need to go in."

. . .

They went around Castelli's office turning on lights. Grassley had the video camera, recording everything. An empty glass sat on the desk's edge. There was no paperwork in sight, no computer; the mayor must have used a laptop. They came behind the desk chair and Cain rolled it back. He switched on the shaded lamp, and the room took on a green glow.

"What's that smell?" Grassley asked. "Bourbon?"

"Someone poured it in the trash," Fischer said. She tapped the wastepaper basket with her foot. "Look."

"That was me," Cain said. "Last night."

Fischer looked around, and he told her the story.

"Get a rise out of him?" she asked.

"Not really."

Cain reached into the trash and found two empty cans of ginger ale and four lime wedges. There was a wadded napkin inside a can that had once held salted nuts. There were two peanuts left in the can.

"Nice work if you can get it," Grassley said. "Knock back some cocktails, have a couple peanuts. Run a city."

"Let's bag it," Cain said. "For all we know, someone else drank these before I came."

The last thing Cain pulled out was a folded piece of ruled notebook paper. It had been at the bottom of the trash, and was soaked with both bourbon and ginger ale. Cain gently unfolded it, taking his time. The edges were soft and stuck together, the paper ready to fall apart. When he had it open, he held it in one palm and pushed up his glasses to look at it.

"Shit," he said.

There had been handwriting, but the black letters had run into illegible spirals, the ink spreading through the bourbon and separating into the spectrum of colors it held. What was left looked like a dark oil slick. There was one dry spot, on the bottom of the page. It was Harry J. Castelli Jr.'s signature, dated yesterday.

"You think that was it?" Grassley asked. "The note?"

"No way to tell. Whatever it was, it's gone."

"We should find the pad he wrote it on," Fischer said. "The notebook — whatever. Maybe there's an impression on the page underneath."

"Check for it."

They started going through the desk drawers, and Fischer found a notebook straight off. The first page had been ripped out.

"Here," Cain said.

He gave her the bourbon-obliterated page, and she held its left side against the notebook. The uneven edges matched like puzzle pieces. She set the wet paper on the desk and put the notebook under the lamp. The three of them leaned in and looked at the blank page that had been beneath the one Castelli ripped out.

"There's nothing," Grassley said. "No imprints — right?"

"Maybe the documents lab," Cain said. "They could look at it with a microscope."

"Unless he ripped it out before he wrote on it — then we've got nothing," Fischer said. She turned to Cain. "Melissa Montgomery might've been the last person to see him alive. But you're a close second."

"I didn't mean to dissolve his note, if that's what you're saying."

"It's not what I'm saying," Fischer said. "I'm just curious about his mood — how'd he seem to you?"

"The same as before," Cain said. "He didn't know anything. He hadn't gotten more photos. This was all a hoax, some guy messing with him."

"That's what he told you."

"And I knew he was lying, but I couldn't shake him from his story."

"Was he drunk?" Fischer asked.

"He was drinking," Cain said. He looked around the office, breathed in the bourbon fumes, and remembered the old man's growl. "A guy like him, there's some ground to cover between drinking and drunk."

Fischer turned around to look at the office. She went over to the curtains and pulled them back, allowing in the dim hum of traffic on Polk Street.

"Where's he keep the liquor?" she asked.

Cain pointed.

"That cabinet."

Fischer went to it and opened the door. There were eight bottles of bourbon, a dozen other spirits. She started pulling out bottles and handing them to Cain. He set them on the floor. When he came up, she gave him an insulated steel ice bucket with the Palace Hotel's insignia emblazoned on the lid.

"Here we go," she said. "We've got a safe."

Grassley came over with the camera and filmed inside the liquor cabinet. When he stepped back, Cain leaned in and looked. At the back of the deep cabinet, there was a hotel-style safe, no higher than a shoebox, but deep enough to hold legal documents without folding them. It had a digital keypad next to its steel handle.

Cain dialed Melissa Montgomery on his cell, and she answered after the first ring.

"Inspector?

"Are you at home?"

"You told me to be here," she answered. "Where are you?

"Standing in Castelli's office, looking at the safe in the back of his liquor cabinet."

There was a long pause. He heard water running, maybe a bathtub filling. Then there was the unmistakable click and grind of a Zippo lighter. She breathed in, then out.

"Eleven sixty-four."

"That's the code?"

"The last time I opened it."

"Which was when?"

"Three months ago," she said. "Is there anything else, Inspector Cain?"

"Was Castelli left-handed?"

"Yes," she said, and hung up.

Cain gave Fischer the code and she punched it in. Grassley filmed as she turned the handle and swung the door open.

"All right," she said. "Safe inventory. You getting this?"

"You don't have to ask," Grassley said.

Fischer began to unload the safe, setting each item on the little shelf that had folded down when she opened the liquor cabinet doors. She set out fifteen envelopes, each thick with unbundled cash. Then came life insurance policies, a will, and a scrap of paper marked with Castelli's scrawl. Cain picked that one up by its corner and studied it. The mayor had listed three Chinatown banks by their addresses. Next to each entry was a date — consecutive days within the last week.

"I can just about guess what these are," Fischer said. "The only question is whether it's him and Melissa, or him and Mona."

Cain looked up. She was setting out five unmarked DVDs, each in a clear plastic jewel case.

"We'll give them to Computer Forensics," Cain said. "Unless you want them."

"You take them," Fischer said. "We'll take the cash — we can run the serial numbers. If it's dirty, and from a known source, we'll want to know."

"That's got to be — what?" Cain said. "A hundred thousand?"

"More," Fischer said. "I used to work bank robberies. That's one seventy-five, two hundred."

"This is a city office. If it's public money, we should find out before we take it."

"Call Melissa back," Fischer said.

Cain redialed, on speaker this time. They listened to the phone ring, five times, six times, before she picked up.

"What now?"

"Castelli's safe — is that his personal stuff, or is there city property in it?"

"If it's in the safe, it's personal. Harry did everything by the book."

"If we found cash, it's not the city's money?"

"I said it's personal," Melissa answered. She hung up, and Cain put his phone away. Grassley and Fischer were each watching him.

"Before we hand that off to you, we should get some kind of receipt, I guess."

Fischer checked her watch.

"There's a kid in the U.S. attorney's office, just sitting on his hands," she said. "I can get him here in an hour with the paperwork."

Cain looked at the stack of cash on the shelf. Giving it to Fischer felt wrong, but he knew it stood a better chance of disappearing if he gave it to his own department.

21

IT WAS ALMOST midnight and Cain was driving alone, Golden Gate Park just a shadow on his left. He could see the rain on his windshield, the shutter-flashes of electricity from the Muni bus in front of him. He hadn't heard back from Chun or Grassley, and Lucy still wasn't picking up the phone. He'd turned on his police scanner, just for the company of the other cops' voices.

There'd been a holdup at the corner of Geary and Van Ness. Two suspects fleeing on foot, and four units responding. A stabbing at the base of the Bay Bridge, but the victim was sitting up in the ambulance and talking. No need even to alert Homicide Detail.

Cain switched off the scanner. Maybe it was better to listen to the rain. But even without the scanner, his head was buzzing. The CSI teams had taken truckloads of evidence from the house, and nearly all of it would be useless. They'd taken less from Castelli's City Hall office, and while some of it might help fill in a picture of the man before he died, nothing explained why or how the shots were fired. Useless information was worse than none at all, because he'd waste weeks figuring out if he needed it or not.

Cain knew he was at an impasse until he could look at the lab results.

Tonight, at 850 Bryant, he'd gone around the building to lean on the forensic lab chiefs. Only the ballistics crew had been cooperative, Dr. Revchuk and his two interns promising a striation report within three days. But otherwise, he'd gotten nothing. No reduction in the waiting times, no bump ahead in line. Six weeks for the toxicology, which had to go to a CHP lab in Sacramento. That put them into March. Three weeks for fingerprints, and nearly the same for DNA. No one could even give him an estimate on the document analysis.

• • •

Standing next to his car in Lucy's driveway, listening to the hood tick as it cooled off, he looked up at the front of the house, scanning for lights inside. Nothing, except the faintest glow from the living room. He smelled the air and caught a hint of wood smoke, and then he understood.

He went up the steps and put his key in the lock. There was a shadow on the doormat, and that stopped him from going any farther. He touched the object with his foot but couldn't identify it in the dark. He clicked on his flashlight and crouched.

She'd left a pair of tennis shoes on the doormat. Women's shoes, size six. He'd seen them in her closet but never on her feet. Now, in the LED glare of his light, he saw why she'd left them outside: they were caked with mud. In the mud were broken leaves and blades of cut grass. He stepped inside and closed the door after himself, then leaned against it with one hand while he took off his own shoes so that he wouldn't wake her.

He found her asleep in an overstuffed chair in front of the fireplace. Her head on the armrest, one palm under her cheek. Legs curled up onto the cushion, and half her body beneath a tartan blanket. He tiptoed upstairs and knelt at the safe to put his gun away. Then he came back downstairs, socked feet silent on the wood floors.

The fire she'd built was mostly burned down to embers, piled high around the andirons and casting their shadows out into the room. He sat on the carpet in front of her and used the poker to stir up the flames. He looked around for another log to put on, but there was nothing. She'd burned through all the wood she'd found, and the fire in front of him was the last of it. She must have used that afternoon's edition of the *Examiner* as tinder, but she'd saved the front section. It was on the floor next to her chair, and even in the soft light he had no trouble reading the headline.

SUICIDE!
CASTELLI TAKES OWN LIFE

It had probably gone to print and been on the stands before Dr. Levy even made her first cut. Cain pulled the paper over and held the front page to the firelight so that he could read the story. There were no official sources; everything was anonymous. But enough people had seen Castelli where he'd fallen that the two reporters were able to paint a clear picture of the scene. They even had two crucial facts that Cain would never have allowed out. The mayor's hands had field-tested positive for gunshot residue, and Mona Castelli's hands were clean.

The one thing missing was a reason — not even a guess at one. The *Examiner*'s reporters hadn't written a word about the blackmail notes or the photographs. Either they didn't know about them or they were waiting until they got a little more.

Cain set the paper down and leaned his head back until it rested against Lucy's shins. After a while, he felt her hand reach out of the blanket and stroke the top of his head. He took her fingers and held them against the side of his neck.

"Should we go up to bed?" he asked. "It'd be more comfortable."

"All right."

She didn't move to get up, though. He turned around to look at her and saw the fire's glow reflected in her eyes.

"Where'd you find the wood?"

"In the park, under the eucalyptuses. And in the redwood grove," she said. "Fallen branches — nothing thicker than my wrist. I broke them over my knee and put them in a bag."

"They must've been wet," Cain said. "All this rain today."

"I had to use two newspapers to get them going."

"How long were you out?"

"Four hours," she said. "Five, maybe. I wasn't feeling good. I thought a walk would help. I read in the book that I'm supposed to walk. But it was so cold, I thought a fire would be nice."

"They've helped before — the walks, I mean?"

"You knew?"

"I'd guessed."

"Is it okay?"

He wasn't sure if she meant the walks or how she hadn't said anything about them.

"I think it's great," Cain said.

"Okay." She sat up and pulled the blanket around her shoulders like a shawl. "It'll be cold upstairs — you should've seen it down here when the fire was going, when it was really going."

She started for the stairs and he followed her.

"I'm sorry I missed it — that I was so late."

"Don't be," she said. "I saw the paper so I knew where you were."

"Still."

"Did they get it right?"

"I don't know," he said. "Probably they did."

Now they were going down the hall. There weren't any lights, but it didn't matter. He was close enough behind her that he could feel the warmth coming from beneath her blanket. He undressed at the foot of the bed. Lucy dropped her blanket and then took off her T-shirt, the high school one she usually slept in. She came up to him and he ran his hands gently along her clavicles and down her chest —

"Careful, Gavin," she whispered. She always whispered when they were this close. "I'm sore."

"I'll be careful — I'm always careful with you."

"I know you are."

— and then his fingers were tracing down her ribs to her stomach, finding the curve that was just beginning to swell from beneath her navel. It was too small to see, this bump. But with his hands, he'd know her body blindfolded. He didn't need to see it to know the ways she'd grown. She put her hands on his and pressed them gently to her skin.

"Do you remember how we got here?" she asked.

"Yes."

"Can you do that again?"

"Of course I can."

Cain was back in the office by four a.m. He'd stopped at a café on the drive down and picked up two large coffees, and now the paper cups were scalding his hands. He set them on the desk, then picked up the folder on his chair. It was two inches thick and had a routing memo stapled to the outside from the SFPD printing shop — the photos from Castelli's house.

He took the lid off the first of the coffees and sat down to study the photographs. After a while, he got out a notebook and started writing, wanting to record the things that weren't in the pictures but were still in his memory. The way the room had smelled when he walked into it — a mixture of spent cordite and drying blood. Closer to Castelli, there'd been an almost visible haze of bourbon fumes, the angel's share rising from his pores.

If he'd put the gun in his mouth and pulled the trigger, what had he been thinking in that last second? The girl, clawing at the coffin lid in the dark? Or maybe he'd only been thinking of himself. He'd seen the second set of photographs; he must have known he couldn't escape what was coming for him. He would have kept tabs on her grave, would have known about the exhumation order.

Everything pointed in one direction, and the *Examiner*'s headline had it right. Suicide. But there'd been two shots, and he still didn't know what to make of the note Castelli left in Melissa Montgomery's inbox: *Get Cain. He needs to know.* Why would he leave a note like that if he'd planned to shoot himself? If he knew he'd die that night, and he wanted Cain to see the second set of photographs, he could have just left them on his desk.

Cain pulled out the photo of the mayor's medicine cabinet. Half the Ambien and tramadol were missing, but the Viagra was unopened. In the next photo, of Castelli's desk, there was the bourbon, nine-tenths empty. Castelli might have been able to drink most men into their graves, but he'd gone through nearly an entire bottle between ten thirty and midnight. He would have been reeling. Blackout drunk. With that much bourbon, he might not have known what he was doing. Instead of a suicide, they could be looking at an accident. Mona said he wasn't a gun person, but that didn't make it true. Castelli might have pursued any number of fascinations behind his locked door.

Picturing it was easy enough.

He comes home, finds his wife gone. He's alone, finally. All day, he's been holding everything back. His rage at the blackmailer, at Cain. He's thinking about the photographs, he's remembering the way Cain dumped his drink and pushed him into his chair. He goes into his study and locks the door. He gets a bottle of bourbon and his gun.

He drinks. One glass, two glasses. He pours more.

He wipes his mouth on his shirtsleeve and coughs into his elbow. He sits in the chair and he holds the gun, and sometimes he points it at his black reflection in the window and imagines the blackmailer standing there. He spins around in his chair and somehow the gun goes off. It blows out the *M* section of his dictionary, but he hardly notices.

He pours one more glass.

The bottle tips over when he sets it down, but he's drunk so much of it now that the bourbon can't spill from the raised neck. He drinks.

He sets the glass down and uses both hands to hold the gun. As it comes up toward his face he sees three barrels, six barrels. Then just black. He closes his eyes. He's so drunk now his thoughts aren't conscious. They're more like the shadows that sometimes float behind his closed eyelids after too many flashbulbs go off at once. Unbidden, unconscious.

He's passing out in his chair, but he could be anywhere. He's an undergraduate, walking down Shattuck Avenue in Berkeley. Nothing in front of him but the future. He sees a sweep of blond hair from the corner of his eye.

There's an easier way out, the blackmailer had said. An unmoored thought, something drifting in a current. It goes by and he hardly notices it, but his fingers must have heard.

Bang.

Cain put the photographs back into the folder and looked at his watch. Five a.m. and still dark outside. He took out his cell phone and dialed. It was early, but that was okay. He wanted to keep Melissa Montgomery on her toes.

"Good morning, Miss Montgomery," he said. "Did I wake you?"

"What do you want?"

"How often did Castelli drink?"

"Every day."

"That's not what I mean — how often did he drink himself stupid? A bottle, two bottles in a sitting."

"Oh," she said. "I don't know."

"You never saw it?"

"I saw it, but I don't know how often he did it."

"When's the last time you know about?"

"Over a year ago. We were in Beijing — the China-Pacific trade conference. I'd just broken it off with him, and then in the hotel he rang down and had bottles delivered to his room. I had to sign the bill."

"You broke it off with him?"

"I told you already."

"You told me you'd stopped. That it was only sometimes, but you'd stopped more than a year ago."

"We stopped because I stopped it."

"Why?"

166

"Does it matter?"

"Right now, everything matters."

"All right." From her end of the line, a door opened and shut. Now he could hear wind. She must have stepped outside to have a more private conversation. He'd forgotten she lived with a roommate. "I broke it off because I'm not stupid. Because a married politician who fucks his chief of staff isn't going anywhere, and if he didn't go anywhere then neither would I."

"That's what you told him?"

"Yes."

"And then he went up to his room and drank himself blind?"

"That was the last day of the conference for us. He didn't leave his room again until it was time to go home."

"Okay," Cain said. "What about Mona?"

"What about her?"

"Could she match Castelli, drink for drink?"

"I wouldn't know," Melissa said. "I tried not to spend time around her. You can imagine why."

"That's all I've got for now."

He hung up and pulled the lid from his second cup of coffee, then started on the folder of scene photos again. He thought about Melissa Montgomery's story and where to fit it into everything else he'd learned. Castelli's public image was armored and ironclad. Tall and fit, he'd lean on a podium and bully anyone who asked questions he didn't like. He was rich, he was tough; his star was rising in the east. But his foundations couldn't hold him. He could be knocked off-balance. He'd strayed from his wife and gotten dumped by his mistress, and he'd reacted to it by locking himself in a Beijing hotel suite and drinking. There was the image, and then there was the man — and the man was vulnerable.

22

HE SPOTTED CHUN and Grassley coming up the Embarcadero toward him, and he waited for them in the long morning shadows, too tired to move toward them and too cold to take his hands from his pockets and wave. He looked over his shoulder to check the clock at the top of the Ferry Building. He'd ask them to meet him at seven thirty. Ten minutes late wasn't bad, considering the short-fused warning he'd given them.

"I didn't call you last night," Chun said once they'd reached him. "You told me to check in, and I forgot. I'm sorry."

"You're okay, so it's nothing. How'd it go?"

"Pretty good. He told me —"

"Let's get breakfast first," Cain said. "It's what we're here for. We'll find a quiet table."

The only quiet place to eat in the Ferry Building turned out to be a bench on the seawall out back. They sat together, drinking their coffee and looking through the iron guardrail at Yerba Buena Island. The falling tide's current ran against the wind, so that the bay's dark water was disturbed with a steep-sided chop.

"They met the week before school started. This was their freshman orientation — August 1984," Chun said. She bit the horned end off her croissant and swallowed it with a sip of her coffee. "They didn't have classes together. Dennis Herrington was premed, a focused kid. Castelli, not so much. But they lived in the same apartment complex. Two doors down from each other."

"They were friends?" Cain asked.

"They were friendly, but that didn't last. How did he put it? Harry Castelli was a decent kid when they met. But then he started hanging around people who gave Dennis the creeps."

"Pi Kappa Kappa," Cain said.

"Castelli was pledging," Chun said. "It was banned from campus, so everything was underground. It wasn't a fraternity so much as a secret society. They partied at a house off Grizzly Peak Boulevard."

"Herrington went?"

"Once, but they never invited him back. He didn't know why — he just didn't make the cut."

"That was when?"

"Fall semester, their freshman year," Chun said.

"This house where they partied," he said. "Did he give you the address?"

"He did, but it's not there anymore — it burned down in 1989," Chun said. "Christmas 1989. I looked it up last night. The firemen found five bodies. Two were Berkeley students, and the other three they never identified."

"Arson?"

"There were empty gas cans in the kitchen. It wasn't just arson — it was premeditated homicide. The bodies were bound up with baling wire."

"I remember that," Cain said. He'd been in middle school, on the other side of the bay. He'd seen it on the news, read about it in his parents' *Chronicle* all through Christmas break. "They never made any arrests. They didn't even have a suspect."

"None," Chun said. She took another bite of her croissant and held her fingers over her mouth as she chewed it. "Herrington told me about the house — the thing was a mansion. Ten bedrooms, twelve baths. A pool, two hot tubs — one inside and one upstairs, on a balcony. There was a basement with a full bar. A library, a billiards room. Art on the walls, none of it crap."

"A lot of money, is what you're saying."

"Piles of it," Chun said. "And this wasn't the house Pi Kappa Kappa used before it got kicked out of Cal. That one's still there; I've seen it. It's your typical frat house — a clapboard piece of shit, with fake Greek columns and weeds for a yard. The Grizzly Peak place was something they picked up after they went underground."

Chun wadded up the waxed paper bag that had held her croissant and put it into her empty coffee cup.

"There were two other things," she said. "A block from their apartment was a park, with a basketball court. Castelli played pickup games there. Herrington used to cut through the park on his way home from class."

"Okay."

"Most of the time, Castelli played without a shirt. Even when it was cold."

"The tattoo," Grassley said. "Herrington knew about it?"

Chun nodded.

"The first time he saw it, it was still fresh — raw and red. That was around spring break."

"You're talking 1985?" Cain asked. "Their freshman year?"

"March, freshman year."

"What about the scars on his forearms? Did you ask about those?"

"That was the other thing," Chun said. "Herrington said they weren't there until the fall semester sophomore year. He saw them when they were moving back in, at the end of the summer. They hadn't healed yet."

Cain had been buzzing on the usual blend of exhaustion and caffeine. Now there was something else in the mix. It was the feeling he got when a piece of the path in front of him suddenly resolved itself and became clear. Castelli had the tattoo inked onto his shoulder blade in the spring of 1985. The girl had gone into Christopher Hanley's casket on July 17, 1985. Sometime during the summer, Castelli had tried to open up his forearm with a razor blade.

"What've you got today?" Cain asked her.

"I take the stand at nine. I'm testifying in the Conroy trial."

"That might go all day," Cain said. "But if it doesn't — if you get out early — you know what to do?"

"Go back to Berkeley, to the police department," she said. "Copy the murder book from the Grizzly Peak fire."

"And see if there's a file on Pi Kappa Kappa. If the Berkeley PD didn't keep one, university police might have. You could ask around, see if the deans know anything." He turned to Grassley. "What about you?"

"I missed the fashion professor," Grassley said. "Last night, she was gone by the time I showed. She's got office hours this morning."

"That's at the building on New Montgomery?"

"Yeah."

"Keep an eye out for Alexa Castelli. She lives across the street, and her mom's staying in the Palace Hotel."

"If I see them, then what?"

"Just keep an eye."

"The dress, I figure it's a dead end anyway."

"But you never know," Cain said. "And if you spot the daughter, stay out of sight. Don't approach her, and whatever you do, don't find yourself in a room alone with her."

"That's trouble I don't need," Grassley said.

"Tell me about it."

Cain stood up and stretched his arms behind his back, joining his fingers together and working his shoulders against the stiffness. "Call me if you learn anything. That goes for both of you."

He walked to his car and sat for a moment before hitting the ignition. From the parking space, he was looking head-on into the traffic coming up the Embarcadero. The bridge was above everything, gray steel hovering over the last of the city before reaching across the water. It was raining again, and most of the cars used their headlights. The drought was done, at least here. Now it rained all the time, while the central valley baked under clouds of dust. He thought sometimes that the city inhabited a different earth, that if the sky ever cleared enough to see the stars, they would be unrecognizable. Uncharted constellations, the long tails of nameless comets.

The city's labs were backed up, and that was choking his investigation. He'd made arrangements to address that. Dr. Henry Newcomb had been the chief medical examiner until a few days after Christmas, when he'd been forced to resign. A case of his had turned out badly for the city, and at the end of it there'd been no one left but Henry to take the blame. He'd been at loose ends when Cain called — no job and no prospect of one, and happy to take anything. Cain hit the ignition and put the car into gear.

A black swan and a single cygnet were gliding near the edge of the lake facing the Palace of Fine Arts, but paddled to the deeper water near the middle when Cain shut his car door and went to get the Styrofoam cooler from his trunk. He stood on the sidewalk with the cooler under one arm, watching the swan and the rotunda's reflection on the rain-dimpled water.

"Cain?"

He turned around. Dr. Newcomb was wearing khakis and an old

Yale sweatshirt. He had a black umbrella tucked under one arm. Cain had never seen him in street clothes. Either he'd been dressed for an autopsy, or he'd been in a suit, testifying.

"Henry."

He shifted the cooler to his other arm and shook Henry Newcomb's hand. Then they headed out across the wet grass and stepped onto a footpath that wound around the lake.

"I wouldn't have bothered you if I had a choice," Cain said. "I'm in a bind."

"You're not worried about bothering me," Henry said. "Admit it."

"I'm not that worried."

"You think I'll taint everything I touch."

"You can't testify," Cain said. "Try seeing it from my perspective."

It was raining again, but Henry didn't open his umbrella. They walked through the stone columns and then beneath the semi-shelter of the open rotunda.

"You can't testify," Cain said. "But maybe you can steer me in the right direction. My hands are tied until I get the lab results, and I can't wait six weeks. I need to move now."

"I don't have a lab."

"But you know people. If no one will do you a favor, you could rent time in one. I read about that."

"Rent time with what budget? The city's?"

"Not the city — the FBI," Cain said. "This case, I'm working it with them."

Henry motioned to the cooler, and Cain handed it to him.

"It's Castelli, isn't it?"

It surprised him that Henry knew. He'd imagined the former medical examiner holed up in his house, the papers piling up outside his front door and the TV unplugged. But he'd picked up the phone on the second ring when Cain called, and he'd agreed to meet right away. He just didn't want to do it in his house. He didn't want to upset his wife.

"Dr. Levy gave me a full set," Cain said. "Liver, blood, urine. You've got ten cc's of fluid from each eye. A slice of his heart, even."

Henry knelt and put the cooler on the polished stone floor. He opened the lid and removed the two ice packs. Beneath them were the glass sample tubes, each sealed with a black rubber stopper.

Henry sorted through them, reading the labels. He got to the last two and looked up.

"What are these?" he asked. "Who's Jane Doe?"

"We opened a casket from the cemetery in El Carmelo. There was a second body—a young woman. We don't know who she was or why she's in there."

"This is something separate?" Henry asked. "Or connected to Castelli?"

Cain shook his head.

"What you've got are two samples. One's a piece of her liver. Run the toxicology, tell me what was in her system when she died. I've got a hunch, but I want to see what you find out before I get into it."

"And the other?" Henry held up the sample tube. "What's this?"

"That's a piece of the fetus," Cain said. "She was in her first trimester. If there's a link to Castelli, you're holding it."

Henry turned the sample tube to the light and looked at the tiny slice of fetal tissue.

"How long ago was this?"

"Thirty years. She was buried alive in the eighties," Cain said. "Can you do it?"

"You want me to do what?" Henry asked. "See if he's the father?"

"That's right."

"Sequencing it would be hard—a lot of the DNA would be destroyed. But paternity shouldn't be much trouble."

Henry loaded the samples back into the cooler, put cold packs on top of them, and closed the lid. He stood up, and Cain followed him across the rotunda to the path that picked up on the other side.

"How long will you need?"

"Give me today to get a lab," Henry said. "Tonight to do the work. If they can't make time for me at Stanford, I can call Slade Ulrich at UCSF. If I can get in there, I'll be able to do it all pretty quickly."

They came out from beneath the protection of the columns, and back into the rain. The black swan and its cygnet were nosing through the leaves on the bank nearby. Cain wondered about the lone offspring. Swans came in clutches of three. Something must have killed the others. A loose dog, a kid with a mean streak. They reached the curve in the path that took them closest to the bank, and the swan saw them. She raised herself up and spread her wings.

They both looked at her, her flight feathers flashing white as she made her threat display. Henry began to walk again. He still hadn't opened his umbrella, and it was raining harder now. They were both soaking wet, the water running down Cain's leather jacket and soaking his pants at the thighs. Henry was so tall that Cain practically had to jog to keep up.

When they reached Baker Street again, they stopped alongside Cain's car.

"They took a pregnant woman and buried her alive?" Henry asked. "Someone really did that?"

"She clawed at the casket lid, ripped her fingernails out."

"You have to catch him, Cain."

"We'll see. I'll need your report before I can do much of anything."

Henry nodded and walked away. He crossed the street and went through the rain. Cain shook the water from his jacket and got into his car. He turned on the wipers, then the heater. By the time he looked up again, Henry Newcomb was gone.

23

HE CUT THROUGH the Presidio, then crossed out of San Francisco and into Marin on the Golden Gate Bridge, hardly any traffic to slow him at this hour. The lanes coming into the city were backed up for miles, a thousand pairs of headlights in an endless blur. It took him forty-five minutes to get to John MacDowell's house in Stinson Beach, most of that on the narrow curves of Shoreline Highway. Crossing the Marin Headlands, he caught glimpses of the Pacific beneath its broken blanket of fog, and then after Muir Beach, the ocean was clear out to the horizon.

MacDowell lived on Seadrift Avenue, out near the end of a private peninsula. Cain stopped at the security booth and rolled down his window. He leaned out to hand the guard his inspector's star, but the man raised the gate and waved him through. He drove up the peninsula, a low spit of sand just feet above the surf, scanning the street numbers. Most of the houses here were designed to take up the entire buildable space of their lots, pressed too close together for Cain to see the ocean beyond. There were sprawling low bungalows built of redwood, and columned concrete monstrosities, and stucco houses in the Spanish style, with tiered tile roofs and ironwork on the upstairs balconies.

The house where MacDowell lived was a modern box, built of unvarnished wood and glass. There was a detached garage, and above that a guest apartment.

Cain pulled into the driveway and checked his phone for messages, then got out and looked around. The garage had a rolling door with five square windows set in it. He went up to the middle one and cupped his hands around his eyes to look inside. There was nothing but a tool bench, though he could tell from the stains on the concrete floor that usually there were two cars here.

Around the side of the garage there was a wooden staircase that led to a little deck with a view over the roof of the main house out to the beach. He stood a moment with his hands on the rail, wondering how a retired cop found his way to a place like this. It wasn't the main house, but the view was probably better. The waves broke in a long line down the beach, the water here unsettled and broken by currents.

"The right time of year, you can see whales out there."

There was a rocking chair in the far corner of the deck, up against the apartment wall, and in it there was an old man who was much smaller than he once had been. His back was bent and his skin hung off him in wrinkled folds where the flesh beneath it had evaporated. There was a blanket folded on his lap and a cup of coffee on the small table next to him. He had been so still, and tucked so far back into the corner, that Cain hadn't noticed him. The waitress at the Western had said John MacDowell moved in with family, but that was probably too strong a term. He was just a guest passing through. This was his next to last stop.

"Gray whales, I guess," the man said. "Going north in the winter and south in the summer."

"I didn't see you there."

"I try to keep out of the way," the man said. "I try to blend."

Cain took out his badge again and handed it over. The man looked at it and gave it back.

"You're Inspector MacDowell?"

"Retired," he said. "Obviously."

"Gavin Cain."

They shook hands and MacDowell slowly stood up.

"We might as well go inside," he said. He picked up his mug in a hand that looked like it was made of knotted wood. "If you came to talk about one of my old cases, we'll want to be out of this wind."

He opened the French doors and they stepped into the apartment's main room. It was polished and spare. There was a glass-topped coffee table with a piece of sun-silvered driftwood in the middle of it. A pair of low white couches on either side of the table. The kitchen had a sit-in dining nook at a bay window that looked out at the ocean. Everything smelled of lemon oil and fresh laundry.

The man saw Cain's gaze and shook his head.

"I'm learning Spanish from my daughter's housekeeper," he said.

"People say old dogs and new tricks, and all that. I don't disagree —but I've got to talk to somebody, don't I?"

"Sure you do."

"Which case did you want to talk about?"

"It's not an old case," Cain said. "Not exactly."

He looked around the room again. There was no television, no radio. There were no bookshelves. There weren't even any magazines on the coffee table. Maybe all those things were in the bedroom, but Cain didn't think so. He'd found the old man sitting on the porch, staring at the waves. It was all he had to do unless it was a cleaning day.

"What is it, then?"

"Do you have time?" Cain asked. "I mean—you're not busy today?"

"Are you kidding me?"

"If you take a ride with me, I'll buy you lunch. You can show me around your old neighborhood."

"My old neighborhood," MacDowell said. "Not where I lived, but where I patrolled."

"You remember it?"

"The Richmond?" He set his blanket on the counter and poured his coffee down the sink. "I put in my twenty on patrol, took a week off, and put in another twenty-five as an inspector. Both tours in the Richmond. From the beach, east to Divisadero—sixty-five blocks long and twenty-two wide. I could tell you stories."

"That's what I want," Cain said. "Stories. What about lunch at the Western?"

"I'll get my coat."

Coming back across the bridge, the city growing in front of them, MacDowell sat up a little straighter. He hadn't spoken since they'd gotten onto the freeway.

"I'd come down more if I still had a car," he said.

"Yeah?"

"Every day, maybe," he said. "This is my town."

"Who took the car?"

"My daughter. Her husband."

"Why?" Cain asked. "You're what—eighty, eighty-one?"

"Ninety-two."

177

He looked like he was a hundred and fifty, like he could tell a credible story about riding into Mexico with the cavalry, looking for signs of Pancho Villa. He'd put on a camelhair coat with plaid patches at the elbows, and wore an SFPD ball cap that he'd probably picked up when Cain was in grade school.

"But your eyes are okay," Cain said. "I see you looking at things."

"Most of the time, sure," MacDowell said. "My eyes were never the problem. But I drive out, and sometimes I get lost. They think my brain's a scrambled egg — my daughter, I mean. And my son-in-law. But it's not my brain, either. It's the map in my head — it's thirty years past its expiration date. I was getting lost on my own street. I didn't recognize the houses anymore."

"You look for a landmark and it's not there."

"They used to be there," MacDowell said. "All the houses, the buildings. The people who lived in them."

"Sure."

"Summertime, they ate their dinners in the backyards and they got it on upstairs with the windows open. They raised children, had fights. But most of the time it was happily ever after. You know what I'm talking about?"

"It's still that way."

"It's how it was for me. But then sometimes they killed each other and we'd come to pick through the wreckage. You know that, too. What you don't know is that the world isn't pausing for you. It just goes on. You don't own anything — it all belongs to time."

"You remember 1985?"

"Like yesterday," he said. "Better than yesterday."

"Now you're just messing with me."

"You wish," MacDowell asked. "That was the year I turned sixty. My daughter married, my wife passed. Five years left till I pulled the pin. The kids on the squad called me the old man. You believe that? I've been an old man almost as long as you've been alive. I could tell you stories."

They came off the bridge and Cain drove them to the Richmond, MacDowell's old neighborhood.

"We'll go down Geary to get to the Western," Cain said. "You can tell me some stories on the way."

• • •

"Pull over here," MacDowell said. "Four blocks, and I finally recognize something."

Cain turned to the curb and parked alongside a fire hydrant. MacDowell was looking through the driver's-side window, at the buildings on the other side of the street. There was a row house, a catastrophe of green-painted redwood. It had been a bar as long as Cain could remember. Next door was a low red house, the sign above the sidewalk mostly in Korean. The English at the bottom said CHARCOAL BARBECUE. Its windows were caked in decades of soot. To the right of that was a single-story stucco building with a dark glass door. No sign out front, and no windows. Aside from the door, the only thing on the front wall was the rusted mechanical bell of a burglar alarm.

"That used to be a church," MacDowell said. "I'm talking 'seventy-nine. A storefront operation, Jim Jones type of shit. We got the call in July. Coldest Sunday I can remember. And rain — you've never seen rain like it."

"What happened?"

"Middle of the sermon, a man walks in that front door, already has his gun out. He plugs the reverend in the forehead. One shot. He steps back out, puts the gun in his waistband, and goes into the bar like nothing happened."

"No kidding."

"Time we show up, he's on his third beer," MacDowell said. "They used to have Pabst on draft. I sit down next to him, casual as anything, and take his gun off him. He doesn't mind a bit. He asks if I want a drink, and I figure what the hell. So I pass his gun to my partner and the two of us have a beer. My partner's standing behind him with a gun in each hand."

"Why'd he do it?"

"He used to have the reverend over for dinner. He had a fifteen-year-old daughter. You can see where this is going."

"She was pregnant?"

"Twins, it turned out."

"What'd he get?"

"Twenty," MacDowell said. "In Folsom. Funny thing was, he turned into a preacher. Ordained, all that."

"Where's he now?"

"I lost track," MacDowell said. He was still looking at the bar. "Half the guys we arrested, they were all right. You know?"

"Sure."

"Kind of guys you could sit down with, have a beer. It wouldn't seem that far out of line. But that was the only time I actually did."

Cain checked his side-view mirror, then pulled back into the right lane. A few blocks later, they stopped again in front of a faded yellow house. In '82 it had been an unlicensed daycare. Ten, fifteen kids under the age of two. Upstairs there was a workshop where eight naked women sat around a long table. Each woman had a metric laboratory scale, a box of glassine bags, and a brick of heroin. There were two televisions in the house. One upstairs and one downstairs. When MacDowell and his partner came in, everyone was watching *Sesame Street*. The kids, the women, the three guards with guns.

Cain drove off again, and they started looking for the scene of a triple homicide MacDowell had caught in '77 but couldn't find it. They looked for twenty minutes, MacDowell shaking his head at every turn, looking at the streets that no longer made any sense to him. The old houses had been cut up into new apartments, and the old apartment buildings gutted and turned into massive single-family homes. A complete inversion of the world MacDowell had known.

When he looked like he was fading, Cain brought them back to Geary and parked in front of a vacant storefront sandwiched between a coffee shop and a used appliance dealer.

"One more, and then lunch," Cain said. "You remember this?"

"Not ringing any bells."

"In 'eighty-five, it was a funeral home," Cain prompted.

MacDowell looked around. He studied the storefronts on the other side of the street, looked in the window of the coffee shop.

"Fonteroy's," MacDowell said. "Sure."

"You ever hear anything about it?"

"Fonteroy's?"

"That's right."

"Pull up. Past the coffee shop."

Cain left the parking spot and went ahead three spaces. MacDowell waved his hand, signaling to stop. There was nowhere to park, so Cain stayed in the lane and put on his hazard lights. They were looking up an alley that accessed the space behind the buildings. A row of grime-coated dumpsters sat beneath the fire escapes.

"I was doing a Saturday shift. Around noon. It's quiet in the station. Pretty much just me and my partner, catching up on paperwork. There was the desk officer, falling asleep over the sports section."

"What year is this?"

MacDowell looked at the ceiling.

"I was one year from pulling the pin," he said. "So this is 1989."

"Okay," Cain said. He tried not to sound disappointed. In 1989, John Fonteroy had been gone for four years. He'd put his wife and daughter in the family car the day of Christopher Hanley's funeral, lit out of the city, and never come back.

"The desk officer gets a call from dispatch. Someone saw a 647b —that's still the dispatch code for a hooker?"

"Yeah."

"So someone saw a 647b running up the sidewalk here."

"That's not so unusual," Cain said.

"But this lady was buck naked, and screaming."

"That's different."

Cain looked back up the sidewalk. It was about a hundred feet to what used to be the front door of Fonteroy's.

"We'd been typing all morning. In 'eighty-nine, in the Richmond station, we were still using typewriters and carbon paper. We hadn't gotten a decent run in a while, and this was just around the corner. So we got in our car and came over."

"You found her?"

"It took some poking around—she was hiding behind the dumpsters. Small, like a mouse, and way back there in the alley. Naked as a baby and drugged out of her skull. Pretty girl, though. Blond and good-looking. And holding a scalpel with blood on the blade."

"What'd you do?"

"My partner tackled her, and I got the scalpel. Then we put a blanket around her and brought her to the car. And don't get any ideas. This was right after all the problems with the vice squad in North Beach. So we did it by the book—got on the radio, said we were transporting a female."

"Then you gave your odometer reading," Cain said.

"That's still in the manual?"

"Same deal," Cain said. "No wandering around when you've got a lady in the back."

"Absolutely no wandering. We took her to the emergency room at UCSF. Gave our odometer again when we got there. Two miles — no detours."

"And her story was what?"

"We never figured it out," MacDowell said. "The caller said she was a 647b, but she wasn't anyone we knew. She was a foreigner. European, I guess. Latvian, Estonian. Something like that. They had to get a translator, but even then we couldn't make sense of it."

"She was drugged?"

"Like you wouldn't believe," MacDowell said. "She had red welts when we picked her up, and by the time we got her to the hospital, they'd turned to bruises. Handprints on her wrists, her neck."

"She was that drugged, and someone saw her running?"

"Her motor skills weren't impaired," MacDowell said. "She could run, she could swing that blade. She nearly kicked out the car window."

"But what?"

"It was her mind that was gone. She didn't know her name, what year it was. She was scared out of her skin — clawing at herself. But she didn't know what she was scared of. Whatever she'd taken, it wiped her mind clean."

"They do a rape exam?"

"First thing — but it was inconclusive. If you'd gotten this today, you'd have checked under her fingernails, see if she fought back and got a piece of him. But we were just getting into DNA back then, and it was only being used in the big cases. The headliners."

"How long was she at the hospital?"

"It took her a day and half just to come down from the drugs —"

Cain started to ask a question but MacDowell waved it away and answered it.

"— they never figured out what it was. She slept a lot. When she was awake, they'd call me and I'd come with the translator and try to talk."

"And nothing?"

"Nothing."

"She didn't remember, or she didn't want to say?"

"I don't know," MacDowell said. "Both, maybe. First the one, and then after the drugs wore off, she knew enough not to talk."

"What'd you think?"

"What else was there to think?" MacDowell asked. "She'd had a close call. She was lucky. We figure she jumped out of a moving car, took off down the street."

But Cain knew she hadn't come from a moving car. She'd come from the funeral home. One of her captors must have turned his back just long enough for her to grab something. There would have been plenty of blades in a mortuary's back room. If the men hadn't chased her down and dragged her back, hadn't shot her down on the sidewalk, then she must have known how to use the scalpel. MacDowell had said it was bloody.

"What happened to her?" Cain asked. "You must've kept tabs."

"Middle of the night, she got up and walked out of UCSF. Nothing but a hospital gown. An EMT out front saw her go but didn't think to stop her. I was so pissed, I would've charged him with something if I could've. Negligence. Criminal stupidity."

"And that was that."

"That's right," MacDowell said. "Case closed."

"You canvassed the area?"

"Sure, but no one saw where she came from. That's why we figured a car. One second there's nothing, and the next second, there's a naked woman running to the alley."

Cain looked back toward the vacant storefront. Maybe she'd jumped out of a moving car. But it was also possible she'd come sprinting out the front door of the funeral home. The years didn't match up, but the story fit too well.

"In 'eighty-nine, what was that?" Cain asked. He pointed out the back window. "It wasn't Fonteroy's anymore. That closed in 'eighty-five."

"After Fonteroy took off, it was empty awhile, and then it was the Eternity Chapel. Another funeral parlor—because what else was the landlord going to do with it? Once a place gets set up for that, that's it."

"Who ran it?"

"I don't know—I never had any trouble with him."

"But you knew Fonteroy."

"Guy had a record as long as your arm. Fonteroy wasn't even his real name. It was Finnegan. He used to drive getaway cars on bank jobs. He trained as an undertaker at San Quentin. We used to roll past in the seventies and drop in, just to make sure he was still straight."

Cain tapped his fingers on the steering wheel, thinking it through. If someone had been looking for a funeral director willing to take cash and look the other way, Fonteroy was the obvious choice. If he'd been in San Quentin for bank jobs, he'd have a reputation. But if MacDowell's nude woman in 1989 had anything to do with the funeral home, then maybe Fonteroy's disappearance hadn't stopped the casket program. Maybe it only slowed it down for a few months, until Eternity Chapel moved in.

"This is why you wanted to talk to me?" MacDowell asked. "Fonteroy?"

"I'll tell you over lunch," he said. "But on the way, I've got to make a call."

He turned off the flashers and started driving again, debating whether to call Chun or Grassley. Chun was better at digging up records, but she was busier. Grassley just had the dress. Cain dialed Grassley and put the call on speaker.

"Cain?"

"You somewhere you can talk?"

"I'm in Union Square —"

"I thought you were seeing the fashion professor at the Academy of Art."

"I wrapped that up, and she told me to go talk to someone at Britex — this fabric store at Geary and Stockton. It's complicated."

"Is it a lead, or a goose chase? Because I got something else for you to work on."

"Let me go in here and see what I can learn."

"All right," Cain said. "When you wrap that up, see what you can find out about Eternity Chapel."

"What's Eternity Chapel?"

"What Fonteroy's turned into — the landlord rented the building to another funeral home after Fonteroy took off. I want the name of the proprietor."

"How do I find that?"

"However you want," Cain answered. Maybe he should have called Chun after all. "If it was me, I'd start by finding out who owned the building. Then you ask for a copy of the lease. Or you could check the mortuary licenses. The tax records. Take your pick."

"You got it."

Cain hung up and looked at MacDowell. The old man was watching through the windshield, hands on his knees.

"Green partner?"

"Pretty much."

"Either they catch on in the first year, or they don't."

"He'll do okay."

He turned on Fillmore and parked down the street from the Western. When he got out, he realized he was in the same parking spot he'd had when Castelli's blackmailer left a note on his windshield. He turned around, checking the area. There were a pair of bent-back women, MacDowell's age or older. One of them was pushing a collapsible grocery cart. MacDowell was on the sidewalk, watching him.

"Someone following you?"

"You never know."

24

THEY HAD LUNCH at the Western and then headed back to Stinson Beach. MacDowell made it halfway across the bridge before falling asleep; he stayed out until they rolled to a stop in his daughter's driveway. Cain got out and helped MacDowell up the stairs.

At the landing, MacDowell shook his hand and let himself in to the little apartment. Cain stood a moment, looking out at the ocean. It was three o'clock, and there was no fog at all. The horizon was fifteen, twenty miles out, but he didn't see any gray whales. Maybe they'd already gone south. He went back down to the car, wondering what the daughter was thinking, keeping a ninety-two-year-old man up a set of steps like that. Why not let him live in the main house? For that matter, why not let him have a book or two?

He backed out of the driveway and then called Lucy. She answered on the second ring.

"Gavin?" she asked. "Is everything okay?"

"It's fine — I just wanted to hear your voice."

"I might take a walk again. Or a nap. I can't decide."

"Either sounds good."

"When will you be back?"

"I don't know."

"If it's late, I'll take a nap now. Then I'll be awake when you get back."

"Do that."

"So you'll be late, is what you're saying."

"I'll be late."

There was traffic coming back, and he didn't reach his desk until five thirty. It was already dark. He called Grassley and got no answer, then tried Chun and got the same. There was a folder on his chair, routed upstairs from the ballistics lab. It was two inches thick. Most reports were just a single page. He went to the kitchenette for a cup of coffee, then came back and opened the report. It took him ten seconds to scan the first two pages, and by the end of them, he'd forgotten all about his coffee.

He flipped the page and kept reading, reaching for his phone without looking up. He left messages for Chun and Grassley, then remembered Fischer. She answered right away.

"Cain," she said. She spoke in a hurried whisper. "I'm about to get on a plane—I'm coming back from L.A. The field office here is the best in the country at tracing currency, so I came down with Castelli's cash. What's up?"

"I'm sitting here looking at the ballistics report and you're not going to believe it."

"Try me."

"You remember the bullet in the dictionary?"

"The perfect bullet."

"They matched it to the gun. So then they ran it on the system, just to see. They got a hit."

"You're serious."

"It's linked to an unsolved homicide."

"When?"

"October 15, 1998."

"We're talking about Castelli's gun," Fischer said. "The thirty-eight S and W that was under the desk."

"That gun."

"We know he owned it in 1998?"

"He registered it in 1991. Maybe when he inherited it."

"Who was the victim?" Fischer asked. "And where was this?"

"I haven't gotten there—but it's all here."

He thumbed the stack and saw handwritten notes, color photographs. A shot of tire tracks in dark mud. A red Cadillac in a dirt parking lot, tall trees behind it.

"You've got a hard copy?"

"Yeah."

"Scan it and email me," she said. "If you can do it in ten minutes, I'll read it in the air."

"All right."

"Shit, Cain," she said.

"I know."

He hung up and took the report with him, still reading as he went through the cubicle farm to the copy room. He loaded the file into the feed tray and ran it through the scanner, then emailed it from his phone to Fischer. He went back to his office, ignoring the three people who said hello. He shut his door, then locked it.

The guy's name was Lester Fennimore.

A state park ranger found his 1997 Cadillac Eldorado at midnight in a trailhead parking lot in Castle Rock State Park. Lester Fennimore was in the driver's seat, his face resting on the steering wheel. He'd been shot six times in his right side, as if the shooter had been sitting in the passenger seat. It had rained at ten o'clock, and there were two sets of tire tracks in the parking lot. One was from the Cadillac coming in. The other must have been the shooter's car. It had pulled up alongside the Cadillac, then backed out to leave.

Cain pulled up a map on his computer monitor. Castle Rock State Park was twenty-three miles from San Jose. In 1998, Castelli had been living down there, getting rich on startup stock options.

Cain's phone rang and he grabbed it.

"This is Cain."

"We might get cut off," Fischer said. "I'm on board now."

"You can talk?"

"Government flight, and all to myself. You saw the stuff on Fennimore?"

"Which part?"

"The interview with his widow, the background — he graduated from Cal in 'eighty-nine. So he was a freshman in 'eighty-five."

"So they might have known each other?"

"Oh, they definitely knew each other. Go to the autopsy photos. The third one."

Cain dug into the documents, flipping through pages of interview notes and laboratory reports until he came to the autopsy. The first photograph showed Lester Fennimore on the steel table. He lay naked on his back, eyes open in dead surprise. Four gunshot wounds were scattered on the right side of his chest. A fifth bullet had smashed his jaw and come out through his left cheek. Cain turned the page. There was a close-up of Fennimore's face. He'd probably been a handsome man. Short dark hair and green eyes. There were healed scars on his left ear and on his throat, but they didn't detract from him overall.

He turned the page. The coroner had turned Fennimore over to photograph his back. There was another bullet wound in his spine. It must have been the last shot, fired after he'd fallen into the steering wheel.

"You get to it?"

"Yeah, I see it," Cain said.

He was looking at a tattoo on Lester Fennimore's right shoulder. Each Greek letter was an inch across. The artist had inked them vertically, following the inside edge of Fennimore's scapula.

Π
K
K

"He was Pi Kappa Kappa," Fischer said. "They were frat brothers."

Cain stared at the dead man's tattoo. He fumbled for his briefcase, clicked it open, and took out his copy of the blackmailer's second set of photographs. The man on top of the girl had never shown his face to the camera. There was just his back. Broad shoulders and short, dark hair. The tattoo trailing his shoulder blade. It could have been Castelli; it could have been Lester Fennimore.

"Yesterday, Chun came up with something," he said. "Fennimore isn't the only Pi Kappa Kappa who got killed — there were five others in 1989."

"What?"

He told her about the house on Grizzly Peak Boulevard, the arson and the five bodies that'd been found in the rubble. By now, Chun should have copied Berkeley PD's murder book on the case. If there was a file on Pi Kappa Kappa, she'd have that, too.

"What do you think?" Cain asked.

From her end of the line, he could hear the whine of the jet's engines. She thought about it for so long that he thought he'd lost her.

"I think this is bigger than we thought," she finally said. "It goes deeper than we thought. We need to find that girl."

"I know it," Cain said. "I'm working on it."

He was pretty sure the girl was in a freezer, seven floors beneath him. Henry Newcomb might be able to point the way by tomorrow, and if he did, then he would have to consider coming clean to Fischer about what he'd found.

"What about the money?" he asked. "What'd you find?"

"It was nothing," Fischer said. "No idea what he meant to do with it, but he'd withdrawn it from his savings account last week. His and Mona's."

"What bank?" Cain asked.

There was a pause while Fischer went into her notes.

"Chase, on McAllister and Van Ness. Right across from City Hall."

"That wasn't on the list."

"Which list?"

"In the safe, with the cash — we found a scrap of paper with the names and addresses of banks. But they were all in Chinatown. If he took the cash out of Chase, we still don't know what the list was for."

"Maybe it's where he was going to put it," Fischer said.

"Either way, we'll have to give it back to Mona Castelli," Cain said. "It's hers unless you've got a reason we need to hold on to it."

"We give it back — there aren't any grounds for civil forfeiture, and we know the money came out of their joint account. But think what else you want to ask her when we do it," Fischer said. "I land in an hour."

"I'll meet you in her lobby."

"Fine."

He hung up and turned back to the report. Lester Fennimore. Shot to death by Castelli's gun sometime after ten o'clock on June 28, 1998. He was sitting in his red Cadillac Eldorado on the loneliest stretch of Skyline Boulevard in Santa Cruz County. Cain looked at the photographs. The car in the lot, rain puddled up in the tire tracks. A measuring tape in the mud, showing the width of the wheelbase. The driver's-side window, blood spattered and punctured by the bullet that had gone through Fennimore's cheek.

An investigator had interviewed Fennimore's wife. Cain scanned the handwritten notes. They lived in Walnut Creek; their daughter had just turned two. Mrs. Fennimore couldn't explain what her husband had been doing in Castle Rock State Park, seventy miles from their house. He'd just lost his job. There was nowhere he had to be, no one he had to meet. She'd gone to bed at eight o'clock, and he'd been home. Sitting in the living room, drinking a beer and watching TV. He must have left as soon as she'd gone to sleep and driven south in a hurry. There was no time in the chronology for any detours, for any aimless wandering. He'd arrived in the trailhead parking lot before ten, before the rain. The dirt under the Cadillac was dry. He'd been waiting in the parking lot for his killer. He was there on business secret enough that he'd kept it from his wife.

Cain thought about the leads he'd gotten from Matt Redding.

In one of the first photographs, there'd been a dozen Thrallinex tablets, a lipstick-marked glass, a whiskey flask, and a set of keys, all sitting on a nightstand. One of the keys fit a 1980s model Cadillac Eldorado. Lester Fennimore died in a 1997 Eldorado. Some people were like that with cars. They'd find a model and stick with it, get a new one every few years.

Cain took out the blackmailer's photograph and looked at the man on top of the girl. He was holding her ankles out, pushing against her as he arched his back and flexed his muscles. He was showing off, performing for the camera. Was that Castelli, or Fennimore? And how many of the men who'd died in the Grizzly Peak house had ΠKK tattooed on their shoulder? Maybe they'd all been there. Taking turns with her, snapping shots of each other. And ever since, Castelli had been trying to bury it.

25

HE STEPPED OUT of the elevator and onto the Palace Hotel's top floor. Officer Combs had angled one of the overstuffed chairs so that in one glance he could keep tabs on the stairs, the elevator doors, and the hall that led to Room 8064. When he saw Cain, the young cop stood up and gestured down the hall.

"She's in there?" Cain asked.

"With the daughter, who got here two hours ago," Combs said. "I recognized her from the paper."

"Alexa," Cain said, and Combs nodded. "Have they come out at all?"

"No, sir — not since they've been together. But Mrs. Castelli left the room on her own before that, at two o'clock."

"She talk to you?"

"Just whispered hello — I could barely hear her. Then she called the elevator and went down. I took the stairs and beat her to the lobby. She didn't see me when she got out."

"Where'd she go?"

"The bar in the lobby," Combs said. "The Pied Piper. She sat at the end and had a martini."

"Anyone talk to her, recognize her?"

"Place was empty. She had her drink alone and got another. I watched her from outside, in the lobby. In the bar, they have a big painting. She stared at that awhile, and drank, and asked for a third. She must've brought a plastic cup in her purse. She poured the last drink into it and took it upstairs."

Cain looked down the hall. He could see the wide double doors of her corner suite, light spilling through the thin gap above the threshold. A room like that must have had a bar. Or Alexa could have brought something from her apartment. It was hard to imagine that she'd gotten all the way through the day on no more than three drinks. He looked back at Combs.

"Did anyone else come to see her?"

"Earlier," Combs said. He took a notepad from his back pocket and looked at what he'd written. "Right after my shift started. Charles Lum — her estate lawyer. He was on the list."

"What list?"

"Last night, she gave us a list, people we could let in."

"Who was on it?"

"The daughter, Melissa Montgomery, and this guy Lum."

Mona either suspected or knew that her husband slept with his campaign manager. She could barely get herself to say the other woman's name. But now that Castelli was in the morgue, Melissa was one of three people allowed in Mona's room. Maybe she wanted Melissa for the same reason Cain did. She'd known Castelli the best. She had all the answers, right down to the combination that opened his office safe.

"How long was Lum with her?" Cain asked.

"An hour."

"And then she went straight to the bar?"

"Yes, sir."

Fischer stepped from the elevator at eight o'clock, the briefcase in her right hand. She nodded a greeting at Combs, then walked with Cain to the suite.

Alexa opened the door, and Cain had never seen her so thoroughly clothed. She wore a long-sleeved black dress, with tiny pearls sewn onto the pale collar. Black tights and patent leather heels. Her hair, still wet from a recent shower, was held back with a simple velvet headband. On her right wrist, she wore the Imogene Bass bracelet her father had given her. She looked like a prim fifth-grader on her way to a funeral, except that she was holding a glass of bourbon.

She looked at Cain for what seemed like a long time, and then turned to speak over her shoulder.

"Mom — it's Inspector Cain and his friend," she said. She whispered carefully, as though something behind her was cracked and her voice alone might shatter it. "That woman, Agent Fischer. Should I let them in?"

There was a murmur from inside the room, audible but incomprehensible. Alexa stepped back and opened the door. She brought up her glass and sipped the bourbon, wrinkling her nose when she swallowed.

Cain and Fischer stepped into the room and Alexa closed the door behind them. They were in the sitting room of a two-bedroom suite. A deep blue couch and two matching chairs were arranged to face a fireplace that probably hadn't seen a burning log since the Harding administration. Mona Castelli lay on the couch, eyes closed, the back of her wrist resting on her forehead. On the coffee table next to her was a bottle of Maker's Mark and an empty glass.

"I'm sorry to bother you so late," Fischer said.

"Can't this wait till morning?" Mona asked. She didn't open her eyes to speak.

"Inspector Cain and I thought you'd want to have some things from Harry's office," Fischer said.

"What things?"

"You knew about his safe?" Fischer asked.

"I don't know what he had in his office," Mona said. "I never went there."

"Not once, the whole time he was mayor?"

"I said I never went," Mona said. She used her hands against the couch cushions, pushing until she was sitting up.

Fischer sat in the chair nearest Mona's head. She pushed the bourbon bottle out of the way and set her briefcase on the coffee table but didn't open it. Mona sat looking at it, her eyes puffy, half focused.

Cain checked behind him.

Alexa stood by the door. She had her bourbon glass in one hand and a cell phone in the other. She was typing a text message with her left thumb. She finished her message and darkened the phone's screen. When she saw Cain watching her, she finished her drink in one long, easy swallow. Cain wondered who she'd be texting right now. There was Patricia, her nightshade-eyed friend. And there was the kid from the paintings, the one who occasionally slept over, though not often enough for Alexa to call him a boyfriend.

"What things?" Alexa asked. She crossed the room and sat opposite Fischer. "I went to his office. I saw the safe but never inside it."

"There were insurance policies and a will," Fischer said. "Also, some cash."

Before either of the Castellis could answer, Cain reached into his jacket and brought out a thick envelope. He set it on the coffee table. Alexa looked inside it, then pushed it across to her mother.

"Those are the originals," Cain said. "You'll want to give them to Mr. Lum. He'll know what to do with them."

He'd already made copies of the will and the insurance policies. He wasn't a lawyer, but he understood the gist. Both policies had two-year suicide riders, but Castelli had bought them ten years ago. Even if he'd put the gun in his mouth and willingly pulled the trigger, there was no bar to a payout. The riders were expired, and the companies would have to get out their checkbooks. The entire estate went to Mona, but she was only the trustee. Alexa was the true beneficiary and would come into everything when Mona died.

Mona looked in the envelope and thumbed weakly through the pages. She looked at Fischer.

"You said something about cash," she said. "The safe had cash?"

"I'll get to that," Fischer said. She put her hand on the briefcase. "But I wanted to ask you —"

"He never said anything about the safe."

"— if you've heard the name Lester Fennimore."

"Lester," Mona said. She looked at Alexa, who shook her head. "Lester Fennimore."

"You've heard the name?"

"He was someone Harry knew?" Mona asked.

"Are you saying that, or asking us?"

She combed her fingers through her hair, then rubbed at her eyes. Drunk, hungover, and no makeup on, but it didn't matter. She looked young. She had a nineteen-year-old daughter, but she was under forty, and she'd had unlimited cash since she was eighteen.

"Asking — saying. I don't know," Mona said. "The name sounds familiar."

"Someone Harry knew?"

"I don't know — yes. I think."

On the table, Alexa's phone lit up with an incoming text. She took it and put it in her lap, screen down. Cain watched her and watched the phone. He waited to see if she'd give some sign. A rise of color in her cheeks, a downward turn of her eyes. But she was too much like her father to reveal anything so easily. She reached across the table and took the bourbon bottle by its neck, then refilled her glass.

"You met him?" Fischer asked.

"Lester Fennimore?" Mona asked. "I don't think I ever met him. I think Harry might have talked about him."

"When?"

"That would've been years ago — before Alexa was born."

The way Mona had told it before, Alexa was born more or less nine months after she'd first gone to work for Harry Castelli. Their house — the house she'd moved into after dropping out of Stanford — had been twenty miles from the trailhead at Castle Rock State Park.

"Alexa was born when?" Cain asked.

"December 12, 1998," Alexa said.

Cain looked at her. She was still holding the phone on her lap, one hand on top of it like it might slip away. He turned back to Mona.

"And after she was born, you never heard about Lester Fennimore again?"

"Not that I remember," Mona said. "He might've said something, but I don't know. I was busy with a baby."

"Okay."

"What's this have to do with?" Mona asked. "Was it Lester who sent Harry the letter?"

"No," Fischer said. "It wasn't Lester. I think we can be pretty sure about that."

Cain's phone began to vibrate in his pocket. He slipped it out and looked at the screen. There wasn't anything Lieutenant Nagata needed from him right now that couldn't wait. He dropped the phone back into his pocket and let it go on silently ringing.

"Did you ever ask Harry about his tattoo?" Cain asked. "The Pi Kappa Kappa tattoo?"

"It was just something he got in college. A fraternity he joined for a while."

"Just a while?"

"He quit. He said after a couple years of partying, he finally got to know the guys. And he didn't like them."

"What do you mean, he didn't like them?" Cain asked.

"He said they scared him," Mona said. "He said they were bad news."

Cain caught Fischer's eyes, and he knew they were both thinking the same thing. Angela Chun's witness, the doctor up in Marin County, had said something similar. He'd told Chun that the Pi Kappa Kappa brothers had given him the creeps.

196

"Then why didn't he get that tattoo removed?" Cain asked. "It's not like he couldn't afford it."

"I don't know," Mona said. "I never asked."

"About that cash," Fischer said. "Does this room have a safe?"

"In the bedroom."

"You'll want to put it in there, probably."

Fischer laid the briefcase down and opened it. She began lifting out the bundled bills, setting them on the coffee table. The field office in L.A. must have repackaged them after scanning the serial numbers. Now the stacks were held together with color-coded currency straps. There were twenty-two bundles, each holding ten thousand dollars. Fischer closed the briefcase and set it on the floor next to her chair.

"What is that?" Mona asked.

"Two hundred and twenty thousand dollars."

"And it was Harry's?"

"He withdrew it from some of your banks last week," Fischer said. "We don't know why."

"Neither do I."

"These were joint accounts," Fischer said. "Yours and his. And you're in the will. So this is yours."

"Okay."

Fischer handed Mona a receipt. She must have had it written up by the same federal prosecutor she'd used for the last one.

"I need you to sign this, to acknowledge you received it from me. You can count the money first, if you want. We can wait."

"I don't need to count it."

Fischer gave Mona a pen, and she sat up enough to scrawl a signature across the bottom of the page. Alexa watched from behind the rim of her glass. She had taken her phone and put it behind her.

"You don't know why he took it out?" Cain asked. "No idea?"

"None."

He took a piece of paper from his pocket and unfolded it. He looked at it, reading through the list again, and then looked up. Mona and Alexa were watching him. He handed the sheet to Mona.

"This is a copy of a document we found in his safe," Cain said. "With the cash."

"Three addresses," Mona said. "Some dates."

"Those are banks in Chinatown," Cain said. "Three banks in three days. Does that mean anything to you?"

Mona looked at the page again, her eyes flicking back and forth as she read the three entries. In his pocket, his phone began to ring again, and he ignored it.

"It doesn't mean anything," she said. "I don't know what it is."

"But that's Harry's writing?"

"It's his."

Fischer stood up, the empty briefcase in her hand. She looked at the table.

"Put that in the safe," she said. "Before you go to sleep tonight. And then tomorrow, go put it back in the bank."

Mona nodded, but she wasn't looking at Fischer. She leaned across to the bottle of Maker's Mark and pulled the cork out. She poured herself a drink, then pushed the bottle toward her daughter.

26

HE WAS AT a red light behind the Century Theater on Mission Street, watching a crowd of moviegoers cross from the theater to the parking garage. The light turned green but the street was still blocked, and as he was waiting for the stragglers to make their way across, his phone rang again.

Nagata's name lit the screen.

He'd forgotten her other calls, had been too focused on Mona's answers and Alexa's furtive interest in her phone. He answered on speaker and dropped the phone into the console between the seats.

"This is Cain."

"And thank god," she said. She was out of breath. Men were shouting in the background. "Where are you?"

"On Mission, going home."

"Then I'll wait for you here."

"Where are you?"

"Standing in your apartment."

"My apartment? In Daly City?"

"You don't really live here, do you?" she said. "That's why it's half packed up."

"What are you doing in my apartment, Lieutenant Nagata?"

"You didn't answer your phone. So we thought —"

"What happened?"

"Grassley and Chun. About an hour ago, they — it looks like maybe they were seeing each other. That's why we found them the way —"

"You're not making any sense," Cain said. He pulled to the curb next to the Hotel Pickwick. A barefooted man with a bottle of wine crossed the street in front of him and stood a second in his head-lights to take a drink. "Start from the beginning."

"Chun called 911," Nagata said. "An hour ago. She could barely talk. She called from Grassley's place. She only got out two words, and then she passed out. *Help Cain.* That's it. The EMTs got there before us. The front door was open, so they went up the stairs —"

"Jesus, Nagata."

"You think I don't know?" she snapped. "You think I'm just Castelli's hack, and I don't get it?"

"I didn't say that."

"It's got to be the Castelli case," Nagata said. Calmer now, or trying hard to be. "It's the only one you were both on. We figure he followed one of them, then went inside and got both."

Cain took the phone from his ear and looked around.

The barefoot wino was crossing the intersection again, ducking through the traffic, attracted like a moth to the *Chronicle* building's white glow. He held the bottle by its neck, waving it over his head. Chun had called 911 but had passed out. His partner had been there but hadn't gotten on the line when she dropped the receiver. Cain was cold all over, and dizzy. He had to check the speedometer to make sure the car wasn't moving.

"Grassley?" he asked.

"There wasn't anything they could do. For Chun, maybe. They took her to UCSF. All they'd say is there's a chance."

"What happened?"

"It wasn't a gun," Nagata said. "A knife, for sure. And something else — a bat, a hammer. We don't know yet. This just happened, and we've been looking for you."

Ahead of him, an endless line of headlights came down Mission Street. He was falling, waiting to land. Trying to understand Nagata's words. Grassley was gone, and Chun was barely hanging on at UCSF. Someone had left her for dead, but she'd saved just enough of herself to make it to the phone. Her attacker must have been in a hurry. He had somewhere else to be, was so desperate to get there that he didn't stay around to see if Chun was finished.

"Cain?" Nagata asked. "Cain, did I lose you?"

There'd been a note on his windshield, a phone call to the restaurant's kitchen. They'd chased the tall kid up California Street, then lost him in the alley behind the Sutter Health medical building. There was only one way the kid could have known where to be with the note. He'd been following Cain all day. But Cain hadn't been to his apartment in Daly City that day, or any day since the first blackmail letter arrived. He'd been at Lucy's house. The tall kid had seen all that.

Cain dropped the car into first gear and peeled through the red light, pressing his hand on his horn, clearing the intersection without even checking for cross traffic.

"Cain?" Nagata was shouting. "Cain, what's going on?"

"If he'd been following me," Cain said, "he wouldn't know about my place. He'd know about Lucy's."

"Lucy's your girlfriend."

"She's on Twenty-Second Avenue," Cain said. "Between Fulton and Cabrillo."

He gave her the address, then slowed as he approached the next intersection. There was nothing coming up Sixth toward him, so he accelerated into the right turn. Whatever Nagata said next was lost to the engine. It was two blocks before he let off the gas, and then he was rolling toward Market at fifty miles an hour, his foot hovering above the brake but not touching it.

"Cain?"

"You got her address?" he said. "You're coming, with your guys?"

"I'm coming—but, Cain?"

"Say it."

"I remember that place; we went there. It's Lucy Bolet, isn't it? You started dating Lucy Bolet. The pianist, the one who was inside Ashbury Heights Elementary."

"Yeah."

"Oh, shit, Cain," she said. "We're coming."

"I'll be there first," he said. "When you get there, I'll be inside."

"Cain—"

He reached to the phone and hung up. Cain shot across Market, the gas pedal flat to the floor. He didn't even hear the sound of the horns until he was through the intersection, coming into the Tenderloin on Taylor Street at fifty miles an hour.

There was a standstill ahead, a bus stuck in the intersection. The driver stood behind the bus, looking up at the overhead catenary cables. He'd already set out a pair of red flares. Cain was three cars back. He switched on the LED flashers hidden behind his car's grille and laid his hand on the horn. Then he turned onto the sidewalk, no concern at all for his car's side-view mirrors and door panels, or for the city's newly planted trees. Their two-inch trunks, held upright

201

with staked wires, went beneath his front bumper one at a time until he came off the curb and crossed the intersection in the pedestrian walk. He saw one of his hubcaps spin away like a lost coin.

If he was driving like everything depended on it, it was because it did.

Cain stopped opposite Lucy's house, his car pointed downhill. He'd coasted the last block with the engine off, his headlights killed. He pulled the parking brake and stepped out, leaving the door open so there'd be no sound of it closing. He'd had sixty-two blocks, racing in the dark, to work it out. He'd sent Chun to Berkeley this morning to copy the murder book on the Pi Kappa Kappa fire, to find out what else she could about the underground brotherhood. That was before he'd even known about the unsolved murder of Lester Fennimore.

Now the Pi Kappa Kappa lead was the hottest thing he had going, but it was also the most dangerous. Chun might have run into any number of people today, asking about the fraternity and the fire. She'd have been talking to desk sergeants and detectives in two police departments. She might have gone to the university to see if the dean of students kept a file. Cain didn't know where she'd been or who she'd seen, but he had to consider this: Someone didn't like the questions she'd been asking. Somebody waited until she was gone, and then picked up the phone and made a call.

He crossed the street with his gun drawn, pausing at the steps that led up to Lucy's porch. Her front door was ajar. Blood was tracked on every other step leading up to it. There were treaded footprints, but he couldn't tell if they were coming or going. Every room of the house facing the street was dark.

Five soundless steps to the porch, the gun in both hands.

He came to the door and slipped sideways through it, then took a breath and looked down. There was blood on the floor, smears of it every four feet. He could hear sirens in the distance now. Nagata was coming with her men, but they were still twenty blocks away. He followed the blood. It tracked through the house to the music room. The French doors stood open, and there was sheet music spread across the floor. The man had stepped on it, had bloodied the score.

Cain went back to the front and climbed the stairs. There was blood there, too. Chun or Grassley must have fought. One of them must have managed a shot, or gotten the knife and used it to open up the guy's leg. Now his right shoe was full of blood, and he was tracking it everywhere he went. At the upstairs landing, the prints went back and forth down the hallway. In and out of the bedrooms, the bathroom.

The master bedroom was lit by the streetlamp outside. A long bar of light angled through the gap in the curtains and fell across the floor. The bed was unmade. The closet door was open. There was blood beneath the window, a small pool of it. He must have stood there a while, looking down at the street.

Maybe she had gone out, had been on one of her exploratory walks. He knelt at the foot of the bed and shone his flashlight underneath it. All he saw was the bare floor, the molding along the back wall under the head of their bed.

"Lucy?"

He stood and went to the closet. Outside, the sirens were getting louder. They were coming down Fulton, a deep phalanx of patrol cars racing toward him. He flicked on the closet light.

"Lucy?"

With his free hand, he checked behind the hanging clothes, the long dresses and the heavy coats. He felt nothing but the cedar-planked wall. He turned off the light, then left the bedroom and went down the hall. He cleared the empty guest bedroom and his closet. The third bedroom, which faced out over the back garden, was empty.

If she hadn't been on a walk, and if she wasn't in the house now, there was only one possibility. But he couldn't think about that yet. He wouldn't let himself until he finished checking the house.

Coming into the bathroom, he immediately felt a change in temperature. It was warmer in here, and he could smell the bath water. He switched on his flashlight again. The tub was full, steam still rising from it. There was a bottle of shampoo floating on the water's surface. The floor was wet and the white bathmat was stained red.

She hadn't been on a walk.

She'd been in the bath, and he'd come in on her. He had shoved through the door and found her, here, where she was the most vulnerable, where —

"Gavin?"

It was just a whisper, from behind him. He turned around. Now he was facing the sink, the mirror behind it so fogged up from the bathwater that his own image was just a blur. Everything that had been on the counter around the basin had been knocked to the floor. There was blood on the wall, blood on the hand towel hanging in the chrome ring by the door.

But the voice had come from inside the room.

He crouched at the cabinet beneath the sink and pulled the two doors open. He wouldn't have thought Lucy could fit in here. Yet there she was, curled behind the sink's U-bend drain.

She blinked against the flashlight beam, then reached for his hand.

He holstered his gun. She was naked, and still wet from the bath. But there was no blood on her at all. She reached for his hand, squeezing his fingers so hard it hurt.

"Gavin — is he gone?"

"You can come out of there," he said. "But stay in this room."

She didn't move.

"Lucy — I'm sorry. I'm so sorry."

He let go of her hand and got his phone. Nagata answered on the first ring. He already knew where she was. The sirens were right outside the house.

27

HE TURNED ON the porch light and stood outside at the top of the steps with his badge in his left hand as the line of patrol cars came down the hill and stopped in front of the house. Nagata came out first. Eight other officers followed her. There was Frank Lee, from the Homicide Detail, and the rest of them were patrol officers he didn't recognize. None of them had his gun drawn, which meant Nagata must have gotten on the radio as soon as she'd hung up with him.

"There's blood," a young cop said.

"I see it," she said. "Wait down here."

She came up the stairs, avoiding the bloody footprints, and stood with Cain near the door. She looked into the house, then at Cain.

"She's upstairs," he said. "In the bathroom. Hiding under the sink where I found her."

"She's lucky," Nagata said. "That's twice now."

"I'm not taking another chance with her," Cain said. "Not like this. She can't live this way. Have your men check the whole thing again. I still haven't gone in the basement or the garage."

He started to go back into the house.

"Cain—"

"We'll talk in the living room," Cain said. "You and Frank and me."

But before he talked to Nagata, he went upstairs. He took clothes from her closet and brought them into the bathroom. He shut the door, then rolled up the bloody bath mat and set it aside. He used the ruined hand towel to clean up the rest of the blood from the wall and the countertop, and then he sat down in front of the cabinet and opened the doors.

Lucy looked out at him, her eyes the color of wet slate.

"I'll help you out of there," he said.

She reached for his hand and he helped lift her from behind the drainpipe and out of the cabinet. He pulled her onto his lap and reached into the cabinet again for a clean towel to put around her. She was shivering with cold or fear, and her skin was covered in goose bumps.

"He wasn't looking for you," Cain said. "He was looking for me."

She put her arms around him and held him tightly.

"This won't happen again," he said. "I promise you that."

"What do we do?" she whispered. "We can't stay here, can we?"

"We can't. We won't."

"I saw him," she said. "Through the crack in the doors."

"What did he look like?"

"He was tall. And hurt. Bleeding all down his leg."

"Did you see his face?"

"He was too tall," she said. She was whispering into the side of his neck. "He stood right here. He was throwing things. I saw his hand —the only skin I saw. He was white. I thought he'd open the cabinet and find me. I was sure he'd find me."

He held on to her, not wanting to press her with any more questions, but knowing he had to.

"Did it sound like it was just the one guy, or did he have someone else?"

"Just one."

If there had been two, they would have talked to each other, and she would have heard them. And even if they hadn't talked, their footsteps would have given them away.

"How long between when he left and when I came home?"

"Not long," she said.

He waited for her to go on, for her to play the memory back and answer his question with precision. She had a perfect sense of time and cadence, knew the length of every note and every rest. At the Ashbury Heights Elementary trial, she had taken the stand before Matt Redding, and Cain had been sitting at the prosecution's table, watching. The cross-examination turned on her ability to recall the timing of shots in a span of five minutes. How long had she spent kneeling under the stairs, using her body to shield the twenty children she'd silently gathered and rushed into that crawlspace? When, exactly, did she put her hand over the crying boy's mouth, clamping so hard to silence him that his lips bled onto her palm and he passed out in her arms?

Lucy was tapping her finger against his back, measuring her time in the dark.

"He left and went down the stairs," Lucy said. "And then you came in. Two and a half minutes."

From downstairs, Nagata's men began to call out as they'd cleared the basement and the garage. Through the bathroom window, Cain heard another officer in the back garden. The blood tracked out the basement door, through the flower beds, and over the back fence. Then Nagata was on the radio, asking for backup, every available unit. She wanted to saturate the avenues, go door-to-door. She needed a CHP helicopter to sweep from above with a searchlight; someone needed to bring dogs.

Cain held Lucy back from him so he could see her face.

"Can you get dressed?"

"Yes."

"I've got to talk to Nagata," Cain said. "I want you to pack a bag. Whatever you need."

"For how long?"

"A week, to start."

She nodded, then used his shoulders to push herself up.

When he came downstairs, Fischer was sitting at the dining room table with Nagata and Frank Lee. A department photographer was setting up lights in the music room to take pictures of the blood-stamped sheet music spread across the floor. Sumida came in the front door, nodded to Cain, and led a team of three technicians down to the basement. Red and blue lights pulsed through the open door and the windows. There was probably half a liter of blood in the house and outside. Plenty for CSI to work with, but they wouldn't get anywhere if the tall kid's DNA hadn't already been uploaded to a searchable database.

Cain pulled out the chair across from Nagata and sat.

"Who shot him—Chun or Grassley?"

"We don't know," she said.

"How is it possible you don't know that?"

"Because he took their weapons," Nagata said. "There was one forty-caliber casing in the bedroom. So one of them got off a shot, but we don't know which."

"You put out a notice to all the hospitals?"

"Of course."

Fischer was looking at the blood below the wainscoting on the dining room wall. He must have stumbled into it. Judging from how high up the wall it was, the wound was above his knee. Maybe it had nicked his femoral artery and he'd hole up in someone's backyard and bleed to death. That would be the best thing, even if it meant they couldn't sit him down in a windowless room and ask him questions. Better that he die with his secrets than spend another hour on his feet with a pair of police-issue guns and nothing on his mind but murder.

"We need a safe house," Cain said to Fischer. "Somewhere Lucy and I can stay until this is over."

"I called as soon as I heard, and they're setting them up," she said. "Two apartments, side by side."

"We just need one."

"I'll be next door," Fischer said. "If they came for you, they could come for me."

He wasn't thinking straight, and it was showing. Nagata hadn't said anything about taking him off the case, but it might still be coming. She couldn't pull him until she talked to the new mayor, and she didn't have an open channel the way she used to. Now there was a chain of command to work through, and that gave him a day or two of leeway before anything changed. That could be enough, if he pushed hard enough. And if he stayed on track right now, she might not even go to the mayor.

He turned to Nagata.

"Lucy saw him, when he came in. Not his face, but his body. He's tall, like the guy Chun and I chased. Caucasian. And he was here less than ten minutes ago."

In the kitchen, the china cabinet began to rattle, and overhead, the chandelier's dangling crystals started to shiver. The CHP helicopter was hovering directly above the house. The pilot switched on his spotlight and suddenly the garden was lit up like home plate on a game night.

"If he came in the front and left over the back fence, he might've ditched his car. Or someone else drove him here from Grassley's place," he said. "If that person was waiting—"

But Nagata stopped him, shaking her head.

"He didn't get a ride—he came in Grassley's car. It's parked out

208

front. Three spots down from yours. The driver's seat is covered in blood."

"Then we'll find him," Frank Lee said. Above them, the helicopter veered off and began to sweep the backyards. The rattling stopped in the kitchen, but the chandelier was still moving, making the shadows dance. "He's on foot, with a bullet in his leg."

"Ten minutes ago he was on foot," Cain said. "But now he's got two guns, a knife, and nothing to lose. He just killed a cop — two cops, as far as he knows. He's got to have found a car to use, which means he's either got a hostage or there's another dead body."

Frank looked at the table, then nodded.

"Lieutenant, you need to get on the radio," Frank said. He slid a handheld unit across to her. "Throw up some roadblocks, lock up this neighborhood. And we've got to watch the bridges — these guys, once they get wheels, they always head for the bridges."

Half an hour passed and they hadn't heard anything, and by then Cain knew they wouldn't. The officers in the backyard followed the blood over the garden fence, and then through a series of yards. They called out each find over the radio, and Cain and Fischer leaned close to Nagata's handheld unit on the dining table.

Dark blood dribbled along a neighbor's steppingstone path. In the white beams of the officers' flashlights, the icy petals of chamomile flowers were spattered. Red streaks and shoeprints ran up the face of a mossy redwood fence and into the next yard. They hopped that fence and found more of the same, and they followed the trail until it brought them out between two houses on Cabrillo. They crossed the sidewalk, following blood between two parked cars at the curb. And then, in the middle of the street, as if their quarry had simply evaporated, there was nothing.

Cain looked up from the radio. The tall kid had a car, and he was gone.

28

KAREN FISCHER'S PEOPLE came in a line of three unmarked
SUVs that picked their way through the parked patrol cars and
stopped directly in front of the house. Cain carried Lucy's suitcase
down the steps as she walked alongside him. Including their trip to
the courthouse for her testimony in the Ashbury Heights trial, it was
only the second time they'd been outside the house together. They
climbed into the back of the middle vehicle. Fischer took the front
seat, next to the driver. When they were moving, going up the hill
and through the SFPD roadblock at the top of Twenty-Second Avenue, she turned around.

"The apartments are secure — nothing safer in the city, unless we
stayed in Alcatraz," she said. She waited until Lucy was looking at
her. "You're going to be just fine."

"What about Gavin? The man was looking for him, not me. The
apartment's safe, but he's not going to be there the whole time, is he?"

"We'll be careful," Fischer said. "We'll work together, Gavin and
me. Like partners. We'll have each other's backs."

Lucy reached over and took Cain's hand but didn't look at him.
Her head was turned to the left. She was watching the helicopter
carve a grid pattern through the sky north of Fulton. Its searchlight
probed downward, lighting the tiny drops of windblown rain.

It wasn't until they made the last turn to the safe house that Cain understood where they were going. They'd taken the bridge out of the
city to the U.S. Coast Guard station on Yerba Buena Island.

The apartments, which must really have been barracks, were in
a low building that faced a small, puddle-strewn parading ground.
Past that, and a jumble of rocks dumped long ago in a protective sea-

wall, was the bay. He put Lucy's suitcase on the bed and then stood next to her by the little window. The curtains had faded to the color of sand but might once have been orange. Lucy pushed them back, and they looked out together. The grounds below were dark, and no one was outside. They hadn't seen anyone at all except the guards at the gate. There were no boats tied up along the quay, though there seemed to be enough docking space for several. Rain pooled on the empty concrete piers. Maybe all the guardsmen were on patrol.

Across the bay, the port of Oakland blinked in and out of the fog. Four-legged cranes with their long necks, ships tied up underneath them as they gave up their loads of Chinese cargo.

"I brought a couple of books," Lucy said. "Thick ones."

"That was a good idea."

"You'll be careful?"

"I promise."

"Are you going back to the house?"

"I'll probably have to."

He might have to go for the investigation; he might have to go because he hadn't thought to pack anything for himself. Not even a toothbrush.

"The back of my calendar has a list of all my students. Their parents' phone numbers."

"I'll call them."

"But don't say what happened," Lucy said. "Or they'll never come back."

He nodded and reminded himself to call Frank Lee. He'd seen the calendar on the music room floor, with blood on it. It probably wasn't in the house anymore. But Frank could pull it from the evidence boxes and make the calls.

The bed was just wide enough for the two of them if they slept on their sides, spooned together. That would be okay. There was a little desk, built into the wall. Next to it was a chest of drawers with a small TV on top of it, the kind with a bunny-ear antenna set on top. He wasn't sure if it would work or not, but it didn't matter. They wouldn't turn it on.

The sink in the bathroom was bolted straight to the wall, the pipes hanging down underneath. Rust showed in scratches at the bottom of the shallow bath. The walls were made of dark-paneled press-board; the light came from a bare sixty-watt incandescent bulb.

He came back and sat on the end of the little bed, next to Lucy.

"What do you have to do now?" she asked.

"Find him."

"But how?"

He thought about that. He thought about Grassley, who was probably in the basement beneath 850 Bryant Street by now. Grassley hadn't liked to be alone down there, but he would be tonight, until Dr. Levy's assistants came in and moved him to the steel table. On the ride from the city, Nagata had called to update them on Chun's status. She was out of surgery, but her brain was swelling. She'd been hit in the head with something. A hammer, a bat. The butt of her own gun, after it had been taken from her. They still didn't know, and Chun was in no position to tell them. The last Nagata had heard, the doctors were debating whether or not to induce a coma.

Cain had only just been getting to know both of them, was just figuring out what each of them had to offer. And he'd overlooked so much, even though it had been right there for him to see. He'd ascribed no significance to the way Grassley always waited for Chun, walked alongside her. It had been right there for him to pick up, but that was true for everything. All of the evidence was sitting in plain sight, waiting to be recognized.

"Gavin?" Lucy said. "What are you going to do?"

"I don't know."

There was a tap on the door. A pause, then two more taps.

Cain got off the bed and walked to the door, then bent down to look through the peephole — Fischer. He let her in, then sat down on the bed again, gesturing for her to take the chair at the built-in desk.

"I'll knock tomorrow morning," she said. "Six thirty. They're bringing my car over, so we'll use that."

"Okay."

"We'll do this, Cain."

"Okay."

"Every day, we get a little closer. Tomorrow, even more."

"What about Lucy?" Cain asked. "She'll need to eat, and there's nothing here."

There was no kitchenette in the room, not even a mini fridge or a

212

plastic cup in the bathroom. If she wanted water, she'd have to drink straight from the tap.

"Downstairs, on the other side of the quad, there's a cafeteria. There are signs pointing the way."

"It'll be open?"

"They do coffee and sandwiches all night—for dispatch, for the fast boat crews," Fischer said. "Breakfast starts at seven."

"She can walk the grounds and no one will bother her?"

"There's no place safer."

"You've stayed here before."

"Twice," she said. She looked at Lucy. "It's not bad. If you go in the cafeteria, you'll find people to talk to, if you want. But if you'd rather be left alone, they'll do that."

"They know why I'm here?"

"Yes."

"That's all they know about me?"

"That's it."

"Okay."

He swung his feet to the floor and sat looking around the unfamiliar room in the dark.

It was only when he stood up and walked to the window, feeling the pilled carpet underfoot, that he remembered what this place was and why they were here. His skin was still damp with sweat from the dream that had woken him. He pulled back the curtains and let in the little bit of light that came across from Oakland. Then he turned around and looked at the room again. He saw the rising curve of Lucy's hip, saw the way her hair spilled across the one pillow. There was a thin bar of greenish light coming from beneath the door, and he could hear the mercury-vapor lamp buzzing in the outdoor hallway.

It was just after three in the morning.

Of course there was no safe in this room. Before going to bed, he'd pulled the magazine from his gun and left the two pieces in separate desk drawers. He checked it now, his fingers on the cold metal in the dark. Then he stood close to the glass, inside the space of chilled air that had built up between the curtains and the pane. He told himself that when he stopped sweating, he'd go back to bed.

"Gavin?"

"I'm sorry."

"You were dreaming," she said. "You can't help that."

He got in next to her.

"I thought you slept through them."

"Not always." She put her arm across his chest. "You've only got a few hours. Three and a half. Not much time."

"So what are you saying?"

"Use it wisely."

She went back to sleep and he lay awake under the heat of her arm. She didn't wear a watch, and there was no clock in the room. If she knew how much time was left until Fischer knocked, it was because her brain's metronome went on clicking, even as she slept.

He woke with just enough time to take a shower and dress before Fischer arrived. He was standing in front of the mirror, fixing the knot in his tie, when he heard Fischer in the walkway outside. He turned off the bathroom light, collected his gun, and went outside quietly so that Lucy could go on sleeping.

The morning sky was purple and black. He thought it had been chilly inside the little Coast Guard apartment, but it was cold enough out here to see Fischer's breath when she spoke.

"We'll check out the cafeteria, get some coffee. Then you'll see it and know she'll be okay here."

"I trust you," he said. "We don't have to check it just for me."

"Still," Fischer said. She began to walk and he followed her. "The coffee's not the worst. And it's free."

They headed down a set of cement steps that he hardly remembered climbing last night, to a path that traversed the back end of the quad.

"How're you holding up?" she asked him.

"Okay," he said.

He hadn't known Grassley well, but he'd liked him. And if this hadn't happened, they would have come to know each other like brothers. He'd been looking forward to that. Not just to arriving at the point of complete trust, but also to the long road they'd have walked to get there. The years of lunches at the Western; the late-night coffee in Mel's or at Lori's. All of it would have been worthwhile.

214

They reached the cafeteria, and he held the door for Fischer.

"The autopsy's this morning," he said. "It's at nine, and I'd like to go."

"Of course."

They were up early, and there was enough time between their coffee and the autopsy to run one other errand. They walked to Fischer's car, each of them carrying a paper cup, and Cain told her about the girl in the casket. He told her about Fonteroy's video, and how he and Grassley had followed it to the grave in El Carmelo. He hadn't meant to share this with her until he had more proof, but now he didn't have a choice. As of last night, he had no partner.

"You were standing next to the excavator when you got the call from Nagata?" Fischer asked.

"That's right."

"And you think the girl in the casket could be the girl in the pictures?"

"We might find that out today, if Henry Newcomb did his job and got a lab."

"So the very moment you found the girl, but before you could open the casket, you got a call. You got reassigned to the blackmail case," Fischer said. "We're supposed to think that's a coincidence?"

"I don't know."

"Of course it's not."

"That's where I am," Cain said. "But I can't figure out what it means. Castelli asked Nagata for a name and got me. He wanted the best inspector in the department, and somehow that's me."

"Who told him?"

"Nagata."

They walked through the half-empty parking lot in silence until they reached Fischer's car. Cain got into the passenger seat.

"We'll need to think about this," Fischer said. "We'll need to think about it very carefully."

"You think it was her."

"I'm not saying that."

"Good," Cain said. "Because Nagata wouldn't be in on something like that. It makes no sense. If Castelli had stayed mayor forever, she would've been the chief of police. If he'd gone back to Washington, or become governor — no telling where she could've gone. But when he died, her star set. If Nagata picked me, it's because I've got the most seniority in Homicide. That's it."

"Which is why we need to think," Fischer said. "Someone wanted SFPD on the blackmail case. That means someone knew that SFPD already had the casket."

"Maybe we're looking at it the wrong way," Cain said. "We're asking: Why did they want me on the blackmail case? But what if that's the wrong question?"

"What's the right one?"

He chose his words carefully, articulating the question for the first time.

"Why did they send the blackmail letter right after I got the exhumation order? Keep in mind, the court's order was a public document. The minute I got it, anyone keeping an eye out would have known."

As Fischer drove past the guard booth, Cain leaned over to see if the man inside was awake. He was upright and alert, and his uniform was crisp. Cain tipped him a two-fingered wave, and then they were on the road that wound around the bluffs, snaking toward the west side of the island to reach the bridge on-ramp.

"That's brilliant," Fischer said. "That's the question."

"You think?"

"They blackmailed Castelli after they knew the body was coming up—because, what if they knew something about the body was going to lead back to him?"

"Then they'd only have a narrow window," Cain said. "If they made it look like he shot himself right before all that came out—a girl in a casket, buried alive—who'd look twice?"

"We nearly didn't," Fischer said. "It almost had us."

"They had to get the ball rolling before we arrested him, or else they wouldn't be able to reach him. They weren't blackmailing him at all. They meant to kill him, and the letter was just cover."

"But what would be on the body?" Fischer asked. "Thirty years underground, what would connect him?"

He looked over at Fischer. He'd forgotten how much he'd kept back from her.

"She was pregnant."

"You think it's his."

"That's what we're going to find out."

She sped up and steered around the curving ramp until they merged onto the bridge. Then the city was stretched out in front of them, the steep hills and the lights glittering against a dark dawn.

29

THEY PARKED ON Bay Street and looked across at Henry New-comb's house. There were no lights burning in the living room, but above it, one window on the top floor was lit. It must have been a kid's bedroom. The master suite would likely be in the back, over-looking the garden.

They got out of the car and crossed the street, then climbed the narrow steps up to Henry's front door. Cain skipped the doorbell and used his fist. Knocking like a beat cop, like Grassley. They waited and listened, and then they heard light feet running down the stairs. The door opened four inches and stopped on its chain.

A pair of small boys' faces looked out from the level of the door-knob. One of them was hyperalert, studying Cain with interest. The other was shy and wary.

"Who are you?" the curious one asked.

Cain took his inspector's star and held it for the boy to see.

"Gavin Cain, SFPD," he said. "I'm here to see your father."

"His father, not mine," the boy said. "This is David Newcomb. I'm his friend, Ross Carver. I don't live here."

Henry's son looked out and said nothing. Then he withdrew from the cracked door and went away. He called out softly from the foot of the stairs.

"Dad?"

When he didn't get an answer, he climbed out of sight and called again.

"Do you like being a cop?" the other boy asked Cain.

"It's okay."

"That's what I'm going to do," the boy said. "When I'm old. I think it looks better than just okay."

"You want to catch the bad guys."

"Or shoot them."

"It's a lot of paperwork, shooting them," Cain said. "So it's better just to catch them."

"Did you ever have to shoot a guy?"

"Once," Cain said.

He looked through the crack in the door, behind the boy. Henry's son was still upstairs, and he thought he could hear Henry and his wife speaking with their child.

"Did he die?" the boy asked, and Cain turned back to him.

"He was fine," Cain said. He was going to leave it at that, but both the boy and Fischer were watching him, waiting for him to explain. "I shot him in the leg and the arm. Twice in the arm."

"On purpose?" the boy asked.

Cain nodded. "I wanted to arrest him."

"What did he do?"

"Why did I shoot him? Or what did he do after I shot him?"

"Both."

"He was a very bad guy," Cain said. This was now the longest conversation he'd ever had on this topic outside of a courtroom. But he didn't mind. It was good practice, talking to a kid about things like this. "He'd walked into a school, the man I shot. He went in so he could hurt a bunch of kids. And five of the teachers. And then he left before we could catch him. It took us four years to figure out who he was and track him down."

The man had done a lot more than hurt the children and the teachers at Ashbury Heights. He'd been shooting to kill. And afterward, when he'd run out of bullets, he'd walked through a shattered window and across the playground. He'd hopped a low chainlink fence and then disappeared. The original inspectors hadn't gotten anywhere, and the worst crime in the city's memory landed on Cain's desk as a cold case. He'd taken the grainy security footage to Menlo Park and met Matt Redding in his threadbare office. In less than a week, he was knocking on Lucy's door with Nagata, the district attorney, and a picture of the guy cuffed to a hospital bed.

But he didn't need to go into all that with this kid, this aspiring homicide inspector.

"You got him, though," the boy said. "You finally found him, and you shot him."

"That's right."

"And what did he do?"

"He cried out, fell down. He tried to grab his gun off the floor, but before he could, I rolled him over and cuffed him."

"That's what I want to do," the boy said. "Just like that."

Henry finally came down and sent the boys back upstairs, and Cain heard a television turn on up there. Then the three of them sat down in the living room. Henry was wearing a terry-cloth bathrobe, and his hair stuck out above his ears. He hadn't shaved in at least three days.

"I haven't written it up yet," he said. "It was a late night."

"You got time in a lab."

"I did. I started with the girl," Henry said. "You wanted to know what she had in her system when she died. You ever heard of a drug called Thrallinex? It came off the market before it ever made much of a name for itself."

Fischer looked at Cain.

"It's what you were looking for," Henry said. "Isn't it?"

"They took a picture of her, before she went into the coffin. They were about to force-feed her a dozen tablets of Thrallinex, the ten-milligram pills. Does that sound about right?"

"It fits."

"What about Castelli?"

"That was a lot easier. If he hadn't shot himself, he might've died from the alcohol and the zolpidem tartrate —"

"Zolpidem what?" Fischer asked.

"— otherwise known as Ambien," Henry said. He looked at Cain. "What was it he liked to drink?"

"Maker's Mark," Cain said.

"That's right," Henry said. "Now I remember."

Castelli had appointed Henry, and then after things had gone south for Henry, he'd asked for his resignation. But Henry had been in Castelli's orbit long enough that he would have seen the man drink.

"How loaded was he?" Cain asked.

"He'd had enough to do the job without the gun — it's a wonder he was conscious to pull the trigger."

"It's a wonder," Cain said. He looked at Fischer. "Isn't it?"

"Sure."

"And the last part?" Cain asked. "The DNA?"

"That tied it all together," Henry said. "The samples you gave me — you had an entire family in the cooler. The mother, who suffocated in a casket. The father, who shot himself in the head. And their child — it was a girl, if you care — who died in the womb."

"So it was his."

"It was his."

"You can write it up for me?"

"Sure, but what for? You can't use it anywhere. And the labs you're waiting on, they'll tell you the same thing when they get around to it."

"All right," Cain said. He stood up, and so did Fischer. "Forget we came here."

"I will, after I send you my bill."

30

THEY ARRIVED AT the station an hour ahead of the autopsy, so he took Fischer up to the sixth floor, and they went into his office. Grassley had left a stack of files on his chair, and Cain put them on the floor so Fischer could sit.

"You've got a theory," Fischer said. "You've known about the girl longer than me, so you're a step ahead. Tell me a story that makes all of it fit."

Cain swiveled toward the window and twisted the rod that worked the blinds, to shut out the gray daylight.

"It has to start with Castelli getting caught up with Pi Kappa Kappa," Cain said. "By the time he was a pledge, they'd gone underground. They must have been into something."

"The skin trade," Fischer said. "Human traffic."

"Maybe the girl was someone they wanted to punish. She broke a rule, she tried to break free. They made it into a party and took pictures."

"But you've got to account for at least eight weeks between the rape and the burial," Fischer said. "She was a couple months along with his baby. Unless the night in the pictures wasn't his first time with her, or it was someone else in the shots."

"Maybe he kept her chained to the bed for eight weeks. The DNA says it was his baby," Cain said. "We've got a picture of a man raping her, and Melissa Montgomery — who's seen him naked — couldn't rule him out. So let's say it was him, and let's say he helped put her in the casket."

"Okay."

"Then he started worrying about it," Cain said. "And he got especially worried after a different girl got away — the one MacDowell found in the alley behind the funeral home. Which meant the fire at the Grizzly Peak frat house was convenient. Everyone who died that night was probably there when the photographs got taken."

"You think Castelli set that fire?"

"You asked me to tell a story that puts everything together," Cain said. "That's what I'm trying to do. I don't know if it's true or not — it just fits."

"Go on."

"So Castelli gets on with his life. He goes to London and does some consulting. When his dad loses the ambassadorship, he comes back to California and gets his MBA. Things are looking up after that, and he's in San Jose making real money."

"And then Lester Fennimore comes along," Fischer said. "His old frat brother."

"Maybe he wants to talk to Castelli about the girl, or the fire."

"Or both."

"So Castelli agrees to meet him," Cain said. "They want a quiet spot — Castle Rock State Park fits the bill. Especially after dark. But Castelli doesn't go there to talk. He's got his thirty-eight, and either he's wearing gloves or he brought a rag to wipe everything down."

"Then who's the blackmailer?" Fischer asked. "And why now?"

"Well, it wasn't really blackmail," Cain said. "Castelli thought the same thing. They weren't asking for money. They were pressuring him to kill himself — which might've just been cover for a plan to kill him. But what if before that, they'd been shaking him down for years?"

"The money in his safe," Fischer said. "You think he was going to pay it to them. But then something changed, and they just wanted him dead."

"What changed was me," Cain said. "I got the exhumation order. And then the secret they'd been holding over him all this time was about to come into the open. They wanted Castelli dead before we could arrest him and make him talk."

"But who are they?"

"If we're right," Cain said, "not everyone who knew about the pictures died in the Grizzly Peak fire. Lester Fennimore lived to the late 1990s. There could be others."

"So you think it's a Pi Kappa Kappa brother."

Cain nodded.

"I think that's what got Grassley killed, what put Chun in the hospital — she was out there, in Berkeley, asking about Pi Kappa Kappa. Someone got scared and decided to shut us down."

At nine o'clock, they buzzed into the secure area behind the reception desk in the ME suite, and soon he was standing next to Rachel Levy in front of a portable cold storage chamber, a quad unit that held four bodies. The door on the top right was Grassley's compartment. Cain looked behind him and nodded to Nagata. Then he took the evidence key from Dr. Levy and unlocked the chamber. He opened the door and rolled the cadaver tray out on its sliders. He and Jim Braun took the head, and Dr. Levy and Frank Lee took the feet. They moved Grassley's tray onto the cart and rolled him into the autopsy suite.

Cain stood back with Nagata and Fischer and watched Dr. Braun pull the sheet off. The natural instinct, the human impulse, would be to turn away from the sight of his dead friend. But when the sheet came off, Cain didn't even let himself blink.

Grassley was naked, his skin pale with death. His mouth was open and his tongue bulged out, as if he'd been choking for air as he died. His throat was cut from ear to ear, a toothless second mouth that opened beneath his chin. One of the morgue assistants had washed the body already, and the only blood was around the wound itself. The edges were clean, the layers of tissue visible. Cain didn't need Dr. Levy to tell him that it had been an unusually sharp blade.

Next to him, Lieutenant Nagata took his hand, gripping it hard. He pressed back, and didn't let go, but never took his eyes from Grassley. Dr. Levy was speaking into her hanging microphone, but he wasn't listening. He looked at Grassley's hands. There were no cuts or bruises on the knuckles, no blade slashes on his forearms or outer wrists. He hadn't thrown any punches, hadn't picked up a defensive wound fending off the knife. But on the right side of his neck, and on his shoulder, there were dozens of small cuts. Most of them had barely gone deep enough to draw blood.

Cain let go of Nagata's hand and stepped around so that he was standing behind Grassley's head.

"What are these?" he said, interrupting Dr. Levy's narration of the surface examination.

She stepped back, then nodded at Jim Braun. He hit a switch on the wall, which paused the recorder.

"What were you pointing to?"

Cain pointed again at the clusters of blade marks on Grassley's neck. Frank Lee came around and studied the cuts. He wrote something in his notebook, then flipped the page.

"These aren't from a fight. They're too shallow," Frank Lee said. "And look at them — they're parallel. All the blade marks are side by side."

Grassley was Frank's case now. They would pursue their investigations separately, and if they came together and landed on the same person, so much the better.

"Superficial pressure cuts," Dr. Levy said.

"How'd they get there?"

"Hold a blade against your arm sometime. Press down, but don't pull it back and forth. We're not talking about a slicing wound."

Fischer asked the next question for Cain.

"If a right-handed man was standing behind him, holding a knife on his neck — threatening, waving the blade around and then putting it back — you'd get marks like this?"

"Yes."

"It was a hostage situation," Fischer said. "Maybe even a standoff. Chun had the gun, and the guy had Grassley."

"That must be it," Frank said. He wrote something else in his notebook. "That's what happened."

"Can I start again?" Dr. Levy asked.

Cain nodded to Dr. Braun, and he hit the wall switch to resume the recording. Dr. Levy continued her surface examination, but Cain wasn't paying attention anymore. There was something about the pressure wounds he didn't like. They didn't make sense, didn't fit some piece of the story he'd been telling Fischer.

He was sure that he'd just hit on something important. But that kind of certainty never lasted long.

"Cain?" Fischer said. "Did you hear her?"

"What?"

"Back up," she whispered. "She's going to open him up now."

He looked at her, not understanding at first. He was too far away from this, grasping too hard at the solution he thought he'd glimpsed.

Then he saw Dr. Levy standing over Grassley with the autopsy saw, and he understood. He wasn't wearing any protective gear. No lab coat over his suit, no safety glasses, no mask. They didn't want him standing here when Dr. Levy put the blade against Grassley's navel and started cutting.

When it was over, he went with Nagata and Fischer and they sat on a smoking bench that faced a chainlink fence and the San Francisco County Jail. None of them smoked, but that didn't matter. They just needed to sit. A strong wind funneled between the jail and the Hall of Justice, and it carried a hard spatter of rain. That didn't matter either.

"I'd like to go see Chun," Cain said. "Can you get me in?"

"She's not out of it yet."

"But can you get me in?"

"I can try," Nagata said.

"That's all I want."

Mount Sutro loomed behind the UCSF Medical Center, its radio tower cutting through the low clouds that were piling against the heights. They rode the elevator up to the intensive care unit, and Fischer hung back with Cain while Nagata talked to the nurse at the triage desk.

"Three minutes," Nagata said when she came back. "And just you."

"All right."

Cain crossed the hall to Chun's room and opened the door. She lay on an angled bed. There were intravenous tubes running into a port on her forearm, oxygen tubes in her nose. Catheter lines ran from beneath the blue sheets, and he saw a urine bag hanging from the end of the bed, its contents the color of weak coffee. Her face and head were bandaged, and it looked like half her hair had been shaved off so the doctors could examine her head wound. There was a line of staples and sutures from her left ear to the base of her throat. The vascular surgeon must have gone through the existing knife wounds to repair her damaged carotid artery.

Cain pulled up a chair and sat next to her. He opened his briefcase and took the gunshot residue field kit he'd brought from his office. He opened the package and put on the gloves that were inside it, then ripped open the cotton swab's foil envelope.

"You hang in there, Angela," he said. "We need you back."

He took her right hand and gently swabbed it, getting the webbing between her thumb and forefinger and the backs of her knuckles. He opened the plastic box and put the swab in, and squeezed the ampule of reactive agent, feeling the thin glass break inside the plastic dropper. He dripped the reactant onto the cotton and then closed the box. He held Angela's hand and waited for the swab to develop. Her skin was cold and there was no reaction at all to his touch. It wasn't like touching a sleeping woman. He thought of the photographs of the drugged girl, the shape she'd taken after the Thrallinex took her.

When he looked through the lensed lid again a moment later, he saw the fine blue specks that had appeared on the surface of the swab, and he knew what they meant.

"You did just fine, Angela," he whispered to her. "You got him high in the leg. He's holed up somewhere, and he's hurting worse than you."

When he let go of her hand, her fingers stayed curled in the same position. He had to look at the flickering green line of her pulse on the EKG to be sure she wasn't dead.

For a moment, in the crowded elevator heading down to the street level, he thought again of the shallow cuts on Grassley's neck. The gunshot residue on Chun's right hand, which meant the single .40 caliber round on the floor had come from her gun.

Something didn't match. He was sure there was a flaw in his story. But once the elevator doors slid open and he'd followed Fischer through the main entrance of the hospital, out into a cold gray noon, he wasn't sure of anything anymore.

"Where to now?" Fischer said.

He didn't know. He wanted to go back to Yerba Buena Island, back to the safe room on the Coast Guard's fenced-off lot. He wanted to put his arms around Lucy and spend all afternoon watching the wind stir up the bay. But he had to keep up the initiative. They had to keep moving, or they'd sink.

"Let's go to Union Square," Cain said. "I've got an idea."

31

THEY PARKED IN the garage buried beneath Union Square, then came up to the street level and crossed Stockton. They followed the sidewalk past a narrow brick building, the façade of which carried the zigzag lattice of a fire escape, and then at the next door, they turned in to Britex Fabrics.

Grassley had been on his way here the last time Cain had spoken to him.

The door closed behind them, and they stood looking at bolts of silk and printed fabric stacked on racks and arranged on shelves. The store was deep, and occupied the entire four-story building. Cain thought there might be enough fabric in here to clothe every woman in the city. A salesperson came over. She looked past Cain at Fischer.

"May I help you find something?"

"Ask him," Fischer said. "He's the one looking."

Cain already had out his phone. He gave it to the woman, and she looked at the photograph of Grassley. He was in his SFPD dress uniform, to the left of a U.S. flag. The woman handed the phone back.

"He was my partner," Cain said. He put the phone in his pocket and then brought out his inspector's star. "He came in here yesterday."

"I remember him."

"Did he talk to you?"

"He asked for the manager. I took him upstairs."

"Is she up there now?"

"I'll take you."

They found the manager on the third floor. She was working with a younger woman to arrange a display of sewing notions.

"Susan?" the saleswoman said. "These officers are here to see you — I think it's about yesterday."

The woman stood up and turned around. She had salt-and-pepper hair and an easy smile. She shook Cain's hand, then Fischer's, and then took a pair of reading glasses from the pocket of her apron to look at the picture of Grassley.

"He came in yesterday," she said. "He'd been talking to Martina Delaney, at the Academy of Art, and she sent him here."

"What did he ask you?" Cain said.

"Is he in trouble? He said he was a policeman, and he showed me his badge."

"He was my partner," Cain said. "I talked to him before he came here, but I don't know why he came."

"You can't ask him?"

Cain shook his head, and the woman's easy smile disappeared.

"He asked me about a girl. He showed me a picture of her — you've seen it, I guess. The girl's in a knockoff Jean Patou dress she made. She's got her hands up in front of her, and she's backed against a wall. She looks scared. It was a horrifying picture."

"What did he ask you?"

"If I'd seen her before."

"Had you?"

She nodded.

"This was my parents' store. I've worked here for years. I remember her."

"Do you remember all your customers?" Fischer asked.

"Of course not — that'd be impossible. But I remember her because she looked like Lauren Bacall, and she was very talented — one of the best I'd seen. And she had the loveliest accent."

"What kind of accent?"

"English."

"What did you know about her?" Cain asked.

"I didn't know anything — I thought she was a housewife, or someone's mistress. Maybe that sounds old fashioned now, but that's what I thought. She didn't have a wedding ring, I don't think. Anyway, she was young, and must not have had anything to do but sew. She came in a lot for a little while —"

"You're talking about 1985."

"Somewhere in there—she came in a lot. She made four or five dresses. Some of them were couture copies. Some of them were her own designs. She'd show me sketches, and I'd help her pick out the right fabrics."

"Did you know her name?"

"If I did, I've forgotten it."

"And you figured she was a rich English girl, one with a lot of time on her hands?"

"I didn't think she was rich, though your partner asked me the same thing."

"What made you think she wasn't wealthy?"

"She paid in cash and didn't have a credit card. She'd pass up the best fabric and look for the sales. When she picked something for me to cut, she'd get exactly what she needed and not an inch more. No room for mistakes. Rich ladies who sew, they generally make a lot of mistakes."

"Did you know where she lived, if she had a place in the city?"

"No idea."

"Did she ever come in with anyone else?"

"Never."

"What else did my partner ask you?"

"He said I should call him if I remembered anything else. He gave me his card, and I put it in my office."

Cain took one of his own cards from behind his badge and handed it to her.

"Call this number instead."

Fischer's office, on the thirteenth floor of the Burton Building, looked across Golden Gate Avenue into the windows of the state office building. She had a narrow desk that was piled with paper. He didn't know what kinds of cases she worked, what else she had going on aside from Castelli. He didn't know if she was married or had a family, but he supposed she must have been alone, because she'd come alone to the safe house. He stood next to the window and looked at the potted jade plant she kept on the sill. She was in the rolling chair behind her desk, turning on her computer.

When she had a browser window open, he pulled out one of the guest chairs and sat.

"What now?" Fischer asked.

"We need to figure out if the British have a national missing persons clearinghouse," Cain said.

Fischer did a search and the first link on the results page was what they wanted. The clearinghouse was called the U.K. Missing Persons Bureau. They didn't bother searching the database of photographs. If she had been in it, Matt Redding would have found her. Instead, Fischer found a general email address.

"I think we should just attach the one photograph," she said. "The first one. I'd rather hold back the rest."

"So would I."

"And I'm giving them your phone number. The body's in your custody, so they should call you."

"That's fine."

She typed for a moment, then let him read the message. Then she attached a scanned copy of the photograph and pressed send.

By two o'clock, a dull thump was growing in Cain's head.

"I'll get lunch," Fischer said. "Nothing special. But I know a good place."

"I don't know."

"You need it, Cain," she said. "You mind walking?"

"That's fine."

They took the elevator down and went out into the early afternoon. He followed Fischer to a French-style brasserie on the edge of Hayes Valley. It was packed and looked expensive, and Cain thought they'd have to wait for a table. Most of the Saturday-afternoon crowd in the converted corner house didn't seem to be here on any kind of business. It wasn't the sort of place Cain would have picked, and he was already turning to go, but then Fischer took his wrist and began leading them through the restaurant.

A waitress said hello, calling Fischer by her first name. Another waitress caught the swinging kitchen door and held it open for them.

The back of the restaurant was all stainless steel and flashes of flame from the line of *chefs de partie*. Fischer led them across the room, toward a massive man kneeling in front of a wooden case of Louvois grand cru champagne. He was holding a bottle up to the light, studying its label.

"Michael."

He stood up and turned around, a single fluid motion, easy in spite of his bulk because everything on him was muscle. He took her hand and kissed her cheek, then nodded toward Cain.

"This is Gavin Cain," she said. "The inspector I told you about."

"Mr. Cain."

He held out his hand and Cain shook it. It was like holding hands with a bench vise.

"This is Michael," Fischer said. "My fiancé."

"Nice to meet you."

"Can we sit at the kitchen table?" Fischer asked. "I told Cain I'd get him lunch."

The kitchen table was wedged between a pair of high wine storage racks. The table itself was an old sherry cask, and there were no seats. They stood on either side of it, and Fischer's fiancé served them. He offered them wine, and they turned it down and took water instead. Cain took the glass and held it against his forehead.

"I wanted to bring you somewhere nice," Fischer said. "I don't want you to feel like I left you hanging."

"Hanging how?"

"I've got to be in D.C. tomorrow morning. I'm on a redeye tonight."

"You can't get out of it?"

"I tried."

"It doesn't have to do with our case?"

"If it did, I'd tell you. But it's nothing to do with us. It's about our office's budget."

"It's bullshit, is what you're saying."

"The purest, uncut strain of bullshit," Fischer said. "Which you can get only in D.C. I'll be back on Tuesday."

Michael brought them a loaf of bread and a saucer of olive oil to dip it in. Cain watched him go back to the kitchen, watched him come up behind one of the apprentice chefs and look over the kid's shoulder.

"He's your fiancé but you don't live together?" Cain asked. "You didn't bring anyone else to Yerba Buena."

"Our relationship is a little bit complicated," Fischer said. "But it makes sense to us."

"What about Castelli?" Cain said. "Does that make sense?"

"I don't know."

"Before the autopsy, we were sitting in my office. I told you my theory of the case," Cain said. "But I had to stop short."

"You think someone killed him, but you can't prove it because he was alone in the house," Fischer said.

Cain nodded. He looked at the bread and the olive oil and watched the line of chefs. It all looked wonderful, but he had no appetite.

"He was locked in the study," Cain said. "GSR on his right hand, his own thirty-eight next to him. And then there's everything we got from the alarm company."

"So maybe he shot himself," Fischer said. "That doesn't mean we're not still looking for someone. The blackmailer's out there, and he tried to close us down last night."

"Say the last set of pictures showed him raping a girl—a girl we found buried alive, with his baby inside her. Say that's true."

"Okay."

"And somebody knew about it, and sent him pictures and said: *I'm going to tell.*"

"Okay."

"And then he shoots himself, because he knows he's about to get caught. Is that even a crime?"

"What are you asking?"

"I'm asking, if that's the story and it's all true, then why would this person go out and kill Grassley, and maybe Chun, and try for me? What did he really do wrong? He threatened to expose a murderer. Castelli couldn't handle the pressure, so he killed himself. This kid might not have done anything wrong, and he tries to kill three cops?"

"Maybe he was there, the night the pictures were taken."

"The kid Chun and I saw running up California Street was barely in his twenties," Cain said. He stepped back and let Michael put shallow bowls of soup on the sherry cask. "In 1985, he hadn't even been born. Which is another big problem in our theory."

"So maybe we've got our story all wrong, you're saying."

"Something doesn't fit."

"What do you want to do?"

Cain picked up his spoon and touched it to the soup. He set it back down without tasting the broth. He'd seen plenty of autopsies, had learned to act casually about them afterward. There were inspectors on Homicide Detail who'd go directly from the morgue to Mo-

Mo's, across from the ballpark. They'd order rare New York strips and prove to each other just how undisturbed they were. Cain had done it too. He'd watched bodies disassembled with saws and pruning shears, every organ brought to a produce scale. And not an hour later, he'd eaten lunch.

But this morning he'd seen his partner on the steel table, Chun might not be far behind, and Lucy had spent the better part of last night hiding in a cabinet while a murderer tore her music room apart.

He put the spoon down and picked up a piece of the bread. He tore it in half and dipped it in the soup, then set it on the edge of the bowl. He checked the time and saw that Fischer was watching him. She put down her spoon and pushed the loaf of bread on its cutting board toward him. The look on her face was suddenly very kind, and he wasn't sure he was ready for that.

"Think of it in terms of physics," she said.

"I don't understand."

"We need to keep running forward so we can catch the guy. But to stay in motion, we need a certain amount of energy."

"Okay."

"So eat," she said. "It's not disrespecting Grassley. It's just calories. That's all this is."

"Okay."

He picked up his bread and dipped it back into his soup, and then he ate it.

32

CAIN'S PHONE RANG as they were leaving the restaurant. It was an unknown number with an East Bay area code. He answered it, using his left hand to shield the mouthpiece from the wind.

"Inspector Cain?" a man asked.

"Who's this?"

"Officer Combs," the man said. "You asked me to call if anyone tried to see Mrs. Castelli, if anything strange happened."

"Where are you?"

"Back at the Palace Hotel," Combs said. "She went for a walk, and now she's in her room. It's— I don't know what it was, or what it means. But I figured you'd want to hear this."

"Sit tight, Combs," he said. "We'll be there in fifteen minutes."

They found Officer Combs in his chair outside the top-floor elevator landing. He stood up when the doors parted. For this assignment, and at Cain's request, he was in plainclothes. They suited him. Putting on the uniform every day wouldn't be part of his ritual for much longer. There were openings on the Homicide Detail, and Cain needed people he could count on.

They shook hands, and Combs hesitated a moment before putting his hand on Cain's shoulder.

"I heard about Inspector Grassley," he said. "And I know Angela. We went through the academy together."

"We saw her today."

"She'll be all right?"

"She's a fighter," Cain said. "More than you know."

"The sonofabitch who did this—"

"I know."

Cain led them to the main stairs and they went down to the first

235

half-landing. They could still see the elevators, and there was no way anyone could go down the hall to Mona Castelli's room without them seeing. But their voices wouldn't carry under her door if they stood down here.

"They came out at noon," Combs said. "Both of them—the daughter spent the night."

"Where'd they go?"

"They took the elevator down. We used the stairs and beat them—"

"We?" Fischer asked.

"Officer Aguilar—she was assigned to watch Alexa."

"Got it."

"They split up in the lobby—no hugs, no words at all. They just went different ways. Aguilar followed the daughter, and I stuck with Mona."

"Did she see you?" Cain asked.

"Not then. But she knows who I am, even without the uniform. And that's important. I'm getting to that."

"Go on."

"Mrs. Castelli went into the Pied Piper. It was mostly empty, and she got a seat at the end of the bar. Back to the door, easy to watch. Three martinis in twenty minutes. Doubles, I think. She didn't talk to anyone but the bartender."

"Dedication," Cain said. "Commitment."

"She ought to be committed. She came out of there, and she wasn't even staggering. I think she was walking straighter than when she went in."

Above them, in the main hallway, a man in a hotel uniform walked past. He was balancing a room service tray on one hand and disappeared with it down the hallway toward Mona Castelli's room. Cain went up the stairs until he could see to the end of the hall. The man was knocking on a door that wasn't Mona Castelli's.

Cain returned to the midlevel landing, and Combs continued.

"She left the hotel, and I followed her at a distance; she was headed up into Chinatown. She stopped outside the Cathay Orient Bank and took something out of her purse. She was holding it in her left hand when she went up the steps."

The Cathay Orient was the only bank Cain knew of with a main branch open on Saturdays. It was also one of three banks listed on the piece of paper they'd found in Castelli's office safe.

"You didn't see what it was?" Fischer asked. "What she had in her hand?"

Combs shook his head.

"I was on the other side of the street," he said. "I'd been hanging back. But not far enough. Before she went in, she stood in the open door and looked back the way she came. Then she checked the other side of the street."

"She wanted to see if she'd been followed," Cain said.

"And she saw me. Her eyes locked on mine, and it took her a second to recognize me. But as soon as she did, she let go of the door. Whatever was in her hand, she put it back in her purse. She went down the steps and walked back to the hotel."

"How big was the purse?"

"Small. You could fit a checkbook, maybe some keys. That's it."

"You're talking about a clutch," Fischer said. "That's what she had?"

"A clutch — yeah."

"What about her clothes?" Fischer asked. "Were they bulky? Pockets?"

"Everything she wears is skin tight."

"And she's been in the room since?"

"She came back from the bank, and she hasn't left."

"All right," Fischer said. "What about the daughter?"

"Officer Aguilar followed her to the apartment. Alexa's been up there since noon, and Aguilar's at the coffee shop across the street, where she can see the door."

Cain looked at Fischer and she flicked her eyes toward the elevators. There wasn't much more they could get here, unless they went down the hall and knocked on Mona Castelli's door. But it wasn't time for that yet; they didn't have enough to work with. The only thing to do was lie back and wait. And watch.

"You did a good job, Officer Combs," Cain said. "Keep it up. Follow her when she goes out. Don't be overt, but if she looks around, make sure she sees you."

"I think I get it."

"When you back people into corners, you don't know what they'll do," Cain said. "So watch her, but watch yourself. You know what happened to Grassley."

"Yes, sir."

"Who's your relief?"

Combs listed the other officers and their shifts, and they went through the same for Aguilar. Cain told him to call each of the others to pass along the word. They were to follow Mona and Alexa Castelli from the shadows, but step into view if either woman looked for a tail. Let them wonder how many eyes were watching them, how many ears were listening when they spoke. Then Cain asked for three more names, reliable patrol officers who could track Melissa Montgomery. A shared house on a residential street in Noe Valley might be harder to watch than a hotel room or a downtown condo. But a good officer would come up with something.

They came out of the hotel and got in Fischer's car, which was parked at the valet stand along New Montgomery. They had to wait for a taxi to finish loading in front of them, and while they were sitting in the cold car, Cain felt the double pulse of an incoming text vibrate in his pocket.

> *Found Chun's car on Alabama St., one block from Grassley's apt. No forced entry, no blood. Some stuff in the trunk that bears on your case. Left copies on your chair.*

After he read it, he passed the phone to Fischer.

"Who's this from?"

"Frank Lee."

"Got it," she said.

She put the car into gear and steered onto New Montgomery, past Alexa's apartment. In a moment, they drove by the coffee shop and Cain got a glimpse of a woman who might have been Aguilar. Then they were passing the front of Alexa's condo, the double-height windows spilling light onto the wet sidewalk, the cut-crystal chandelier glittering. Her school was on the left. Grassley had been lucky that the fashion professor had sent him to Britex. They'd gotten some valuable information from the manager. But Cain wished he hadn't sent Chun alone to Berkeley, that he'd gotten Grassley to go with her. He had no idea who she'd been talking to, where she'd gone after the police station.

And he was still bothered by the shallow cuts on Grassley's neck; his car abandoned in front of Lucy's house, the driver's seat soaked in blood.

"We're missing something," Cain said.

"I know." She turned right onto Mission. "We'll work it out."

"She had two hundred thousand in cash in her room, and she went to a bank but didn't bring it."

"We'll work it out, Cain."

The Hall of Justice was dark when they came to it, and there was a crowd out front. Cain caught the story in snippets of conversation as they passed the knots of office workers waiting on the sidewalk: a flooded utility tunnel, a shorted electrical main. The backup generators were offline, again. A young woman in a white lab coat said, "If the stiffs thaw out, it'll reek for ten blocks."

He led Fischer past the out-of-commission metal detectors, holding his badge up for the guards. An even bigger crowd had gathered in front of the nonfunctional elevators. He turned to the fire stairs and pushed the door open. Battery-powered emergency lamps gave a dull red light, reminding Cain of dark rooms. Maybe the Pi Kappa Kappa brothers had shot and developed the film without leaving the mansion. The brick wall in the first photograph could have been in the basement. He wondered what other prints they had developed, where all those images had gone.

They came out on the sixth floor and then crossed the cubicle farm to his office. On Cain's chair were two copies of the Grizzly Peak murder book from the Berkeley Police Department—the files Frank Lee had found in Chun's trunk. Cain set them side by side on his desk and flipped through them to be sure they were the same. Then he gave one of them to Fischer.

"Let's get out of here," he said.

"Yerba Buena?'

"She doesn't have a phone. I hate to be gone so long with no way to check in."

They parked in the half-empty lot and looked through the windshield at the Coast Guard outpost. The buildings were low and squat, hunkering against the rain. As they watched, the streetlights began to blink on, one and then another.

"You're going to the airport tonight?"

"Midnight."

"In this car?"

"Shit," Fischer said. "I forgot about that."

Cain's car was parked outside Lucy's house, unless the city had towed it. He wasn't sure if he'd left it parked in front of a neighbor's driveway. At the time, it hadn't mattered.

"I can take a cab tomorrow, or have a patrolman come out and get me."

"Forget it — use this one," she said. She took the keys from the ignition and handed them to him. "Michael can take me to the airport."

"You're sure?"

"Just don't drive it on the sidewalk. I saw what you did to yours."

They got out of the car and walked through the rain to the barracks.

He found Lucy on the desk chair, which she'd moved to the window. A wool blanket covered her shoulders. She didn't turn around when he came in, and it wasn't until he was by her side that he realized she was asleep. He put his briefcase and his copy of the murder book on the desk, then sat down on the end of the bed and took off his shoes. He removed his jacket and unholstered his gun. After he'd unloaded it and put it into the drawer, Lucy stirred and turned to him.

"Did you get him?"

"Not yet."

"When?"

"I don't know," he said. The room was so small that he could reach out and put his hands on her shoulders without getting off the bed. "Have you eaten anything today?"

"I went to the café."

"Do you need dinner?"

"No."

"What's wrong?" he asked, regretting it before the words were out of his mouth.

They hadn't gotten in many fights, but questions like this were a good way to start. It was obvious what was wrong. She got off the chair and came around to the other side of the bed. She sat with her back against the headboard, the blanket still wrapped around her.

When he put his hand on her leg, she immediately bent her knee to get away from his touch.

"It's only been one day," she said. "And everyone is very nice. But I hate it here, Gavin."

"I know."

"Promise me you'll fix this," she said. "I want to go home."

"I promise."

"Take your briefcase and your binder, and work in the café. You can read in there without bothering me."

"Okay."

"It's cold war cuisine, seven nights a week. Tonight you get Salisbury steak and carrot salad. With raisins."

"Are you okay?" he asked, and regretted asking that, too.

She looked at him, her hands folded on the gentle rise in her belly.

"I just want to sleep until I can go home," she said. "Or anywhere. Anywhere but here."

33

HE WAS IN bed next to Lucy, on top of the covers and still wearing his clothes. He was half awake, thinking of getting out of bed and driving into the city to begin again, but not sure what good that would do. It was four thirty in the morning when his phone began vibrating in his pants pocket. The long, sustained pulses of an incoming call. He got out of the bed and went quickly to the bathroom.

He shut the door and answered the call. It was from a blocked number.

"Hello?"

"I'm calling for DI Gavin Cain."

A man's deep voice. He sounded older than Cain, in his sixties at least. And he had an English accent.

"DI?"

"Sorry — Detective Gavin Cain."

"Inspector Cain," he said. "This is San Francisco you're calling."

"All right."

"Who is this?"

"You and the FBI agent, Fischer, sent an email to the Missing Persons Bureau. It found its way to me."

Cain sat on the edge of the tub. When they'd sent the email to the U.K., they thought they might get a hit. But they'd never imagined it would come so quickly. It had taken just over twelve hours.

"You're in the U.K.," Cain said. He was covering his mouth with his hand, and whispering. "Scotland Yard? The Metropolitan Police?"

"I was with the Met back then, but now I'm somewhere else. I do the same sorts of things now as I did back then, but with a bigger budget," the man said. "Which means I have more reasons to be careful. I'll only have this conversation face to face. How soon can you come?"

"I don't even know where you are."

"London."

"Or who you are."

"I know who your girl is," the man said. "Which is what matters. I can tell you her name. I can tell you why she was in San Francisco."

Cain wished he could record the call, that he had the ability to trace it. But he was half awake and whispering in a bathroom, and he wasn't even sure his phone had enough battery to finish the conversation. It was already making warning tones. It might die at any second.

"What do you want?" he asked.

"I want to bring her home," the man said. "And I want to know what happened to her."

"I'm not getting on a plane," Cain said. "All I've got is a thirty-year-old dead body, is what you think. I can drop everything and go to London because you tell me to."

"Look—"

"You've got no idea how much other shit is going on right now. No fucking idea. I am not getting on a plane. Sir."

"It's true—I've no idea," the man said. "But if you want to know about the girl, I'm the man who can tell you."

"You're talking to me right now."

"Not on the phone—if you're keeping up with the papers, you must understand."

"If you want to meet, then come here."

"What I'm going to tell you, I can't say in California."

"Because I could arrest you."

"And I can't risk that."

"Then think of a place where that's off the table," Cain said. "You can figure one out."

The line was silent for nearly thirty seconds. When the man spoke again, his voice wasn't nearly so confident.

"I'll be in touch," he said. "There's an afternoon flight—"

Cain's phone died. He sat on the tub and looked at its black screen.

Ten minutes later, he was in the Coast Guard café with his briefcase and the murder book. Fischer's plane was probably coming down

243

through the clouds, descending toward Washington. There was no way to contact her, and no way to reach the man from London. Instead, he poured a cup of coffee from the all-night urn and found a table close to a wall outlet. He took the phone's charger from his briefcase and plugged it in, then opened the Grizzly Peak murder book and flipped a third of the way through it, to the autopsy reports.

There had been five men in the house, but only three of them had ever been identified. The medical examiner made those IDs with partial dental records, which matched three Berkeley juniors who'd gone missing. The other two bodies were older men, in their thirties or forties, but the medical examiner found nothing on them. There was no national database of dental records; those were only available if a family turned them over to the police and the police had uploaded them into a missing persons database. The conclusion was obvious. If these dead men had families, they weren't especially concerned about finding them. At the time, in 1989, there'd been no DNA testing done. As John MacDowell had said, back then DNA was only for the celebrity cases. The headliners. But as far as Cain could tell, no one had ever gone back later and tried it.

That meant two of the bodies from the rubble had always been mystery men.

All five corpses were found with their hands bound behind their backs with heavy-gauge wire. There were possible gunshot wounds laterally across the men's throats, but it was hard for the medical examiner to be sure. If there had been bullets, they'd passed through soft tissue and missed any bone. After the fire, there wasn't much soft tissue left. It was all speculation from that point. The medical examiner found trace entry wounds, possible gunpowder stippling from a point-blank shot. He guessed the men had been shot, but that's all it was: a guess. If he was right, then the killer's intent was clear enough. Bind them so they couldn't leave, and shoot out their throats so they couldn't scream. The fire would take care of the rest.

He looked to his left. A Coast Guard enlistee carrying his breakfast on a tray was staring openly at the murder book. The page was a black-and-white photograph, a burnt corpse on an autopsy table. He closed the cover but kept his finger between the pages like a bookmark.

"Sorry, sir. Caught my eye."

"These do that."

He opened the binder again and tried to catch hold of his thoughts before he lost them. Castelli hadn't registered his gun until 1991, two years after the Grizzly Peak fire. But even if he'd owned the gun then, there was no consistency with the way Lester Fennimore had died. That had been wild, indiscriminate shooting. The shooter had fired all six shots, striking Fennimore's face and torso. That was blind firing. All the hallmarks of fear and panic. The man who'd set the Grizzly Peak fire was more calculating. He'd taken the time to bind his victims, had shot each one only once. It made no sense that someone who could kill five people so methodically in 1989 would make such a mess of a single murder in 1998.

There had to be two different shooters. He poured a packet of powdered creamer into his coffee and drank the first few sips without thinking much of anything. Sometimes a blank mind had the space to make a leap, as though it needed the room to get a running start.

Lester Fennimore.

Something about him, something Cain had seen the first night he'd learned the man's name, sitting in his half-dark office and talking to Fischer as she flew out of Los Angeles. He took the ballistics report out of his briefcase, the one with Fennimore's autopsy attached. He wasn't sure what he was looking for but knew exactly which picture he needed. It was the initial headshot, from the shoulders up. He flipped through the report until he found it, and then he pushed his glasses up onto his forehead and held the page close so that he could study it.

After a minute, he was sure he knew what he was looking at, but he went to the text anyway. He found the coroner's surface examination. He usually just skimmed these, because they were routine. This time, he read it word for word, and three-quarters of the way through, the coroner verified what the picture clearly showed.

... there are matching scars on either side of the laryngeal prominence. Each scar is a circular indentation, approximately 1/4 inch in diameter, consistent with a well-healed previous gunshot wound. Decedent's left ear is lightly deformed with scarification consistent with an old burn. Decedent's medical records do not reflect having ever sought treatment for either a burn or a gunshot. Contacted following the autopsy, the decedent's widow did not know the origin of these scars.

However, she confirmed to this examiner that her husband could not speak above a whisper.

These were healed wounds. This examiner concludes that neither the damage to the voice box, nor the burns on the left ear, contributed in any way . . .

Maybe the Santa Cruz County Coroner was convinced the old scars had nothing to do with Lester Fennimore's murder, but Cain wasn't so sure. The man had a Pi Kappa Kappa tattoo on his shoulder, a bullet hole through his larynx, and a half-burned left ear. He'd died in a Cadillac Eldorado, a few model years down the line from the one someone had driven to the English girl's rape. In 1989, he'd crawled out of the Grizzly Peak fire with his throat shot out, and he'd been a marked man ever since.

By now Cain's phone was charged enough to use. He went to the SFPD's secure server and ran a trace on Lester Fennimore's widow. Her social security number was in the prior investigator's notes, and with a lead like that, it didn't take long to find her. She had moved out of Walnut Creek and into a house outside of Mendocino. He found the place on a satellite map and zoomed in on it, but the image was no good. There was just a blur deep in the woods along the North Fork of the Albion River. He wondered how much she'd be willing to tell him about Lester.

He put the key in the ignition and started the engine, then drove Fischer's car over to the guard booth. He nodded to the man inside, went over the one-way traffic spikes, and then wound through Yerba Buena's predawn darkness to reach the bridge. It took twenty minutes to get from Yerba Buena to his apartment in Daly City; most of the city was asleep at this time on a Sunday morning.

Nagata must have gotten the landlady to unlock his front door, or one of the men with her knew his way around a set of picking tools, because the jamb wasn't splintered and the lock slid back without catching. He went in and looked around, and couldn't tell that Nagata had been in here two nights ago with a squad of men. There were half-packed boxes on the floor. All the clothes were out of the closet and piled on the bed in folded stacks. He stripped off his suit and dropped it in a box, then put on a fresher one. He threw another two changes into a duffel bag before he left again.

He got in Fischer's car and drove back to the Coast Guard station, and on the way over he called Frank Lee. It was six in the morning, but Frank was awake.

"Gavin, how're you doing?"

"Holding up."

"What about Angela?"

"I saw her yesterday — have you been there?"

"Not yet."

Frank was breathing hard, and wherever he was, it was windy. Cain guessed he'd caught him in the middle of a morning jog.

"Listen," Cain said. "I'm going to leave town today. There are a couple people in Marin I want to talk to. If I find anything that helps with Grassley and Chun, I'll call you first. But I think this is just Castelli."

"Okay."

"If you don't hear from me by tomorrow morning, call Agent Fischer."

"You okay, Cain?"

"Sometimes it's like walking on water," Cain said. "You move fast or you sink."

"Seriously, Cain. You okay?"

"I'm fine. I'm keeping ahead of it. Can I ask you a favor?"

"Anything."

"When you're done with the house, send in a cleaning service and put the bill on my desk."

"Nagata will pay for it."

"Either way, put it on my desk."

"All right," Frank said. "Now, let me tell you what I've got. You were right about the guy. He jumped your girlfriend's fence, and he made it to Cabrillo and jacked a car. Oakland PD found it about two a.m."

"The driver?"

"In the trunk."

"I'm sorry."

"How's this your fault?"

"I don't know."

"The driver was a retired school principal. Seventy-five years old. He lived on Twenty-Fourth Avenue. He was two blocks from home."

"But the kid ditched the car in Oakland?"

247

"Yeah."

"Where?"

"Saint Augustine's, on Alcatraz Avenue. There's a parking lot next to the church."

Cain drew a map of Oakland in his mind, found Alcatraz Avenue and followed it east. Past Shattuck, past Telegraph, until he pulled to a mental stop in front of the church.

"That's practically in Berkeley."

"What's that mean to you?" Frank said.

"Maybe nothing," Cain said. "But we've got a theory about Castelli. There's a connection to a frat that got kicked off the Cal campus in the eighties. Pi Kappa Kappa — you heard of it?"

"Never."

"Castelli pledged it — but only after it went underground."

Frank took his time before answering, the wind blowing unimpeded across his receiver.

"And the kid who killed Grassley jacked a car and dropped it in Oakland," he finally said. "Right on the edge of Berkeley. Close enough to limp home, maybe. That's what you're thinking. That there's still a chapter, and he's a member."

"Or maybe it's nothing."

"You want me to follow up while you're gone?"

"If you can — but watch your back."

"After I heard about Grassley and Chun? I strapped on my ankle piece," Frank said. "I haven't done that since my first year in plainclothes."

Cain said goodbye and hung up. He didn't want to tell Frank what he thought about the ankle holster. Two guns wouldn't see behind him any more than one. He checked his rearview mirror, then took a left on Fulton. The rest of the way to Yerba Buena was a straight shot east, the sun finally lighting up the sky ahead of him. All at once, the clouds were pink and orange. But he knew in ten minutes the color would be gone and everything would be gray again.

He came along the walkway and fit his key into the barrack door, taking care to enter their room without waking her. He put his things down on the desk and sat in the chair. He'd left a voicemail for Fischer and now, when he checked his phone, he saw that she'd responded with a text.

248

Do you want to wait for some backup?

The answer, of course, was no. He wasn't sure what would happen, either in Mendocino or when the man from London called again. But he wasn't waiting for anything. From the beginning, they'd all understood that without the girl's name, they had nothing. Until they knew who she was, everything else was under a shroud. Who buried her, and why. What Castelli was hiding, and whether he'd been paying someone for years. He was breaking the protocols now, leaving town to see a witness without giving his lieutenant a heads-up; moving toward a meeting with the man in London without filing any reports.

But following the rules would only matter if this case went to trial and he had to testify, and he knew it would never get that far. Not after what they did to Grassley and Chun, and not after Lucy had to hide in her own house. This wasn't going to finish in a courtroom. It would end with bullets, with a body in the morgue and a board of inquiry. Cain didn't care if they ruled it a good shooting.

He picked up his phone and answered Fischer's text. When he looked up, Lucy was awake and watching him. He saw her eyes shift to the desk, to the duffel bag he'd packed.

"What is it?" she asked. "What's going on?"

"I don't want to leave you alone," he said. "It's bad enough you to have to stay here. But if I'm out of town, it's even worse. I want to bring you with me."

"Where?"

"North," he said. "Up the coast, to Mendocino. We'll stay in a bed and breakfast."

"But you'll be working."

"I'll be talking to someone," he said. "You can stay in the room, or go for a walk around the town if you're up for it. Can you do it?"

She looked around the little room. The dingy carpet, the dented walls. Then she pushed back the covers and got out of bed, one hand holding her stomach beneath the navel.

"I'd been getting ready for this. You know I have been."

"I know."

"I want to be the way I was."

"It'll be easier if we're somewhere nice. A couple more days, and then you can go home. Frank Lee's going to get it cleaned."

249

"But will it be safe?"

"A couple more days, and it'll be safe."

"You're getting closer?"

"Yes."

"Then give me five minutes."

In the time he'd known Lucy, and especially in the last few months, he'd thought a lot about all the things they'd never done. All the things they might never do. They'd never taken a walk together, or a drive along the coast. They'd never gone to a friend's house for dinner, never walked into a restaurant together. She'd never held his hand when the lights went down in a movie at a theater, never shouted into his ear to be heard in a club. They survived all right without all those things, their relationship unconstrained within the walls of her house. She played the piano and they read books aloud to each other, and they cooked meals with groceries from her delivery service or ate takeout that he brought from the places she missed the most.

But he regretted everything that had been closed off, and he knew that she did too. He'd seen her standing in the upstairs rooms, where the windows were high enough to look out across some of the other rooftops, into the foreclosed distance. Even her posture spoke of something missing. He had thought she was probably ready for it, had guessed about her secret excursions. But now she was getting it all at once, like jumping from a cliff above deep water. No choice at all about the outcome after her feet left the ground.

They were in Fischer's car, Lucy in the passenger seat and Cain behind the wheel. They'd passed through the city and now they were on the bridge, the Marin Headlands rising ahead of them.

"This is the last one," he said. "I have to finish. But after it's done, then so am I."

"What are you saying?"

"That we can go anywhere. We can do anything."

"Okay."

"You're staying here for me," Cain said. "Since we met, that's what you've been doing. But that's never been fair. So after this, I'm done. We can go wherever you want."

"Gavin—"

"You had that offer in Lausanne. We could go there."

"If it's still open," she said. "And what would you do in Lausanne? What would you do if you didn't do this?"

"Whatever it took."

She took her hand from his knee and pivoted sideways in her seat, leaning against the door handle as she studied his face.

"Let me think about it," she said.

34

LUCY HAD GONE into Ashbury Heights Elementary one day four years ago to talk to the students about music. She wasn't a teacher there, didn't belong in the school at all except that she'd been asked by a friend of a friend to come and give a presentation. It was Career Day; she was supposed to talk about the places she'd traveled, the concerts she'd played. How she had walked alone onto the stages of Europe's greatest halls, had looked up past the lights and met the eyes of kings and queens. But it didn't go like that. Half an hour after she'd stepped inside the school, another man had followed. He wasn't from the city; he had no connections to the school or the children inside it. He had two pistols in his jacket pockets and a backpack full of ammunition. Five minutes later, Lucy was the only adult survivor. Her career as a pianist was at an end. But in four years of exile, giving piano lessons in the home that had become both a refuge and a prison, she hadn't forgotten the world she'd known.

"What's the name of the hotel?" she asked.

"It's just a bed and breakfast."

"Is it the Palisades?"

"No — I just found it online."

"Did you pay already?"

"Not yet."

"Let me have your phone."

He dug it from his pocket and handed it to her, watching in glances as he steered through the curves. The coastal highway was narrow, and on the left the cliffs dropped all the way down to the ocean. But he could see that Lucy was searching the Internet, and soon she put the phone to her ear.

"It's still there," she said to him. "So I'm changing us."

"All right."

"You'll like it."

Then she was on the line with the desk clerk at the Palisades, and Cain was thinking how easy it would have been to do this months ago. He could have just made the reservation and packed her bag. He could have held her hand going down the front steps to the car, and now, looking at her sitting there, he knew she would have done it gladly. But this wasn't the right way. Now they were running away from the man who'd broken into her house, and Cain was working on a case. He should have brought her for the simple sake of going. It would have been so easy, and yet he'd never thought of it.

After they turned in to the driveway and came through the screen of redwood trees that hid the Palisades from the road, Cain saw the place and couldn't believe he'd never heard of it. It looked like a California robber baron's idea of a castle. A wild and tangled rose garden grew in the sloped lawn, and the house towered at the top of a low rise. Cain pulled under the porte cochère before parking and getting out, leaning back to look up at the building's stone turrets. He counted seven chimneys and forty windows. The air was scented with roses and wet bark, with the ocean's tang and the sweet tinge of wood smoke. They went up the stairs and opened the front door, then crossed a Persian carpet the size of a basketball court. Lucy trailed her finger along the keyboard of a Steinway as she went to the front desk and rang the bell.

An old man came out and glanced at Cain a moment before turning back to Lucy. His black bow tie was hand-knotted, and his green wool cardigan looked as old as the house.

"You're Miss Bolet?"

"That's right."

"Lucy Bolet," the man said, taking his time as he spoke her name, letting it rest in the air between them as he pulled at his memory. "You stayed with us before. Five years ago — or was it six?"

"Five and change."

"Will you play?" he asked, nodding toward the Steinway. "A lot of us remember when you were here before. To hear you play again — that would really be something."

"Has it been tuned?"

"Last week."

"This evening, then. Before dinner."

253

"I'll put out word."

"Just in the hotel," Lucy said. "Not around town."

"Of course," the man said. And then, in a much quieter voice, he added, "I heard what happened. I prayed for you."

"Thank you."

"Are you coming back now?"

"Coming back?" Lucy asked. She seemed to consider the different meanings. "Yes—I think so."

She reached into her purse, but Cain stepped to her side.

"Let me."

In the room, they set their bags on the bed, then went across to the window and opened the curtains. They were looking down on the rose garden. Between the trees, at the far edge of the lawn, they could see the Pacific, blue water and white foam out to the horizon.

"Now what?" Lucy asked, just as Cain's phone rang.

The caller's number was blocked, and Cain answered, reflexively cupping his hand over his mouth.

"Is this Cain?"

"Yes."

The caller had an English accent, but his voice was decades too smooth to be the man who'd contacted Cain this morning.

"Tomorrow at noon," the man said. "He'll be here, waiting for you."

"Where?"

"The British consulate general," the man said. "Bring your passport and leave your gun."

The man hung up, and Cain stood looking at his phone. It would take a well-connected man to set up a meeting in the British consulate. And he'd chosen the location well. Foreign consulates were the only places in the city off-limits to Cain. He would have to come unarmed, and would lose all of his jurisdiction when he stepped through the door.

"Are you all right?" Lucy asked.

"Fine," he said. They would have to check out tomorrow so that he could get back to the city in time for the meeting. He would have to find another hotel in the city where Lucy could stay.

There was a stone fireplace facing the bed. Kindling and logs were stacked nearby in a pair of wicker baskets. "Do you want me to light that before I go?"

"Please."

"I'll be back before dinner."

She pulled the ottoman over to the fireplace and sat down to watch as the flames crackled up through the dry kindling and into the split oak logs. She had a book in her lap, its jacket flap tucked into the page where she'd left off.

By three in the afternoon, he was driving again. Back through the village of Mendocino, and then east, into the wooded foothills. After he turned off the paved road, he followed a set of mud and gravel ruts for five miles, and then his phone told him he'd arrived. The driveway was so overgrown that if not for the heavy chain blocking the entrance, he might have overlooked it altogether. Past the chain, the driveway curved up a hill and disappeared into the redwood trees. He parked against a mossy embankment and walked to the chain. It was rusted down its length, each end locked around a tree. One of the locks was pitted with corrosion and covered with green lichen; the other showed bright brass around the keyhole.

He stepped over the chain and went up the driveway, reaching into his coat to unsnap the strap on the top of his holster. He had no idea what Susan Fennimore had been doing up here these last ten years.

When he came to the end of the driveway, there was a clearing. A red pickup truck was parked under a wood-shake roof, and next to that was the cabin. He didn't make it across the clearing before the front door opened and Susan stepped halfway out. She kept her left hand inside the house, and Cain supposed she was holding a rifle or a shotgun.

"What do you want?"

"To ask you a few questions, about your former husband."

"Lester or Malcolm?"

"Lester."

"Who are you?"

"Inspector Cain, with the SFPD."

He reached into his jacket, slowly, not taking his eyes from her. He took out his badge and held it up.

"Lester got himself killed in Santa Clara. We lived in Walnut Creek. How does the SFPD have anything to do with that?"

"The gun that shot him turned up in another crime scene."

He took another ten steps toward the house. Susan looked to be about forty-five. She had dark blond hair, hints of gray at the roots. Her eyes were focused and clear. She was wearing a chambray shirt and blue jeans, a pair of doeskin work gloves in her hip pocket. On the porch next to her front door was a pair of mud-covered rubber galoshes. Gardening tools were leaning against the wood plank wall. There weren't any flowers or vegetable plots in the clearing around the cabin, but he'd seen the satellite picture before coming out here. He knew that farther back in the woods behind the cabin, there was another structure. He figured it must be a greenhouse, but he wasn't here to investigate what she might be growing there.

"I'm not going to ask about anything but Lester," Cain said. "Can I come up to the porch?"

She leaned back into the cabin and he heard her set something down. Then she came out, empty-handed, and closed the door behind her. There were a few wooden chairs at one end of the porch and she sat in one, pulling the gloves from her pocket and setting them on her knee. Cain came up the steps and took the other chair, angling it so that he could sit facing her. He had a notebook and pen with him but didn't take them out.

"I saw the investigator's notes, from 1998," Cain said. "You and Lester had a daughter?"

"Cari."

"Now she's what — twenty-one, twenty-two?"

"Twenty-two. She's at Humboldt State."

"She was two when Lester was killed," Cain said. "And he'd just lost his job?"

"That's right. I wasn't working either."

"So things weren't easy."

"*Desperate* would be a good word. You've got a toddler. You have a mortgage. Two car payments to make."

"What did he do — before he lost his job, what did he do?"

"He was a software engineer."

"So he was looking for jobs in Silicon Valley?"

"That's right."

"Did he say where?"

"Everywhere."

"He had a bachelor's in computer science from Cal, isn't that right?"

"That's right."

"Is that where you met him?"

She shook her head.

"We met after college."

"Did you know anything about his friends in college? His frat brothers?"

"I knew he was in a fraternity. He had the tattoo."

"Did he tell you about it?"

"No."

"Did you ask?"

"I guess I might have."

"But what? He changed the subject? Went silent?"

"That's right."

"What about the burn on his ear and the scar on his throat?"

"There was a fire in his dorm," Susan said. "He was asleep when it started. He made it out, but some of the other kids didn't."

"That's what he told you?"

She nodded.

"He spoke in a whisper — is that right?"

"He said —" She paused and looked at her lap, her eyebrows pressing toward each other. "He was stumbling down a staircase. There was smoke. He fell and he hit something and crushed his throat. That was just a story? Is that what you're telling me?"

"I don't know."

"What crime scene was it, where you found the gun? Or can't you say?"

"It made the paper this week. I can tell you that," Cain said. He watched her face for recognition, but when there wasn't any, he moved on. "When Lester was shot, he was in a red Cadillac Eldorado. Had he always been an Eldorado man?"

Now Susan smiled, some memory lighting upon her face.

"I made fun of him for that. I couldn't decide what he looked like more, driving those cars of his — a retiree, headed down to the VFW for steak night? Or was it a pimp? He hated that, me making fun of him. He'd always had Eldorados. His grandfather gave him one when he turned sixteen."

"So he had one in college."

"That's right."

"Was Lester a good man?"

"I thought so at the time. As far as husbands go, as far as fathers go, I didn't have anything to compare him to."

"And later?"

"Later on, the comparison didn't help him."

"Do you still have any pictures of him?"

"I've got one box. It's in a box of his things. I kept it for Cari, in case she ever wanted to know about her dad. She looked through it, but she never kept anything. She latched on to Malcolm when I married him."

"Where's Malcolm now?"

"He had a heart attack, ten years ago. He was older than me."

"The box with Lester's things — may I look through it?"

"What are you looking for?"

"I don't know," Cain said, honestly.

"I'll give it to you," she said. "You can keep it. But then I need to get back to work."

She went into the cabin, and he sat looking at the gardening tools lined up by the door. Maybe she was just growing hothouse tomatoes back there, selling them at farmers' markets for a little cash on the side. Maybe Malcolm had left her with enough money to put Cari Fennimore through Humboldt State. He'd told her that he was only here to ask questions about Lester. Prying into her greenhouse wasn't part of the deal.

She came out holding a cardboard file box. She set it on the porch rail, next to the steps.

"I forgot your name," she said. "Mr. Detective."

"It's Cain," he said. He came over and handed her his card. "Gavin Cain. If I find something, and we know what happened to Lester, do you want me to come and tell you?"

She took her time thinking about that. Lester must not have stacked up well against Malcolm at all.

"All right," she said. "That would be fine."

He put the box into the backseat, pushed it over, and then climbed in next to it. He took off the lid and set it in the foot well, then leaned over to look in while he put on his gloves. Lester Fennimore must have been a heavy smoker. Twenty years on, and his things still smelled like an ashtray. He pulled out a black fabric bag first, its opening cinched closed with a pull string. He knew what was in it from the weight and the shape, and when he loosened the string and reached into the bag, he wasn't surprised to be holding a Nikon single lens reflex camera. It was an F3, a film model, and it was fitted with a good lens. He checked the back and turned the gears to advance the frame, but didn't think there was any film inside. He opened the back and saw that the camera was empty.

There was a photograph of Lester as an eight- or nine-year-old kid. He was standing near a creek. Big smile, bowl-cut hair, a rainbow trout in his hands. There was a diploma from UC Berkeley, rolled up in a cardboard tube. An engraved pewter whiskey flask, but not the one from the blackmail photographs. He found a baseball cap with the name of some high school Cain had never heard of, a pocketknife with a polished teak handle, a Seiko watch that hadn't ticked in two decades, a little plastic box with half a dozen hand-tied fishing flies, a Zippo lighter engraved *L.R.F.* in cursive script.

And then, at the bottom, a stack of faux-leather daily planners, each one embossed on the front, in gold leaf, with the year it covered. Cain took them out and looked through them. He had the last decade of Lester Fennimore's life, his daily schedule from 1988 to 1998.

He took the top book and flipped to June 28, the day Lester was shot. The page was blank. If Lester had any appointments that day, he'd decided not to write them down. Cain began flipping backward. On the twenty-sixth, Lester had gone to an interview at SUN Microsystems, in Santa Clara. He had a dental appointment on June twenty-second, but that was scratched out. Maybe he'd scheduled it before he lost his job, then canceled it to save money. Two days before that, he'd driven down to San Jose for an interview. There wasn't a company name, but there was an address. Cain got out his phone and looked it up.

The address in Fennimore's planner had been the corporate headquarters of NavSoft.

Cain set the planner on his knees and looked out the window, tapping his knuckle against the glass as he thought. On June 20, 1998, Harry Castelli was the vice president of NavSoft. Fennimore came down for an interview, but didn't get the job. There was no way to know if the frat brothers saw each other that day. But eight days later, Fennimore drove back through San Jose in the dark on his way to a rendezvous at Castle Rock State Park. By ten o'clock that night, he was dead, six bullets from Castelli's Smith and Wesson scattered through him.

Maybe Lester hadn't gotten the job but while he was inside Castelli's company, he'd thought of another way to make money. He and Susan were desperate by then. A mortgage and two cars. A toddler to feed. Cain put the books back in the box and then fit the lid over the top. He got out of the backseat and came up to the driver's door. The sun was getting low now, and these roads were no good in the dark.

35

CAIN CAME UP the steps of the Palisades, balancing Lester Fennimore's box under his left arm. He paused before he opened the front
door, looking through the cut-crystal window at the small crowd
gathered in the lobby. He pushed the door open and stepped inside.
There were thirty people in the room, most of them in varying degrees of evening attire. Cain spotted the desk clerk. He'd shed his
green cardigan in favor of an evening jacket. A waiter came through
a door, carrying a tray of champagne flutes above his right shoulder.

"—and then she didn't leave the house for four *years,*" a woman
was saying. "This—"

"Champagne, sir?"

"Sure."

Cain took the glass and moved toward the center of the room.
There was a single light above the piano. Then Lucy came down the
steps. She paused on the landing, looking at the crowd. She wore a
simple dress made of black jersey, and she was barefoot. She had tied
her hair into a knot at the back of her head, and wore no makeup and
no jewelry. The room went still when she appeared, thirty pairs of
eyes on her. She nodded at the crowd, and then she came the rest of
the way down the steps and crossed to the piano.

"—it was in 2010," the desk clerk was whispering to a group behind Cain. "At the Royal Albert Hall, in London. That was the last
time. Until tonight."

Lucy pulled out the piano bench, sat down, and ran her fingers
silently along the tops of the keys. She had no sheet music, but that
didn't matter. She drew a breath and the crowd went silent, and then
she bent toward the keyboard, her eyes closed.

"Liszt," the desk clerk whispered, when Lucy had made it through
the first few bars.

261

"Oh my god," an old man breathed, as Lucy took off into a long run of notes, right hand only, her left hand curled in her lap.

And then there was nothing, except for the music.

They ate dinner at a low table set up in front of their fireplace.

"I'm always this way, after," she said. Their plates were empty now, and Cain was finishing his beer. The waiter had brought a glass of mineral water for her, but she hadn't touched it.

"What way?"

"Rattled," she said. "Quiet."

"Okay."

"It's not because it was the first time back. It's because it was like any other time."

"That's good," Cain said.

"You probably know the feeling even better than I do," she answered. "You're under the lights all the time. Every eye in the house on you, waiting for you to make a mistake. And if you do, it really matters. So that when you're done for the day, you're quiet. It takes you a while to decide that you're okay. That you didn't make any mistakes."

He took a sip of his beer and watched her in the firelight.

"But you're not going to do that," she said. "Make mistakes."

"No," he answered.

At eleven the next morning, he checked her into the Marriott at Union Square. He went with her up to the eighth floor, watching the lobby shrink away as the glass elevator rose upward. There were people in the third-floor bar, but no one was watching the elevators. No one had followed them back from Mendocino, either. In the room, he slipped off his shoulder holster and locked his gun in the safe.

"Will you be okay?" he asked.

"I still have my book."

"They'll probably take my phone at the consulate. If you need me —"

"I'll be okay," Lucy said. She wrapped her arms around herself and looked out the arched window. "What do you think he wants to say?"

"I don't know."

"But you have a hunch," she said. "You always do."

He looked at the gray sky, at the traffic moving down Post Street toward the square.

"He sounded like a man who wanted to confess."

"Confess what?"

"I don't know," Cain said. "But he feels guilty about something. I'm sure about that."

"And you think it's safe to meet him?"

"It's in a consulate. And they must know I told people—"

"Fischer, you mean. You told her."

"—so they'd be crazy to do anything."

"All right," she said.

They both knew there were plenty of crazy people. Neither of them had to say it to the other. But there were a thousand times as many people who were perfectly decent. The odds were with him on this.

The day had been getting darker since dawn, and the next wave of rain was almost here. He stood in a thinning lunch-hour crowd near the corner of Sansome and Sutter. The consulate's marble columns were stained dark with water. Nearby, a young tourist couple held their cell phones at arm's length, taking a few last photos of themselves before they fled the weather.

"You look just like your picture," a man said. "Maybe we should go inside before the rain comes, eh?"

Cain turned around. The man facing him was a few years into his seventies. He wore a dark cashmere overcoat that was unbuttoned enough to show the crimson knot of his tie. His brimmed black hat was pulled low over his brow.

"Too conspicuous to do this on the street?" Cain asked him.

"Obviously," the man said, and Cain knew his voice. It was the refined baritone he'd heard on the first call. "And the weather. Mostly the weather."

They looked together up the street. A wall of storm clouds was advancing along Sutter, a cold whiteout. Everything behind it was already gone.

"You didn't fly here just to give me all the answers," Cain said. "You have your own agenda. Tell me about that first."

"I want to know how she died," the man said. "That's the first thing. I want to know what happened."

263

Now the first rain came with the wind, big and icy drops that speckled the pavement around them. They could play games with each other and get soaked. Or they could get to the point and move on.

"She was buried alive."

"On top of a corpse — in another man's casket?"

"You're not guessing. You know that."

"It's what we were afraid of," the man said. His paused to loosen his tie, as though the knot had been the thing blocking his throat. "After everything that happened in 'eighty-nine, we guessed it. But we didn't want to believe."

"You didn't have anything to do with it, did you?"

"I had everything to do with it — I sent her, and I shouldn't have."

"You said the first thing you wanted was to know what happened," Cain said. "What's the second?"

"The body. I want to bring her home."

Cain looked at him. This choked-up old man in his cashmere overcoat, the rain already soaking into it.

"Let's go, then," Cain said. "Show me in."

The heavy rain arrived as they were coming into the consulate's security lobby. Even when the door closed behind them, they could hear it hitting the bulletproof glass. A guard checked Cain's passport against a list on his clipboard, then took Cain's phone and put it in a drawer. Cain went through the metal detector, and the guard met him on the other side with a visitor's badge.

His host had sidestepped the security station and was waiting next to a steel door. He opened it with a key card and held it for Cain.

"How much do you know about the Metropolitan Police?"

"Nothing," Cain said. He was looking down a short hallway. There was a door on each side, a slate-gray concrete wall at the end. A CCTV camera, mounted near the ceiling, watched him. "It's the London police, but it's got a mandate that goes beyond the city. It's got a building called Scotland Yard. That's it."

"There've been articles about Special Branch," the man said. He stepped around Cain and opened the door on the right. "Some of the things we did back in the eighties — did you see those?"

"No."

"The undercover operations? The infiltrations of animal rights groups?"

Now they were in a windowless conference room. The man sat down, elbows on the table. Cain pulled out a chair and sat facing him.

"You're saying this has to do with animal rights?"

"It's nothing to do with that," the man said. "I'm giving you background. People know about the animal rights groups, but it went beyond that. Far beyond that."

"Undercover operations. Infiltrations."

"Yes."

Yesterday morning, on the phone, the man had hinted that he'd moved on from Special Branch to something even more secretive. He looked the part, with his fine coat and his weary face.

"You were running agents, weren't you?"

"Yes."

"She was one of them."

"She wasn't an agent. She was an officer of the Metropolitan Police, Special Branch. She was in California on an undercover assignment."

The man reached into his coat and brought out a slim envelope. He opened the flap and slid out a three-by-five photograph, then put it on the table. Cain bent forward to look at it. The young woman wore a cadet uniform, and looked into the camera with the thinnest of smiles. She stood next to a Union Jack, hands at her sides. The plaque on the wall behind her said HENDON POLICE COLLEGE. Cain turned the photograph over. On the back, in a neat pencil script, was a name.

Carolyn Stone.

She was the girl from the photographs. There was no doubt of it, unless she had a twin sister. He turned to the old man.

"You sent a London police officer undercover to San Francisco," he said. "Did you follow any of the protocols?"

"It was too sensitive. Only three people in Special Branch knew what we were doing. There was way too much of that, back then. Special Branch confused itself for another agency."

"What were you doing?"

The man took the photograph from the table and put it back into the envelope. He had strong-looking hands, but they were trembling. Age, maybe, or a recent stroke. He was doing everything he could to hide it, but his hands were a tell.

"What do you know about Harry J. Castelli?" the old man asked.

"He died this week," Cain said. "I was one of the last two people to see him alive."

"Not the son. I'm talking about the father. What do you know about him?"

"He was the ambassador."

"What else have you turned up about him?"

"I haven't been focused on the father. He hasn't come up at all."

"He's gone now, or you could sit him down and ask him. He died in 'ninety-one. In Thailand."

"Ask him what?"

"Let me put it this way — I flew in here yesterday afternoon, came through immigration, and got my passport stamped. To go home, I'd do the same thing in reverse. But what would I do if I lost my passport today? What then?"

"You'd come here," Cain said. "To your consulate. They'd issue a temporary passport."

"And I might not even miss my plane," the old man said. "Because they can print a temporary passport onsite. Right here in San Francisco."

"It's not going to do me any good if you talk in circles," Cain said.

"Harry Castelli Sr., your ambassador, could have done the same thing. And once he set someone up with a temporary passport, she'd be a U.S. citizen as far as immigration is concerned — whatever nationality she'd had when she woke up that morning, it wouldn't matter."

"Castelli was issuing false passports?" Cain asked. "We're talking about the ambassador to the U.K., issuing false passports."

"Temporary passports. But that's not how we got into it. We weren't investigating passport fraud — it wasn't our jurisdiction, however broad a view we might have had on that subject. We were looking into missing girls. And then one thing led to another."

"How many missing girls?"

"Twenty-two," the old man said. He hadn't paused to think about it. He had the number right there, because it had been weighing on him for thirty years. "Immigrants, mostly. Eastern Europeans, Russians. The youngest was seventeen and the oldest was twenty-six."

"Immigrants, but living in London?"

"In London, or near it," the man said. "This was the early eighties. We didn't have computers like we do now. No program crosscheck-

266

ing the files, flagging related cases. Which meant that back then, these things could go on and on. Like a coal fire, underground—by the time you notice, it's out of control. It took a sharp young man in Missing Persons to put it together."

"Who?"

"It doesn't matter. A man saw the pattern and brought it to me. In every instance, the young woman had been gone for weeks before the families came to us. Months, sometimes. Because the girls had said they'd got jobs. That they had to move away to start."

"What kind of jobs?"

This time, the man did pause.

"We don't know what they were promised," he said. "But we know what they got."

He opened the envelope again and set a flash memory drive on the table next to Cain's saucer.

"You won't want to watch this," he said. "But you'll probably have to."

"What is it?"

"You might not have ever thought about this. But it's obvious, once you start looking into it—back then, after VCRs but before the Internet, there was a lot of money in a certain kind of video."

"You're talking about pornography."

"That word covers a lot of ground. There's plenty that's fairly mundane, but then there's the rest of the spectrum. So many needs to suit, fantasies people can't say out loud. Everything from simple meanness to open brutality. And here's another thing you probably never wanted to think about. On the worst of those films—the dark end, so to speak—what you see on the screen isn't acting. It isn't consensual."

"Then what is it?" Cain asked.

"It's rape. It's murder. And it's real."

"It's Carolyn Stone on this?"

He was holding out the flash drive. But the old man shook his head.

"It's an Estonian girl. Katarina Vesik."

"Who?"

"She was an immigrant, from Tallinn. Her family came over in 'eighty-two, when she was sixteen. She wanted to model, so she was hanging around the agencies, the fashion shops. Trying to get into parties, trying to get noticed. Someone noticed her, I suppose — she went missing in September. Her brother brought us the tape in February of 'eighty-four. There was no telling how long he'd had it, no guessing how he'd come by it — and we worked him hard."

"But you must have had a hunch."

"We thought he ordered it from a magazine ad. Or he got it in exchange for something in his own collection — which he would have tossed out before coming to us. We thought he would've liked it just fine, the video, except it was his little sister. And it seems like they kept her for a while, made a few others."

"You saw other videos?" Cain asked.

"Never — but in this one, she's half starved. Wounds, all over her, that are weeks old. Some of them almost healed."

"Jesus," Cain said.

"We said that too. The state she was in — you know it must have taken the brother a while to put it together. He might've watched it two or three times."

Cain looked out the wall and saw the strange symmetry in the way everything had presented itself. The Met and the SFPD had each come into this case because of videos that had landed on their laps. The brother and his snuff-porn tape, John Fonteroy and his dying confession. In the end, the cancerous undertaker hadn't been able to say what he'd really seen. What he'd been a part of for so long. The guilt was too great to look the camera in its eye and say that he'd seen Carolyn Stone go into the casket alive. He knew how many had come before her and could only guess how many would follow.

"After he came in with the tape — at least we understood what we were looking at. What we had on our hands."

"This was before you knew about the temporary passports. Before you had any connection to Castelli," Cain said.

"Well before," the man said. "Making the connection was old-fashioned police work. Interviewing the girls' friends, their closest confidantes. None of them had ever talked about who had hired them, how they'd found their new job. But one of girls rang her friend from Heathrow. She had a temporary U.S. passport, is what she said. She was getting on a flight to San Francisco. Then she hung up and no one heard a word from her again — except the men who bought the video, if hers was the sort where they made her talk."

Now the man was opening his envelope again. He brought out

a folded sheet of paper and laid it on the table. When he unfolded it, Cain could see that this was old paper. Tattered at the corners, slightly yellowed by the decades in a hanging file somewhere. The man turned it around and slid it across. It was a photocopy of Carolyn Stone's U.K. passport.

"We made a decision, inside Special Branch. We were already doing the undercover work in other groups — we had an officer who took it so far that he married an animal rights activist, had a baby with her. All so he could report on her, on her friends. Around Special Branch, we all thought that was a good piece of work. We weren't thinking. So this, the missing girls and the videos, was an easy decision. Until we started seeing links to Castelli."

"Because he was the ambassador," Cain said. "That made it more complicated."

"Until we thought what it could mean. What if we had something on him? Something so terrible that if we came to him and asked a favor, he couldn't say no?"

"You meant to blackmail him."

The man looked at Cain, considering that. Then he nodded.

"We sent Carolyn to San Francisco, on a student visa. She enrolled in the University of California."

"You picked her because she looked young. And because she fit the type."

"Also because she was very good. Top of her class at Hendon," he said. "She went over in the autumn of 1984, so that she enrolled in the son's year. She managed to sit next to him in a French class."

"Her job was to get close to the son?"

"And the fraternity, too. You know about Pi Kappa Kappa?"

"I know."

"That was an insular brotherhood. And secretive. We knew Castelli Sr. had been a member, and that he'd put his son in touch before packing him off to university. Carolyn had to be patient before she could get anything out of him."

"Was she reporting to you?" Cain asked.

"Daily, when it was safe."

"When's the last time you heard from her?"

"July seventeen, 1985."

"That's when they killed her," Cain said. "They buried Christopher Hanley that day, and she was in the casket."

It was almost a comforting thought. She couldn't have suffered more than twenty-four hours.

"What did she report that day?"

"Nothing much. It was a phone call, and she talked to me. The son was back in town that day. Classes ended in June, and he'd spent most of the summer in London. We kept her in Berkeley to watch the fraternity, because we could put people on the son. But many of those kids were on holiday — it was a slow summer for her."

"And she spent her downtime sewing, didn't she?" Cain asked.

The man arched one gray eyebrow above the frame of his tortoise-shell glasses.

"She did like to sew. That wasn't in her reports. It was in her file — she had to list her pastimes on a form when she applied. After she disappeared, I went over everything a thousand times. How did you know?"

"The photograph of her," Cain said. "She'd made the dress she was wearing. And she was very good."

The man thought about that, taking the new information and comparing it with what he already knew.

"There'd have been times she would have needed to be striking. To stand out, more than she already did," the man said. "Some of the older Pi Kappa Kappa men moved in high circles. But there was no budget for that sort of thing. She had to make it work with what she had."

There was a rush of noise from the hallway, and then it was quiet again. The man was staring at the backs of his hands on the table and never looked up.

"Was it any use sending her? Did she get anything, before she disappeared?" Cain asked.

"Not much. She was there just under a year. Two girls disappeared while she was there. She never saw them on the other side, never saw any of the Pi Kappa Kappa brothers with them. But she logged the activity, and when we went back and compared it against the last day the girls had been seen, there were anomalies — five of the core group dropped out of sight, and she didn't see them again for two weeks."

"They'd taken the girls somewhere to make the film."

"The films, yes."

"Did she connect Castelli to it?" Cain asked. "Was he one of the five who disappeared?"

"No."

"Could it be possible that the ambassador was part of it, but not the son — not Harry Castelli Jr.?"

"Anything was possible," the man said. "But we hadn't proved anything yet."

"Were you her only point of contact with Special Branch?"

"Yes."

"So her reports — they weren't just business. She would have told you other things. How she was holding up. Whether she was scared, lonely. That kind of thing."

"She talked about quitting," the man said. He had tented his fingers in front his forehead. He used his thumbs to rub against his white eyebrows. "She said she was tired and didn't know if she could keep going. I had to plead with her to stay on."

"She wanted to come home?"

"Quite the opposite, in fact — she talked about staying there but dropping the mission."

"Did she say why?"

"She lost her taste for it, is what I think — what she was doing, it bothered her somehow."

Cain thought about the methods Special Branch had condoned. Infiltrations through sexual relationships. Maybe she'd bought into it and that was how she got in trouble. Or maybe it was why she wanted to quit.

"If she had met someone — if she'd become involved romantically, is what I'm talking about — would she have told you?"

"I don't know."

"Did she have anyone back in England?"

"Anyone how?"

"A boyfriend, a fiancé."

"There was a man she was seeing when she was at the police college. We saw that when we did background on her. But that didn't go far. It was over before she left for the States."

"Before she disappeared, did she tell you she was pregnant?"

"What?"

"She was in her first trimester. She'd have been starting to show, but only just."

The old man's fingers caught hold of the table's edge, flexing as he steadied himself.

"She'd been on the assignment for a year by then," he said.

"So it happened while she was here."

"She never said anything."

"Would she have, if she'd known?"

"I don't know."

"Are you okay?"

The old man shook his head, but Cain had no way to gauge what any of this meant to him — whether it was one mistake among many, a career painted with errors, or something that stood alone. It was clear that Carolyn Stone was important to this man. He'd taken a risk, sending her without protection to infiltrate men who were infinitely more dangerous than he'd imagined. Losing her had carried a price, and he was still paying it.

"It took us a long while to get another officer in place. We were waiting to see if Carolyn might turn up. We made quiet inquiries — there was only so much we could do. And meanwhile, the disappearances went on and on. Four more years of them."

"And then you sent another officer."

"In 1989. Another woman, but a little older. We thought she was better trained. We may have been wrong about that."

Earlier, the man had said that after 1989, Special Branch knew Carolyn Stone had probably been buried alive. Now Cain understood how they'd reached that conclusion.

"I talked to a retired homicide inspector on Friday. In 1989, he picked up a naked woman running down an alley behind Eternity Chapel. She was drugged — she could move, but she couldn't think straight, and couldn't speak. He got her to a hospital, and then she disappeared. She was your officer, wasn't she?"

"She was."

"So then she knew. She had proof — who they were and what they were doing. What did she do next?"

The old man waited a long time until he answered. He looked at the street outside, watched the office workers with their black umbrellas. He looked at Cain and didn't blink.

"She dropped out of sight too. We never saw her again, but we think we know what she did."

"You're talking about the Grizzly Peak fire. Five bodies, a bullet through each man's trachea."

"If that was her, she did it on her own. We didn't order it."

272

"But you didn't particularly mind, either," Cain said. "You didn't pick up the phone."

"No, we didn't."

"And that was the end for you?" Cain asked. "When you heard about the fire, you ended the investigation."

"After the fire, the girls stopped disappearing."

"And you never tied Harry Castelli Jr. to anything at all?"

"Just the father," the man said. "His son was clean."

The man stood, but left his hat on the table.

"Carolyn had a sister, and she's still in London. I'll have someone at the Met contact you through the normal channels with a DNA sample."

"If the lab says they're sisters, we'll release her to the family."

The man put on his hat now and came around to open the door.

"We're done here, I think."

36

OUTSIDE THE CONSULATE, he sat in Fischer's car and watched the front door. He'd never gotten the man's name, but that might not matter. He had a photograph of Carolyn Stone and a memory stick with a snuff film on it. He took out his phone and turned it back on. There was a missed call from Nagata, but it was Officer Combs he needed to talk to. He called the patrolman's cell.

"Combs — where are you?"

"The Palace."

"What's your status?"

Combs gave his report in a low whisper. He had just taken over a double shift watching Mona Castelli. Since coming back from the Cathay Orient bank on Saturday afternoon, she hadn't taken a step outside the hotel's walls. She'd left her room three times on Sunday, but only to visit the Pied Piper. She drank her martinis and talked to no one. She'd had no visitors except the man who carried in her room service trays. It was early in the afternoon. Her day hadn't even begun yet, and probably wouldn't for a few more hours. Mona Castelli didn't strike Combs as an early riser.

Cain hung up and pocketed his phone.

In front of him, there was a swarm of yellow cabs. A crowd of pedestrians, invisible beneath the protection of their umbrellas, crossed the intersection. He saw the old man among them, slipping through the rain like a knife blade until he disappeared down the escalator of Montgomery Street Station. Cain wondered if there was other business for the man here, or if he'd come only for Carolyn Stone.

He drove west, listening to the wiper blades, trying to put everything together. One fact stood above all the others. When Carolyn Stone died, she was carrying Castelli's child. She had spoken to her handler in Special Branch right up to the day of her murder. Not once, in over a year of undercover work, had she ever singled out Castelli as a criminal. Most likely, she'd gone to his bed without force.

Maybe it had begun as part of her work. What better way to get close to Castelli than to take him to bed?

It was hard for him to picture Harry Castelli as a young man. Particularly one who might have attracted a woman like Carolyn Stone. Cain only saw the gravel-voiced, bourbon-swilling politician. But Castelli must have been different then. At eighteen, he might have believed the slogans on his own campaign signs.

Harry J. Castelli Sr. was a monster, but it was possible he'd shielded his son from the worst of his inclinations. That wasn't so unusual. If the ambassador's crimes had been merely financial, he might have brought his son inside the circle. But this wasn't simply a matter of cooking the embassy's books, or using the diplomatic pouch to move black market goods. He'd been trafficking girls and women so they could be raped on film and then disposed of. The ambassador was a man used to keeping secrets. He put on his tailored suits, and carried his calfskin briefcase, and no one around him would have seen the darkness.

But it all came apart in 1985.

A teenaged Harry left London for Berkeley. He'd never lived outside his father's shadow, and at first, before he pledged Pi Kappa Kappa, he must have felt like the world was awash in light and air. Right away, he met Carolyn Stone. He was eighteen. His head must have ached with the future. Nothing about Carolyn would have struck him as strange. Not the ease of meeting her, not the strength of her immediate interest in him. He was an ambassador's son; he was rich. He was hardwired to accept every blessing as his destiny. Of course he didn't understand how extraordinary she was. Of course he didn't understand how dangerous he was to her.

Cain parked on the street at UCSF and walked up the hill toward the medical center. There was a momentum beneath him now, a groundswell tilting his feet and propelling him. He had put a name to the girl in the casket; he knew why she'd come to San Francisco. The only person he knew who could give him the rest was Angela Chun. If she would wake up, if she could talk to him for ten seconds, she could close the circle.

He went through the main entrance and took the elevator up to the ICU, and stepped out into chaos. There were uniformed cops milling near the duty nurse. He didn't recognize anyone until Nagata turned around.

"I tried calling you," she said.

There were black streaks of mascara underneath Nagata's eyes. Cain looked around the room again and saw three officers in a group huddle. Their arms around each other's waists, their heads bowed.

"What's happening?" Cain asked.

"There was a complication—they missed something, in the first surgery. They took her in for a second try. And they botched it."

"Botched it how?"

"She's gone, Cain."

"Just now?"

Nagata nodded, and Cain looked across the hall. The door to Angela's room stood open. There was no light inside. He walked in and sat in the chair by the empty bed. The room smelled of daisies and roses. No one had thrown away the bouquets yet. He hadn't asked where she was, and Nagata hadn't said. Maybe she was still on the operating table. Maybe they'd already zipped her in a bag and taken her down to the morgue. It didn't matter, because Nagata was right. Angela was gone.

Cain closed his eyes and pressed his thumbs into his temples.

37

FISCHER WAS WAITING on the curb outside the main terminal at SFO. While he brought them back into the city on 101, he told her about his meetings with Susan Fennimore and the man from Special Branch.

"The guys in Washington lied to me," Fischer said when Cain was finished. "They didn't call me up there to look at a budget ledger. They wanted to tell me something about Castelli. Not the mayor, but his father. The ambassador."

"He was under investigation?"

She nodded.

"Short of the secretary of state, he had the highest position in U.S. diplomacy. Yet he was a wildcard. The Counterintelligence Division thought something was wrong, that he was selling secrets. But they could never prove anything."

"Did they know about the temporary passports?"

"If they did, they didn't tell me."

"Then they didn't know about the girls, either."

"I don't think so. But they might not have been telling me every-thing—counterintelligence guys are cagey. They sit in their dark of-fices and collect information, but they never share it."

"Why did they tell you?"

"Maybe to nudge us to look at London connections—they didn't know how far ahead of them you already were," Fisher said.

"We're close now," Cain said. "We need one or two more pieces, and then it'll all make sense."

Cain parked at the valet stand at the Palace Hotel and they went in-side to meet Officer Combs in the lobby. He led them down the long marble hallway, past the empty ballroom and to the Market Street doors. The bar was to the left, and Cain saw Mona Castelli sitting there, her back to the entrance.

"She went out two hours ago," Combs said. "She took a cab, but I called Officer Renton, and he beat her to the bank. He bumped into her going up the steps. Very casual, but then he acted like he just recognized her. 'Aren't you Mona Castelli?' She turned around and got back in the cab —"

"She'd asked it to wait?" Cain asked.

"Yeah — and she got in, and had the driver take her back to the hotel."

"What was she carrying?" Fischer asked.

"Just her handbag. The small one."

"Is Officer Aguilar still watching Alexa?"

"That's right."

"Anything going on there?"

"She's been staying in her studio. No visitors."

They left Combs and went out to the street. Curtains of mist blew down the street toward the bay, and there were clusters of smokers and homeless men huddled under all of the awnings.

"What do you think?" Fischer asked.

"It's got to be a safe deposit box," Cain said. "She's got something in there and she wants to get it out. But she doesn't want anyone to see her with it."

"What is it?"

"We'll need to find out," Cain said. "You had that kid at the U.S. attorney's office draft a receipt for Castelli's cash. How good is he at writing search warrants?"

"You want it coming from us?"

"If it lands in front of a judge who'll sign it, I'll take it from anyone."

"It has to say what we expect to find," Fischer said. "Even a friendly judge won't sign an open-ended warrant."

"We'll explain the note we found in Castelli's safe. It had bank addresses, and dates. We'll explain what Combs and Renton saw, the two times she tried to get to her box."

"Castelli's note — you think he knew something about Mona. Knew that she was keeping something in a safe deposit box."

"I think he suspected. I think he wanted to find out. He wasn't telling us anything about the blackmail notes because he wanted to do his own homework first. But he was nervous enough that he was withdrawing cash and stashing it in his office."

Fischer's car was around the corner. Cain checked behind him for traffic, then stepped out into New Montgomery. From there he could see the brickwork side of Alexa's building. He counted up the floors until he saw her windows. They were lit up, three bright panes above the latticework of an iron fire escape.

Alexa stepped into view.

She was nude, and she was tying her hair into a loose knot at the top of her head. When she finished, she cupped her hands around her eyes and pressed against the glass to look out. Cain turned his face away and stepped back to the sidewalk.

Fischer's kid at the U.S. attorney's office was as fast as he was good. They met him at eight p.m. outside the district court. He came running down the front steps, tie flipped over his shoulder, and got into the backseat. He loosened his tie, opened his briefcase, and handed a signed and sealed search warrant up to Cain.

"Ryan Harding," he said. "You're Cain? Inspector Cain?"

Cain reached around and shook the kid's hand.

"This is good to go?"

"Tonight," the kid said. "This second. I called the general counsel at Cathay Orient Bank and told her what I had. I said we'd come in the morning with fifty guys. SWAT jackets and rifles — scare the shit out of her customers, if that's what she wants. Or she could let us in right now, after hours."

"All right," Cain said. "I like it. Let's go."

They came into Chinatown, moving at a walking pace through dense late-evening traffic. Regular taxis and pedicabs, families on foot walking half in the street because the sidewalks were too crowded.

Fischer parked in a bus stop and put her law enforcement placard on the dash. They got out of the car and walked back to the Cathay Orient Bank, the only pedestrians in sight who weren't hiding under black umbrellas. When they reached the bank, they went up the steps and found four people waiting between the carved stone columns. Two uniformed security guards stood near the bronze doors. A man in a brown suit came up to them.

"I'm Warren Lee," he said. "The vice president. This is Cindy Wang, our in-house counsel."

Cain shook the vice president's hand and nodded to the lawyer. She was wearing a black dress and a three-strand pearl necklace. Ryan Harding's call about the search warrant must have pulled her out of a dinner somewhere.

"I'll let us in—"

"Let's read the warrant first," the lawyer said. She pointed to the papers in Ryan Harding's hand. "Is that it?"

He handed it to her and she stood on the top step, using the light from the phone screen to read the document. She checked the judge's signature, and then she read through the entire thing again.

"Is this my copy?" she asked.

"Yes, ma'am."

"Go ahead and let us in, Warren," she said. She folded the search warrant in half and put it in her purse. "Do we even know if this woman has a safe deposit box with us?"

"She does," the vice president said. "I looked it up when you called."

He stepped to the left of the door and lifted back the cover on a keypad and print reader. He punched in a code and then held his thumb over the scanner until the lights on the keys turned from red to green. Then he used a key to open the metal gates that covered the doors, and a second key to open the front door. He held it open and all seven of them stepped into the bank's dark lobby. When the man closed the door and locked it, the only light came from an exit sign on the wall above the door.

"She rented the box in 1998," the vice president said. He had gone off through the dark, and then he hit a light switch. High above, in the arched marble ceiling, bulbs blinked on with hollow glassy clicks. "She's had it ever since."

"Do you know what month she rented it?" Cain asked.

"I think it was October. I can get you the signature card. It'll have the exact date."

There was a long teller counter in the back of the room, and behind it, lit now by overhead spotlights, was the door to the vault.

"You understand I need to document this," the lawyer said. "Since you're basically breaking into the safe and taking something that belongs to a customer."

"You didn't call her, did you?" Fischer asked.

Cain saw the vice president glance downward but didn't catch what he said.

"What was that?"

"It's policy," the vice president said.

"You tipped her off."

"On the phone, you didn't say not to," the lawyer said, looking at Ryan Harding. "I'll need photographs of your badges and IDs."

She nodded at one of the security guards, who was holding a small video camera. "And this gentleman will film us. No objections?"

"None," Cain said. "But let's do this. We haven't got much time now."

He got out his badge and his driver's license and held them side by side while the lawyer photographed them. While she was doing the same with Fischer, and then with Ryan Harding, Cain went to the counter and leaned on it to watch the vice president open the vault. He dialed the combination, then spun the polished steel spindle wheel. The round door, when he pulled it back, was a foot thick.

Everyone moved into the vault now, stepping over the high threshold and then down a set of stone stairs to the polished concrete floor. There may have been other rooms in the back of the vault, but the doorway there was blocked off by a velvet rope hanging between two brass poles. The first room was where the safe deposit boxes were. Hundreds of them lined the walls on either side of the entrance.

"It's 1206," the vice president said. "Here."

He took another set of keys from his pocket and unlocked the front panel. He pulled it open, then slid a steel drawer out of the wall and carried it to a high wooden table in the center of the vault. He set the drawer down and Cain and Fischer came next to him so they could see. It was a little larger than a shoebox. The guard with the video camera came around the other side, filming.

The only thing in the drawer was a legal-size manila envelope.

"May I?" Cain asked.

"Go ahead," Fischer said. "Let's see."

Cain took a set of latex gloves from his coat pocket and pulled them on. He picked up the envelope and knew what was inside from its weight and stiffness. When he turned it over, the other side was speckled with brown-black stains.

"Is that blood?" the vice president said. "Dried blood?"

"Probably," Cain said.

He unwound the string clasp and opened the flap. He tilted the envelope, letting its contents slide out onto the table. There were a dozen black-and-white photographs and a small plastic canister with the negatives. The photographs that had come to Castelli with the blackmail notes were copies. These were the originals. The first print was one he knew well. Carolyn Stone was backed against the brick wall, her hands held up in fear. Cain set it to the side, going quickly through the first eight pictures because he'd seen them all before. The lawyer and the vice president hadn't seen them, though, and he saw the way they each stepped back when he came to the rape.

"Is this what you were looking for?" Cindy Wang asked.

"It is."

He turned to the ninth photograph, one he hadn't seen yet. It must have been taken in the preparation room at the Fonteroy Mortuary. Carolyn Stone was holding herself up, leaning over a steel under-taker's table. She wore nothing but bruises, and her eyes were half closed. There was fresh blood on her lips. She held her left arm pro-tectively across the front of her stomach.

An open casket waited on the table behind her.

"Jesus," Fischer said. "They even photographed this."

Cain turned to the tenth photograph. Three men were manhan-dling Carolyn into the casket. They wore pantyhose over their heads to hide their faces. Two of them had her arms and shoulders, and a third was struggling with her legs. Her feet were a blur of motion. She had gone in kicking. Cain turned the picture over. The eleventh photograph showed the men pushing the casket lid down. One of Carolyn's hands was visible through the crack. Part of her face rose into the last light she would ever see, her mouth open in a scream.

In the twelfth photograph, it was all over.

The casket was closed. There was a small metal plaque on the lid, engraved with Christopher Hanley's name. The dates of his birth and death. Cain turned the photograph over. There was handwriting on the back, in faded pencil.

Harry,

We'll need to talk about this, and agree on a price. You have a young wife who doesn't know, and that's worth something, isn't it?

If they dig her up, they'll find out about the baby. And if they find that, they'll find you.

— L.F.

Cain eased everything back into the envelope and looked up. "We need to go," he said to Fischer. "Right now."

38

CAIN'S PHONE RANG as they were getting into Fischer's car. He answered it, standing on the sidewalk, covering his free ear with his palm so that he could hear over the street noise.

"Inspector Cain? It's Officer Combs."

"What's going on?"

"They're on the move — both of them. Mona got in a taxi a minute ago, and Officer Aguilar just called me. Alexa did the same."

"Where are you?"

"At the Palace — but I lost her. I thought she was heading out on foot, but she jumped in a cab before I knew what was happening."

"All right."

"She had a bag with her this time. A shopping bag, but I don't know what was in it."

Cain hung up and got in the car.

They had to take Ryan Harding back to the federal building, and then they sat in Fischer's car and looked at the rain in the headlights.

"You knew the photographs would be in there," Fischer said.

"I guessed it — Castelli didn't have anything to do with his dad's snuff videos, and didn't rape Carolyn Stone. He didn't know she was an undercover cop. She was just a girl he met in college — his girl-friend, he thought. But his frat brothers must have found out about her, and they killed her."

"I'm following you so far, but what about Lester Fennimore?"

"He had the pictures — he might have taken some of them, and he might have been in some of them. He had the tattoo. He crawled out of the Grizzly Peak fire and lived, but by 1998 he'd hit hard times. He'd lost his job, and he needed cash. He knew Castelli was in Silicon Valley, raking it in."

"So he decided to blackmail Castelli, in 1998. That's what you're saying. It could be Castelli in the pictures, and that was Fennimore's angle. You can't tell it isn't Castelli — even Melissa Montgomery, who'd slept with him, wasn't sure."

"And Fennimore had a wildcard," Cain said.

"Which was what?"

"He knew Carolyn Stone was pregnant, that it was Castelli's baby. She probably told him, begging for her life. They didn't have DNA testing in 1985, but they did in 1998. He would've known about it."

"But why did Mona have the pictures?"

"Because however Fennimore sent the note to Castelli, Mona found it first. She'd just dropped out of Stanford and married him. She was pregnant with Alexa. And she comes home one day and finds this."

"It was her at Castle Rock State Park," Fischer said. "She shot Fennimore with Castelli's gun. But why did she hold on to the pictures? Why not destroy them? Or confront her husband, if she thought he'd raped a girl?"

"Because he was on the upswing," Cain said. "He was getting rich, going places. The pictures were insurance, in case things stopped going so well."

Fischer had her hands on the wheel. She was looking through the windshield, her eyes flicking back and forth as she sorted through the details. He saw that she agreed with him, that she knew he'd put the facts together the only way they'd fit.

"She knew Christopher Hanley's name from the plaque on the casket — it was in the photo," Fischer said. "All she had to do was find the grave and then keep tabs on it — an exhumation order is a public document, so she was watching for that."

"Which, by now, she could have done online," Cain said. "She just had to set up an alert on the court's electronic docket."

"And when she saw that you got one, it was now or never," Fischer said. "Carolyn Stone was coming out of the ground, and if Castelli's DNA was in a database, it'd only be a matter of time before we connected him to her. It would have been the end of him."

Cain nodded. That was exactly what he thought.

"So she decided to cash out while she was still ahead. Hound him into suicide, and collect."

"But she must have had an accomplice."

"We'll get that out of her when we pick her up," he said. He thought about it for a moment. If Mona and Alexa were both on the move at the same time, there was one place they'd probably want to go. "Let's go up to Sea Cliff Avenue."

Then he did what he always did when he knew he was about to make an arrest. He patted the left side of his jacket, to check his gun.

"Shit."

"What?"

"Nothing — I left my weapon in Lucy's hotel. I couldn't take it to the consulate."

"Do you want to go get it?"

"There's no time. Let's just go."

They parked down the street and walked up to the house. Upstairs, in the study, the curtains were open and the lights were on. Through the brightly lit windows, they could see see the bookcases along the far wall. They went along the steppingstones, through the herb garden, to reach the front door. Cain was about to knock, but Fischer grabbed his wrist. She pointed at the door, and then, when his eyes adjusted to the dark, he saw why. It wasn't completely shut. He pushed it with his fingers and it swung open.

They stood looking into the dark entry hall. The house was completely silent, until Cain called into it.

"Mona Castelli?"

They waited for an answer, but there was none.

"Do you smell that?" Fischer asked.

Cain nodded. It was wafting out the front door, now that they'd opened it. Cordite smoke was biting and unmistakable. Fischer drew her gun. She held it in both hands, pointed at the ground.

"Stay behind me," she whispered.

She stepped into the house and he followed her. They checked in both downstairs bathrooms and the empty kitchen. Then the den and the library. They looked in the sunroom, where Cain had sat with Mona Castelli the first time he'd met her. The silver martini pitcher was still on the glass table.

They came back toward the front of the house and went upstairs. The master bedroom was massive, but everything was in its place. The bed was made. Everything in the closets was either folded or hung. The next bedroom they entered must have been Alexa's. There was a cherry wood easel, and a mirror on a wooden stand. Nude self-portraits crowded the walls, arranged in a chronological progression. In every portrait, Alexa stood reflected in the mirror, a brush in her right hand as she studied herself. She was patient, observant, and her favorite subject was herself. But looking from one painting to the next, Cain understood something else. She was damaged beyond repair, and had been from the very beginning.

When they backed out of the room, they went down the hall to the study. Cain tried the door and found it unlocked. He pushed it open, and they stood in the doorway looking.

"Oh, shit," Fischer said.

It was all either of them said for a long moment.

Mona Castelli was on the floor in front of the desk. She had come to her death wearing a white blouse and dark jeans. The blouse was soaked in blood; the bullet had hit the center of her sternum, between her breasts. A perfect heart shot. She might have been dead before she hit the carpet.

The young man who'd shot her hadn't gone so easily.

He lay on the other side of the room. His hand was still reaching for the .40 caliber automatic that he must have used to shoot Mona. But while Mona had died with a single shot to the chest, this kid was riddled. His shirt and jeans were soaked in blood. He'd been shot in the hip, the groin, and both shoulders. Twice in the stomach. The wall behind him was bloody and punched up with bullet holes. Spackled with bone and blood, with small bits of fabric from the boy's clothes.

Cain went across the room and knelt next to him, as Alexa must have done, when she put the gun to his temple and fired the last shot. His brain was fanned out on the carpet, but Cain ignored that. He was looking at the kid, putting the pieces back together and patching the holes, trying to picture him alive. He was long and lean, this kid. Built to run. And kneeling there, Cain recognized him.

He'd posed nude for Alexa. There had been half a dozen paintings of him hanging in her studio. The kid on China Beach, sitting on the rocks. The kid on Alexa's bed, face-down and arms dangling toward the floor. When Cain had gone to Grassley's autopsy, he'd seen the parallel cuts on the side of his partner's neck. Now he understood what had bothered him about those. He'd assumed Grassley and Chun were attacked because Chun had been asking questions about

Pi Kappa Kappa in Berkeley. But that had been wrong. This kid had seen Grassley in the Academy of Art, going into professors' offices and asking questions. Grassley had just been there to ask about the dress, but the kid wouldn't have known that. He'd followed Grassley to his car, had sat behind the driver's seat with a knife on his neck. It was Chun's bad luck that she was waiting for Grassley in his bedroom.

"Is that Grassley's gun?" Fischer asked.

He looked around. She was standing behind him.

"Or Angela's. I'm not sure."

She offered her hand and helped him back to his feet.

"Are you okay?"

"I'm good," he said.

"We saw him," Fischer said.

"What?"

"In the coffee shop, by Alexa's studio. We were having coffee with Melissa Montgomery, and he was right next to us."

Cain closed his eyes and pictured it. Melissa had given him the envelope, the new set of pictures and the second blackmail note. *Get Cain*, Castelli had told her. Maybe he'd been ready to come clean, to tell them who Carolyn was. To say what he suspected about his wife. But there hadn't been time for it. His life had run out that same night. Right here, in this room.

"He was by the window," Cain said. "The tall kid, listening to music on his headphones."

"That's right."

"He was watching us the whole time — maybe they all were."

"Alexa must have called him after her mom got the call from the bank," Fischer said. "He knew it was over. He told them to come here. Whatever excuse he gave, what he really wanted was to have them in the same place. They were the only ones who could point to him."

Cain looked around the study again. Mona Castelli's fresh blood was splashed across the dried stains from her husband's murder. Their marriage had been dead from the day she'd opened Lester Fennimore's envelope. But if she'd just confronted her husband instead of Fennimore, it might have all been different.

"Where are you going?" Fischer asked.

"Outside for a second," Cain said. "I need some air. I'll call Nagata.

We need the ME, the CSI team. We need the photographers — everything."

"Okay."

He left her in the study and went downstairs. Castelli had died because his wife despised him, because she never knew the truth and hadn't tried to learn it. She'd spent nineteen years believing what Lester Fennimore had put in her mind. She thought she was sleeping next to a rapist, and she was fine with that as long as he kept bringing in money.

Cain didn't like it, but he could live with it.

It was Grassley and Chun that he couldn't stand. It was the fact that the dead kid upstairs had smashed into Lucy's house, and only luck had kept him from killing her.

He stood in the kitchen and steadied himself. Upstairs, he'd told Fischer that he was going to call Nagata. But he didn't get out his phone. Instead he went toward the rear of the house, through the den and into the sunroom. There was a sliding glass door here that led out to the cliff steps. He wasn't surprised when it slid back easily. It hadn't been locked. He looked at the handle and saw a single, bloody fingerprint.

Later, he would think that this was the moment that he should have called upstairs, that he should have stopped and asked for backup. He'd chided Chun for this kind of thing. It's the guys who rush in without looking who always get killed, he'd told her. But he wasn't thinking about backup, wasn't thinking about the fact that he wasn't carrying his gun. Maybe that's how it happened to everyone else. He thought he saw a trail, and he wanted to follow it.

The bridge's foghorn greeted him when he stepped outside, and then there was the wind and the sound of the ocean from down below. The wooden steps were soaked and slippery. He walked down them carefully, holding the handrail and feeling his way around the corners where the shadows were so dark that he couldn't see his feet. It was a long, zigzagging descent to the beach. He could smell the wet sand and the seaweed, and then he reached the beach and there was just enough light from the cloud-covered moon that he could make out fresh footsteps. He followed them, the tracks skirting the edge of the tide pools and sticking to the soft sand. He came to a print that was in clean, hard-packed sand and he knelt to look at it.

She was barefoot.

He stood up and looked along the empty length of China Beach, then saw her silhouette on the promontory of rock where he'd spoken to her before. He walked the rest of the way to her and stopped when she turned around to face him.

She was wearing another of her gingham dresses, the thin fabric printed with black and white checks, and splattered from the neckline down with blood. There was blood on her face and blood on her bare arms. She held a pistol off to her right side, pointing it at the ground and not at him.

"Don't come any closer, Inspector Cain."

"All right."

"I shot him," she said. "He shot my mom, so I had to. It's not like I had a choice, did I?"

"Sure," he said.

He took another step toward her, and this time she raised the gun.

"Not any closer."

"All right," Cain said. He wanted to keep her talking to him, wanted her to lower the gun. "Did he shoot your father, too? Was it his idea?"

"My father was a rapist," she said. "He killed a girl. Him, and his friends. They took pictures of her, and then they buried her alive."

"Your mom told you that. But it's not true."

"Yes, it is," she said. "I've seen the pictures. She showed them to me when I was ten."

"You didn't find them in his study. She showed you."

"She needed me to know."

"She'd been planning this for nine years," Cain said.

"At least."

Cain tried not to look back along the beach, or up the cliff to the house. Fischer didn't know he was down here. She thought he was standing in the front yard, on the phone with his lieutenant.

"You didn't answer — did your boyfriend shoot your father?"

Alexa came a step toward him, then another two. Now he could reach out and grab her if he wanted to. Tackle her onto the rocks and rip the gun from her hand, if she didn't shoot him first. She must have known the danger, but she took another step. She was daring herself to do it. Proving that she could. She'd already shot one person tonight. A second wouldn't be any harder. She lowered the gun, and he understood what she was doing. Now she was daring him.

"Yes," she said. She was close enough now that she had to look up at him. "He shot my father."

"Your mom let him into the house when she left to go to Monterey," Cain said. "She came out, and he went in. The door only opened once. When your father got home, he made him drink bourbon. Made him swallow pills, and then he put the gun in his mouth."

"Yes."

"When your mom came home, he left the house when she opened the front door. That's how you did it. That's how you beat the alarm log."

"Yes."

"Whose idea was it?"

"I knew he'd do it if I asked him to—he'd killed a boy when he was thirteen. They said that was an accident too. Two kids in a garage, playing with a gun. Someone's finger slips on the trigger. But he wondered if it was really an accident, what he did. If maybe, deep down, he just wanted to see what would happen. So when he said he'd do anything for me, I knew he would."

"What happened to the money?"

She flicked her eyes to the right. He turned carefully to look, not wanting to let her out of his sight. There was a shopping bag on the beach, fifty feet away. She'd set it down past the high tide line.

"Was it always just about the money?" Cain asked.

"It was always about him. Getting rid of him."

"Did you know he was withdrawing cash and stashing it?"

Alexa nodded. She was holding the gun one-handed, her index finger curled tightly on the trigger. He wondered how many bullets were left in the magazine. She'd used plenty upstairs, on her boyfriend.

"But he had it all wrong. We weren't going to take the money and run away from him. We were going to stay right here. He was the one who was going to leave."

With her free hand, she reached behind her neck. She raised the gun again and kept it pointed at his stomach as she undid the tie on her dress. She'd stripped naked in front of him nearly every time he'd seen her. He didn't see why this time had to be any different.

"You should have come swimming with me that night," Alexa said. "That was your chance. I'm not inviting you again."

She pulled her dress off and took a step backward to be free of it. It lay in a circle on the rocks between them.

"Your girlfriend is Lucy Bolet. The pianist. The one who saved all the children."

"Yes."

"You would have come swimming with me, except you have her."

"Miss Castelli—"

"You'll never know what it would have been like now. You'll just have to imagine it."

She backed up to the end of the rock. A wave broke behind her, an eruption of bright foam and dark water that exploded upward around her and left her soaked. White water streamed off the rock and back into the ocean, and she stood looking at him. She hadn't even moved. She used her free hand to sweep the water from her breasts, from her stomach.

Then she raised the gun and aimed it at him.

"You're a good man. You have a good girlfriend. I would have been like her, if I'd had a chance like she did. Saving all those kids — a hero, but still so delicate."

"Alexa."

"I liked getting to know you," she said. "Goodbye, Inspector Cain."

He thought she would fire. He was bracing for it, stuck on his feet instead of diving for the sand. But she didn't pull the trigger. Instead, in a single clean motion, she turned and dove into the black water. It was a perfect dive, long practiced from this same rock. Her fingertips broke the surface ahead of her, and then the whole slender length of her body disappeared without a sound or a splash.

Cain ran to the edge of the rock in time to be knocked on his back by another breaking wave. He scrabbled backward on his hands and his feet, then got to his knees. He stared into the dark.

Ten yards out, she surfaced.

She was swimming face-down, her feet a white blur. She was heading away from the shore, out to sea. She went up the face of an approaching wave, then disappeared down its back. In ten seconds, the wave crashed against the rock. When it was gone, just foam running back into the water, he'd lost her.

He called to her for a minute, but there was no answer. There was the wind, and the foghorn's low note, and the waves breaking on the beach. He took out his phone and felt it. It had been in an inside pocket and was mostly dry. He hit the button and the screen lit up. But for a long moment, he couldn't think of anyone to dial.

He stared out into the dark and called her name.

Acknowledgments

I might never have written this book had it not been for a series of conversations involving my agent, Alice Martell, and my editors, Naomi Gibbs and Bill Massey. I owe each of them the greatest of thanks. In February of 2015, I had submitted a manuscript for a novel called *The Night Market*. Everyone was excited about the book, but Alice, Naomi, and Bill agreed that before *The Night Market* is published in 2018, I needed to tell another story. What I ended up with is *The Dark Room,* which serves as the center panel in a triptych of San Francisco's nighttime scenery.

Once again, Dawn Barbour and her colleagues at the Sausalito Police Department were extremely helpful on police procedure and investigative techniques. Steve Goodenow, the private investigator I have used for years in my legal practice, helped me understand the tools that can be used to search for missing persons. Nathaniel Boyer, MD, came through with arcane medical knowledge, as always.

And finally there was my wife, Maria Wang. While I was writing *The Dark Room,* she was teaching me about the most important things of all. I hope some of those lessons made it into the book unscathed.